The People of
HOTEL

Warren Trent
The St. Gregory's aristocratic, irascible owner.

Peter McDermott
The hotel's handsome general manager
who was still haunted by the sins of his youth.

Marsha Preyscott
The teenage New Orleans heiress
who wanted to make life an endless dream.

Curtis O'Keefe
The tough, fun-loving tycoon
who schemed to buy the St. Gregory for a song.

Duke of Croydon
The internationally famous
statesman who hid behind the
skirts of his arrogant, ice-maiden wife.

and

Keycase Milne
The oddly lovable thief
whose fumbling misadventures provided
the catalyst that brought them all together.

HOTEL
"A RIP-SNORTING STORY."
Bestsellers

Arthur Hailey
Hotel

BANTAM BOOKS · TORONTO · LONDON · NEW YORK

All of the characters in this book are fictitious and any
resemblance to actual persons, living or dead, is
purely coincidental.

*This low-priced Bantam Book
has been completely reset in a type face
designed for easy reading, and was printed
from new plates. It contains the complete
text of the original hard-cover edition.*
NOT ONE WORD HAS BEEN OMITTED.

HOTEL
*A Bantam Book / published by arrangement with
Doubleday & Company, Inc.*

PRINTING HISTORY
Doubleday edition published January 1965
11 printings through March 1966
Literary Guild of America edition published February 1965
2nd printing .... May 1965
Doubleday One Dollar Book Club edition published March 1965
Reader's Digest Condensed Books edition published April 1965
This book has been published in the following foreign languages:
*Danish, Dutch, Finnish, French, German, Icelandic, Italian,
Japanese, Norwegian, Portuguese, Serbo-Croatian, Swedish*
Bantam edition published July 1966
47 printings through June 1979

CONTENTS

Traveller, pray lodge in this unworthy house.
The bath is ready. A peaceful room awaits
you. Come in! Come in!

—Translation of a sign at the doorway of an inn, Takamatsu, Japan.

MONDAY EVENING

1

If he had had his way, Peter McDermott thought, he would have fired the chief house detective long ago. But he had not had his way and now, once more, the obese ex-policeman was missing when he was needed most.

McDermott leaned down from his husky six-and-a-half feet and jiggled the desk telephone impatiently. "Fifteen things break loose at once," he told the girl by the window of the wide, broadloomed office, "and nobody can find him."

Christine Francis glanced at her wrist watch. It showed a few minutes before eleven P.M. "There's a bar on Baronne Street you might try."

Peter McDermott nodded. "The switchboard's checking Ogilvie's hangouts." He opened a desk drawer, took out cigarettes and offered them to Christine.

Coming forward, she accepted a cigarette and McDermott lit it, then did the same for himself. He watched as she inhaled.

Christine Francis had left her own smaller office in the St. Gregory Hotel executive suite a few minutes earlier. She had been working late and was on the point of going home when the light under the assistant general manager's door had drawn her in.

"Our Mr. Ogilvie makes his own rules," Christine said. "It's always been that way. On W.T.'s orders."

McDermott spoke briefly into the telephone, then waited again. "You're right," he acknowledged. "I tried to reor-

1

ganize our tame detective force once, and my ears were properly pinned back."

She said quietly, "I didn't know that."

He looked at her quizzically. "I thought you knew everything."

And usually she did. As personal assistant to Warren Trent, the unpredictable and irascible owner of New Orleans' largest hotel, Christine was privy to the hotel's inner secrets as well as its day-to-day affairs. She knew, for example, that Peter, who had been promoted to assistant general manager a month or two ago, was virtually running the big, bustling St. Gregory, though at an ungenerous salary and with limited authority. She knew the reasons behind that, too, which were in a file marked *Confidential* and involved Peter McDermott's personal life.

Christine asked, "What *is* breaking loose?"

McDermott gave a cheerful grin which contorted his rugged, almost ugly features. "We've a complaint from the eleventh floor about some sort of sex orgy; on the ninth the Duchess of Croydon claims her Duke has been insulted by a room-service waiter; there's a report of somebody moaning horribly in 1439; and I've the night manager off sick, with the other two house officers otherwise engaged."

He spoke into the telephone again and Christine returned to the office window which was on the main mezzanine floor. Head tilted back to keep the cigarette smoke from her eyes, she looked casually across the city. Directly ahead, through an avenue of space between adjoining buildings, she could see into the tight, crowded rectangle of the French Quarter. With midnight an hour away, it was early yet for the Quarter, and lights in front of late night bars, bistros, jazz halls, and strip joints—as well as behind darkened shutters—would burn well into tomorrow morning.

Somewhere to the north, over Lake Pontchartrain probably, a summer storm was brewing in the darkness. The beginnings of it could be sensed in muted rumblings and an occasional flash of light. With luck, if the storm moved south toward the Gulf of Mexico, there might be rain in New Orleans by morning.

The rain would be welcome, Christine thought. For three

2

weeks the city had sweltered in heat and humidity, producing tensions all around. There would be relief in the hotel too. This afternoon the chief engineer had complained again, "If I canna' shut down part of the air conditioning soon, I willna' be responsible for my bearings."

Peter McDermott put down the telephone and she asked, "Do you have a name for the room where the moaning is?"

He shook his head and lifted the phone again. "I'll find out. Probably someone having a nightmare, but we'd better make sure."

As she dropped into an upholstered leather chair facing the big mahogany desk, Christine realized suddenly how very tired she was. In the ordinary way she would have been home at her Gentilly apartment hours ago. But today had been exceptionally full, with two conventions moving in and a heavy influx of other guests, creating problems, many of which had found their way to her desk.

"All right, thanks." McDermott scribbled a name and hung up. "Albert Wells, Montreal."

"I know him," Christine said. "A nice little man who stays here every year. If you like, I'll check that one out."

He hesitated, eying Christine's slight, trim figure.

The telephone shrilled and he answered it. "I'm sorry, sir," the operator said, "we can't locate Mr. Ogilvie."

"Never mind. Give me the bell captain." Even if he couldn't fire the chief house detective, McDermott thought, he would do some hell raising in the morning. Meanwhile he would send someone else to look after the disturbance on the eleventh and handle the Duke and Duchess incident himself.

"Bell captain," the phone said, and he recognized the flat nasal voice of Herbie Chandler. Chandler, like Ogilvie, was another of the St. Gregory's old-timers and reputedly controlled more sideline rackets than anyone else on staff.

McDermott explained the problem and asked Chandler to investigate the complaint about an alleged sex orgy. As he had half expected, there was an immediate protest. "That ain't my job, Mr. Mac, and we're still busy down here." The tone was typical Chandler—half fawning, half insolent.

McDermott instructed, "Never mind the argument, I

3

want that complaint attended to." Making another decision: "And something else: send a boy with a pass key to meet Miss Francis on the main mezzanine." He replaced the phone before there could be any more discussion.

"Let's go." His hand touched Christine's shoulders lightly. "Take the bellboy with you, and tell your friend to have his nightmares under the covers."

2

Herbie Chandler, his weasel-face betraying an inner uneasiness, stood thoughtfully by the bell captain's upright desk in the St. Gregory lobby.

Set centrally, beside one of the fluted concrete columns which extended to the heavily ornamented ceiling high above, the bell captain's post commanded a view of the lobby's comings and goings. There was plenty of movement now. The conventioneers had been in and out all evening and, as the hours wore on, their determined gaiety had increased with their liquor intake.

As Chandler watched out of habit, a group of noisy revelers came through the Carondelet Street door: three men and two women; they held drinking glasses, the kind that Pat O'Brien's bar charged tourists a dollar for over in the French Quarter, and one of the men was stumbling badly, supported by the others. All three men wore convention name tags. GOLD CROWN COLA the cards said, with their names beneath. Others in the lobby made way good-naturedly and the quintet weaved into the main floor bar.

Occasional new arrivals were still trickling in—from late planes and trains, and several were being roomed now by Chandler's platoon of bellboys, though the "boys" was a figure of speech since none was younger than forty, and several graying veterans had been with the hotel a quarter century or more. Herbie Chandler, who held the power of hiring and firing his bell staff, preferred older men. Someone who had to struggle and grunt a bit with heavy luggage was likely to earn bigger tips than a youngster who swung bags as if they contained nothing more than balsa wood.

4

One old-timer, who actually was strong and wiry as a mule, had a way of setting bags down, putting a hand over his heart, then picking them up with a shake of his head and carrying on. The performance seldom earned less than a dollar from conscience-stricken guests who were convinced the old man would have a coronary around the next corner. What they did not know was that ten per cent of their tip would find its way into Herbie Chandler's pocket, plus the flat two dollars daily which Chandler exacted from each bellboy as the price of retaining his job.

The bell captain's private toll system caused plenty of low-toned growlings, even though a fast-moving bellboy could still make a hundred and fifty dollars a week for himself when the hotel was full. On such occasions, as tonight, Herbie Chandler often stayed at his post well beyond the usual hour. Trusting no one, he liked to keep an eye on his percentage and had an uncanny knack of sizing up guests, estimating exactly what each trip to the upstairs floors would yield. In the past a few individualists had tried holding out on Herbie by reporting tips to be less than they really were. Reprisals were unfailingly swift and ruthless, and a month's suspension on some trumped-up charge usually brought non-conformists into line.

There was another cause, too, for Chandler's presence in the hotel tonight, and it accounted for his unease which had been steadily growing since Peter McDermott's telephone call a few minutes earlier. McDermott had instructed: investigate a complaint on the eleventh floor. But Herbie Chandler had no need to investigate because he knew roughly what was happening on the eleventh. The reason was simple: he had arranged it himself.

Three hours earlier the two youths had been explicit in their request and he had listened respectfully since the fathers of both were wealthy local citizens and frequent guests of the hotel. "Listen, Herbie," one of them said, "there's a fraternity dance tonight—the same old crap, and we'd like something different."

He had asked, knowing the answer, "How different?"

"We've taken a suite." The boy flushed. "We want a couple of girls."

It was too risky, Herbie decided at once. Both were little

more than boys, and he suspected they had been drinking. He began, "Sorry, gentlemen," when the second youth cut in.

"Don't give us any crap about not being able to, because we know you run the call girls here."

Herbie had bared his weasel teeth in what passed for a smile. "I can't imagine where you got that idea, Mr. Dixon."

The one who had spoken first insisted, "We can pay, Herbie. You know that."

The bell captain hesitated, despite his doubts his mind working greedily. Just lately his sideline revenues had been slower than usual. Perhaps, after all, the risk was slight.

The one named Dixon said, "Let's quit horsing around. How much?"

Herbie looked at the youths, remembered their fathers, and multiplied the standard rate by two. "A hundred dollars."

There was a momentary pause. Then Dixon said decisively, "You got a deal." He added persuasively to his companion, "Listen we've already paid for the booze. I'll lend you the rest of your split."

"Well . . ."

"In advance, gentlemen." Herbie moistened his thin lips with his tongue. "Just one other thing. You'll have to make sure there's no noise. If there is, and we get complaints, there could be trouble for all of us."

There would be no noise, they had assured him, but now, it seemed, there had been, and his original fears were proving uncomfortably true.

An hour ago the girls had come in through the front entrance as usual, with only an inner few of the hotel's staff aware that they were other than registered hotel guests. If all had gone well, both should have left by now, as unobtrusively as they had come.

The eleventh floor complaint, relayed through McDermott and specifically referring to a sex orgy, meant that something had gone seriously wrong. What? Herbie was reminded uncomfortably of the reference to booze.

It was hot and humid in the lobby despite the overworked air conditioning, and Herbie took out a silk handkerchief to mop his perspiring forehead. At the same time he silently cursed his own folly, wondering whether, at this stage, he should go upstairs or stay well away.

3

Peter McDermott rode the elevator to the ninth floor, leaving Christine who was to continue to the fourteenth with her accompanying bellboy. At the opened elevator doorway he hesitated. "Send for me if there's any trouble."

"If it's essential I'll scream." As the sliding doors came between them her eyes met his own. For a moment he stood thoughtfully watching the place where they had been, then, long legged and alert, strode down the carpeted corridor toward the Presidential Suite.

The St. Gregory's largest and most elaborate suite—known familiarly as the brasshouse—had, in its time, housed a succession of distinguished guests, including presidents and royalty. Most had liked New Orleans because after an initial welcome the city had a way of respecting its visitors' privacy, including indiscretions, if any. Somewhat less than heads of state, though distinguished in their way, were the suite's present tenants, the Duke and Duchess of Croydon, plus their retinue of secretary, the Duchess's maid, and five Bedlington terriers.

Outside the double padded leather doors, decorated with gold fleur-de-lis, Peter McDermott depressed a mother-of-pearl button and heard a muted buzz inside, followed by a less muted chorus of barkings. Waiting, he reflected on what he had heard and knew about the Croydons.

The Duke of Croydon, scion of an ancient family, had adapted himself to the times with an instinct for the common touch. Within the past decade, and aided by his Duchess—herself a known public figure and cousin of the Queen—he had become ambassador-at-large and successful troubleshooter for the British government. More recently, however, there had been rumors that the Duke's career had reached a critical point, perhaps because his touch had become a shade too common in some areas, notably those of liquor and other men's wives. There were

7

other reports, though, which said the shadow over the Duke was minor and temporary, and that the Duchess had the situation well in hand. Supporting this second view were predictions that the Duke of Croydon might soon be named British Ambassador to Washington.

From behind Peter a voice murmured, "Excuse me, Mr. McDermott, can I have a word with you?"

Turning abruptly he recognized Sol Natchez, one of the elderly room-service waiters, who had come quietly down the corridor, a lean cadaverous figure in a short white coat, trimmed with the hotel's colors of red and gold. The man's hair was slicked down flatly and combed forward into an old-fashioned forelock. His eyes were pale and rheumy, and the veins in the back of his hands, which he rubbed nervously, stood out like cords with the flesh sunk deep between them.

"What is it, Sol?"

His voice betraying agitation, the waiter said, "I expect you've come about the complaint—the complaint about me."

McDermott glanced at the double doors. They had not yet opened, nor, apart from the barking, had there been any other sound from within. He said, "Tell me what happened."

The other swallowed twice. Ignoring the question, he said in a pleading hurried whisper, "If I lose this job, Mr. McDermott, it's hard at my age to find another." He looked toward the Presidential Suite, his expression a mixture of anxiety and resentment. "They're not the hardest people to serve . . . except for tonight. They expect a lot, but I've never minded, even though there's never a tip."

Peter smiled involuntarily. British nobility seldom tipped, assuming perhaps that the privilege of waiting on them was a reward in itself.

He interjected, "You still haven't told me . . ."

"I'm gettin' to it, Mr. McDermott." From someone old enough to be Peter's grandfather, the other man's distress was almost embarrassing. "It was about half an hour ago. They'd ordered a late supper, the Duke and Duchess— oysters, champagne, shrimp Creole."

"Never mind the menu. What happened?"

8

"It was the shrimp Creole, sir. When I was serving it
. . . well, it's something, in all these years it's happened
very rarely."

"For heaven's sake!" Peter had one eye on the suite
doors, ready to break off the conversation the moment they
opened.

"Yes, Mr. McDermott. Well, when I was serving the
Creole the Duchess got up from the table and as she came
back she jogged my arm. If I didn't know better I'd have
said it was deliberate."

"That's ridiculous!"

"I know, sir, I know. But what happened, you see, was
there was a small spot—I swear it was no more than a
quarter inch—on the Duke's trousers."

Peter said doubtfully, "Is that *all* this is about?"

"Mr. McDermott, I swear to you that's all. But you'd
think—the fuss the Duchess made—I'd committed murder. I apologized, I got a clean napkin and water to get
the spot off, but it wouldn't do. She insisted on sending for
Mr. Trent . . ."

"Mr. Trent is not in the hotel."

He would hear the other side of the story, Peter decided,
before making any judgment. Meanwhile he instructed,
"If you're all through for tonight you'd better go home.
Report tomorrow and you'll be told what will happen."

As the waiter disappeared, Peter McDermott depressed
the bell push again. There was barely time for the barking
to resume before the door was opened by a moon-faced,
youngish man with pince-nez. Peter recognized him as the
Croydons' secretary.

Before either of them could speak a woman's voice
called out from the suite's interior. "Whoever it is, tell
them not to *keep* buzzing." For all the peremptory tone,
Peter thought, it was an attractive voice with a rich huski-
ness which excited interest.

"I beg your pardon," he told the secretary. "I thought
perhaps you hadn't heard." He introduced himself, then
added, "I understand there has been some trouble about
our service. I came to see if I could help."

The secretary said, "We were expecting Mr. Trent."

"Mr. Trent is away from the hotel for the evening."

9

While speaking they had moved from the corridor into the hallway of the suite, a tastefully appointed rectangle with deep broadloom, two upholstered chairs, and a telephone side table beneath a Morris Henry Hobbs engraving of old New Orleans. The double doorway to the corridor formed one end of the rectangle. At the other end, the door to the large living room was partially open. On the right and left were two other doorways, one to the self-contained kitchen and another to an office-cum-bed-sitting room, at present used by the Croydons' secretary. The two main, connecting bedrooms of the suite were accessible both through the kitchen and living room, an arrangement contrived so that a surreptitious bedroom visitor could be spirited in and out by the kitchen if need arose.

"Why can't he be sent for?" The question was addressed without preliminary as the living-room door opened and the Duchess of Croydon appeared, three of the Bedlington terriers enthusiastically at her heels. With a swift finger-snap, instantly obeyed, she silenced the dogs and turned her eyes questioningly on Peter. He was aware of the handsome, high-cheekboned face, familiar through a thousand photographs. Even in casual clothes, he observed, the Duchess was superbly dressed.

"To be perfectly honest, Your Grace, I was not aware that you required Mr. Trent personally."

Gray-green eyes regarded him appraisingly. "Even in Mr. Trent's absence I should have expected one of the *senior* executives."

Despite himself, Peter flushed. There was a superb hauteur about the Duchess of Croydon which—in a perverse way—was curiously appealing. A picture flashed into his memory. He had seen it in one of the illustrated magazines—the Duchess putting a stallion at a high fence. Disdainful of risk, she had been securely and superbly in command. He had an impression, at this moment, of being on foot while the Duchess was mounted.

"I'm assistant general manager. That's why I came personally."

There was a glimmer of amusement in the eyes which held his own. "Aren't you somewhat young for that?"

"Not really. Nowadays a good many young men are

10

engaged in hotel management." The secretary, he noticed, had disappeared discreetly.

"How old *are* you?"

"Thirty-two."

The Duchess smiled. When she chose—as at this moment—her face became animated and warm. It was not difficult, Peter thought, to become aware of the fabled charm. She was five or six years older than himself, he calculated, though younger than the Duke who was in his late forties. Now she asked, "Do you take a course or something?"

"I have a degree from Cornell University—the School of Hotel Administration. Before coming here I was an assistant manager at the Waldorf." It required an effort to mention the Waldorf, and he was tempted to add: *from where I was fired in ignominy, and black-listed by the chain hotels, so that I am fortunate to be working here, which is an independent house.* But he would not say it, of course, because a private hell was something you lived with alone, even when someone else's casual questions nudged old, raw wounds within yourself.

The Duchess retorted, "The Waldorf would never have tolerated an incident like tonight's."

"I assure you, ma'am, that if we are at fault the St. Gregory will not tolerate it either." The conversation, he thought, was like a game of tennis, with the ball lobbed from one court to the other. He waited for it to come back.

"If you were at fault! Are you aware that your waiter poured shrimp Creole over my husband?"

It was so obviously an exaggeration, he wondered why. It was also uncharacteristic since, until now, relations between the hotel and the Croydons had been excellent.

"I was aware there had been an accident which was probably due to carelessness. In that event I'm here to apologize for the hotel."

"Our entire evening has been ruined," the Duchess insisted. "My husband and I decided to enjoy a quiet evening in our suite here, by ourselves. We were out for a few moments only, to take a walk around the block, and we returned to supper—and this!"

Peter nodded, outwardly sympathetic but mystified by

the Duchess's attitude. It seemed almost as if she wanted to impress the incident on his mind so he would not forget it.

He suggested, "Perhaps if I could convey our apologies to the Duke . . ."

The Duchess said firmly, "That will not be necessary."

He was about to take his leave when the door to the living room, which had remained ajar, opened fully. It framed the Duke of Croydon.

In contrast to his Duchess, the Duke was untidily dressed, in a creased white shirt and the trousers of a tuxedo. Instinctively Peter McDermott's eyes sought the tell-tale stain where Natchez, in the Duchess's words, had "poured shrimp Creole over my husband." He found it, though it was barely visible—a tiny spot which a valet could have removed instantly. Behind the Duke, in the spacious living room a television set was turned on.

The Duke's face seemed flushed, and more lined than some of his recent photographs showed. He held a glass in his hand and when he spoke his voice was blurry. "Oh, beg pardon." Then, to the Duchess: "I say, old girl. Must have left my cigarettes in the car."

She responded sharply, "I'll bring some." There was a curt dismissal in her voice and with a nod the Duke turned back into the living room. It was a curious, uncomfortable scene and for some reason it had heightened the Duchess's anger.

Turning to Peter, she snapped, "I insist on a full report being made to Mr. Trent, and you may inform him that I expect a personal apology."

Still perplexed, Peter went out as the suite door closed firmly behind him.

But he was allowed no more time for reflection. In the corridor outside, the bellboy who had accompanied Christine to the fourteenth floor was waiting. "Mr. McDermott," he said urgently, "Miss Francis wants you in 1439, and please hurry!"

4

Some fifteen minutes earlier, when Peter McDermott had left the elevator on his way to the Presidential Suite, the bellboy grinned at Christine. "Doing a bit of detectiving, Miss Francis?"

"If the chief house officer was around," Christine told him, "I wouldn't have to."

The bellboy, Jimmy Duckworth, a balding stubby man whose married son worked in the St. Gregory accounting department, said contemptuously, "Oh, him!" A moment later the elevator stopped at the fourteenth floor.

"It's 1439, Jimmy," Christine said, and automatically both turned right. There was a difference, she realized, in the way the two of them knew the geography of the hotel: the bellboy through years of ushering guests from the lobby to their rooms; herself, from a series of mental pictures which familiarity with the printed plans of each floor of the St. Gregory had given her.

Five years ago, she thought, if someone at the University of Wisconsin had asked what twenty-year-old Chris Francis, a bright co-ed with a flair for modern languages, was likely to be doing a lustrum later, not even the wildest guess would have had her working in a New Orleans hotel. That long ago her knowledge of the Crescent City was of the slightest, and her interest less. She had learned in school about the Louisiana Purchase and had seen *A Streetcar Named Desire*. But even the last was out of date when she eventually came. The streetcar had become a diesel bus, and Desire was an obscure thoroughfare on the east side of town, which tourists seldom saw.

She supposed, in a way, it was this lack of knowledge which brought her to New Orleans. After the accident in Wisconsin, dully and with only the vaguest of reasoning, she had sought a place where she could be unknown and which, as well, was unfamiliar to herself. Familiar things, their touch and sight and sound, had become an ache of heart—all encompassing—which filled the waking day and penetrated sleep. Strangely—and in a way it shamed her

13

at the time—there were never nightmares; only the steady procession of events as they had been that memorable day at Madison airport. She had been there to see her family leave for Europe: her mother, gay and excited, wearing the *bon voyage* orchid which a friend had telegraphed; her father, relaxed and amiably complacent that for a month the real and imagined ailments of his patients would be someone else's concern. He had been puffing a pipe which he knocked out on his shoe when the flight was called. Babs, her elder sister, had embraced Christine; and even Tony, two years younger and hating public affection, consented to be kissed.

"So long, Ham!" Babs and Tony had called back, and Christine smiled at the use of the silly, affectionate name they gave her because she was the middle of their trio sandwich. And they had all promised to write, even though she would join them in Paris two weeks later when term ended. At the last her mother had held Chris tightly, and told her to take care. And a few minutes later the big prop-jet had taxied out and taken off with a roar, majestically, though it barely cleared the runway before it fell back, one wing low, becoming a whirling, somersaulting Catherine wheel, and for a moment a dust cloud, and then a torch, and finally a silent pile of fragments—machinery and what was left of human flesh.

It was five years ago. A few weeks after, she left Wisconsin and had never returned.

Her own footsteps and the bellboy's were muffled in the carpeted corridor. A pace ahead, Jimmy Duckworth ruminated, "Room 1439—that's the old gent, Mr. Wells. We moved him from a corner room a couple of days ago."

Ahead, down the corridor, a door opened and a man, well dressed and fortyish, came out. Closing the door behind him, and ready to pocket the key, he hesitated, eying Christine with frank interest. He seemed about to speak but, barely perceptibly, the bellboy shook his head. Christine, who missed nothing of the exchange, supposed she should be flattered to be mistaken for a call girl. From rumors she heard, Herbie Chandler's list embraced a glamorous membership.

When they had passed by she asked, "Why was Mr. Wells's room changed?"

"The way I heard it, miss, somebody else had 1439 and raised a fuss. So what they did was switch around."

Christine remembered 1439 now; there had been complaints before. It was next to the service elevator and appeared to be the meeting place of all the hotel's pipes. The effect was to make the place noisy and unbearably hot. Every hotel had at least one such room—some called it the ha-ha room—which usually was never rented until everything else was full.

"If Mr. Wells had a better room why was he asked to move?"

The bellboy shrugged. "You'd better ask the room clerks that."

She persisted, "But you've an idea."

"Well, I guess it's because he never complains. The old gent's been coming here for years with never a peep out of him. There are some who seem to think it's a bit of a joke." Christine's lips tightened angrily as Jimmy Duckworth went on, "I did hear in the dining room they give him that table beside the kitchen door, the one no one else will have. He doesn't seem to mind, they say."

Christine thought grimly: Someone would mind tomorrow morning; she would guarantee it. At the realization that a regular guest, who also happened to be a quiet and gentle man, had been so shabbily treated, she felt her temper bristle. Well, let it. Her temper was not unknown around the hotel and there were some, she knew, who said it went with her red hair. Although she curbed it mostly, once in a while it served a purpose in getting things done.

They turned a corner and stopped at the door of 1439. The bellboy knocked. They waited, listening. There was no acknowledging sound and Jimmy Duckworth repeated the knock, this time more loudly. At once there was a response: an eerie moaning that began as a whisper, reached a crescendo, then ended suddenly as it began.

"Use your pass key," Christine instructed. "Open the door—quickly!"

She stood back while the bellboy went in ahead; even

15

in apparent crisis a hotel had rules of decorum which must be observed. The room was in darkness and she saw Duckworth snap on the ceiling light and go around a corner out of sight. Almost at once he called back, "Miss Francis, you'd better come."

The room, as Christine entered, was stiflingly hot, though a glance at the air-conditioning regulator showed it set hopefully to "cool." But that was all she had time to see before observing the struggling figure, half upright, half recumbent in the bed. It was the birdlike little man she knew as Albert Wells. His face ashen gray, eyes bulging and with trembling lips, he was attempting desperately to breathe and barely succeeding.

She went quickly to the bedside. Once, years before, in her father's office she had seen a patient *in extremis,* fighting for breath. There were things her father had done then which she could not do now, but one she remembered. She told Duckworth decisively, "Get the window open. We need air in here."

The bellboy's eyes were focused on the face of the man in bed. He said nervously, "The window's sealed. They did it for the air conditioning."

"Then force it. If you have to, break the glass."

She had already picked up the telephone beside the bed. When the operator answered, Christine announced, "This is Miss Francis. Is Dr. Aarons in the hotel?"

"No, Miss Francis; but he left a number. If it's an emergency I can reach him."

"It's an emergency. Tell Dr. Aarons room 1439, and to hurry, please. Ask how long he'll take to get here, then call me back."

Replacing the phone, Christine turned to the still-struggling figure in the bed. The frail, elderly man was breathing no better than before and she perceived that his face, which a few moments earlier had been ashen gray, was turning blue. The moaning which they had heard outside had begun again; it was the effort of exhaling, but obviously most of the sufferer's waning strength was being consumed by his desperate physical exertion.

"Mr. Wells," she said, trying to convey a confidence she was far from feeling, "I think you might breathe more

16

easily if you kept perfectly still." The bellboy, she noticed, was having success with the window. He had used a coat hanger to break a seal on the catch and now was inching the bottom portion upward.

As if in response to Christine's words, the little man's struggles subsided. He was wearing an old-fashioned flannel nightshirt and Christine put an arm around him, aware of his scrawny shoulders through the coarse material. Reaching for pillows, she propped them behind, so that he could lean back, sitting upright at the same time. His eyes were fixed on hers; they were doe-like, she thought, and trying to convey gratitude. She said reassuringly, "I've sent for a doctor. He'll be here at any moment." As she spoke, the bellboy grunted with an extra effort and the window, suddenly freed, slid open wide. At once a draft of cool fresh air suffused the room. So the storm *had* moved south, Christine thought gratefully, sending a freshening breeze before it, and the temperature outside must be lower than for days. In the bed Albert Wells gasped greedily at the new air. As he did the telephone rang. Signaling the bellboy to take her place beside the sick man, she answered it.

"Dr. Aarons is on his way, Miss Francis," the operator announced. "He was in Paradis and said to tell you he'll be at the hotel in twenty minutes."

Christine hesitated. Paradis was across the Mississippi, beyond Algiers. Even allowing for fast driving, twenty minutes was optimistic. Also, she sometimes had doubts about the competence of the portly, Sazerac-drinking Dr. Aarons who, as house physician, lived free in the hotel in return for his availability. She told the operator, "I'm not sure we can wait that long. Would you check our own guest list to see if we have any doctors registered?"

"I already did that." There was a touch of smugness in the answer, as if the speaker had studied stories of heroic telephone operators and was determined to live up to them. "There's a Dr. Koenig in 221, and Dr. Uxbridge in 1203."

Christine noted the numbers on a pad beside the telephone. "All right, ring 221, please." Doctors who registered in hotels expected privacy and were entitled to it.

Once in a while, though, emergency justified a break with protocol.

There were several clicks as the ringing continued. Then a sleepy voice with a Teutonic accent answered, "Yes, who is it?"

Christine identified herself. "I'm sorry to disturb you, Dr. Koenig, but one of our other guests is extremely ill." Her eyes went to the bed. For the moment, she noticed, the blueness around the face had gone, but there was still an ashen-gray pallor, with breathing as difficult as ever. She added, "I wonder if you could come."

There was a pause, then the same voice, soft and agreeable: "My dearest young lady, it would be a matter of utmost happiness if, however humbly, I could assist. Alas, I fear that I could not." A gentle chuckle. "You see, I am a doctor of music, here in your beautiful city to 'guest conduct'—it is the word, I think—its fine symphony orchestra."

Despite the urgency, Christine had an impulse to laugh. She apologized, "I'm sorry for disturbing you."

"Please do not concern yourself. Of course, if my unfortunate fellow guest becomes—how shall I put it?—beyond the help of the *other* kind of doctors, I could bring my violin to play for him." There was a deep sigh down the telephone. "What finer way to die than to an adagio by Vivaldi or Tartini—superbly executed."

"Thank you. I hope that won't be necessary." She was impatient now to make the next call.

Dr. Uxbridge in 1203 answered the telephone at once in a no-nonsense tone of voice. In reply to Christine's first question he responded, "Yes, I'm a doctor of medicine—an internist." He listened without comment while she described the problem, then said tersely, "I'll be there in a few minutes."

The bellboy was still at the bedside. Christine instructed him, "Mr. McDermott is in the Presidential Suite. Go there, and as soon as he's free ask him to come here quickly." She picked up the telephone again. "The chief engineer, please."

Fortunately there was seldom any doubt about the chief's availability. Doc Vickery was a bachelor who lived in the hotel and had one ruling passion: the St. Gregory's mechanical equipment extending from foundations to the roof. For a quarter century, since leaving the sea and his native Clydeside, he had overseen the installation of most of it and, in lean times when money for replacement equipment was scarce, had a way of coaxing extra performance out of tired machinery. The chief was a friend of Christine's, and she knew that she was one of his favorites. In a moment his Scottish burr was on the line. "Aye?"

In a few words she told him about Albert Wells. "The doctor isn't here yet, but he'll probably want oxygen. We've a portable set in the hotel, haven't we?"

"Aye, we've oxygen cylinders, Chris, but we use them just for gas welding."

"Oxygen is oxygen," Christine argued. Some of the things her father had told her were coming back. "It doesn't matter how you wrap it. Could you order one of your night people to have whatever's necessary sent up?"

The chief gave a grunt of agreement. "I will; and soon as I get my breeks on, lassie, I'll be along mysel'. If I don't, some clown will likely open an acetylene tank under yon man's nose, and that'll finish him for sure."

"Please hurry!" She replaced the phone, turning back to the bed.

The little man's eyes were closed. No longer struggling, he appeared not to be breathing at all.

There was a light tap at the opened door and a tall, spare man stepped in from the corridor. He had an angular face, and hair graying at the temples. A dark blue suit, conservatively cut, failed to conceal beige pajamas beneath. "Uxbridge," he announced in a quiet, firm voice.

"Doctor," Christine said, "just this moment . . ."

The newcomer nodded and from a leather bag, which he put down on the bed, swiftly produced a stethoscope. Without wasting time he reached inside the patient's flannel nightshirt and listened briefly to the chest and back. Then, returning to the bag, in a series of efficient movements he took out a syringe, assembled it, and snapped off the neck of a small glass vial. When he had drawn the fluid from the vial into the syringe, he leaned over the bed and pushed a sleeve of the nightshirt upward, twisting it into a rough

19

tourniquet. He instructed Christine, "Keep that in place; hold it tightly."

With an alcohol swab Dr. Uxbridge cleansed the forearm above a vein and inserted the syringe. He nodded to the tourniquet. "You can release it now." Then, glancing at his watch, he began to inject the liquid slowly.

Christine turned, her eyes seeking the doctor's face. Without looking up, he informed her, "Aminophylline; it should stimulate the heart." He checked his watch again, maintaining a gradual dosage. A minute passed. Two. The syringe was half empty. So far there was no response.

Christine whispered, "What is it that's wrong?"

"Severe bronchitis, with asthma as a complication. I suspect he's had these attacks before."

Suddenly the little man's chest heaved. Then he was breathing, more slowly than before, but with fuller, deeper breaths. His eyes opened.

The tension in the room had lessened. The doctor withdrew the syringe and began to disassemble it.

"Mr. Wells," Christine said. "Mr. Wells, can you understand me?"

She was answered by a series of nods. As they had been earlier, the doe-like eyes were fixed on her own.

"You were very ill when we found you, Mr. Wells. This is Dr. Uxbridge who was staying in the hotel and came to help."

The eyes shifted to the doctor. Then, with an effort: "Thank you." The words were close to a gasp, but they were the first the sick man had spoken. A small amount of color was returning to his face.

"If there's anyone to thank it should be this young lady." The doctor gave a cool, tight smile, then told Christine, "The gentleman is still very sick and will need further medical attention. My advice is for immediate transfer to a hospital."

"No, no! I don't want that." The words came—a swift and urgent response—from the elderly man in the bed. He was leaning forward from the pillows, his eyes alert, hands lifted from beneath the covers where Christine had placed them earlier. The change in his condition within the space of a few minutes was remarkable, she thought. He was still breathing wheezily, and occasionally with effort, but the acute distress had gone.

For the first time Christine had time to study his appearance. Originally she had judged him to be in his early sixties; now she revised the guess to add a half dozen years. His build was slight, and shortness, plus thin peaked features and the suggestion of a stoop, created the sparrowlike effect she remembered from previous encounters. His hair, what little was left of it, was usually combed in sparse gray strands, though now it was disarranged, and damp from perspiration. His face habitually held an expression which was mild and inoffensive, almost apologetic, and yet underneath, she suspected, was a ridge of quiet determination.

The first occasion she had met Albert Wells had been two years earlier. He had come diffidently to the hotel's executive suite, concerned about a discrepancy in his bill which he had been unable to settle with the front office. The amount involved, she recalled, was seventy-five cents and while—as usually happened when guests disputed small sums—the chief cashier had offered to cancel the charge, Albert Wells wanted to prove that he had not incurred it at all. After patient inquiry, Christine proved that the little man was right and, since she herself sometimes had bouts of parsimony—though alternating with wild feminine extravagance—she sympathized and respected him for his stand. She also deduced—from his hotel bill, which showed modest spending, and his clothes which were obviously ready-to-wear—that he was a man of small means, perhaps a pensioner, whose yearly visits to New Orleans were high points of his life.

Now Albert Wells declared, "I don't like hospitals. I never have liked them."

"If you stay here," the doctor demurred, "you'll need medical attention, and a nurse for twenty-four hours at least. You really should have intermittent oxygen too."

The little man insisted, "The hotel can arrange about a nurse." He urged Christine, "You can, can't you, miss?"

"I suppose we could." Obviously Albert Wells's dislike of hospitals must be strong. For the moment it had overcome his customary attitude of not wishing to cause trouble. She wondered, though, if he had any idea of the high cost of private nursing.

There was an interruption from the corridor. A coveralled mechanic came in, wheeling an oxygen cylinder on a trolley. He was followed by the burly figure of the chief engineer, carrying a length of rubber tubing, some wire and a plastic bag.

"This isn't hospital style, Chris," the chief said. "I fancy it'll work, though." He had dressed hurriedly—an old tweed jacket and slacks over an unbuttoned shirt, revealing an expanse of hairy chest. His feet were thrust into loose sandals and beneath his bald, domed head a pair of thick-rimmed spectacles were, as usual, perched at the tip of his nose. Now, using the wire, he was fashioning a connection between the tube and plastic bag. He instructed the mechanic who had stopped uncertainly, "Set up the cylinder beside the bed, laddie. If you move any slower, I'll think it's you should be getting the oxygen."

Dr. Uxbridge seemed surprised. Christine explained her original idea that oxygen might be needed, and introduced the chief engineer. With his hands still busy, the chief nodded, looking briefly over the top of his glasses. A moment later, with the tube connected, he announced, "These plastic bags have suffocated enough people. No reason why one shouldna' do the reverse. Do you think it'll answer, Doctor?"

Some of Dr. Uxbridge's earlier aloofness had disappeared. "I think it will answer very well." He glanced at Christine. "This hotel appears to have some highly competent help."

She laughed. "Wait until we mix up your reservations. You'll change your mind."

The doctor returned to the bed. "The oxygen will make you more comfortable, Mr. Wells. I imagine you've had this bronchial trouble before."

Albert Wells nodded. He said throatily, "The bronchitis I picked up as a miner. Then the asthma came later." His eyes moved on to Christine. "I'm sorry about all this, miss "

"I'm sorry too, but mostly because your room was changed."

The chief engineer had connected the free end of the rubber tube to the green painted cylinder. Dr. Uxbridge told him, "We'll begin with five minutes on oxygen and five minutes off." Together they arranged the improvised mask around the sick man's face. A steady hiss denoted that the oxygen was on.

The doctor checked his watch, then inquired, "Have you sent for a local doctor?"

Christine explained about Dr. Aarons.

Dr. Uxbridge nodded approval. "He'll take over when he arrives. I'm from Illinois and not licensed to practice in Louisiana." He bent over Albert Wells. "Easier?" Beneath the plastic mask the little man moved his head confirmingly.

There were firm footfalls down the corridor and Peter McDermott strode in, his big frame filling the outer doorway. "I got your message," he told Christine. His eyes went to the bed. "Will he be all right?"

"I think so, though I believe we owe Mr. Wells something." Beckoning Peter into the corridor, she described the change in rooms which the bellboy had told her about. As she saw Peter frown, she added, "If he does stay, we ought to give him another room, and I imagine we could get a nurse without too much trouble."

Peter nodded agreement. There was a house telephone in a maid's closet across the hallway. He went to it and asked for Reception.

"I'm on the fourteenth," he informed the room clerk who answered. "Is there a vacant room on this floor?"

There was a perceptible pause. The night room clerk was an old-timer, appointed many years ago by Warren Trent. He had an autocratic way of doing his job which few people ever contested. He had also made known to Peter McDermott on a couple of occasions that he resented newcomers, particularly if they were younger, senior to himself, and from the north.

"Well," Peter said, "is there a room or isn't there?"

"I have 1410," the clerk said with his best southern planter's accent, "but I'm about to allocate it to a gentleman who has this moment checked in." He added, "In case you're unaware, we are very close to a full house."

Number 1410 was a room Peter remembered. It was large and airy and faced St. Charles Avenue. He asked reasonably, "If I take 1410, can you find something else for your man?"

"No, Mr. McDermott. All I have is a small suite on five, and the gentleman does not wish to pay a higher rate."

Peter said crisply, "Let your man have the suite at the room rate for tonight. He can be relocated in the morning. Meanwhile I'll use 1410 for a transfer from 1439, and please send a boy up with the key right away."

"Just one minute, Mr. McDermott." Previously the clerk's tone had been aloof; now it was openly truculent. "It has always been Mr. Trent's policy . . ."

"Right now we're talking about my policy," Peter snapped. "And another thing: before you go off duty leave word for the day clerks that tomorrow I want an explanation of why Mr. Wells was shifted from his original room to 1439, and you might add that the reason had better be good."

He grimaced at Christine as he replaced the phone.

5

"You must have been insane," the Duchess of Croydon protested. "Absolutely, abysmally insane." She had returned to the living room of the Presidential Suite after Peter McDermott's departure, carefully closing the inner door behind her.

The Duke shifted uncomfortably as he always did under one of his wife's periodic tongue lashings. "Damn sorry, old girl. Telly was on. Couldn't hear the fellow. Thought he'd cleared out." He took a deep draught from the whiskey and soda he was holding unsteadily, then added plaintively, "Besides, with everything else I'm bloody upset."

"Sorry! Upset!" Unusually there was an undernote of hysteria in his wife's voice. "You make it sound as if it's all some sort of game. As if what happened tonight couldn't be the ruination . . ."

"Don't think anything of sort. Know it's all serious. Bloody serious." Hunched disconsolately in a deep leather armchair he seemed a little man, akin to the bowler-hatted mousy genus which English cartoonists were so fond of drawing.

The Duchess went on accusingly, "I was doing the best I could. The very best, after your incredible folly, to establish that both of us spent a quiet evening in the hotel. I even invented a walk that we went for in case anyone saw us come in. And then crassly, stupidly, you blunder in to announce you left your cigarettes in the car."

"Only one heard me. That manager chap. Wouldn't notice."

"He noticed. I was watching his face." With an effort the Duchess retained her self-control. "Have you any notion of the ghastly mess we're in?"

"Already said so." The Duke drained his drink, then contemplated the empty tumbler. "Bloody ashamed too. 'F you hadn't persuaded me . . . 'F I hadn't been fuddled . . ."

"You were drunk! You were drunk when I found you, and you still are."

He shook his head as if to clear it. "Sober now." It was his own turn to be bitter. "You *would* follow me. Butt in. Wouldn't leave things be . . ."

"Never mind that. It's the other that matters."

He repeated, *"You* persuaded me . . ."

"There was nothing we could do. Nothing! And there was a better chance my way."

"Not so sure. 'F the police get their teeth in . . ."

"We'd have to be suspected first. That's why I made that trouble with the waiter and followed through. It isn't an alibi but it's the next best thing. It's set in their minds we were here tonight . . . or would have been if you hadn't thrown it all away. I could weep."

"Be interesting that," the Duke said. "Didn't think you were enough of a woman." He sat upright in the chair and had somehow thrown off the submissiveness, or most of it. It was a chameleon quality which sometimes bewildered those who knew him, setting them to wondering which was the real person.

The Duchess flushed, the effect heightening her statuesque beauty. "That isn't necessary."

"P'raps not." Rising, the Duke went to a side table

25

where he splashed Scotch generously into his glass, followed by a short snort of soda. With his back turned, he added, "All same, must admit 's'at bottom most of our troubles."

"I admit nothing of the kind. Your habits are, perhaps, but not mine. Going to that disgusting gambling joint tonight was madness; and to take that woman . . ."

"Y'already covered that," the Duke said wearily. "Exhaustively. On our way back. Before it happened."

"I wasn't aware that what I said had penetrated."

"Your words, old girl, penetrate thickest mists. I keep trying make them impenetrable. So far haven't succeeded." The Duke of Croydon sipped his fresh drink. "Why'd you marry me?"

"I suppose it was mostly that you stood out in our circle as someone who was doing something worth while. People said the aristocracy was effete. You seemed to be proving that it wasn't."

He held up his glass, studying it like a crystal ball. "Not proving it now. Eh?"

"If you appear to be, it's because I prop you up."

"Washington?" The word was a question.

"We could manage it," the Duchess said. "If I could keep you sober and in your own bed."

"Aha!" Her husband laughed hollowly. "A damn cold bed at that."

"I already said that isn't necessary."

"Ever wondered why I married *you?*"

"I've formed opinions."

"Tell you most important." He drank again, as if for courage, then said thickly, "Wanted you in that bed. Fast. Legally. Knew was only way."

"I'm surprised you bothered. With so many others to choose from—before and since."

His bloodshot eyes were on her face. "Didn't want others. Wanted you. Still do."

She snapped, "That's enough! This has gone far enough."

He shook his head. "Something you should hear. Your pride, old girl. Magnificent. Savage. Always appealed to me. Didn't want to break it. Share it. You on your back. Thighs apart. Passionate. Trembling . . ."

"Stop it! Stop it! You . . . you lecher!" Her face was white, her voice high pitched. "I don't care if the police catch you! I hope they do! I hope you get ten years!"

6

After his quickly concluded dispute with Reception, Peter McDermott recrossed the fourteenth floor corridor to 1439.

"If you approve," he informed Dr. Uxbridge, "we'll transfer your patient to another room on this floor."

The tall, sparely built doctor who had responded to Christine's emergency call nodded. He glanced around the tiny ha-ha room with its mess of heating and water pipes. "Any change can only be an improvement."

As the doctor returned to the little man in the bed, beginning a new five-minute period of oxygen, Christine reminded Peter, "What we need now is a nurse."

"We'll let Dr. Aarons arrange that." Peter mused aloud: "The hotel will have to make the engagement, I suppose, which means we'll be liable for payment. Do you think your friend Wells is good for it?"

They had returned to the corridor, their voices low.

"I'm worried about that. I don't think he has much money." When she was concentrating, Peter noticed, Christine's nose had a charming way of crinkling. He was aware of her closeness and a faint, fragrant perfume.

"Oh well," he said, "we won't be too deep in debt by morning. We'll let the credit department look into it then."

When the key arrived, Christine went ahead to open the new room, 1410. "It's ready," she announced, returning.

"The best thing is to switch beds," Peter told the others. "Let's wheel this one into 1410 and bring back a bed from there." But the doorway, they discovered, was an inch too narrow.

Albert Wells, his breathing easier and with returning color, volunteered, "I've walked all my life, I can do a little bit now." But Dr. Uxbridge shook his head decisively.

The chief engineer inspected the difference in widths.

27

"I'll take the door off its hinges," he told the sick man. "Then ye'll go out like a cork from a bottle."

"Never mind," Peter said. "There's a quicker way—if you're agreeable, Mr. Wells."

The other smiled, and nodded.

Peter bent down, put a blanket around the elderly man's shoulders and picked him up bodily.

"You've strong arms, son," the little man said.

Peter smiled. Then, as easily as if his burden were a child, he strode down the corridor and into the new room.

Fifteen minutes later all was functioning as if on nyloned bearings. The oxygen equipment had been successfully transferred, though its use was now less urgent since the air conditioning in the more spacious quarters of 1410 had no competition from hot pipes, hence the air was sweeter. The resident physician, Dr. Aarons, had arrived, portly, jovial, and breathing bourbon in an almost-visible cloud. He accepted with alacrity the offer of Dr. Uxbridge to drop in in a consultant capacity the following day, and also grasped eagerly a further suggestion that cortisone might prevent a recurrence of the earlier attack. A private duty nurse, telephoned affectionately by Dr. Aarons ("Such wonderful news, my dear! We're going to be a team again.") was reportedly on the way.

As the chief engineer and Dr. Uxbridge took their leave, Albert Wells was sleeping gently.

Following Christine into the corridor, Peter carefully closed the door on Dr. Aarons who, while waiting for his nurse, was pacing the room in his own accompaniment, *pianissimo,* of the Toreador Song from *Carmen.* ("*Pom, pom, pom, pom-pom; pom-pom-pom, pom-pom . . .*") The latch clicked, cutting the minstrelsy off.

It was a quarter to twelve.

Walking toward the elevators, Christine said, "I'm glad we let him stay."

Peter seemed surprised. "Mr. Wells? Why wouldn't we?"

"Some places wouldn't. You know how they are: the least thing out of the ordinary, and no one can be bothered. All they want is people to check in, check out, and pay the bill; that's all."

"Those are sausage factories. A real hotel is for hospi-

28

tality; and succor if a guest needs it. The best ones started that way. Unfortunately too many people in this business have forgotten."

She regarded him curiously. "You think we've forgotten here?"

"You're damn right we have! A lot of the time, anyway. If I had my way there'd be a good many changes . . ." He stopped, embarrassed at his own forcefulness. "Never mind. Most of the time I keep such traitorous thoughts to myself."

"You shouldn't, and if you do you should be ashamed." Behind Christine's words was the knowledge that the St. Gregory *was* inefficient in many ways and in recent years had coasted under the shadow of its former glories. Currently, too, the hotel was facing a financial crisis which might force drastic transitions whether its proprietor, Warren Trent, was in favor or not.

"There's heads and brick walls," Peter objected. "Beating one against the other doesn't help. W.T. isn't keen on new ideas."

"That's no reason for giving up."

He laughed. "You sound like a woman."

"I *am* a woman."

"I know," Peter said. "I've just begun to notice."

It was true, he thought. For most of the time he had known Christine—since his own arrival at the St. Gregory —he had taken her for granted. Recently, though, he had found himself increasingly aware of just how attractive and personable she was. He wondered what she was doing for the rest of the evening.

He said tentatively, "I didn't have dinner tonight; too much going on. If you feel like it, how about joining me for a late supper?"

Christine said, "I love late suppers."

At the elevator he told her, "There's one more thing I want to check. I sent Herbie Chandler to look into that trouble on the eleventh but I don't trust him. After that I'll be through." He took her arm, squeezing it lightly. "Will you wait on the main mezzanine?"

His hands were surprisingly gentle for someone who might have been clumsy because of his size. Christine

29

glanced sideways at the strong, energetic profile with its jutting jaw that was almost lantern-like. It was an interesting face, she thought, with a hint of determination which could become obstinacy if provoked. She was aware of her senses quickening.

"All right," she agreed. "I'll wait."

7

Marsha Preyscott wished fervently that she had spent her nineteenth birthday some other way, or at least had stayed at the Alpha Kappa Epsilon fraternity ball on the hotel's convention floor, eight stories below. The sound of the ball, muted by distance and competing noises, came up to her now, drifting through the window of the eleventh-floor suite, which one of the boys had forced open a few minutes ago when the warmth, cigarette smoke, and general odor of liquor in the tightly packed room became overly oppressive, even for those whose grasp of such details was rapidly diminishing.

It had been a mistake to come here. But as always, and rebelliously, she had sought something different, which was what Lyle Dumaire had promised, Lyle whom she had known for years and dated occasionally, and whose father was president of one of the city's banks as well as a close friend of her own father. Lyle had told her while they were dancing, "This is kid stuff, Marsha. Some of the guys have taken a suite and we've been up there most of the evening. A lot of things are going on." He essayed a manly laugh which somehow became a giggle, then asked directly, "Why don't you come?"

Without thinking about it she had said yes, and they had left the dancing, coming upstairs to the small, crowded suite 1126–7, to be enveloped as they went in by stale air and high-pitched clamor. There were more people than she expected, and the fact that some of the boys were already very drunk was something she had not bargained for.

There were several girls, most of whom she knew, though none intimately, and she spoke to them briefly, though it

30

was hard to hear or be heard. One who said nothing, Sue Phillipe, had apparently passed out and her escort, a boy from Baton Rouge, was pouring water over her from a shoe he kept replenishing in the bathroom. Sue's dress of pink organdy was already a sodden mess.

The boys greeted Marsha more effusively, though almost at once returning to the improvised bar, set up by turning a glass-fronted cabinet upon its side. Someone— she wasn't sure who—put a glass clumsily into Marsha's hand.

It was obvious too that something was happening in the adjoining room, to which the door was closed, though a knot of boys whom Lyle Dumaire had joined—leaving Marsha alone—was clustered around it. She heard snatches of talk, including the question, "What was it like?" but the answer was lost in a shout of ribald laughter.

When some further remarks made her realize, or at least suspect, what was happening, disgust made her want to leave. Even the big lonely Garden District mansion was preferable to this, despite her dislike of its emptiness, with just herself and the servants when her father was away, as he had been for six weeks now, and would continue to be for at least two more.

The thought of her father reminded Marsha that if he had come home as he originally expected and promised, she would not have been here now, or at the fraternity ball either. Instead, there would have been a birthday celebration, with Mark Preyscott presiding in the easy jovial way he had, with a few of his daughter's special friends who, she knew, would have declined the Alpha Kappa Epsilon invitation if it had conflicted with her own. But he had not come home. Instead, he had telephoned, apologetically as he always did, this time from Rome.

"Marsha, honey, I really tried but I couldn't make it. My business here is going to take two or three weeks more, but I'll make it up to you, honey, I really will when I come home." He inquired tentatively if Marsha would like to visit her mother and her mother's latest husband in Los Angeles, and when she declined without even thinking about it, her father had urged, "Well, anyway, have a wonderful birthday, and there's something on the way I

31

think you'll like." Marsha had felt like crying at the sweet sound of his voice, but hadn't because she had long ago taught herself not to. Nor was there any point in wondering why the owner of a New Orleans department store, with a platoon of highly paid executives, should be more inflexibly tied to business than an office boy. Perhaps there were other things in Rome which he wouldn't tell her about, just as she would never tell him what was happening in room 1126 right now.

When she made her decision to leave she had moved to put her glass on a window ledge and now, down below, she could hear them playing *Stardust*. At this time of evening the music always moved on to the old sentimental numbers, especially if the band leader was Moxie Buchanan with his All-Star Southern Gentlemen who played for most of the St. Gregory's silver-plated social functions. Even if she had not been dancing earlier she would have recognized the arrangement—the brass warm and sweet, yet dominant, which was the Buchanan trademark.

Hesitating at the window, Marsha pondered a return to the dance floor, though she knew the way it would be there now: the boys increasingly hot in their tuxedoes, some fingering their collars uncomfortably, a few hobbledehoys wishing they were back in jeans and sweatshirt, and the girls shuttling to and from the powder room, behind its doors sharing giggled confidences; the whole affair, Marsha decided, as if a group of children were dressed to play charades. Youth was a dull time, Marsha often thought, especially when you had to share it with others the same age as yourself. There were moments—and this was one— when she longed for companionship that was more mature.

She would not find it though in Lyle Dumaire. She could see him, still in the group by the communicating door, his face flushed, starched shirtfront billowed and black tie askew. Marsha wondered how she could ever have taken him seriously, as she had for a while.

Others as well as herself were beginning to leave the suite, heading for the outer doorway in what seemed to be a general exodus. One of the older boys whom she knew as Stanley Dixon came out from the other room. As he nodded toward the door which he carefully closed behind

32

him, she could hear snatches of his words. ". . . girls say they're going . . . had enough . . . scared . . . disturbance."

Someone else said, ". . . told you we shouldn't have had all this . . ."

"Why not somebody from here?" It was Lyle Dumaire's voice, much less under control than it had been earlier.

"Yeah, but who?" The eyes of the small group swung around the room appraisingly. Marsha studiedly ignored them.

Several friends of Sue Phillipe, the girl who had passed out, were trying to help her to her feet, but not succeeding. One of the boys, more steady than the rest, called out concernedly, "Marsha! Sue's in pretty bad shape. Can you help her?"

Reluctantly Marsha stopped, looking down at the girl who had opened her eyes and was leaning back, her child-like face pallid, mouth slack, with its lipstick smeared messily. With an inward sigh Marsha told the others, "Help me get her to the bathroom." As three of them lifted her, the drunken girl began to cry.

At the bathroom one of the boys seemed inclined to follow, but Marsha closed the door firmly and bolted it. She turned to Sue Phillipe who was staring at herself in the mirror with an expression of horror. At least, Marsha thought gratefully, the shock had been sobering.

"I wouldn't worry too much," she remarked. "They say it has to happen once to all of us."

"Oh, God! My mother will *kill* me." The words were a moan, ending with a dive to the toilet bowl in order to be sick.

Seating herself on the edge of the bathtub, Marsha said practically, "You'll feel a lot better after that. When you're through I'll bathe your face and we can try some fresh make-up."

Her head still down, the other girl nodded dismally.

It was ten or fifteen minutes before they emerged and the suite was almost cleared, though Lyle Dumaire and his cronies were still huddled together. If Lyle planned to escort her, Marsha thought, she would turn him down. The only other occupant was the boy who had appealed for help. He came forward, explaining hurriedly, "We've

33

arranged for a girl friend of Sue's to take her home, and Sue can probably spend the night there." As he took the other girl's arm, she went with him compliantly. Over his shoulder the boy called back, "We've a car waiting downstairs. Thanks a lot, Marsha." Relieved, she watched them go.

She was retrieving her wrap, which she had put down to help Sue Phillipe, when she heard the outer door close. Stanley Dixon was standing in front of it, his hands behind him. Marsha heard the lock click softly.

"Hey, Marsha," Lyle Dumaire said. "What's the big rush?"

Marsha had known Lyle since childhood, but now there was a difference. This was a stranger, with the mien of a drunken bully. She answered, "I'm going home."

"Aw, come on." He swaggered toward her. "Be a good sport and have a drink."

"No, thank you."

As if he had not heard: "You're going to be a good sport, kid, aren't you?"

"Just privately," Stanley Dixon said. He had a thick nasal voice with a built-in leer. "Some of us have had a good time already. It's made us want more of the same." The other two, whose names she didn't know, were grinning.

She snapped, "I'm not interested in what you want." Though her voice was firm, she was aware of an underlying note of fear. She went toward the door, but Dixon shook his head. "Please," she said, "please let me go."

"Listen, Marsha," Lyle blustered. "We know you want to." He gave a coarse giggle. "All girls want to. They never really mean no. What they mean is 'come and get it.'" He appealed to the others. "Eh, fellas?"

The third boy crooned softly, "That's the way it is. You gotta get in there and get it."

They began to move closer.

She wheeled. "I'm warning you: if you touch me I shall scream."

"Be a pity if you did that," Stanley Dixon murmured. "You might miss all the fun." Suddenly, without seeming to move, he was behind her, clapping a big sweaty hand

34

across her mouth, another pinioning her arms. His head was close to hers, the smell of rye whiskey overpowering.

She struggled, and tried to bite the hand, but without success.

"Listen, Marsha," Lyle said, his face twisted into a smirk, "you're going to get it, so you might as well enjoy it. That's what they always say, isn't it? If Stan lets go, will you promise not to make any noise?"

She shook her head furiously.

One of the others seized her arm. "Come on, Marsha. Lyle says you're a good sport. Why don't you prove it?"

She was struggling madly now, but unavailingly. The grip around her was unyielding. Lyle had the other arm and together they were forcing her toward the adjoining bedroom.

"The hell with it," Dixon said. "Somebody grab her feet." The remaining boy took hold. She tried to kick, but all that happened was her high-heeled pumps came off. With a sense of unreality Marsha felt herself being carried through the bedroom doorway.

"This is the last time," Lyle warned. The veneer of good humor had vanished. "Are you going to co-operate or not?"

Her answer was to struggle more violently.

"Get her things off," someone said. And another voice —she thought it was from whoever was holding her feet— asked hesitantly, "Do you think we should?"

"Quit worrying." It was Lyle Dumaire. "Nothing'll happen. Her old man's whoring it up in Rome."

There were twin beds in the room. Resisting wildly, Marsha was forced backward onto the nearest. A moment later she lay across it, her head pressed back cruelly until all she could see was the ceiling above, once painted white but now closer to gray, and ornamented in the center where a light fitting glowed. Dust had accumulated on the fitting and beside it was a yellowed water stain.

Abruptly the ceiling light went out, but there was a glow in the room from another lamp left on. Dixon had shifted his grip. Now he was half sitting on the bed, near her head, but the grasp on her body as well as across her mouth was inflexible as ever. She felt other hands, and hysteria swept

35

over her. Contorting herself, she attempted to kick but her legs were pinned down. She tried to roll over and there was a rending sound as her Balenciaga gown tore.

"I'm first," Stanley Dixon said. "Somebody take over here." She could hear his heavy breathing.

Footsteps went softly on the rug around the bed. Her legs were still held firmly, but Dixon's hand on her face was moving, another taking its place. It was an opportunity. As the new hand came over, Marsha bit fiercely. She felt her teeth go into flesh, meeting bone.

There was an anguished cry, and the hand withdrawn.

Inflating her lungs, Marsha screamed. She screamed three times and ended with a desperate cry. "Help! Please help me!"

Only the last word was cut off as Stanley Dixon's hand slammed back into place with a force that made her senses swim. She heard him snarl, "You fool! You stupid goon!"

"She bit me!" The voice was sobbing with pain. "The bitch bit my hand."

Dixon said savagely, "What did you expect her to do, kiss it? Now we'll have the whole goddamned hotel on our necks."

Lyle Dumaire urged, "Let's get out of here."

"Shut up!" Dixon commanded. They stood listening.

Dixon said softly, "There's nothing stirring. I guess nobody heard."

It was true, Marsha thought despairingly. Tears clouded her vision. She seemed to have lost the power to struggle any more.

There was a knock on the outside door. Three taps, firm and assertive.

"Christ!" the third boy said. "Somebody did hear." He added with a moan, "Oh God!—my hand!"

The fourth asked nervously, "What do we do?"

The knocking was repeated, this time more vigorously.

After a pause a voice from outside called, "Open the door, please. I heard someone shout for help." The caller's speech had a soft, southern accent.

Lyle Dumaire whispered, "There's only one; he's by himself. Maybe we can stall."

"It's worth a try," Dixon breathed. "I'll go." He mur-

36

mured to one of the others, "Hold her down and this time don't make any mistake."

The hand on Marsha's mouth changed swiftly and another held her body.

A lock clicked, followed by a squeak as the door opened partially. Stanley Dixon, as if surprised, said, "Oh."

"Excuse me, sir. I'm an employee of the hotel." It was the voice they had heard a moment earlier. "I happened to be passing and heard someone cry out."

"Just passing, eh?" Dixon's tone was oddly hostile. Then, as if deciding to be diplomatic, he added, "Well, thanks anyway. But it was only my wife having a nightmare. She went to bed before me. She's all right now."

"Well . . ." The other appeared to hesitate. "If you're sure there's nothing."

"Nothing at all," Dixon said. "It's just one of those things that happen once in a while." He was convincing, and in command of the situation. In a moment, Marsha knew, the door would close.

Since she had relaxed she had become aware that the pressure on her face had lessened also. Now she tensed herself for one final effort. Twisting her body sideways, momentarily she freed her mouth. "Help!" she called. "Don't believe him! Please help!" Once more, roughly, she was stopped.

There was a sharp exchange outside. She heard the new voice say, "I'd like to come in, please."

"This is a private room. I told you my wife is having a nightmare."

"I'm sorry, sir; I don't believe you."

"All right," Dixon said. "Come in."

As if not wishing to be witnessed, the hands upon Marsha removed themselves. As they did, she rolled over, pushing herself partially upright facing the door. A young Negro was entering. In his early twenties, he had an intelligent face and was neatly dressed, his short hair parted and carefully brushed.

He took in the situation at once and said sharply, "Let the young lady go."

"Take a look, fellas," Dixon said. "Take a look at who's giving orders."

37

Dimly, Marsha was aware that the door to the corridor was still partially open.

"All right, nigger boy," Dixon snarled. "You asked for it." His right fist shot out expertly, the strength of his big broad shoulders behind the blow which would have felled the young Negro if it had found its target. But in a single movement, agile as a ballet step, the other moved sideways, the extended arm going harmlessly past his head, with Dixon stumbling forward. In the same instant the Negro's own left fist snapped upward, landing with a hard, sharp crack at the side of his attacker's face.

Somewhere along the corridor another door opened and closed.

A hand on his cheek, Dixon said, "You son-of-a-bitch!" Turning to the others, he urged, "Let's get him!"

Only the boy with the injured hand held back. As if with a single impulse, the other three fell upon the young Negro and, before their combined assault, he went down. Marsha heard the thud of blows and also—from outside— a growing hum of voices in the corridor.

The others heard the voices too. "The roof is falling in," Lyle Dumaire warned urgently. "I told you we should get out of here."

There was a scramble to the door, led by the boy who had not joined in the fighting, the others hastily behind him. Marsha heard Stanley Dixon stop to say, "There's been some trouble. We're going for help."

The young Negro was rising from the floor, his face bloody.

Outside, a new, authoritative voice rose above the others. "Where is the disturbance, please?"

"There was screaming and a fight," a woman said excitedly. "In there."

Another grumbled, "I complained earlier, but no one took any notice."

The door opened wide. Marsha caught a glimpse of peering faces, a tall, commanding figure entering. Then the door was closed from the inside and the overhead light snapped on.

Peter McDermott surveyed the disordered room. He inquired, "What happened?"

Marsha's body was racked with sobs. She attempted to stand, but fell back weakly against the headboard of the bed, gathering the torn disheveled remnants of her dress in front of her. Between sobs her lips formed words: "Tried . . . rape . . ."

McDermott's face hardened. His eyes swung to the young Negro, now leaning for support against the wall, using a handkerchief to stem the bleeding from his face.

"Royce!" Cold fury flickered in McDermott's eyes.

"No! No!" Barely coherent, Marsha called pleadingly across the room. "It wasn't him! He came to help!" She closed her eyes, the thought of further violence sickening her.

The young Negro straightened. Putting the handkerchief away, he mocked, "Why don't you go ahead, Mr. McDermott, and hit me. You could always say afterward it was a mistake."

Peter spoke curtly. "I already made a mistake, Royce, and I apologize." He had a profound dislike of Aloysius Royce who combined the role of personal valet to the hotel owner, Warren Trent, with the study of law at Loyola University. Years before, Royce's father, the son of a slave, had become Warren Trent's body servant, close companion, and confidant. A quarter century later, when the old man died, his son Aloysius, who had been born and raised in the St. Gregory, stayed on and now lived in the hotel owner's private suite under a loose arrangement by which he came and went as his studies required. But in Peter McDermott's opinion Royce was needlessly arrogant and supercilious, seeming to combine a distrust of any proffered friendliness with a perpetual chip on his shoulder.

"Tell me what you know," Peter said.

"There were four of them. Four nice white young gentlemen."

"Did you recognize anyone?"

Royce nodded. "Two."

"That's good enough." Peter crossed to the telephone beside the nearer bed.

"Who you calling?"

"The city police. We've no choice but to bring them in."

There was a half-smile on the young Negro's face. "If you want some advice, I wouldn't do it."

"Why not?"

"Fo' one thing," Aloysius Royce drawled, accenting his speech deliberately, "I'd have to be a witness. An' let me tell you, Mr. McDermott, no court in this sovereign State of Louisiana is gonna take a nigger boy's word in a white rape case, attempted or otherwise. No, sir, not when four upstanding young white gentlemen say the nigger boy is lying. Not even if Miss Preyscott supports the nigger boy, which I doubt her pappy'd let her, considering what all the newspapers and such might make of it."

Peter had picked up the receiver; now he put it down. "Sometimes," he said, "you seem to want to make things harder than they are." But he knew that what Royce had said was true. His eyes swinging to Marsha, he asked, "Did you say 'Miss Preyscott'?"

The young Negro nodded. "Her father is Mr. Mark Preyscott. *The* Preyscott. That's right, miss, isn't it?"

Unhappily, Marsha nodded.

"Miss Preyscott," Peter said, "did you know the people who were responsible for what happened?"

The answer was barely audible. "Yes."

Royce volunteered, "They were all from Alpha Kappa Epsilon, I think."

"Is that true, Miss Preyscott?"

A slight movement of her head, assenting.

"And did you come here with them—to this suite?"

Again a whisper. "Yes."

Peter looked questioningly at Marsha. At length, he said, "It's up to you, Miss Preyscott, whether you make an official complaint or not. Whatever you decide, the hotel will go along with. But I'm afraid there's a good deal of truth in what Royce said just now about publicity. There would certainly be some—a good deal, I imagine—and not pleasant." He added: "Of course, it's really something for your father to decide. Don't you think I should call, and have him come here?"

Marsha raised her head, looking directly at Peter for the first time. "My father's in Rome. Don't tell him, please —ever."

40

"I'm sure something can be done privately. I don't believe anyone should get away with this entirely." Peter went around the bed. He was startled to see how much of a child she was, and how very beautiful. "Is there anything I can do now?"

"I don't know. I don't know." She began to cry again, more softly.

Uncertainly, Peter took out a white linen handkerchief which Marsha accepted, wiped the tears, then blew her nose.

"Better?"

She nodded. "Thank you." Her mind was a turmoil of emotions: hurt, shame, anger, an urge to fight back blindly whatever the consequences, and a desire—which experience told her would not be fulfilled—to be enfolded in loving and protective arms. But beyond the emotions, and exceeding them, was an overwhelming physical exhaustion.

"I think you should rest a while." Peter McDermott turned down the coverlet of the unused bed and Marsha slipped under it, lying on the blanket beneath. The touch of the pillow to her face was cool.

She said, "I don't want to stay here. I couldn't."

He nodded understandingly. "In a little while we'll get you home."

"No! Not that either! Please, isn't there somewhere else . . . in the hotel?"

He shook his head. "I'm afraid the hotel is full."

Aloysius Royce had gone into the bathroom to wash the blood from his face. Now he returned and stood in the doorway of the adjoining living room. He whistled softly, surveying the mess of disarranged furniture, overflowing ash trays, spilled bottles, and broken glass.

As McDermott joined him, Royce observed, "I guess it was quite a party."

"It seems to have been." Peter closed the communicating door between the living room and bedroom.

Marsha pleaded, "There must be some place in the hotel. I couldn't face going home tonight."

Peter hesitated. "There's 555, I suppose." He glanced at Royce.

Room 555 was a small one which went with the assistant

41

general manager's job. Peter rarely used it, except to change. It was empty now.

"It'll be all right," Marsha said. "As long as someone phones my home. Ask for Anna the housekeeper."

"If you like," Royce offered, "I'll go get the key."

Peter nodded. "Stop in there on the way back—you'll find a dressing gown. I suppose we ought to call a maid."

"You let a maid in here right now, you might as well put it all on the radio."

Peter considered. At this stage nothing would stop gossip. Inevitably when this kind of incident happened any hotel throbbed backstairs like a jungle telegraph. But he supposed there was no point in adding postscripts.

"Very well. We'll take Miss Preyscott down ourselves in the service elevator."

As the young Negro opened the outer door, voices filtered in, with a barrage of eager questions. Momentarily, Peter had forgotten the assemblage of awakened guests outside. He heard Royce's answers, quietly reassuring, then the voices fade.

Her eyes closed, Marsha murmured, "You haven't told me who you are."

"I'm sorry. I should have explained." He told her his name and his connection with the hotel. Marsha listened without responding, aware of what was being said, but for the most part letting the quiet reassuring voice flow easily over her. After a while, eyes still closed, her thoughts wandered drowsily. She was aware dimly of Aloysius Royce returning, of being helped from the bed into a dressing gown, and being escorted quickly and quietly down a silent corridor. From an elevator there was more corridor, then another bed on which she laid down quietly. The reassuring voice said, "She's just about all in."

The sound of water running. A voice telling her that a bath was drawn. She roused herself sufficiently to pad to the bathroom where she locked herself in.

There were pajamas in the bathroom, neatly laid out, and afterward Marsha put them on. They were men's, in dark blue, and too large. The sleeves covered her hands and even with the trouser bottoms turned up it was hard not to trip over them.

She went outside where hands helped her into bed. Snuggling down in the crisp, fresh linen, she was aware of Peter McDermott's calm, restoring voice once more. It was a voice she liked, Marsha thought—and its owner also. "Royce and I are leaving now, Miss Preyscott. The door to this room is self-locking and the key is beside your bed. You won't be disturbed."

"Thank you." Sleepily she asked, "Whose pajamas?"

"They're mine. I'm sorry they're so big."

She tried to shake her head but was too tired. "No matter . . . nice . . ." She was glad they were his pajamas. She had a comforting sense of being enfolded after all.

"Nice," she repeated softly. It was her final waking thought.

8

Peter waited alone for the elevator on the fifth floor. Aloysius Royce had already taken the service elevator to the fifteenth floor, where his quarters adjoined the hotel owner's private suite.

It had been a full evening, Peter thought—with its share of unpleasantness—though not exceptional for a big hotel, which often presented an exposed slice of life that hotel employees became used to seeing.

When the elevator arrived he told the operator, "Lobby, please," reminding himself that Christine was waiting on the main mezzanine, but his business on the main floor would take only a few minutes.

He noted with impatience that although the elevator doors were closed, they had not yet started down. The operator—one of the regular night men—was jockeying the control handle back and forth. Peter asked, "Are you sure the gates are fully closed?"

"Yes, sir, they are. It isn't that; it's the connections I think, either here or up top." The man angled his head in the direction of the roof where the elevator machinery was housed, then added, "Had quite a bit of trouble lately. The chief was probing around the other day." He worked

43

the handle vigorously. With a jerk the mechanism took hold and the elevator started down.

"Which elevator is this?"

"Number four."

Peter made a mental note to ask the chief engineer exactly what was wrong.

It was almost half-past twelve by the lobby clock as he stepped from the elevator. As was usual by this time, some of the activity in and around the lobby had quieted down, but there was still a fair number of people in evidence, and the strains of music from the nearby Indigo Room showed that supper dancing was in progress. Peter turned right toward Reception but had gone only a few paces when he was aware of an obese, waddling figure approaching him. It was Ogilvie, the chief house officer, who had been missing earlier. The heavily jowled face of the ex-policeman—years before he had served without distinction on the New Orleans force—was carefully expressionless, though his little pig's eyes darted sideways, sizing up the scene around him. As always, he was accompanied by an odor of stale cigar smoke, and a line of fat cigars, like unfired torpedoes, filled the top pocket of his suit.

"I hear you were looking for me," Ogilvie said. It was a flat statement, unconcerned.

Peter felt some of his earlier anger return. "I certainly was. Where the devil were you?"

"Doing my job, Mr. McDermott." For an outsize man Ogilvie had a surprisingly falsetto voice. "If you want to know, I was over at police headquarters reporting some trouble we had here. There was a suitcase stolen from the baggage room today."

"Police headquarters! Which room was the poker game in?"

The piggy eyes glowered resentfully. "If that's the way you feel, maybe you should do some checking. Or speak to Mr. Trent."

Peter nodded resignedly. It would be a waste of time, he knew. The alibi was undoubtedly well established, and Ogilvie's friends in headquarters would back him up. Besides, Warren Trent would never take action against Ogilvie, who had been at the St. Gregory as long as the hotel proprietor himself. There were some who said that the fat detective knew where a body or two was buried, and thus had a hold over Warren Trent. But whatever the reason, Ogilvie's position was unassailable.

"Well, you just happen to have missed a couple of emergencies," Peter said. "But both are taken care of now." Perhaps after all, he reflected, it was as well that Ogilvie had not been available. Undoubtedly the house officer would not have responded to the Albert Wells crisis as efficiently as Christine, nor handled Marsha Preyscott with tact and sympathy. Resolving to put Ogilvie out of his mind, with a curt nod he moved on to Reception.

The night clerk whom he had telephoned earlier was at the desk. Peter decided to try a conciliatory approach. He said pleasantly, "Thank you for helping me out with that problem on the fourteenth. We have Mr. Wells settled comfortably in 1410. Dr. Aarons is arranging nursing care, and the chief has fixed up oxygen."

The room clerk's face had frozen as Peter approached him. Now it relaxed. "I hadn't realized there was anything that serious."

"It was touch and go for a while, I think. That's why I was so concerned about why he was moved into that other room."

The room clerk nodded sagely. "In that case I'll certainly pursue inquiries. Yes, you can be sure of that."

"We've had some trouble on the eleventh, too. Do you mind telling me whose name 1126-7 is in?"

The room clerk flipped through his records and produced a card. "Mr. Stanley Dixon."

"Dixon." It was one of the two names Aloysius Royce had given him when they talked briefly after leaving Marsha.

"He's the car dealer's son. Mr. Dixon senior is often in the hotel."

"Thank you." Peter nodded. "You'd better list it as a checkout, and have the cashier mail the bill." A thought occurred to him. "No, have the bill sent to me tomorrow, and I'll write a letter. There'll be a claim for damages after we've figured out what they are."

"Very well, Mr. McDermott." The change in the night

clerk's attitude was most marked. "I'll tell the cashier to do as you ask. I take it the suite is available now."

"Yes." There was no point, Peter decided, in advertising Marsha's presence in 555, and perhaps she could leave unnoticed early. The thought reminded him of his promise to telephone the Preyscott home. With a friendly "good night" to the room clerk he crossed the lobby to an unoccupied desk, used in daytime by one of the assistant managers. He found a listing for Mark Preyscott at a Garden District address and asked for the number. The ringing tone continued for some time before a woman's voice answered sleepily. Identifying himself, he announced, "I have a message for Anna from Miss Preyscott."

The voice, with a Deep South accent, said, "This is Anna. Is Miss Marsha all right?"

"She's all right, but she asked me to tell you that she will stay the night at the hotel."

The housekeeper's voice said, "Who did you say that was again?"

Peter explained patiently. "Look," he said, "if you want to check, why don't you call back? It's the St. Gregory, and ask for the assistant manager's desk in the lobby."

The woman, obviously relieved, said, "Yes, sir, I'll do that." In less than a minute they were reconnected. "It's all right," she said, "now I know who it is for sure. We worry about Miss Marsha a bit, what with her daddy being away and all."

Replacing the telephone, he found himself thinking again about Marsha Preyscott. He decided he would have a talk with her tomorrow to find out just what happened before the attempted rape occurred. The disorder in the suite, for example, posed several unanswered questions.

He was aware that Herbie Chandler had been glancing at him covertly from the bell captain's desk. Now, walking over to him, Peter said curtly, "I thought I gave instructions about checking a disturbance on the eleventh."

Chandler's weasel face framed innocent eyes. "But I went, Mr. Mac. I walked right around and everything was quiet."

And so it had been, Herbie thought. In the end he had gone nervously to the eleventh and, to his relief, whatever disturbance there might have been earlier had ended by the time he arrived. Even better, on returning to the lobby, he learned that the two call girls had left the hotel without detection.

"You couldn't have looked or listened very hard."

Herbie Chandler shook his head obstinately. "All I can say is, I did what you asked, Mr. Mac. You said to go up, and I did, even though that isn't our job."

"Very well." Though instinct told him that the bell captain knew more than he was saying, Peter decided not to press the point. "I'll be making some inquiries. Maybe I'll talk to you again."

As he recrossed the lobby and entered an elevator, he was conscious of being watched both by Herbie Chandler and the house officer, Ogilvie. This time he rode up one floor only, to the main mezzanine.

Christine was waiting in his office. She had kicked off her shoes and curled her feet under her in the upholstered leather chair she had occupied an hour and a half before. Her eyes were closed, her thoughts far away in time and distance. She summoned them back, looking up as Peter came in.

"Don't marry a hotel man," he told her. "There's never an end to it."

"It's a timely warning," Christine said. "I hadn't told you, but I've a crush on that new sous-chef. The one who looks like Rock Hudson." She uncurled her legs, reaching for her shoes. "Do we have more troubles?"

He grinned, finding the sight and sound of Christine immensely cheering. "Other people's, mostly. I'll tell you as we go."

"Where to?"

"Anywhere away from the hotel. We've both had enough for one day."

Christine considered. "We could go to the Quarter. There are plenty of places open. Or if you want to come to my place, I'm a whiz at omelets."

Peter helped her up and steered her to the door where he switched off the office lights. "An omelet," he declared, "is what I really wanted and didn't know it."

They walked together, skirting pools of water which the rain had left, to a tiered parking lot a block and a half from the hotel. Above, the sky was clearing after its interlude of storm, with a three-quarter moon beginning to break through, and around them the city center was settling down to silence, broken by an occasional late taxi and the sharp tattoo of their footsteps echoing hollowly through the canyon of darkened buildings.

A sleepy parking attendant brought down Christine's Volkswagen and they climbed in, Peter jackknifing his length into the right-hand seat. "This is the life! You don't mind if I spread out?" He draped his arm along the back of the driver's seat, not quite touching Christine's shoulders.

As they waited for the traffic lights at Canal Street, one of the new air-conditioned buses glided down the center mall in front of them.

She reminded him, "You were going to tell me what happened."

He frowned, bringing his thoughts back to the hotel, then in crisp short sentences related what he knew about the attempted rape of Marsha Preyscott. Christine listened in silence, heading the little car northeast as Peter talked, ending with his conversation with Herbie Chandler and the suspicion that the bell captain knew more than he had told.

"Herbie always knows more. That's why he's been around a long time."

Peter said shortly, "Being around isn't the answer to everything."

The comment, as both he and Christine knew, betrayed Peter's impatience with inefficiencies within the hotel which he lacked authority to change. In a normally run establishment, with clearly defined lines of command, there would be no such problem. But in the St. Gregory, a good deal of organization was unwritten, with final judgments depending upon Warren Trent, and made by the hotel owner in his own capricious way.

In ordinary circumstances, Peter—an honors graduate of Cornell University's School of Hotel Administration— would have made a decision months ago to seek more satisfying work elsewhere. But circumstances were not ordinary. He had arrived at the St. Gregory under a cloud, which was likely to remain—hampering his chance of other employment—for a long time to come.

Sometimes he reflected glumly on the botchery he had made of his career, for which no one—he admitted candidly—was to blame except himself.

At the Waldorf, where he had gone to work after graduation from Cornell, Peter McDermott had been the bright young man who appeared to hold the future in his hand. As a junior assistant manager, he had been selected for promotion when bad luck, plus indiscretion, intervened. At a time when he was supposedly on duty and required elsewhere in the hotel, he was discovered *in flagrante* in a bedroom with a woman guest.

Even then, he might have escaped retribution. Good-looking young men who worked in hotels grew used to receiving overtures from lonely women, and most, at some point in their careers, succumbed. Managements, aware of this, were apt to punish a single transgression with a stern warning that a similar thing must never happen again. Two factors, however, conspired against Peter. The woman's husband, aided by private detectives, was involved in the discovery, and a messy divorce case resulted, with attendant publicity, which all hotels abhorred.

As if this was not enough, there was a personal retribution. Three years before the Waldorf debacle, Peter McDermott had married impulsively and the marriage, soon after, ended in separation. To an extent, his loneliness and disillusion had been a cause of the incident in the hotel. Regardless of the cause, and utilizing the ready-made evidence, Peter's estranged wife sued successfully for divorce.

The end result was ignominious dismissal and blacklisting by the major chain hotels.

The existence of a black list, of course, was not admitted. But at a long series of hotels, most with chain affiliations, Peter McDermott's applications for employ-

49

ment were peremptorily rejected. Only at the St. Gregory, an independent house, had he been able to obtain work, at a salary which Warren Trent shrewdly adjusted to Peter's own desperation.

Therefore when he had said a moment ago, *Being around isn't the answer to everything,* he had pretended an independence which did not exist. He suspected that Christine realized it too.

Peter watched as she maneuvered the little car expertly through the narrow width of Burgundy Street, skirting the French Quarter and paralleling the Mississippi a half mile to the south. Christine slowed momentarily, avoiding a group of unsteady wassailers who had wandered from the more populous and brightly lighted Bourbon Street, two blocks away. Then she said, "There's something I think you should know. Curtis O'Keefe is arriving in the morning."

It was the kind of news that he had feared, yet half-expected.

Curtis O'Keefe was a name to conjure with. Head of the world-wide O'Keefe hotel chain, he bought hotels as other men chose ties and handkerchiefs. Obviously, even to the sparsely informed, the appearance of Curtis O'Keefe in the St. Gregory could have only one implication: an interest in acquiring the hotel for the constantly expanding O'Keefe chain.

Peter asked, "Is it a buying trip?"

"It could be." Christine kept her eyes on the dimly lighted street ahead. "W.T. doesn't want it that way. But it may turn out there isn't any choice." She was about to add that the last piece of information was confidential, but checked herself. Peter would realize that. And as for the presence of Curtis O'Keefe, that electrifying news would telegraph itself around the St. Gregory tomorrow morning within minutes of the great man's arrival.

"I suppose it had to come." Peter was aware, as were other executives in the hotel, that in recent months the St. Gregory had suffered severe financial losses. "All the same, I think it's a pity."

Christine reminded him, "It hasn't happened yet. I said W.T. doesn't want to sell."

Peter nodded without speaking.

They were leaving the French Quarter now, turning left on the boulevarded and tree-lined Esplanade Avenue, deserted except for the receding taillights of another car disappearing swiftly toward Bayou St. John.

Christine said, "There are problems about refinancing. W.T. has been trying to locate new capital. He still hopes he may."

"And if he doesn't?"

"Then I expect we shall be seeing a lot more of Mr. Curtis O'Keefe."

And a whole lot less of Peter McDermott, Peter thought. He wondered if he had reached the point where a hotel chain, such as O'Keefe, might consider him rehabilitated and worth employing. He doubted it. Eventually it could happen if his record remained good. But not yet.

It seemed likely that he might soon have to search for other employment. He decided to worry when it happened.

"The O'Keefe-St. Gregory," Peter ruminated. "When shall we know for sure?"

"One way or the other by the end of this week."

"That soon!"

There were compelling reasons, Christine knew, why it had to be that soon. For the moment she kept them to herself.

Peter said emphatically, "The old man won't find new financing."

"What makes you so sure?"

"Because people with that kind of money want a sound investment. That means good management, and the St. Gregory hasn't got it. It could have, but it hasn't."

They were headed north on Elysian Fields, its wide dual lanes empty of other traffic, when abruptly a flashing white light, waving from side to side, loomed directly ahead. Christine braked and, as the car stopped, a uniformed traffic officer walked forward. Directing his flashlight onto the Volkswagen, he circled the car, inspecting it. While he did, they could see that the section of road immediately ahead was blocked off by a rope barrier. Beyond the barrier other uniformed men, and some in plain clothes, were examining the road surface with the aid of powerful lights.

Christine lowered her window as the officer came to her side of the car. Apparently satisfied by his inspection, he told them, "You'll have to detour, folks. Drive slowly through the other lane, and the officer at the far end will wave you back into this one."

"What is it?" Peter said. "What's happened?"

"Hit and run. Happened earlier tonight."

Christine asked, "Was anyone killed?"

The policeman nodded. "Little girl of seven." Responding to their shocked expressions, he told them, "Walking with her mother. The mother's in the hospital. Kid was killed outright. Whoever was in the car must have known. They drove right on." Beneath his breath he added, "Bastards!"

"Will you find out who it is?"

"We'll find out." The officer nodded grimly, indicating the activity behind the barrier. "The boys usually do, and this one's upset them. There's glass on the road, and the car that did it must be marked." More headlights were approaching from behind and he motioned them on.

They were silent as Christine drove slowly through the detour and, at the end of it, was waved back into the regular lane. Somewhere in Peter's mind was a nagging impression, an errant half-thought he could not define. He supposed the incident itself was bothering him, as sudden tragedy always did, but a vague uneasiness kept him preoccupied until, with surprise, he heard Christine say, "We're almost home."

They had left Elysian Fields for Prentiss Avenue. A moment later the little car swung right, then left, and stopped in the parking area of a modern, two-story apartment building.

"If all else fails," Peter called out cheerfully, "I can go back to bartending." He was mixing drinks in Christine's living room, with its soft tones of moss-green and blue, to the accompanying sound of breaking eggshells from the kitchen adjoining.

"Were you ever one?"

"For a while." He measured three ounces of rye whiskey, dividing it two ways, then reached for Angostura and

Peychaud's bitters. "Sometime I'll tell you about it." As an afterthought he increased the proportion of rye, using a handkerchief to mop some extra drops which had fallen on the Wedgwood-blue rug.

Straightening up, he cast a glance around the living room, with its comfortable mixture of furnishings and color —a French provincial sofa with a leaf-design tapestry print in white, blue, and green; a pair of Hepplewhite chairs near a marble-topped chest, and the inlaid mahogany sideboard on which he was mixing drinks. The walls held some Louisiana French prints and a modern impressionist oil. The effect was of warmth and cheerfulness, much like Christine herself, he thought. Only a cumbrous mantel clock on the sideboard beside him provided an incongruous note. The clock, ticking softly, was unmistakably Victorian, with brass curlicues and a moisture-stained, timeworn face. Peter looked at it curiously.

When he took the drinks to the kitchen, Christine was emptying beaten eggs from a mixing dish into a softly sizzling pan.

"Three minutes more," she said, "that's all."

He gave her the drink and they clinked glasses.

"Keep your mind on my omelet," Christine said. "It's ready now."

It proved to be everything she had promised—light, fluffy, and seasoned with herbs. "The way omelets should be," he assured her, "but seldom are."

"I can boil eggs too."

He waved a hand airily. "Some other breakfast."

Afterward they returned to the living room and Peter mixed a second drink. It was almost two A.M.

Sitting beside her on the sofa he pointed to the odd-appearing clock. "I get the feeling that thing is peering at me—announcing the time in a disapproving tone."

"Perhaps it is," Christine answered. "It was my father's. It used to be in his office where patients could see it. It's the only thing I saved."

There was a silence between them. Once before Christine had told him, matter-of-factly, about the airplane accident in Wisconsin. Now he said gently, "After it happened, you must have felt desperately alone."

She said simply, "I wanted to die. Though you get over that, of course—after a while."

"How long?"

She gave a short, swift smile. "The human spirit mends quickly. That part—wanting to die, I mean—took just a week or two."

"And after?"

"When I came to New Orleans," Christine said, "I tried to concentrate on not thinking. It got harder, and I had less success as the days went by. I knew I had to do something but I wasn't sure what—or where."

She stopped and Peter said, "Go on."

"For a while I considered going back to university, then decided not. Getting an arts degree just for the sake of it didn't seem important and besides, suddenly it seemed as if I'd grown away from it all."

"I can understand that."

Christine sipped her drink, her expression pensive. Observing the firm line of her features, he was conscious of a quality of quietude and self-possession about her.

"Anyway," Christine went on, "one day I was walking on Carondelet and saw a sign which said 'Secretarial School.' I thought—that's it! I'll learn what I need to, then get a job involving endless hours of work. In the end that's exactly what happened."

"How did the St. Gregory fit in?"

"I was staying there. I had since I came from Wisconsin. Then one morning the *Times-Picayune* arrived with breakfast, and I saw in the classifieds that the managing director of the hotel wanted a personal secretary. It was early, so I thought I'd be first, and wait. In those days W.T. arrived at work before everyone else. When he came, I was waiting in the executive suite."

"He hired you on the spot?"

"Not really. Actually, I don't believe I ever was hired. It was just that when W.T. found out why I was there he called me in and began dictating letters, then firing off instructions to be relayed to other people in the hotel. By the time more applicants arrived I'd been working for hours, and I took it on myself to tell them the job was filled."

54

Peter chuckled. "It sounds like the old man."

"Even then he might never have known who I was, except about three days later I left a note on his desk. I think it read 'My name is Christine Francis,' and I suggested a salary. I got the note back without comment—just initialed, and that's all there's ever been."

"It makes a good bedtime story." Peter rose from the sofa, stretching his big body. "That clock of yours is staring again. I guess I'd better go."

"It isn't fair," Christine objected. "All we've talked about is me." She was conscious of Peter's masculinity. And yet, she thought, there was a gentleness about him too. She had seen something of it tonight in the way that he had picked up Albert Wells and carried him to the other room. She found herself wondering what it would be like to be carried in his arms.

"I enjoyed it—a lovely antidote to a lousy day. Anyway, there'll be other times." He stopped, regarding her directly. "Won't there?"

As she nodded in answer, he leaned forward, kissing her lightly.

In the taxi for which he had telephoned from Christine's apartment, Peter McDermott relaxed in comforting weariness, reviewing the events of the past day, which had now spilled over into the next. The daytime hours had produced their usual quota of problems, culminating in the evening with several more: the brush with the Duke and Duchess of Croydon, the near demise of Albert Wells, and the attempted rape of Marsha Preyscott. There were also unanswered questions concerning Ogilvie, Herbie Chandler, and now Curtis O'Keefe, whose advent could be the cause of Peter's own departure. Finally there was Christine, who had been there all the time, but whom he had not noticed before in quite the way he had tonight.

But he warned himself: women had been his undoing twice already. Whatever, if anything, developed between Christine and himself should happen slowly, with caution on his own part.

On Elysian Fields, heading back toward the city, the taxi moved swiftly. Passing the spot where he and Christine had been halted on the outward journey, he observed that the barrier across the road had disappeared and the police were gone. But the reminder produced once again the vague uneasiness he had experienced earlier, and it continued to trouble him all the way to his own apartment a block or two from the St. Gregory Hotel.

TUESDAY

1

As with all hotels, the St. Gregory stirred early, coming awake like a veteran combat soldier after a short, light sleep. Long before the earliest waking guest stumbled drowsily from bed to bathroom, the machinery of a new innkeeping day slid quietly into motion.

Near five A.M., night cleaning parties which for the past eight hours had toiled through public rooms, lower stairways, kitchen areas and the main lobby, tiredly began dissembling their equipment, preparatory to storing it for another day. In their wake floors gleamed and wood and metalwork shone, the whole smelling pleasantly of fresh wax.

One cleaner, old Meg Yetmein, who had worked nearly thirty years in the hotel, walked awkwardly, though anyone noticing might have taken her clumsy gait for tiredness. The real reason, however, was a three-pound sirloin steak taped securely to the inside of her thigh. Half an hour ago, choosing an unsupervised few minutes, Meg had snatched the steak from a kitchen refrigerator. From long experience she knew exactly where to look, and afterward how to conceal her prize in an old polishing rag en route to the women's toilet. There, safe behind a bolted door, she brought out an adhesive bandage and fixed the steak in place. The hour or so's cold, clammy discomfort was well worth the knowledge that she could walk serenely past the house detective who guarded the staff entrance and suspiciously checked outgoing packages or bulging pockets.

The procedure—of her own devising—was foolproof, as she had proven many times before.

Two floors above Meg and behind an unmarked, securely locked door on the convention mezzanine, a switchboard operator put down her knitting and made the first morning wake-up call. The operator was Mrs. Eunice Ball, widow, grandmother, and tonight senior of the three operators who maintained the graveyard shift. Sporadically, between now and seven A.M., the switchboard trio would awaken other guests whose instructions of the night before were recorded in a card-index drawer in front of them, divided into quarter hours. After seven o'clock the tempo would increase.

With experienced fingers, Mrs. Ball flipped through the cards. As usual, she observed, the peak would be 7:45, with close to a hundred and eighty calls requested. Even working at high speed, the three operators would have trouble completing that many in less than twenty minutes, which meant they would have to start early, at 7:35—assuming they were through with the 7:30 calls by then—and continue until 7:55, which would take them smack into the eight o'clock batch.

Mrs. Ball sighed. Inevitably today there would be complaints from guests to management alleging that some stupid, asleep-at-the-switchboard operator had called them either too early or too late.

One thing was to the good, though. Few guests at this time of morning were in a mood for conversation, or were likely to be amorous, the way they sometimes were at night—the reason for the locked, unmarked outer door. Also, at eight A.M., the day operators would be coming in —a total of fifteen by the day's peak period—and by nine the night shift, including Mrs. Ball, would be home and abed.

Time for another wake-up. Once more abandoning her knitting, Mrs. Ball pressed a key, letting a bell far above her ring out stridently.

Two floors below street level, in the engineering control room, Wallace Santopadre, third-class stationary engineer, put down a paperback copy of Toynbee's *Greek Civilization* and finished a peanut butter sandwich he had begun earlier. Things had been quiet for the past hour and he had read intermittently. Now it was time for the final stroll of his watch around the engineers' domain. The hum of machinery greeted him as he opened the control-room door.

He checked the hot-water system, noting a stepped-up temperature which indicated, in turn, that the time-controlled thermostat was doing its job. There would be plenty of hot water during the heavy demand period soon to come, when upwards of eight hundred people might decide to take morning baths or showers at the same time.

The massive air conditioners—twenty-five hundred tons of specialized machinery—were running more easily as the result of a comfortable drop in outside air temperature during the night. The comparative coolness had made it possible to shut down one compressor, and now the others could be relieved alternately, permitting maintenance work which had had to be delayed during the heat wave of the past few weeks. The chief engineer, Wallace Santopadre thought, would be pleased about that.

The old man would be less happy, though, about news of an interruption in the city power supply which had occurred during the night—around two A.M. and lasting eleven minutes, presumably due to the storm up north.

There had been no real problem in the St. Gregory, and only the briefest of blackouts which most guests, soundly asleep, were unaware of. Santopadre had switched over to emergency power, supplied by the hotel's own generators which had performed efficiently. It had, however, taken three minutes to start the generators and bring them to full power, with the result that every one of the St. Gregory's electric clocks—some two hundred all told—was now three minutes slow. The tedious business of resetting each clock manually would take a maintenance man most of the following day.

Not far from the engineering station, in a torrid, odorous enclosure, Booker T. Graham totted up the substance of a long night's labor amid the hotel garbage. Around him the reflection of flames flickered fitfully on smoke-grimed walls.

Few people in the hotel, including staff, had ever seen Booker T.'s domain, and those who did declared it was like an evangelist's idea of hell. But Booker T., who looked not unlike an amiable devil himself—with luminous eyes and flashing teeth in a sweat-shining black face—enjoyed his work, including the incinerator's heat.

One of the very few hotel staff whom Booker T. Graham ever saw was Peter McDermott. Soon after his arrival at the St. Gregory, Peter set out to learn the geography and workings of the hotel, even to its remotest parts. In the course of one expedition he discovered the incinerator.

Occasionally since then—as he made a point of doing with all departments—Peter had dropped in to inquire at firsthand how things were going. Because of this, and perhaps through an instinctive mutual liking, in the eyes of Booker T. Graham, young Mr. McDermott loomed somewhere close to God.

Peter always studied the grimed and greasy exercise book in which Booker T. proudly maintained a record of his work results. The results came from retrieving items which other people threw away. The most important single commodity was hotel silverware.

Booker T., an uncomplicated man, had never questioned how the silverware got into the garbage. It was Peter McDermott who explained to him that it was a perennial problem which management fretted about in every large hotel. Mostly the cause was hurrying waiters, busboys, and others who either didn't know, or didn't care, that, along with the waste food they shoveled into bins, a steady stream of cutlery was disappearing too.

Until several years earlier the St. Gregory compressed and froze its garbage, then sent it to a city dump. But in time the silverware losses became so appalling that an internal incinerator was built and Booker T. Graham employed to hand feed it.

What he did was simple. Garbage from all sources was deposited in bins on trolleys. Booker T. wheeled each trolley in and, a little at a time, spread the contents on a large flat tray, raking the mess back and forth like a gardener preparing topsoil. Whenever a trophy presented itself —a returnable bottle, intact glassware, cutlery, and sometimes a guest's valuables—Booker T. reached in, retrieving it. At the end, what was left was pushed into the fire and a new portion spread out.

Today's totting up showed that the present month, almost ended, would prove average for recoveries. So far, silverware had totalled nearly two thousand pieces, each of which was worth a dollar to the hotel. There were some four thousand bottles worth two cents each, eight hundred intact glasses, value a quarter apiece, and a large assortment of other items including—incredibly—a silver soup tureen. Net yearly saving to the hotel: some forty thousand dollars.

Booker T. Graham, whose take-home pay was thirty-eight dollars weekly, put on his greasy jacket and went home.

By now, traffic at the drab brick staff entrance—located in an alley off Common Street—was increasing steadily. In ones and twos, night workers were trickling out while the first day shift, converging from all parts of the city, was arriving in a swiftly flowing stream.

In the kitchen area, lights were snapping on as early duty helpers made ready for cooks, already changing street clothes for fresh whites in adjoining locker rooms. In a few minutes the cooks would begin preparing the hotel's sixteen hundred breakfasts and later—long before the last egg and bacon would be served at mid-morning—start the two thousand lunches which today's catering schedule called for.

Amid the mass of simmering cauldrons, mammoth ovens and other appurtenances of bulk food production, a single packet of Quaker Oats provided a homey touch. It was for the few stalwarts who, as every hotel knew, demanded hot porridge for breakfast whether the outside temperature was a frigid zero or a hundred in the shade.

At the kitchen fry station Jeremy Boehm, a sixteen-year-old helper, checked the big, multiple deep-fryer he had switched on ten minutes earlier. He had set it to two hundred degrees, as his instructions called for. Later the temperature could be brought quickly to the required three hundred and sixty degrees for cooking. This would be a busy day at the fryer, since fried chicken, southern style, was featured as a luncheon special on the main restaurant menu.

The fat in the fryer had heated all right, Jeremy observed, though he thought it seemed quite a bit smokier than usual, despite the overhanging hood and vent fan, which was on. He wondered if he should report the smokiness to someone, then remembered that only yesterday an assistant chef had reprimanded him sharply for showing an interest in sauce preparation which, he had been informed, was none of his business. Jeremy shrugged. This was none of his business either. Let someone else worry.

Someone *was* worrying—though not about smoke—in the hotel laundry half a block away.

The laundry, a bustling steamy province occupying an elderly two-story building of its own, was connected to the main St. Gregory structure by a wide basement tunnel. Its peppery, rough-tongued manageress, Mrs. Isles Schulder, had traversed the tunnel a few minutes earlier, arriving as usual ahead of most of her staff. At the moment the cause of her concern was a pile of soiled tablecloths.

In the course of a working day the laundry would handle some twenty-five thousand pieces of linen, ranging from towels and bed sheets through waiters' and kitchen whites to greasy coveralls from Engineering. Mostly these required routine handling, but lately a vexing problem had grown infuriatingly worse. Its origin: businessmen who did figuring on tablecloths, using ball-point pens.

"Would the bastards do it at home?" Mrs. Schulder snapped at the male night worker who had separated the offending tablecloths from a larger pile of ordinarily dirty ones. "By God!—if they did, their wives'd kick their arses from here to craptown. Plenty of times I've told those jerk head waiters to watch out and put a stop to it, but what do they care?" Her voice dropped in contemptuous mimicry. "Yessir, yessir, I'll kiss you on both cheeks, sir. By all means write on the cloth, sir, and here's another ball-point pen, sir. As long as I get a great fat tip, who cares about the goddam laundry?"

Mrs. Schulder stopped. To the night man, who had been staring open mouthed, she said irritably, "Go on home! All you've given me is a headache to start the day."

Well, she reasoned when he was gone, at least they'd caught this batch before they got into water. Once ball-point ink got wet, you could write a cloth off because, after that, nothing short of blasting would ever get the ink out. As it was, Nellie—the laundry's best spotter—would have to work hard today with the carbon tetrachloride. With luck they might salvage most of this pile, even though— Mrs. Schulder thought grimly—she would still relish a few words with the slobs who made it necessary.

And so it went, through the entity of the hotel. Upon stage, and behind—in service departments, offices, carpenters' shop, bakery, printing plant, housekeeping, plumbing, purchasing, design and decorating, storekeeping, garage, TV repair and others—a new day came awake.

2

In his private six-room suite on the hotel's fifteenth floor, Warren Trent stepped down from the barber's chair in which Aloysius Royce had shaved him. A twinge of sciatica jabbed savagely in his left thigh like hot lancets—a warning that this would be another day during which his mercurial temper might need curbing. The private barber parlor was in an annex adjoining a capacious bathroom, the latter complete with steam cabinet, sunken Japanese-style tub and built-in aquarium from which tropical fish watched, broody-eyed, through laminated glass. Warren Trent walked stiffly into the bathroom now, pausing before a wall-width mirror to inspect the shave. He could find no fault with it as he studied the reflection facing him.

It showed a deep-seamed, craggy face, a loose mouth which could be humorous on occasion, beaked nose and deep-set eyes with a hint of secretiveness. His hair, jet-black in youth, was now a distinguished white, thick and curly still. A wing collar and neatly tied cravat complemented the picture of an eminent southern gentleman.

At other times the carefully cultivated appearance would have given him pleasure. But today it failed to, the mood of depression which had grown upon him over the past few weeks eclipsing all else. So now it was Tuesday of the final week, he reminded himself. He calculated, as he had on so many other mornings. Including today, there were only four more days remaining: four days in which to prevent his lifetime's work from dissolving into nothingness.

Scowling at his own dismal thoughts, the hotel proprietor limped into the dining room where Aloysius Royce had laid a breakfast table. The oak refectory table, its starched napery and silverware gleaming, had a heated trolley beside it which had come from the hotel kitchen at top speed a few moments earlier. Warren Trent eased awkwardly into the chair which Royce held out, then gestured to the opposite side of the table. At once the young Negro laid a second place, slipping into the vacant seat himself. There was a second breakfast on the trolley, available for such occasions when the old man's whim changed his usual custom of breakfasting alone.

Serving the two portions—shirred eggs with Canadian bacon and hominy grits—Royce remained silent, knowing his employer would speak when ready. There had been no comment so far on Royce's bruised face or the two adhesive patches he had put on, covering the worst of the damage from last night's fracas. At length, pushing away his plate, Warren Trent observed, "You'd better make the most of this. Neither of us may be enjoying it much longer."

Royce said, "The trust people haven't changed their mind about renewing?"

"They haven't and they won't. Not now." Without warning the old man slammed his fist upon the table top. "By God!—there was a time when I'd have called the tune, not danced a jig to theirs. Once they were lined up— banks, trust companies, all the rest—trying to lend their money, urging me to take it."

"Times change for all of us." Aloysius Royce poured coffee. "Some things get better, others worse."

Warren Trent said sourly, "It's easy for you. You're young. You haven't lived to see everything you've worked for fall apart."

And it had come to that, he reflected despondently. In four days from now—on Friday before the close of business—a twenty-year-old mortgage on the hotel property was due for redemption and the investment syndicate holding the mortgage had declined to renew. At first, on learning of the decision, his reaction had been surprise, though not concern. Plenty of other lenders, he assumed, would willingly take over—at a higher interest rate, no doubt—but, on whatever terms, producing the two million dollars needed. It was only when he had been decisively turned down by everyone approached—banks, trusts, insurance companies, and private lenders—that his original confidence waned. One banker whom he knew well advised him frankly, "Hotels like yours are out of favor, Warren. A lot of people think the day of the big independents is over, and nowadays the chain hotels are the only ones which can show reasonable profit. Besides, look at your balance sheet. You've been losing money steadily. How can you expect lending houses to go along with that kind of situation?"

His protestations that present losses were temporary and would reverse themselves when business improved, achieved nothing. He was simply not believed.

It was at this impasse that Curtis O'Keefe had telephoned suggesting their meeting in New Orleans this week. "Absolutely all I have in mind is a friendly chat, Warren," the hotel magnate had declared, his easy Texan drawl coming smoothly down the long-distance phone. "After all, we're a couple of aging innkeepers, you and me. We should see each other sometimes." But Warren Trent was not deceived by the smoothness; there had been overtures from the O'Keefe chain before. The vultures are hovering, he thought. Curtis O'Keefe would arrive today and there was not the slightest doubt that he was fully briefed on the St. Gregory's financial woes.

With an inward sigh, Warren Trent switched his thoughts to more immediate affairs. "You're on the night report," he told Aloysius Royce.

"I know," Royce said. "I read it." He had skimmed the report when it came in early as usual, observing the notation, *Complaint of excessive noise in room 1126,* and then, in Peter McDermott's handwriting, *Dealt with by A. Royce and P. McD. Separate memo later.*

65

"Next thing," Warren Trent growled, "I suppose you'll be reading my private mail."

Royce grinned. "I haven't yet. Would you like me to?"

The exchange was part of a private game they played without admitting it. Royce was well aware that if he had failed to read the report the old man would have accused him of lack of interest in the hotel's affairs.

Now Warren Trent inquired sarcastically, "Since everyone else is aware of what went on, would it be taken amiss if I asked for a few details?"

"I shouldn't think so." Royce helped his employer to more coffee. "Miss Marsha Preyscott—daughter of *the* Mr. Preyscott—was almost raped. Do you want me to tell you about it?"

For a moment, as Trent's expression hardened, he wondered if he had gone too far. Their undefined, casual relationship was based for the most part upon precedents set by Aloysius Royce's father many years earlier. The elder Royce, who served Warren Trent first as body servant and later as companion and privileged friend, had always spoken out with a sprightly disregard of consequences which, in their early years together, drove Trent to white hot fury and later, as they traded insult for insult, had made the two inseparable. Aloysius was little more than a boy when his father had died over a decade ago, but he had never forgotten Warren Trent's face, grieving and tear stained, at the old Negro's funeral. They had walked away from Mount Olivet cemetery together, behind the Negro jazz band which was playing festively *Oh, Didn't He Ramble,* Aloysius with his hand in Warren Trent's, who told him gruffly, "You'll stay on with me at the hotel. Later we'll work something out." The boy agreed trustingly— his father's death had left him entirely alone, his mother having died at his birth—and the "something" had turned out to be college followed by law school, from which he would graduate in a few weeks' time. In the meanwhile, as the boy became a man, he had taken over the running of the hotel owner's suite and, though most of the physical work was done by other hotel employees, Aloysius performed personal services which Warren Trent accepted, either without comment or quarrelsomely as the mood took

66

him. At other times they argued heatedly, mostly when Aloysius rose—as he knew he was expected to—to conversational hooks which Warren Trent baited.

And yet, despite their intimacy and the knowledge that he could take liberties which Warren Trent would never tolerate in others, Aloysius Royce was conscious of a hairline border never to be crossed. Now he said, "The young lady called for help. I happened to hear." He described his own action without dramatizing, and Peter McDermott's intervention, which he neither commended nor criticized.

Warren Trent listened, and at the end said, "McDermott handled everything properly. Why don't you like him?"

Not for the first time Royce was surprised by the old man's perception. He answered, "Maybe there's some chemistry between us doesn't mix. Or perhaps I don't like big white football players proving how kind they are by being nice to colored boys."

Warren Trent eyed Royce quizzically. "You're a complicated one. Have you thought you might be doing McDermott an injustice?"

"Just as I said, maybe it's chemical."

"Your father had an instinct for people. But he was a lot more tolerant than you."

"A dog likes people who pat him on the head. That's because his thinking isn't complicated by knowledge and education."

"Even if it were, I doubt he'd choose those particular words." Trent's eyes, appraising, met the younger man's and Royce was silent. The remembrance of his father always disturbed him. The elder Royce, born while his parents were still in slavery, had been, Aloysius supposed, what Negroes nowadays contemptuously called an "Uncle Tom nigger." The old man had always accepted cheerfully whatever life brought, without question or complaint. Knowledge of affairs beyond his own limited horizon rarely disturbed him. And yet he had possessed an independence of spirit, as witness his relationship with Warren Trent, and an insight into fellow human beings too deep to be dismissed as cotton-patch wisdom. Aloysius had loved his father with a deep love which at moments like this trans-

67

formed itself to yearning. He answered now, "Maybe I used wrong words, but it doesn't change the sense."

Warren Trent nodded without comment and took out his old-fashioned fob watch. "You'd better tell young McDermott to come and see me. Ask him to come here. I'm a little tired this morning."

The hotel proprietor mused, "Mark Preyscott's in Rome, eh? I suppose I ought to telephone him."

"His daughter was insistent that we shouldn't," Peter McDermott said.

The two were in the lavishly furnished living room of Warren Trent's suite, the older man relaxed in a deep, soft chair, his feet raised upon a footstool. Peter sat facing him.

Warren Trent said huffily, "I'll be the one to decide that. If she gets herself raped in my hotel she must accept the consequences."

"Actually we prevented the rape. Though I do want to find out just what happened earlier."

"Have you seen the girl this morning?"

"Miss Preyscott was sleeping when I checked. I left a message asking to see her before she leaves."

Warren Trent sighed and waved a hand in dismissal. "You deal with it all." His tone made clear that he was already tired of the subject. There would be no telephone call to Rome, Peter reasoned with relief.

"Something else I'd like to deal with concerns the room clerks." Peter described the Albert Wells incident and saw Warren Trent's face harden at the mention of the arbitrary room change.

The older man growled, "We should have closed off that room years ago. Maybe we'd better do it now."

"I don't think it need be closed, providing it's understood we use it as a last resort and tell the guest what he's getting into."

Warren Trent nodded. "Attend to it."

Peter hesitated. "What I'd like to do is give some specific instructions on room changes generally. There have been other incidents and I think it needs pointing out that our guests aren't to be moved around like checkers on a board."

"Deal with the one thing. If I want general instructions I'll issue them."

The curt rejoinder, Peter thought resignedly, typified much that was wrong with the hotel's management. Mistakes were dealt with piecemeal after they happened, with little or no attempt to correct their root cause. Now he said, "I thought you should know about the Duke and Duchess of Croydon. The Duchess asked for you personally." He described the incident of the spilled shrimp Creole and the differing version of the waiter Sol Natchez.

Warren Trent grumbled, "I know that damn woman. She won't be satisfied unless the waiter's fired."

"I don't believe he should be fired."

"Then tell him to go fishing for a few days—with pay— but to keep the hell out of the hotel. And warn him from me that next time he spills something, to be sure it's boiling and over the Duchess's head. I suppose she still has those damn dogs."

"Yes." Peter smiled.

A strictly enforced Louisiana law forbade animals in hotel rooms. In the Croydons' case, Warren Trent had conceded that the presence of the Bedlington terriers would not be noticed officially, provided they were smuggled in and out by a rear door. The Duchess, however, paraded the dogs defiantly each day through the main lobby. Already, two irate dog lovers were demanding to know why, when their own pets had been refused admittance.

"I had some trouble with Ogilvie last night." Peter reported the chief house officer's absence and their subsequent exchange.

Reaction was swift. "I've told you before to leave Ogilvie alone. He's responsible directly to me."

"It makes things difficult if there's something to be done . . ."

"You heard what I said. Forget Ogilvie!" Warren Trent's face was red, but less from anger, Peter suspected, than embarrassment. The hands-off-Ogilvie rule didn't make sense and the hotel proprietor knew it. What *was* the hold, Peter wondered, that the ex-policeman had over his employer?

Abruptly changing the subject, Warren Trent announced, "Curtis O'Keefe is checking in today. He wants two adjoining suites and I've sent down instructions. You'd better make sure that everything's in order, and I want to be informed as soon as he arrives."

"Will Mr. O'Keefe be staying long?"

"I don't know. It depends on a lot of things."

For a moment Peter felt a surge of sympathy for the older man. Whatever criticisms might be leveled nowadays at the way the St. Gregory was run, to Warren Trent it was more than a hotel; it had been his lifetime's work. He had seen it grow from insignificance to prominence, from a modest initial building to a towering edifice occupying most of a city block. The hotel's reputation, too, had for many years been high, its name ranking nationally with traditional hostelries like the Biltmore, or Chicago's Palmer House or the St. Francis in San Francisco. It must be hard to accept that the St. Gregory, for all the prestige and glamour it once enjoyed, had slipped behind the times. It was not that the slippage had been final or disastrous, Peter thought. New financing and a firm, controlling hand on management could work wonders, even, perhaps, restoring the hotel to its old competitive position. But as things were, both the capital and control would have to come from outside—he supposed through Curtis O'Keefe. Once more Peter was reminded that his own days here might well be numbered.

The hotel proprietor asked, "What's our convention situation?"

"About half the chemical engineers have checked out; the rest will be clear by today. Coming in—Gold Crown Cola is in and organized. They've taken three hundred and twenty rooms, which is better than we expected, and we've increased the lunch and banquet figures accordingly." As the older man nodded approval, Peter continued, "The Congress of American Dentistry begins tomorrow, though some of their people checked in yesterday and there'll be more today. They should take close to two hundred and eighty rooms."

Warren Trent gave a satisfied grunt. At least, he reflected, the news was not all bad. Conventions were the lifeblood of hotel business and two together were a help, though unfortunately not enough to offset other recent losses. All the same, the dentistry convention was an achievement. Young McDermott had acted promptly on a hot tip that earlier arrangements by the Dental Congress had fallen through, and had flown to New York, successfully selling New Orleans and the St. Gregory to the convention organizers.

"We had a full house last night," Warren Trent said. He added, "In this business it's either feast or famine. Can we handle today's arrivals?"

"I checked on the figures first thing this morning. There should be enough checkouts, though it'll be close. Our over-bookings are a little high."

Like all hotels, the St. Gregory regularly accepted more reservations than it had rooms available. But also like all hotels, it gambled on the certain foreknowledge that some people who made reservations would fail to show up, so the problem resolved itself into guessing the true percentage of non-arrivals. Most times, experience and luck allowed the hotel to come out evenly, with all rooms occupied—the ideal situation. But once in a while an estimate went wrong, in which event the hotel was seriously in trouble.

The most miserable moment in any hotel manager's life was explaining to indignant would-be guests, who held confirmed reservations, that no accommodation was available. He was miserable both as a fellow human being and also because he was despondently aware that never again—if they could help it—would the people he was turning away ever come back to his hotel.

In Peter's own experience the worst occasion was when a baker's convention, meeting in New York, decided to remain an extra day so that some of its members could take a moonlight cruise around Manhattan. Two hundred and fifty bakers and their wives stayed on, unfortunately without telling the hotel, which expected them to check out so an engineers' convention could move in. Recollection of the ensuing shambles, with hundreds of angry engineers and their women folk encamped in the lobby, some waving reservations made two years earlier, still caused Peter to shudder when he thought of it. In the end, the city's other hotels being already filled, the new arrivals were dispersed to motels in outlying New York until next day when the bakers went innocently away. But the monumental taxi bills of the engineers, plus a substantial cash settlement to avoid a lawsuit, were paid by the hotel—more than wiping out the profit on both conventions.

Warren Trent lit a cigar, motioning to McDermott to take a cigarette from a box beside him. When he had done so, Peter said, "I talked with the Roosevelt. If we're in a jam tonight they can help us out with maybe thirty rooms." The knowledge, he thought, was reassuring—an ace-in-the-hole, though not to be used unless essential. Even fiercely competitive hotels aided each other in that kind of crisis, never knowing when the roles would be reversed.

"All right," Warren Trent said, a cloud of cigar smoke above him, "now what's the outlook for the fall?"

"It's disappointing. I've sent you a memo about the two big union conventions falling through."

"Why have they fallen through?"

"It's the same reason I warned you about earlier. We've continued to discriminate. We haven't complied with the Civil Rights Act, and the unions resent it." Involuntarily, Peter glanced toward Aloysius Royce who had come into the room and was arranging a pile of magazines.

Without looking up the young Negro said, "Don't yo' worry about sparing my feelings, Mistuh McDermott"— Royce was using the same exaggerated accent he had employed the night before—"because us colored folks are right used to that."

Warren Trent, his face creased in thought, said dourly, "Cut out the comic lines."

"Yessir!" Royce left his magazine sorting and stood facing the other two. Now his voice was normal. "But I'll tell you this: the unions have acted the way they have because they've a social conscience. They're not the only ones, though. More conventions, and just plain folks, are going to stay away until this hotel and others like it admit that times have changed."

Warren Trent waved a hand toward Royce. "Answer him," he told Peter McDermott. "Around here we don't mince words."

"It so happens," Peter said quietly, "that I agree with what he said."

"Why so, Mr. McDermott?" Royce taunted. "You think it'd be better for business? Make your job easier?"

"Those are good reasons," Peter said. "If you choose to think they're the only ones, go ahead."

Warren Trent slammed down his hand hard upon the chair arm. "Never mind the reasons! What matters is, you're being damn fools, both of you."

It was a recurring question. In Louisiana, though hotels with chain affiliations had nominally integrated months before, several independents—spearheaded by Warren Trent and the St. Gregory—had resisted change. Most, for a brief period, complied with the Civil Rights Act, then, after the initial flurry of attention, quietly reverted to their long-established segregation policies. Even with legal test cases pending, there was every sign that the hold-outs, aided by strong local support, could fight a delaying action, perhaps lasting years.

"No!" Viciously, Warren Trent stubbed out his cigar. "Whatever's happening anywhere else, I say we're not ready for it here. So we've lost the union conventions. All right, it's time we got off our backsides and tried for something else."

From the living room, Warren Trent heard the outer door close behind Peter McDermott, and Aloysius Royce's footsteps returning to the small book-lined sitting room which was the young Negro's private domain. In a few minutes Royce would leave, as he usually did around this time of day, for a law-school class.

It was quiet in the big living room, with only a whisper from the air conditioning, and occasional stray sounds from the city below, which penetrated the thick walls and insulated windows. Fingers of morning sunshine inched their way across the broadloomed floor and, watching them, Warren Trent could feel his heart pounding heavily—an effect of the anger which for several minutes had consumed him. It was a warning, he supposed, which he should heed more often. Yet nowadays, it seemed, so many things frustrated him, making emotions hard to control and to remain

73

silent, harder still. Perhaps such outbursts were mere testiness—a side effect of age. But more likely it was because he sensed so much was slipping away, disappearing forever beyond his control. Besides, anger had always come easily —except for those few brief years when Hester had taught him otherwise: to use patience and a sense of humor, and for a while he had. Sitting quietly here, the memory stirred him. How long ago it seemed!—more than thirty years since he had carried her, as a new, young bride, across the threshold of this very room. And how short a time they had had: those few brief years, joyous beyond measure, until the paralytic polio struck without warning. It had killed Hester in twenty-four hours, leaving Warren Trent, mourning and alone, with the rest of his life to live—and the St. Gregory Hotel.

There were few in the hotel who remembered Hester now, and even if a handful of old-timers did, it would be dimly, and not as Warren Trent himself remembered her: like a sweet spring flower, who had made his days gentle and his life richer, as no one had before or since.

In the silence, a swift soft movement and a rustle of silk seemed to come from the doorway behind him. He turned his head, but it was a quirk of memory. The room was empty and, unusually, moisture dimmed his eyes.

He rose awkwardly from the deep chair, the sciatica knifing as he did. He moved to the window, looking across the gabled rooftops of the French Quarter—the Vieux Carré as people called it nowadays, reverting to the older name—toward Jackson Square and the cathedral spires, glinting as sunlight touched them. Beyond was the swirling, muddy Mississippi and, in midstream, a line of moored ships awaiting their turn at busy wharves. It was a sign of the times, he thought. Since the eighteenth century New Orleans had swung like a pendulum between riches and poverty. Steamships, railways, cotton, slavery, emancipation, canals, wars, tourists . . . all at intervals had delivered quotas of wealth and disaster. Now the pendulum had brought prosperity—though not, it seemed, to the St. Gregory Hotel.

But did it really matter—at least to himself? Was the hotel worth fighting for? Why not give up, sell out—as he could, this week—and let time and change engulf them both? Curtis O'Keefe would make a fair deal. The O'Keefe chain had that kind of reputation, and Trent himself could emerge from it well. After paying the outstanding mortgage, and taking care of minor stockholders, there would be ample money left on which he could live, at whatever standard he chose, for the remainder of his life.

Surrender: perhaps that was the answer. Surrender to changing times. After all, what was a hotel except so much brick and mortar? He had tried to make it more, but in the end he had failed. Let it go!

And yet . . . if he did, what else was left?

Nothing. For himself there would be nothing left, not even the ghosts that walked this floor. He waited, wondering, his eyes encompassing the city spread before him. It too had seen change, had been French, Spanish, and American, yet had somehow survived as itself—uniquely individual in an era of conformity.

No! He would not sell out. Not yet. While there was still hope, he would hold on. There were still four days in which to raise the mortgage money somehow, and beyond that the present losses were a temporary thing. Soon the tide would turn, leaving the St. Gregory solvent and independent.

Matching movement to his resolution, he walked stiffly across the room to an opposite window. His eyes caught the gleam of an airplane high to the north. It was a jet, losing height and preparing to land at Moisant Airport. He wondered if Curtis O'Keefe was aboard.

3

When Christine Francis located him shortly after 9:30 A.M., Sam Jakubiec, the stocky, balding credit manager, was standing at the rear of Reception, making his daily check of the ledger account of every guest in the hotel. As usual, Jakubiec was working with the quick, nervous haste which sometimes deceived people into believing he was less than thorough. Actually there was almost nothing that the credit chief's shrewd, encyclopedic mind missed, a fact which in the past had saved the hotel thousands of dollars in bad debts.

His fingers were dancing now over the machine accounting cards—one for each guest and room—as he peered at names through his thick-lensed spectacles, glancing at the itemized accounts and, once in a while, making a notation on a pad beside him. Without stopping, he glanced up briefly, then down again. "I'll be just a few minutes, Miss Francis."

"I can wait. Anything interesting this morning?"

Without pausing, Jakubiec nodded. "A few things."

"For instance?"

He made a new note on the pad. "Room 512, H. Baker. Check-in 8:10 A.M. At 8:20 a bottle of liquor ordered and charged."

"Maybe he likes to brush his teeth with it."

His head down, Jakubiec nodded. "Maybe."

But it was more likely, Christine knew, that H. Baker in 512 was a deadbeat. Automatically the guest who ordered a bottle of liquor a few minutes after arrival aroused the credit manager's suspicion. Most new arrivals who wanted a drink quickly—after a journey or a tiring day— ordered a mixed drink from the bar. The immediate bottle-orderer was often starting on a drunk, and might not intend to pay, or couldn't.

She knew, too, what would follow next. Jakubiec would ask one of the floor maids to enter 512 on a pretext and make a check of the guest and his luggage. Maids knew what to look for: reasonable luggage and good clothes, and if the guest had these the credit manager would probably do nothing more, aside from keeping an eye on the account. Sometimes solid, respectable citizens rented a hotel room for the purpose of getting drunk and, providing they could pay and bothered no one else, that was their own business.

But if there was no luggage or other signs of substance, Jakubiec himself would drop in for a chat. His approach would be discreet and friendly. If the guest showed ability to pay, or agreed to put a cash deposit on his bill, their parting would be cordial. However, if his earlier suspicions were confirmed, the credit manager could be tough and ruthless, with the guest evicted before a big bill could be run up.

"Here's another," Sam Jakubiec told Christine. "Sanderson, room 1207. Disproportionate tipping."

She inspected the card he was holding. It showed two room-service charges—one for $1.50, the other for two dollars. In each case a two-dollar tip had been added and signed for.

"People who don't intend to pay often write the biggest tips," Jakubiec said. "Anyway, it's one to check out."

As with the other query, Christine knew the credit manager would feel his way warily. Part of his job—equally important with preventing fraud—was *not* offending honest guests. After years of experience a seasoned credit man could usually separate the sharks and sheep by instinct, but once in a while he might be wrong—to the hotel's detriment. Christine knew that was why credit managers occasionally risked extending credit or approved checks in slightly doubtful cases, walking a mental tightrope as they did. Most hotels—even the exalted ones—cared nothing about the morals of those who stayed within their walls, knowing that if they did a great deal of business would pass them by. Their concern—which a credit manager reflected—involved itself with a single basic question: Could a guest pay?

With a single, swift movement Sam Jakubiec flipped the ledger cards back in place and closed the file drawer containing them. "Now," he said, "what can I do?"

"We've hired a private duty nurse for 1410." Briefly Christine reported the previous night's crisis concerning Albert Wells. "I'm a little worried whether Mr. Wells can afford it, and I'm not sure he realizes how much it will cost." She might have added, but didn't, that she was more concerned for the little man himself than for the hotel.

Jakubiec nodded. "That private nursing deal can run into big money." Walking together, they moved away from Reception, crossing the now-bustling lobby to the credit manager's office, a small square room behind the concierge's counter. Inside, a dumpy brunette secretary was working against a wall which consisted solely of trays of file cards.

77

"Madge," Sam Jakubiec said, "see what we have on Wells, Albert."

Without answering, she closed a drawer, opened another and flipped over cards. Pausing, she said in a single breath, "Albuquerque, Coon Rapids, Montreal, take your pick."

"It's Montreal," Christine said, and Jakubiec took the card the secretary offered him. Scanning it, he observed, "He looks all right. Stayed with us six times. Paid cash. One small query which seems to have been settled."

"I know about that," Christine said. "It was our fault."

The credit man nodded. "I'd say there's nothing to worry about. Honest people leave a pattern, same as the dishonest ones." He handed the card back and the secretary replaced it, along with the others which provided a record of every guest who had stayed in the hotel in recent years. "I'll look into it, though; find out what the charge is going to be, then have a talk with Mr. Wells. If he has a cash problem we could maybe help out, give him a little time to pay."

"Thanks, Sam." Christine felt relieved, knowing that Jakubiec could be just as helpful and sympathetic with a genuine case, as he was tough with the bad ones.

As she reached the office doorway the credit manager called after her, "Miss Francis, how are things going upstairs?"

Christine smiled. "They're raffling off the hotel, Sam. I didn't want to tell you, but you forced it out of me."

"If they pull my ticket," Jakubiec said, "have 'em draw again. I've troubles enough already."

Beneath the flippancy, Christine suspected, the credit manager was as worried about his job as a good many others. The hotel's financial affairs were supposed to be confidential, but seldom were, and it had been impossible to keep the news of recent difficulties from spreading like a contagion.

She recrossed the main lobby, acknowledging "good mornings" from bellboys, the hotel florist, and one of the assistant managers, seated self-importantly at his centrally located desk. Then, bypassing the elevators, she ran lightly up the curved central stairway to the main mezzanine.

The sight of the assistant manager was a reminder of his

immediate superior, Peter McDermott. Since last night Christine had found herself thinking about Peter a good deal. She wondered if the time they had spent together had produced the same effect in him. At several moments she caught herself wishing that this was true, then checked herself with an inward warning against an involvement emotionally which might be premature. Over the years in which she had learned to live alone there had been men in Christine's life, but none she had taken seriously. At times, she sometimes thought, it seemed as if instinct were shielding her from renewing the kind of close relationship which five years ago had been snatched away so savagely. All the same, at this moment she wondered where Peter was and what he was doing. Well, she decided practically, sooner or later in the course of the day their ways would cross.

Back in her own office in the executive suite, Christine looked briefly into Warren Trent's, but the hotel proprietor had not yet come down from his fifteenth-floor apartment. The morning mail was stacked on her own desk, and several telephone messages required attention soon. She decided first to complete the matter which had taken her downstairs. Lifting the telephone, she asked for room 1410.

A woman's voice answered—presumably the private duty nurse. Christine identified herself and inquired politely after the patient's health.

"Mr. Wells passed a comfortable night," the voice informed her, "and his condition is improved."

Wondering why some nurses felt they had to sound like official bulletins, Christine replied, "In that case, perhaps I can drop in."

"Not for some time, I'm afraid." There was the impression of a guardian hand raised firmly. "Dr. Aarons will be seeing the patient this morning, and I wish to be ready for him."

It sounded, Christine thought, like a state visit. The idea of the pompous Dr. Aarons being attended by an equally pompous nurse amused her. Aloud she said, "In that case, please tell Mr. Wells I called and that I'll see him this afternoon."

4

The inconclusive conference in the hotel owner's suite left Peter McDermott in a mood of frustration. Striding away down the fifteenth-floor corridor, as Aloysius Royce closed the suite door behind him, he reflected that his encounters with Warren Trent invariably went the same way. As he had on other occasions, he wished fervently that he could have six months and a free hand to manage the hotel himself.

Near the elevators he stopped to use a house phone, inquiring from Reception what accommodation had been reserved for Mr. Curtis O'Keefe's party. There were two adjoining suites on the twelfth floor, a room clerk informed him, and Peter used the service stairway to descend the two flights. Like all sizable hotels, the St. Gregory pretended not to have a thirteenth floor, naming it the fourteenth instead.

All four doors to the two reserved suites were open and, from within, the whine of a vacuum cleaner was audible as he approached. Inside, two maids were working industriously under the critical eye of Mrs. Blanche du Quesnay, the St. Gregory's sharp-tongued but highly competent housekeeper. She turned as Peter came in, her bright eyes flashing.

"I might have known that one of you men would be checking up to see if I'm capable of doing my own job, as if I couldn't figure out for myself that things had better be just so, considering who's coming."

Peter grinned. "Relax, Mrs. Q. Mr. Trent asked me to drop in." He liked the middle-aged red-haired woman, one of the most reliable department heads. The two maids were smiling. He winked at them, adding for Mrs. du Quesnay, "If Mr. Trent had known you were giving this your personal attention he'd have wiped the whole thing from his mind."

"And if we run out of soft soap in the laundry we'll send for you," the housekeeper said with the trace of a smile as she expertly plumped the cushions of two long settees.

He laughed, then inquired, "Have flowers and a basket of fruit been ordered?" The hotel magnate, Peter thought, probably grew weary of the inevitable fruit basket—standard salutation of hotels to visiting VIPs. But its absence might be noticed.

"They're on the way up." Mrs. du Quesnay looked up from her cushion arranging and said pointedly, "From what I hear, though, Mr. O'Keefe brings his own flowers, and not in vases either."

It was a reference—which Peter understood—to the fact that Curtis O'Keefe was seldom without a feminine escort on his travels, the composition of the escort changing frequently. He discreetly ignored it.

Mrs. du Quesnay flashed him one of her quick, pert looks. "Have a look around. There's no charge."

Both suites, Peter saw as he walked through them, had been gone over thoroughly. The furnishings—white and gold with a French motif—were dustless and orderly. In bedrooms and bathrooms the linen was spotless and correctly folded, handbasins and baths were dry and shining, toilet seats impeccably scoured and the tops down. Mirrors and windows gleamed. Electric lights all worked, as did the combination TV-radios. The air conditioning responded to changes of thermostats, though the temperature now was a comfortable 68. There was nothing else to be done, Peter thought, as he stood in the center of the second suite surveying it.

Then a thought struck him. Curtis O'Keefe, he remembered, was notably devout—at times, some said, to the point of ostentation. The hotelier prayed frequently, sometimes in public. One report claimed that when a new hotel interested him he prayed for it as a child did for a Christmas toy; another, that before negotiations a private church service was held which O'Keefe executives attended dutifully. The head of a competitive hotel chain, Peter recalled, once remarked unkindly, "Curtis never misses an opportunity to pray. That's why he urinates on his knees."

The thought prompted Peter to check the Gideon Bibles —one in each room. He was glad he did.

As usually happened when they had been in use for any length of time, the Bibles' front pages were dotted with call girls' phone numbers, since a Gideon Bible—as experienced travelers knew—was the first place to seek that kind of information. Peter showed the books silently to Mrs. du Quesnay. She clucked her tongue. "Mr. O'Keefe won't be needing these, now will he? I'll have new ones sent up."

Taking the Bibles under her arm, she regarded Peter questioningly. "I suppose what Mr. O'Keefe likes or doesn't is going to make a difference to people keeping their jobs around here."

He shook his head. "I honestly don't know, Mrs. Q. Your guess is as good as mine."

He was aware of the housekeeper's eyes following him interrogatively as he left the suite. Mrs. du Quesnay, he knew, supported an invalid husband and any threat to her job would be cause for anxiety. He felt a genuine sympathy for her as he rode an elevator to the main mezzanine.

In the event of a management change, Peter supposed, most of the younger and brighter staff members would have an opportunity to stay on. He imagined that most would take it since the O'Keefe chain had a reputation for treating its employees well. Older employees, though, some of whom had grown soft in their jobs, had a good deal more to worry about.

As Peter McDermott approached the executive suite, the chief engineer, Doc Vickery, was leaving it. Stopping, Peter said, "Number four elevator was giving some trouble last night, chief. I wondered if you knew."

The chief nodded his bald, domed head morosely. "It's a puir business when machinery that needs money spending on it doesna' get it."

"Is it really that bad?" The engineering budget, Peter knew, had been pared recently, but this was the first he had heard of serious trouble with the elevators.

The chief shook his head. "If you mean shall we have a big accident, the answer's no. I watch the safety guards like I would a bairn. But we've had small breakdowns and sometime there'll be a bigger one. All it needs is a couple of cars stalled for a few hours to throw this building out of joint."

Peter nodded. If that was the worse that could happen,

there was no point in worrying unduly. He inquired, "What is it you need?"

The chief peered over his thick-rimmed spectacles. "A hundred thousand dollars to start. With that I'd rip out most of the elevator guts and replace them, then some other things as well."

Peter whistled softly.

"I'll tell you one thing," the chief observed. "Good machinery's a lovely thing, and sometimes well nigh human. Most times it'll do more work than you think it could, and after that you can patch it and coax it, and it'll work for you some more. But somewhere along there's a death point you'll never get by, no matter how much you—and the machinery—want to."

Peter was still thinking about the chief's words when he entered his own office. What was the death point, he wondered, for an entire hotel? Certainly not yet for the St. Gregory, though for the hotel's present regime he suspected the point was already passed.

There was a pile of mail, memos and telephone messages on his desk. He picked up the top one and read: *Miss Marsha Preyscott returned your call and will wait in room 555 until she hears from you.* It was a reminder of his intention to find out more about last night's events in 1126–7.

Another thing: he must drop in soon to see Christine. There were several small matters requiring decisions from Warren Trent, though not important enough to have brought up at this morning's meeting. Then, grinning, he chided himself: Stop rationalizing! You want to see her, and why not?

As he debated which to do first, the telephone bell shrilled. It was Reception, one of the room clerks. "I thought you'd want to know," he said. "Mr. Curtis O'Keefe has just checked in."

5

Curtis O'Keefe marched into the busy, cavernous lobby swiftly, like an arrow piercing an apple's core. And a slightly decayed apple, he thought critically. Glancing around, his experienced hotel man's eye assimilated the signs. Small signs, but significant: a newspaper left in a chair and uncollected; a half-dozen cigarette butts in a sand urn by the elevators; a button missing from a bellboy's uniform; two burned-out light bulbs in the chandelier above. At the St. Charles Avenue entrance a uniformed doorman gossiped with a news vendor, a tide of guests and others breaking around them. Closer at hand an elderly assistant manager sat brooding at his desk, eyes down.

In a hotel of the O'Keefe chain, in the unlikely event of all such inefficiencies occurring at once, there would have been whip-cracking action, slashing reprimands and perhaps dismissals. But the St. Gregory isn't my hotel, Curtis O'Keefe reminded himself. Not yet.

He headed for Reception, a slender, dapper six-foot figure in precisely pressed charcoal gray, moving with dance-like, almost mincing, steps. The last was an O'Keefe characteristic whether on a handball court, as he often was, a ballroom floor or on the rolling deck of his ocean-going cruiser *Innkeeper IV*. His lithe athlete's body had been his pride through most of the fifty-six years in which he had manipulated himself upward from a lower-middle-class nonentity to become one of the nation's richest—and most restless—men.

At the marble-topped counter, barely looking up, a room clerk pushed a registration pad forward. The hotelier ignored it.

He announced evenly, "My name is O'Keefe and I have reserved two suites, one for myself, the other in the name of Miss Dorothy Lash." From the periphery of his vision he could see Dodo entering the lobby now: all legs and breasts, radiating sex like a pyrotechnic. Heads were turning, with breath indrawn, as always happened. He had left her at the car to supervise the baggage. She enjoyed doing things like that occasionally. Anything requiring more cerebral strain passed her by.

His words had the effect of a neatly thrown grenade.

The room clerk stiffened, straightening his shoulders. As he faced the cool gray eyes which, effortlessly, seemed to bore into him, the clerk's attitude changed from indifference to solicitous respect. With nervous instinct, a hand went to his tie.

"Excuse me, sir. Mr. Curtis O'Keefe?"

The hotelier nodded, with a hovering half smile, his face composed, the same face which beamed benignly from a half-million book jackets of *I Am Your Host,* a copy placed prominently in every hotel room of the O'Keefe chain. *(This book is for your entertainment and pleasure. If you would like to take it with you, please notify the room clerk and $1.25 will be added to your bill.)*

"Yes, sir. I'm sure your suites are ready, sir. If you'll wait one moment, please."

As the clerk shuffled reservation and room slips, O'Keefe stepped back a pace from the counter, allowing other arrivals to move in. The reception desk, which a moment ago had been fairly quiet, was beginning one of the periodic surges which were part of every hotel day. Outside, in bright, warm sunshine, airport limousines and taxis were discharging passengers who had traveled south—as he himself had done—on the breakfast jet flight from New York. He noticed a convention was assembling. A banner suspended from the vaulted lobby roof proclaimed:

WELCOME DELEGATES
CONGRESS OF AMERICAN DENTISTRY

Dodo joined him, two laden bellboys following like acolytes behind a goddess. Under the big floppy picture hat, which failed to conceal the flowing ash-blond hair, her baby blue eyes were wide as ever in the flawless child-like face.

"Curtie, they say there's a lotta dentists staying here."

He said drily, "I'm glad you told me. Otherwise I might never have known."

"Geez, well maybe I should get that filling done. I always mean to, then somehow never . . ."

"They're here to open their own mouths, not other people's."

Dodo looked puzzled, as she did so often, as if events around her were something she ought to understand but somehow didn't. An O'Keefe Hotels manager, who hadn't known his chief executive was listening, had declared of Dodo not long ago: "Her brains are in her tits; only trouble is, they're not connected."

Some of O'Keefe's acquaintances, he knew, wondered about his choice of Dodo as a traveling companion when, with his wealth and influence, he could—within reason— have anyone he chose. But then, of course, they could only guess—and almost certainly underestimate—the savage sensuality which Dodo could turn on or obligingly leave quietly simmering, according to his own mood. Her mild stupidities, as well as the frequent gaucheries which seemed to bother others, he thought of as merely amusing—perhaps because he grew tired at times of being surrounded by clever, vigilant minds, forever striving to match the astuteness of his own.

He supposed, though, he would dispense with Dodo soon. She had been a fixture now for almost a year— longer than most of the others. There were always plenty more starlets to be plucked from the Hollywood galaxy. He would, of course, take care of her, using his ample influence to arrange a supporting role or two and, who knew, perhaps she might even make the grade. She had the body and the face. Others had risen high on those commodities alone.

The room clerk returned to the front counter. "Everything is ready, sir."

Curtis O'Keefe nodded. Then, led by the bell captain Herbie Chandler, who had swiftly materialized, their small procession moved to a waiting elevator.

6

Shortly after Curtis O'Keefe and Dodo had been escorted to their adjoining suites, Julius "Keycase" Milne obtained a single room.

Keycase telephoned at 10:45 A.M., using the hotel's direct line from Moisant Airport (*Talk to us Free at New Orleans Finest*) to confirm a reservation made several days earlier from out of town. In reply he was assured that his booking was in order and, if he would kindly hasten cityward, he could be accommodated without delay.

Since his decision to stay at the St. Gregory had been made only a few minutes earlier, Keycase was pleased at the news, though not surprised, for his advance planning had taken the form of making reservations at all of New Orleans' major hotels, employing a different name for each. At the St. Gregory he had reserved as "Byron Meader," a name he had selected from a newspaper because its rightful owner had been a major sweepstake winner. This seemed like a good omen, and omens were something which impressed Keycase very much indeed.

They had seemed to work out, in fact, on several occasions. For example, the last time he had come up for trial, immediately after his plea of guilty, a shaft of sunlight slanted across the judge's bench and the sentence which followed—the sunlight still remaining—had been a lenient three years when Keycase was expecting five. Even the string of jobs which preceded the plea and sentencing seemed to have gone well for the same sort of reason. His nocturnal entry into various Detroit hotel rooms had proceeded smoothly and rewardingly, largely—he decided afterward—because all room numbers except the last contained the numeral two, his lucky number. It was this final room, devoid of the reassuring digit, whose occupant awakened and screamed stridently just as he was packing her mink coat into a suitcase, having already stowed her cash and jewelry in one of his specially capacious topcoat pockets.

It was sheer bad luck, perhaps compounded by the number situation, that a house dick had been within hearing of the screams and responded promptly. Keycase, a philosopher, had accepted the inevitable with grace, not bothering even to use the ingenious explanation—which worked so well at other times—as to why he was in a room other than his own. That was a risk, though, which anyone who lived by being light-fingered had to take, even a skilled specialist like Keycase. But now, having served his time (with maximum remission for good behavior) and, more recently having enjoyed a successful ten-day foray in Kansas City, he was anticipating keenly a profitable fortnight or so in New Orleans.

It had started well.

He had arrived at Moisant Airport shortly before 7:30 A.M., driving from the cheap motel on Chef Menteur Highway where he had stayed the night before. It was a fine, modern terminal building, Keycase thought, with lots of glass and chrome as well as many trash cans, the latter important to his present purpose.

He read on a plaque that the airport was named after John Moisant, an Orleanian who had been a world aviation pioneer, and he noted that the initials were the same as his own, which could be a favorable omen too. It was the kind of airport he would be proud to thunder into on one of the big jets, and perhaps he would soon if things continued the way they had before the last spell inside had put him out of practice for a while. Although he was certainly coming back fast, even if nowadays he occasionally hesitated where once he would have operated coolly, almost with indifference.

But that was natural. It came from knowing that if he was caught and sent down again, this time it would be from ten to fifteen years. That would be hard to face. At fifty-two there were few periods of that length left.

Strolling inconspicuously through the airport terminal, a trim, well-dressed figure, carrying a folded newspaper beneath his arm, Keycase stayed carefully alert. He gave the appearance of a well-to-do businessman, relaxed and confident. Only his eyes moved ceaselessly, following the movements of the early rising travelers, pouring into the terminal from limousines and taxis which had delivered them from downtown hotels. It was the first northbound exodus of the day, and a heavy one since United, National, Eastern, and Delta each had morning jet flights scheduled variously for New York, Washington, Chicago, Miami and Los Angeles.

Twice he saw the beginning of the kind of thing he was looking for. But it turned out to be just the beginning, and no more. Two men, reaching into pockets for tickets or change, encountered a hotel room key which they had carried away in error. The first took the trouble to locate a postal box and mail the key, as suggested on its plastic tag. The other handed his to an airline clerk who put it in a cash drawer, presumably for return to the hotel.

Both incidents were disappointing, but an old experience. Keycase continued to observe. He was a patient man. Soon, he knew, what he was waiting for would happen.

Ten minutes later his vigil was rewarded.

A florid-faced, balding man, carrying a topcoat, bulging flight bag and camera, stopped to choose a magazine on his way to the departure ramp. At the newsstand cash desk he discovered a hotel key and gave an exclamation of annoyance. His wife, a thin mild woman, made a quiet suggestion to which he snapped, "There isn't time." Keycase, overhearing, followed them closely. Good! As they passed a trash can, the man threw the key in.

For Keycase the rest was routine. Strolling past the trash can, he tossed in his own folded newspaper, then, as if abruptly changing his mind, turned back and recovered it. At the same time he looked down, observed the discarded key and palmed it unobtrusively. A few minutes later in the privacy of the men's toilet he read that it was for room 641 of the St. Gregory Hotel.

Half an hour later, in a way that often happened when the breaks began, a similar incident terminated with the same kind of success. The second key was also for the St. Gregory—a convenience which prompted Keycase to telephone at once, confirming his own reservation there. He decided not to press his luck by loitering at the terminal any longer. He was off to a good start and tonight he would check the railroad station, then, in a couple of days, maybe, the airport again. There were also other ways to obtain hotel keys, one of which he had set in motion last night.

It was not without reason that a New York prosecuting attorney years before had observed in court, "Everything this man becomes involved in, your honor, is a key case. Frankly, I've come to think of him as 'Keycase' Milne."

The observation had found its way into police records and the name stuck, so that even Keycase himself now used it with a certain pride. It was a pride seasoned by such expert knowledge that given time, patience, and luck, the chances of securing a key to almost anything were extremely good.

His present specialty-within-a-specialty was based on people's indifference to hotel keys, an indifference—Keycase long ago learned—which was the constant despair of hoteliers everywhere. Theoretically, when a departing guest paid his bill, he was supposed to leave his key. But countless people left a hotel with their room keys forgotten in pocket or purse. The conscientious ones eventually dropped the keys in a mailbox, and a big hotel like the St. Gregory regularly paid out fifty dollars or more a week in postage due on keys returned. But there were other people who either kept the keys or discarded them indifferently.

This last group kept professional hotel thieves like Keycase steadily in business.

From the terminal building Keycase returned to the parking lot and the five-year-old Ford sedan which he had bought in Detroit and driven first to Kansas City, then New Orleans. It was an ideally inconspicuous car for Keycase, a dull gray, and neither old nor new enough to be unduly noticed or remembered. The only feature which bothered him a little were the Michigan license plates— an attractive green on white. Out-of-state plates were not unusual in New Orleans, but the small distinctive feature was something he would have preferred to be without. He had considered using counterfeit Louisiana plates, but this seemed to be a greater risk, besides which, Keycase was shrewd enough not to step too far outside his own specialty.

Reassuringly, the car's motor started at a touch, purring smoothly as the result of an overhaul he had performed himself—a skill learned at federal expense during one of his various incarcerations.

He drove the fourteen miles to town, carefully observing speed limits, and headed for the St. Gregory which he had located and reconnoitered the day before. He parked near Canal Street, a few blocks from the hotel, and removed two suitcases. The rest of his baggage had been left in the motel room on which he had paid several days' rent in advance. It was expensive to maintain an extra room. It was also prudent. The motel would serve as a cache for whatever he might acquire and, if disaster struck, could be abandoned entirely. He had been careful to leave nothing there which was personally identifiable. The motel key was painstakingly hidden in the carburetor air filter of the Ford.

He entered the St. Gregory with a confident air, surrendering his bags to a doorman, and registered as B. W. Meader of Ann Arbor, Michigan. The room clerk, conscious of well-cut clothes and firm chiseled features which bespoke authority, treated the newcomer with respect and allocated room 830. Now, Keycase thought agreeably, there would be three St. Gregory keys in his possession— one the hotel knew about and two it didn't.

Room 830, into which the bellboy ushered him a few moments later, turned out to be ideal. It was spacious and comfortable and the service stairway, Keycase observed as they came in, was only a few yards away.

When he was alone he unpacked carefully. Later, he decided, he would have a sleep in preparation for the serious night's work ahead.

7

By the time Peter McDermott reached the lobby, Curtis O'Keefe had been efficiently roomed. Peter decided not to follow; there were times when too much attention could be as bothersome to a guest as too little. Besides, the St. Gregory's official welcome would be extended by Warren Trent and, after making sure the hotel proprietor had been informed of O'Keefe's arrival, Peter went on to see Marsha Preyscott in 555.

As she opened the door, "I'm glad you came," she said. "I was beginning to think you wouldn't."

She was wearing a sleeveless apricot dress, he saw, which obviously she had sent for this morning. It touched her body lightly. Her long black hair hung loosely about her shoulders in contrast to the more sophisticated—though disordered—hairdo of the previous night. There was something singularly provoking—almost breathtaking—in the half-woman, half-child appearance.

"I'm sorry it took so long." He regarded her approvingly. "But I see you've used the time."

She smiled. "I thought you might need the pajamas."

91

"They're just for emergency—like this room. I use it very rarely."

"That's what the maid told me," Marsha said. "So if you don't mind, I thought I'd stay on for tonight, at least."

"Oh! May I ask why?"

"I'm not sure." She hesitated as they stood facing each other. "Maybe it's because I want to recover from what happened yesterday, and the best place to do it is here." But the real reason, she admitted to herself, was a wish to put off her return to the big, empty Garden District mansion.

He nodded doubtfully. "How do you feel?"

"Better."

"I'm glad of that."

"It isn't the kind of experience you get over in a few hours," Marsha admitted, "but I'm afraid I was pretty stupid to come here at all—just as you reminded me."

"I didn't say that."

"No, but you thought it."

"If I did, I should have remembered we all get into tough situations sometimes." There was a silence, then Peter said, "Let's sit down."

When they were comfortable he began, "I was hoping you'd tell me how it all started."

"I know you were." With the directness he was becoming used to, she added, "I've been wondering if I should."

Last night, Marsha reasoned, her overwhelming feelings had been shock, hurt pride, and physical exhaustion. But now the shock was gone and her pride, she suspected, might suffer less from silence than by protest. It was likely, too, that in the sober light of morning Lyle Dumaire and his cronies would not be eager to boast of what they had attempted.

"I can't persuade you if you decide to keep quiet," Peter said. "Though I'd remind you that what people get away with once they'll try again—not with you, perhaps, but someone else." Her eyes were troubled as he continued, "I don't know if the men who were in that room last night were friends of yours or not. But even if they were, I can't think of a single reason for shielding them."

"One was a friend. At least, I thought so."

"Friend or not," Peter insisted, "the point is what they tried to do—and would have, if Royce hadn't come along. What's more, when they were close to being caught, all four scuttled off like rats, leaving you alone."

"Last night," Marsha said tentatively, "I heard you say you knew the names of two."

"The room was registered in the name of Stanley Dixon. Another name I have is Dumaire. Were they two?"

She nodded.

"Who was the leader?"

"I think . . . Dixon."

"Now then, tell me what happened beforehand."

In a way, Marsha realized, the decision had been taken from her. She had a sense of being dominated. It was a novel experience, and even more surprisingly, she found herself liking it. Obediently she described the sequence of events beginning with her departure from the dance floor and ending with the welcome arrival of Aloysius Royce.

Only twice was she interrupted. Had she, Peter McDermott asked, seen anything of the women in the adjoining room whom Dixon and the others had referred to? Had she observed anyone from the hotel staff? To both questions she shook her head negatively.

At the end she had an urge to tell him more. The whole thing, Marsha said, probably would not have happened if it had not been her birthday.

He seemed surprised. "Yesterday was your birthday?"

"I was nineteen."

"And you were alone?"

Now that she had revealed so much, there was no point in holding back. Marsha described the telephone call from Rome and her disappointment at her father's failure to return.

"I'm sorry," he said when she had finished. "It makes it easier to understand a part of what happened."

"It will never happen again. Never."

"I'm sure of that." He became more businesslike. "What I want to do now is make use of what you've told me."

She said doubtfully, "In what way?"

"I'll call the four people—Dixon, Dumaire and the other two—into the hotel for a talk."

"They may not come."

"They'll come." Peter had already decided how to make sure they would.

Still uncertain, Marsha said, "That way, wouldn't a lot of people find out?"

"I promise that when we're finished there'll be even less likelihood of anyone talking."

"All right," Marsha agreed. "And thank you for all you've done." She had a sense of relief which left her curiously lightheaded.

It had been easier than he expected, Peter thought. And now he had the information, he was impatient to use it. Perhaps, though, he should stay a few minutes more, if only to put the girl at ease. He told her, "There's something I should explain, Miss Preyscott."

"Marsha."

"All right, I'm Peter." He supposed the informality was all right, though hotel executives were trained to avoid it, except with guests they knew very well.

"A lot of things go on in hotels, Marsha, that we close our eyes to. But when something like this happens we can be extremely tough. That includes anyone on our staff, if we find out they were implicated."

It was one area, Peter knew—involving the hotel's reputation—where Warren Trent would feel as strongly as himself. And any action Peter took—providing he could prove his facts—would be backed solidly by the hotel proprietor.

The conversation, Peter felt, had gone as far as it need. He rose from his chair and walked to the window. From this side of the hotel he could see the busy mid-morning activity of Canal Street. Its six traffic lanes were packed with vehicles, fast and slow moving, the wide sidewalks thronged by shoppers. Knots of transit riders waited on the palm-fronded center boulevard where air-conditioned buses glided, their aluminum panels shining in the sunlight. The N.A.A.C.P. was picketing some business again, he noticed. *THIS STORE DISCRIMINATES. DO NOT PATRONIZE,* one placard advised, and there were others, their bearers pacing stolidly as the tide of pedestrians broke around them.

"You're new to New Orleans, aren't you?" Marsha said.

She had joined him at the window. He was conscious of a sweet and gentle fragrance.

"Fairly new. In time I hope to know it better."

She said with sudden enthusiasm, "I know lots about local history. Would you let me teach you?"

"Well . . . I bought some books. It's just I haven't had time."

"You can read the books after. It's much better to see things first, or be told about them. Besides, I'd like to do something to show how grateful . . ."

"There isn't any need for that."

"Well then, I'd like to anyway. Please!" She put a hand on his arm.

Wondering if he was being wise, he said, "It's an interesting offer."

"Good! That's settled. I'm having a dinner party at home tomorrow night. It'll be an old-fashioned New Orleans evening. Afterward we can talk about history."

He protested, "Whoa! . . ."

"You mean you've something already arranged?"

"Well, not exactly."

Marsha said firmly, "Then that's settled too."

The past, the importance of avoiding involvement with a young girl who was also a hotel guest, made Peter hesitate. Then he decided: it would be churlish to refuse. And there was nothing indiscreet about accepting an invitation to dinner. There would be others present, after all. "If I come," he said, "I want you to do one thing for me now."

"What?"

"Go home, Marsha. Leave the hotel and go home."

Their eyes met directly. Once more he was aware of her youthfulness and fragrance.

"All right," she said. "If you want me to, I will."

Peter McDermott was engrossed in his own thoughts as he re-entered his office on the main mezzanine a few minutes later. It troubled him that someone as young as Marsha Preyscott, and presumably born with a gold-plated list of advantages, should be so apparently neglected. Even with her father out of the country and her mother decamped—he had heard of the former Mrs. Preyscott's

95

multiple marriages—he found it incredible that safeguards for a young girl's welfare would not be set up. If I were her father, he thought . . . or brother . . .

He was interrupted by Flora Yates, his homely freckle-faced secretary. Flora's stubby fingers, which could dance over a typewriter keyboard faster than any others he had ever seen, were clutching a sheaf of telephone messages. Pointing to them, he asked, "Anything urgent?"

"A few things. They'll keep until this afternoon."

"We'll let them, then. I asked the cashier's office to send me a bill for room 1126–7. It's in the name of Stanley Dixon."

"It's here." Flora plucked a folder from several others on his desk. "There's also an estimate from the carpenters' shop for damages in the suite. I put the two together."

He glanced over them both. The bill, which included several room service charges, was for seventy-five dollars, the carpenters' estimate for a hundred and ten. Indicating the bill, Peter said, "Get me the phone number for this address. I expect it'll be in his father's name."

There was a folded newspaper on his desk which he had not looked at until now. It was the morning *Times-Picayune*. He opened it as Flora went out and black head-lines flared up at him. The hit-and-run fatality of the night before had become a double tragedy, the mother of the slain child having died in the hospital during the early hours of the morning. Peter read quickly through the report which amplified what the policeman had told them when he and Christine had been stopped at the roadblock. "So far," it revealed, "there are no firm leads as to the death vehicle or its driver. However, police attach credence to the report of an unnamed bystander that a 'low black car moving very fast' was observed leaving the scene seconds after the accident." City and state police, the *Times-Picayune* added, were collaborating in a state-wide search for a presumably damaged automobile fitting this description.

Peter wondered if Christine had seen the newspaper report. Its impact seemed greater because of their own brief contact at the scene.

The return of Flora with the telephone number he had asked for brought his mind back to more immediate things.

He put the newspaper aside and used a direct outside line to dial the number himself. A deep male voice answered, "The Dixon residence."

"I'd like to speak to Mr. Stanley Dixon. Is he at home?"

"May I say who is calling, sir?"

Peter gave his name and added, "The St. Gregory Hotel."

There was a pause, and the sound of unhurried footsteps retreating, then returning at the same pace.

"I'm sorry, sir. Mr. Dixon, junior, is not available."

Peter let his voice take on an edge. "Give him this message: Tell him if he doesn't choose to come to the telephone I intend to call his father directly."

"Perhaps if you did that . . ."

"Get on with it! Tell him what I said."

There was an almost audible hesitation. Then: "Very well, sir." The footsteps retreated again.

There was a click on the line and a sullen voice announced, "This's Stan Dixon. What's all the fuss?"

Peter answered sharply, "The fuss concerns what happened last night. Does it surprise you?"

"Who are you?"

He repeated his name. "I've talked with Miss Preyscott. Now I'd like to talk to you."

"You're talking now," Dixon said. "You got what you wanted."

"Not this way. In my office at the hotel." There was an exclamation which Peter ignored. "Four o'clock tomorrow, with the other three. You'll bring them along."

The response was fast and forceful. "Like hell I will! Whoever you are, buster, you're just a hotel slob and I don't take orders from you. What's more you'd better watch out because my old man knows Warren Trent."

"For your information I've already discussed the matter with Mr. Trent. He left it for me to handle, including whether or not we shall start criminal proceedings. But I'll tell him you prefer to have your father brought in. We'll carry on from there."

"Hold it!" There was the sound of heavy breathing, then, with noticeably less belligerence, "I got a class tomorrow at four."

"Cut it," Peter told him, "and have the others do the

97

same. My office is on the main mezzanine. Remember—four o'clock sharp."

Replacing the telephone, he found himself looking forward to tomorrow's meeting.

8

The disarranged pages of the morning newspaper lay scattered around the Duchess of Croydon's bed. There was little in the news that the Duchess had not read thoroughly and now she lay back, propped against pillows, her mind working busily. There had never been a time, she realized, when her wits and resourcefulness were needed more.

On a bedside table a room-service tray had been used and pushed aside. Even in moments of crisis the Duchess was accustomed to breakfasting well. It was a habit carried over from childhood at her family's country seat of Fallingbrook Abbey where breakfast had always consisted of a hearty meal of several courses, often after a brisk cross-country gallop.

The Duke, who had eaten alone in the living room, had returned to the bedroom a few moments earlier. He too had read the newspaper avidly as soon as it arrived. Now, wearing a belted scarlet robe over pajamas, he was pacing restlessly. Occasionally he passed a hand through his still disordered hair.

"For goodness sake, keep still!" The tenseness they shared was in his wife's voice. "I can't possibly think when you're parading like a stallion at Ascot."

He turned, his face lined and despairing in the bright morning light. "What bloody good will thinking do? Nothing's going to change."

"Thinking always helps—if one does enough and it's the right kind. That's why some people make a success of things and others don't."

His hand went through his hair once more. "Nothing looks any better than it did last night."

"At least it isn't any worse," the Duchess said practically, "and that's something to be thankful for. We're still here—intact."

He shook his head wearily. He had had little sleep during the night. "How does it help?"

"As I see it, it's a question of time. Time is on our side. The longer we wait and nothing happens . . ." She stopped, then went on slowly, thinking aloud, "What we desperately need is to have some attention focused on you. The kind of attention that would make the other seem so fantastic it wouldn't even be considered."

As if by consent, neither referred to their acrimony of the night before.

The Duke resumed his pacing. "Only thing likely to do that is an announcement confirming my appointment to Washington."

"Exactly."

"You can't hurry it. If Hal feels he's being pushed, he'll blow the roof off Downing Street. The whole thing's damn touchy, anyway . . ."

"It'll be touchier still if . . ."

"Don't you think I bloody well know! Do you think I haven't thought we might as well give up!" There was a trace of hysteria in the Duke of Croydon's voice. He lit a cigarette, his hand shaking.

"We shall not give up!" In contrast to her husband, the Duchess's tone was crisp and businesslike. "Even prime ministers respond to pressure if it's from the right quarter. Hal's no exception. I'm going to call London."

"Why?"

"I shall speak to Geoffrey. I intend to ask him to do everything he can to speed up your appointment."

The Duke shook his head doubtfully, though not dismissing the idea out of hand. In the past he had seen plenty of evidence of the remarkable influence exerted by his wife's family. All the same he warned, "We could be spiking our own guns, old girl."

"Not necessarily. Geoffrey's good at pressure when he wants to be. Besides, if we sit here and wait it may be worse still." Matching action to her words, the Duchess picked up the telephone beside the bed and instructed the operator, "I wish to call London and speak to Lord Selwyn." She gave a Mayfair number.

The call came through in twenty minutes. When the

Duchess of Croydon had explained its purpose, her brother, Lord Selwyn, was notably unenthusiastic. From across the bedroom the Duke could hear his brother-in-law's deep protesting voice as it rattled the telephone diaphragm. "By golly, sis, you could be stirring a nest of vipers, and why do it? I don't mind telling you, Simon's appointment to Washington is a dashed long shot right now. Some of those in Cabinet feel he's the wrong man for the time. I'm not saying I agree, but there's no good wearing blinkers, is there?"

"If things are left as they are, how long will a decision take?" .

"Hard to say for sure, old thing. The way I hear, though, it could be weeks."

"We simply cannot wait weeks," the Duchess insisted. "You'll have to take my word, Geoffrey, it would be a ghastly mistake not to make an effort now."

"Can't see it myself." The voice from London was distinctly huffy.

Her tone sharpened. "What I'm asking is for the family's sake as well as our own. Surely you can accept my assurance on that."

There was a pause, then the cautious question, "Is Simon with you?"

"Yes."

"What's behind all this? What's he been up to?"

"Even if there were an answer," the Duchess of Croydon responded, "I'd scarcely be so foolish as to give it on the public telephone."

There was a silence once more, then the reluctant admission, "Well, you usually know what you're doing. I'll say that."

The Duchess caught her husband's eye. She gave a barely perceptible nod before inquiring of her brother, "Am I to understand, then, that you'll act as I ask?"

"I don't like it, sis. I still don't like it." But he added, "Very well, I'll do what I can."

In a few more words they said goodbye.

The bedside telephone had been replaced only a moment when it rang again. Both Croydons started, the Duke moistening his lips nervously. He listened as his wife answered.

"Yes?"

A flat nasal voice inquired, "Duchess of Croydon?"

"This is she."

"Ogilvie. Chief house officer." There was the sound of heavy breathing down the line, and a pause as if the caller were allowing time for the information to sink in.

The Duchess waited. When nothing further was said she asked pointedly, "What is it you want?"

"A private talk. With your husband and you." It was a blunt unemotional statement, delivered in the same flat drawl.

"If this is hotel business I suggest you have made an error. We are accustomed to dealing with Mr. Trent."

"Do that this time, and you'll wish you hadn't." The cold, insolent voice held an unmistakable confidence. It caused the Duchess to hesitate. As she did, she was aware her hands were shaking.

She managed to answer, "It is not convenient to see you now."

"When?" Again a pause and heavy breathing.

Whatever this man knew or wanted, she realized, he was adept at maintaining a psychological advantage.

She answered, "Possibly later."

"I'll be there in an hour." It was a declaration, not a question.

"It may not be . . ."

Cutting off her protest, there was a click as the caller hung up.

"Who was it? What did they want?" The Duke approached tensely. His gaunt face seemed paler than before.

Momentarily, the Duchess closed her eyes. She had a desperate yearning to be relieved of leadership and responsibility for them both; to have someone else assume the burden of decision. She knew it was a vain hope, just as it had always been for as long as she could remember. When you were born with a character stronger than those around you, there was no escaping. In her own family, though strength was a norm, others looked to her instinctively, following her lead and heeding her advice. Even

101

Geoffrey, with his real ability and headstrong ways, always listened to her in the end, as he had just now. As reality returned, the moment passed. Her eyes opened.

"It was a hotel detective. He insists on coming here in an hour."

"Then he knows! My God—he knows!"

"Obviously he's aware of something. He didn't say what."

Unexpectedly the Duke of Croydon straightened, his head moving upright and shoulders squaring. His hands became steadier, his mouth a firmer line. It was the same chameleon change he had exhibited the night before. He said quietly, "It might go better, even now, if I went . . . if I admitted . . ."

"No! Absolutely and positively no!" His wife's eyes flashed. "Understand one thing. Nothing you can possibly do could improve the situation in the slightest." There was a silence between them, then the Duchess said broodingly, "We shall do nothing. We will wait for this man to come, then discover what he knows and intends."

Momentarily it seemed as if the Duke would argue. Then, changing his mind, he nodded dully. Tightening the scarlet robe around him, he padded out to the adjoining room. A few minutes later he returned carrying two glasses of neat Scotch. As he offered one to his wife she protested, "You know it's much too early . . ."

"Never mind that. You need it." With a solicitousness she was unused to, he pressed the glass into her hand.

Surprised, yet yielding, she held the glass and drained it. The undiluted liquor burned, snatching away her breath, but a moment later flooded her with welcome warmth.

9

"Whatever it is can't be all that bad."

At her desk in the outer office of the managing director's suite, Christine Francis had been frowning as she read a letter in her hand. Now she looked up to see Peter McDermott's cheerful rugged face peering around the doorway.

Brightening, she answered, "It's another sling and arrow. But with so many already, what's one more?"

"I like that thought." Peter eased his big frame around the door.

Christine regarded him appraisingly. "You appear remarkably awake, considering how little sleep you must have had."

He grinned. "I had an early morning session with your boss. It was like a cold shower. Is he down yet?"

She shook her head, then glanced at the letter she had been reading. "When he comes he won't like this."

"Is it secret?"

"Not really. You were involved, I think."

Peter seated himself in a leather chair facing the desk.

"You remember a month ago," Christine said, "—the man who was walking on Carondelet Street when a bottle dropped from above. His head was cut quite badly."

Peter nodded. "Damn shame! The bottle came from one of our rooms, no question of that. But we couldn't find the guest who did it."

"What sort of a man was he—the one who got hit?"

"Nice little guy, as I recall. I talked to him after, and we paid his hospital bill. Our lawyers wrote a letter making clear it was a goodwill gesture, though, and not admitting liability."

"The goodwill didn't work. He's suing the hotel for ten thousand dollars. He charges shock, bodily harm, loss of earnings and says we were negligent."

Peter said flatly, "He won't collect. I guess in a way it's unfair. But he hasn't a chance."

"How can you be so sure?"

"Because there's a raft of cases where the same kind of thing has happened. It gives defending lawyers all kinds of precedents they can quote in court."

"Is that enough to affect a decision?"

"Usually," he assured her. "Over the years the law's been pretty consistent. For example, there was a classic case in Pittsburgh—at the William Penn. A man was hit by a bottle which was thrown from a guest room and went through the roof of his car. He sued the hotel."

"And he didn't win?"

"No. He lost his case in a lower court, then appealed to the Supreme Court of Pennsylvania. They turned him down."

"Why?"

"The court said that a hotel—any hotel—is not responsible for the acts of its guests. The only exception might be if someone in authority—say, the hotel manager—knew in advance what was going to happen but made no attempt to prevent it." Peter went on, frowning at the effort of memory. "There was another case—in Kansas City, I think. Some conventioneers dropped laundry bags filled with water from their rooms. When the bags burst, people on the sidewalk scrambled to get out of the way and one was pushed under a moving car. He was badly injured. Afterward he sued the hotel, but couldn't collect either. There are quite a few other judgments—all the same way."

Christine asked curiously, "How do you know all this?"

"Among other things, I studied hotel law at Cornell."

"Well, I think it sounds horribly unjust."

"It's hard on anyone who gets hit, but fair to the hotel. What ought to happen, of course, is that the people who do these things should be held responsible. Trouble is, with so many rooms facing a street it's next to impossible to discover who they are. So mostly they get away with it."

Christine had been listening intently, an elbow planted on her desk, chin cupped lightly in the palm of one hand. Sunlight, slanting through half-opened venetian blinds, touched her red hair, highlighting it. At the moment a line of puzzlement creased her forehead and Peter found himself wanting to reach out and erase it gently.

"Let me get this straight," she said. "Are you saying that a hotel isn't responsible legally for anything its guests may do—even to other guests?"

"In the way we've been talking about, it certainly isn't. The law's quite clear on that and has been for a long time. A lot of our law, in fact, goes back to the English inns, beginning with the fourteenth century."

"Tell me."

"I'll give you the shortened version. It starts when the English inns had one great hall, warmed and lighted by a fire, and everyone slept there. While they slept it was the landlord's business to protect his guests from thieves and murderers."

"That sounds reasonable."

"It was. And the same thing was expected of the landlord when smaller chambers began to be used, because even these were always shared—or could be—by strangers."

"When you think about it," Christine mused, "it wasn't much of an age for privacy."

"That came later when there *were* individual rooms, and guests had keys. After that the law looked at things differently. The innkeeper was obliged to protect his guests from being broken in upon. But beyond that he had no responsibility, either for what happened to them in their rooms or what they did."

"So the key made the difference."

"It still does," Peter said. "On that, the law hasn't changed. When we give a guest a key it's a legal symbol, just as it was in an English inn. It means the hotel can no longer use the room, or quarter anyone else there. On the other hand, the hotel isn't responsible for the guest once he's closed the door behind him." He pointed to the letter which Christine had put down. "That's why our friend from outside would have to find whoever dropped the bottle on him. Otherwise he's out of luck."

"I didn't know you were so encyclopedic."

"I didn't mean to sound that way," Peter said. "I imagine W.T. knows the law well enough, though if he wants a list of cases I have one somewhere."

"He'll probably be grateful. I'll clip a note on the letter." Her eyes met Peter's directly. "You like all this, don't you? Running a hotel; the other things that go with it."

He answered frankly, "Yes, I do. Though I'd like it more if we could rearrange a few things here. Maybe if we'd done it earlier we wouldn't be needing Curtis O'Keefe now. By the way, I suppose you know he's arrived."

"You're the seventeenth to tell me. I think the phone started ringing the moment he stepped on the sidewalk."

"It's not surprising. By now a good many are wondering why he's here. Or rather, when we shall be told officially why he's here."

Christine said, "I've just arranged a private dinner for tonight in W.T.'s suite—for Mr. O'Keefe and friend. Have you seen her? I hear she's something special."

He shook his head. "I'm more interested in my own dinner plan—involving you, which is why I'm here."

"If that's an invitation for tonight, I'm free and hungry."

"Good!" He jumped up, towering over her. "I'll collect you at seven. Your apartment."

Peter was leaving when, on a table near the doorway, he observed a folded copy of the *Times-Picayune*. Stopping, he saw it was the same edition—with black headlines proclaiming the hit-and-run fatalities—which he had read earlier. He said somberly, "I suppose you saw this."

"Yes, I did. It's horrible, isn't it? When I read it I had an awful sensation of watching the whole thing happen because of going by there last night."

He looked at her strangely. "It's funny you should say that. I had a feeling too. It bothered me last night and again this morning."

"What kind of feeling?"

"I'm not sure. The nearest thing is—it seems as if I know something, and yet I don't." Peter shrugged, dismissing the idea. "I expect it's as you say—because we went by." He replaced the newspaper where he had found it.

As he strode out he turned and waved back to her, smiling.

As she often did for lunch, Christine had room service send a sandwich and coffee to her desk. During the course of it Warren Trent appeared, but stayed only to read the mail before setting out on one of his prowls of the hotel which, as Christine knew, might last for hours. Observing the strain in the hotel proprietor's face, she found herself concerned for him, and noticed that he walked stiffly, a sure sign that sciatica was causing him pain.

At half-past two, leaving word with one of the secretaries in the outer office, Christine left to visit Albert Wells.

She took an elevator to the fourteenth floor then, turning down the long corridor, saw a stocky figure approaching. It was Sam Jakubiec, the credit manager. As he came nearer, she observed that he was holding a slip of paper and his expression was dour.

Seeing Christine, he stopped. "I've been to see your invalid friend, Mr. Wells."

"If you looked like that, you couldn't have cheered him up much."

"Tell you the truth," Jakubiec said, "he didn't cheer me up either. I got this out of him, but lord knows how good it is."

Christine accepted the paper the credit manager had been holding. It was a soiled sheet of hotel stationery with a grease stain in one corner. On the sheet, in rough sprawling handwriting, Albert Wells had written and signed an order on a Montreal bank for two hundred dollars.

"In his quiet sort of way," Jakubiec said, "he's an obstinate old cuss. Wasn't going to give me anything at first. Said he'd pay his bill when it was due, and didn't seem interested when I told him we'd allow some extra time if he needed it."

"People are sensitive about money," Christine said. "Especially being short of it."

The credit man clucked his tongue impatiently. "Hell!— most of us are short of money. I always am. But people go around thinking it's something to be ashamed of when if they'd only level, a lot of the time they could be helped out."

Christine regarded the improvised bank draft doubtfully. "Is this legal?"

"It's legal if there's money in the bank to meet it. You can write a check on sheet music or a banana skin if you feel like it. But most people who have cash in their accounts at least carry printed checks. Your friend Wells said he couldn't find one."

As Christine handed the paper back, "You know what I think," Jakubiec said, "I think he's honest and he has the money—but only just and he's going to put himself in a hole finding it. Trouble is, he already owes more than half of this two hundred, and that nursing bill is soon going to swallow the rest."

"What are you going to do?"

The credit manager rubbed a hand across his baldness.

"First of all, I'm going to invest in a phone call to Montreal to find out if this is a good check or a dud."

"And if it isn't good, Sam?"

"He'll have to leave—at least as far as I'm concerned. Of course, if you want to tell Mr. Trent and he says differently"—Jakubiec shrugged—"that's something else again."

Christine shook her head. "I don't want to bother W.T. But I'd appreciate it if you'd tell me before you do anything."

"Be glad to, Miss Francis." The credit manager nodded, then, with short vigorous steps, continued down the corridor.

A moment later Christine knocked at the door of room 1410.

It was opened by a uniformed, middle-aged nurse, serious-faced and wearing heavy horn-rimmed glasses. Christine identified herself and the nurse instructed, "Wait here, please. I'll inquire if Mr. Wells will see you."

There were footsteps inside and Christine smiled as she heard a voice say insistently, "Of course I'll see her. Don't keep her waiting."

When the nurse returned, Christine suggested, "If you'd like to have a few minutes off, I can stay until you come back."

"Well . . ." The older woman hesitated, thawing a little.

The voice from inside said, "You do that. Miss Francis knows what she's up to. If she didn't I'd have been a goner last night."

"All right," the nurse said. "I'll just be ten minutes and if you need me, please call the coffee shop."

Albert Wells beamed as Christine came in. The little man was reclining, diminutively, against a mound of pillows. His appearance—the scrawny figure draped by a fresh old-fashioned nightshirt—still conveyed the impression of a sparrow, but today a perky one, in contrast to his desperate frailness of the night before. He was still pale, but the ashen pallor of the previous day had gone. His breathing, though occasionally wheezy, was regular and apparently without great effort.

He said, "This is good of you to come 'n see me, miss."

"It isn't a question of being good," Christine assured him. "I wanted to know how you were."

"Thanks to you, much better." He gestured to the door as it closed behind the nurse. "But she's a dragon, that one."

"She's probably good for you." Christine surveyed the room approvingly. Everything in it, including the old man's personal belongings, had been neatly rearranged. A tray of medication was set out efficiently on a bedside table. The oxygen cylinder they had used the previous night was still in place, but the improvised mask had been replaced by a more professional one.

"Oh, she knows what she's up to all right," Albert Wells admitted, "though another time I'd like a prettier one."

Christine smiled. "You are feeling better." She wondered if she should say anything about her talk with Sam Jakubiec, then decided not. Instead she asked, "You said last night, didn't you, that you started getting these attacks when you were a miner?"

"The bronchitis, I did; that's right."

"Were you a miner for very long, Mr. Wells?"

"More years'n I like to think about, miss. Though there's always things to remind you of it—the bronchitis for one, then these." He spread his hands, palms uppermost, on the counterpane and she saw they were gnarled and toughened from the manual work of many years.

Impulsively she reached out to touch them. "It's something to be proud of, I should think. I'd like to hear about what you did."

He shook his head. "Sometime maybe when you've a lot of hours and patience. Mostly, though, it's old men's tales, 'n old men get boring if you give 'em half a chance."

Christine sat on a chair beside the bed. "I do have patience, and I don't believe about it being boring."

He chuckled. "There are some in Montreal who'd argue that."

"I've often wondered about Montreal. I've never been there."

"It's a mixed-up place—in some ways a lot like New Orleans."

She asked curiously, "Is that why you come here every year? Because it seems the same?"

The little man considered, his bony shoulders deep in the pile of pillows. "I never thought about that, miss—one way or the other. I guess I come here because I like things old-fashioned and there aren't too many places left where they are. It's the same with this hotel. It's a bit rubbed off in places—you know that. But mostly it's homely, 'n I mean it the best way. I hate chain hotels. They're all the same—slick and polished, and when you're in 'em it's like living in a factory."

Christine hesitated, then, realizing the day's events had dispelled the earlier secrecy, told him, "I've some news you won't like. I'm afraid the St. Gregory may be part of a chain before long."

"If it happens I'll be sorry," Albert Wells said. "Though I figured you people were in money trouble here."

"How did you know that?"

The old man ruminated. "Last time or two I've been here I could tell things were getting tough. What's the trouble now—bank tightening up, mortgage foreclosing, something like that?"

There were surprising sides to this retired miner, Christine thought, including an instinct for the truth. She answered, smiling, "I've probably talked too much already. What you'll certainly hear, though, is that Mr. Curtis O'Keefe arrived this morning."

"Oh no!—not him." Albert Wells' face mirrored genuine concern. "If that one gets his hands on this place he'll make it a copy of all his others. It'll be a factory, like I said. This hotel needs changes, but not his kind."

Christine asked curiously, "What kind of changes, Mr. Wells?"

"A good hotel man could tell you better'n me, though I've a few ideas. I do know one thing, miss—just like always, the public's going through a fad. Right now they want the slickness 'n the chrome and sameness. But in time they'll get tired and want to come back to older things —like real hospitality and a bit of character and atmosphere; something that's not exactly like they found in fifty other cities 'n can find in fifty more. Only trouble is, by the time they get around to knowing it, most of the good places—including this one maybe—will have gone." He stopped, then asked, "When are they deciding?"

"I really don't know," Christine said. The little man's depth of feeling had startled her. "Except I don't suppose Mr. O'Keefe will be here long."

Albert Wells nodded. "He doesn't stay long anywhere from all I've heard. Works fast when he sets his mind on something. Well, I still say it'll be a pity, and if it happens here's one who won't be back."

"We'd miss you, Mr. Wells. At least I would—assuming I survived the changes."

"You'll survive, and you'll be where you want to be, miss. Though if some young fellow's got some sense it won't be working in any hotel."

She laughed without replying and they talked of other things until, preceded by a short staccato knock, the guardian nurse returned. She said primly, "Thank you, Miss Francis." Then, looking pointedly at her watch: "It's time for my patient to have his medication and rest."

"I have to go anyway," Christine said. "I'll come to see you again tomorrow if I may, Mr. Wells."

"I'd like it if you would."

As she left, he winked at her.

A note on her office desk requested Christine to call Sam Jakubiec. She did, and the credit manager answered.

"I thought you'd like to know," he said. "I phoned that bank at Montreal. It looks like your friend's okay."

"That's good news, Sam. What did they say?"

"Well, in a way it was a funny thing. They wouldn't tell me anything about a credit rating—the way banks usually do. Just said to present the check for payment. I told them the amount, though, and they didn't seem worried, so I guess he's got it."

"I'm glad," Christine said.

"I'm glad too, though I'll watch the room account to see it doesn't get too big."

"You're a great watchdog, Sam." She laughed. "And thanks for calling."

Curtis O'Keefe and Dodo had settled comfortably into their communicating suites, with Dodo unpacking for both of them as she always enjoyed doing. Now, in the larger of the two living rooms, the hotelier was studying a financial statement, one of several in a blue folder labeled *Confidential—St. Gregory, preliminary survey*.

Dodo, after a careful inspection of the magnificent basket of fruit which Peter McDermott had ordered delivered to the suite, selected an apple and was slicing it as the telephone at O'Keefe's elbow rang twice within a few minutes.

The first call was from Warren Trent—a polite welcome and an inquiry seeking assurance that everything was in order. After a genial acknowledgment that it was—"Couldn't be better, my dear Warren, even in an O'Keefe hotel"—Curtis O'Keefe accepted an invitation for himself and Dodo to dine privately with the St. Gregory's proprietor that evening.

"We'll be truly delighted," the hotelier affirmed graciously, "and, by the way, I admire your house."

"That," Warren Trent said drily down the telephone, "is what I've been afraid of."

O'Keefe guffawed. "We'll talk tonight, Warren. A little business if we must, but mostly I'm looking forward to a conversation with a great hotel man."

As he replaced the telephone Dodo's brow was furrowed. "If he's such a great hotel man, Curtie, why's he selling out to you?"

He replied seriously as he always did, though knowing in advance the answer would elude her. "Mostly because we've moved into another age and he doesn't know it. Nowadays it isn't sufficient to be a good innkeeper; you must become a cost accountant too."

"Gee," Dodo said, "these sure are big apples."

The second call, which followed immediately, was from a pay telephone in the hotel lobby. "Hullo, Ogden," Curtis O'Keefe said when the caller identified himself, "I'm reading your report now."

In the lobby, eleven floors below, a balding sallow man who looked like an accountant which—among other things —he was, nodded confirmation to a younger male companion waiting outside the glass-paneled phone booth. The caller, whose name was Ogden Bailey and his home Long Island, had been registered in the hotel for the past two weeks as Richard Fountain of Miami. With characteristic caution he had avoided using a house phone or calling from his own room on the fourth floor. Now, in precise clipped tones he stated, "There are some points we'd like to amplify, Mr. O'Keefe, and some later information I think you'll want."

"Very well. Give me fifteen minutes, then come to see me."

Hanging up, Curtis O'Keefe said amusedly to Dodo, "I'm glad you enjoy the fruit. If it weren't for you, I'd put a stop to all these harvest festivals."

"Well, it isn't that I like it so much." The baby blue eyes were turned widely upon him. "But you never eat any, and it just seems awful to waste it."

"Very few things in a hotel are wasted," he assured her. "Whatever you leave, someone else will take—probably through the back door."

"My mom's mad about fruit." Dodo broke off a cluster of grapes. "She'd go crazy with a basket like this."

He had picked up the balance sheet again. Now he put it down. "Why not send her one?"

"You mean now?"

"Of course." Lifting the telephone once more, he asked for the hotel florist. "This is Mr. O'Keefe. I believe you delivered some fruit to my suite."

A woman's voice answered anxiously, "Yes, sir. Is anything wrong?"

"Nothing at all. But I would like an identical fruit basket telegraphed to Akron, Ohio, and charged to my bill. One moment." He handed the telephone to Dodo. "Give them the address and a message for your mother."

When she had finished, impulsively she flung her arms around him. "Gee, Curtie, you're the sweetest!"

He basked in her genuine pleasure. It was strange, he reflected, that while Dodo had proven as receptive to ex-

113

pensive gifts as any of her predecessors, it was the small things—such as at this moment—which seemed to please her most.

He finished the papers in the folder and, in fifteen minutes precisely, there was a knock on the door which Dodo answered. She showed in two men, both carrying briefcases—Ogden Bailey who had telephoned, and the second man, Sean Hall, who had been with him in the lobby. Hall was a younger edition of his superior and in ten years or so, O'Keefe thought, would probably have the same sallow, concentrated look which came, no doubt, from poring over endless balance sheets and drafting financial estimates.

The hotelier greeted both men cordially. Ogden Bailey —alias Richard Fountain in the present instance—was an experienced key figure in the O'Keefe organization. As well as having the usual qualifications of an accountant, he possessed an extraordinary ability to enter any hotel and, after a week or two of discreet observation—usually unknown to the hotel's management—produce a financial analysis which later would prove uncannily close to the hotel's own figures. Hall, whom Bailey himself had discovered and trained, showed every promise of developing the same kind of talent.

Both men politely declined the offer of a drink, as O'Keefe had known they would. They seated themselves on a settee, facing him, refraining from unzippering their briefcases, as if knowing that other formalities must be completed first. Dodo, across the room, had returned her attention to the basket of fruit and was peeling a banana.

"I'm glad you could come, gentlemen," Curtis O'Keefe informed them, as if this meeting had not been planned weeks ahead. "Perhaps, though, before we begin our business it would benefit all of us if we asked the help of Almighty God."

As he spoke, with the ease of long practice the hotelier slipped agilely to his knees, clasping his hands devoutly in front of him. With an expression bordering on resignation, as if he had been through this experience many times before, Ogden Bailey followed suit and, after a moment's hesitation, the younger man Hall assumed the same position. O'Keefe glanced toward Dodo, who was eating her banana. "My dear," he said quietly, "we are about to ask a blessing on our intention."

Dodo put down the banana. "Okay," she said co-operatively, slipping from her chair, "I'm on your channel."

There was a time, months earlier, when the frequent prayer sessions of her benefactor—often at unlikely moments—had disturbed Dodo for reasons she never fully understood. But eventually, as was her way, she had adjusted to the point where they no longer bothered her. "After all," she confided to a friend, "Curtie's a doll, and I guess if I go on my back for him I might as well get on my knees, too."

"Almighty God," Curtis O'Keefe intoned, his eyes closed and pink-cheeked, leonine face serene, "grant us, if it be thy will, success in what we are about to do. We ask thy blessing and thine active help in acquiring this hotel, named for thine own St. Gregory. We plead devoutly that we may add it to those already enlisted—by our own organization —in thy cause and held for thee in trust by thy devoted servant who speaketh." Even when dealing with God, Curtis O'Keefe believed in coming directly to the point.

He continued, his face uplifted, the words rolling onward like a solemn flowing river: "Moreover if this be thy will —and we pray it may—we ask that it be done expeditiously and with economy, such treasure as we thy servants possess, not being depleted unduly, but husbanded to thy further use. We invoke thy blessing also, O God, on those who will negotiate against us, on behalf of this hotel, asking that they shall be governed solely according to thy spirit and that thou shalt cause them to exercise reasonableness and discretion in all they do. Finally, Lord, be with us always, prospering our cause and advancing our works so that we, in turn, may dedicate them to thy greater glory, Amen. Now, gentlemen, how much am I going to have to pay for this hotel?"

O'Keefe had already bounced back into his chair. It was a second or two, however, before the others realized that the last sentence was not a part of the prayer, but the opening of their business session. Bailey was first to recover and, springing back adroitly from his knees to the settee, brought out the contents of his briefcase. Hall, with a startled look, scrambled to join him.

Ogden Bailey began respectfully, "I won't speak as to price, Mr. O'Keefe. As always, of course, you'll make that decision. But there's no question that the two-million-dollar mortgage due on Friday should make bargaining a good deal easier, at least on our side."

"There's been no change in that, then? No word of renewal, or anyone else taking it over?"

Bailey shook his head. "I've tapped some fairly good sources here, and they assure me not. No one in the financial community will touch it, mostly because of the hotel's operating losses—I gave you an estimate of those—coupled with the poor management situation, which is quite well known."

O'Keefe nodded thoughtfully, then opened the folder he had been studying earlier. He selected a single typewritten page. "You're unusually optimistic in your ideas about potential earnings." His bright, shrewd eyes met Bailey's directly.

The accountant produced a thin, tight smile. "I'm not prone to extravagant fancies, as you know. There's absolutely no doubt that a good profit position could be established quickly, both with new revenue sources and overhauling existing ones. The key factor is the management situation here. It's incredibly bad." He nodded to the younger man, Hall. "Sean has been doing some work in that direction."

A shade self-consciously, and glancing at notes, Hall began, "There is no effective chain of command, with the result that department heads in some cases have gained quite extraordinary powers. A case in point is in food purchasing where . . ."

"Just a moment."

At the interruption from his employer, Hall stopped abruptly.

Curtis O'Keefe said firmly, "It isn't necessary to give me all the details. I rely on you gentlemen to take care of those eventually. What I want at these sessions is the broad picture." Despite the comparative gentleness of the rebuke,

Hall flushed and, from across the room, Dodo shot him a sympathetic glance.

"I take it," O'Keefe said, "that along with the weakness in management there is a good deal of staff larceny which is siphoning off revenue."

The younger accountant nodded emphatically. "A great deal, sir, particularly in food and beverages." He was about to describe his undercover studies in the various bars and lounges of the hotel, but checked himself. That could be taken care of later, after completion of the purchase and when the "wrecking crew" moved in.

In his own brief experience Sean Hall knew that the procedure for acquiring a new link in the O'Keefe hotel chain invariably followed the same general pattern. First, weeks ahead of any negotiations, a "spy team"—usually headed by Ogden Bailey—would move into the hotel, its members registering as normal guests. By astute and systematic observation, supplemented by occasional bribery, the team would compile a financial and operating study, probing weaknesses and estimating potential, untapped strengths. Where appropriate—as in the present case— discreet inquiries would be made outside the hotel, among the city's business community. The magic of the O'Keefe name, plus the possibility of future dealings with the nation's largest hotel chain, was sufficient to elicit any information sought. In financial circles, Sean Hall had long ago learned, loyalty ran a poor second to practical self-interest.

Next, armed with this accumulated knowledge, Curtis O'Keefe would direct negotiations which, more often than not, were successful. Then the wrecking crew moved in.

The wrecking crew, headed by an O'Keefe Hotels vice-president, was a tough-minded and swift-working group of management experts. It could, and did, convert any hotel to the standard O'Keefe pattern within a remarkably short time. The early changes which the wrecking crew made usually affected personnel and administration; more wholesale measures, involving reconstruction and physical plant, came later. Above all, the crew worked smilingly, with reassurance to all concerned that there were to be no drastic innovations, even as it made them. As one team member expressed it: "When we go in, the first thing we announce is that no staff changes are contemplated. Then we get on with the firings."

Sean Hall supposed the same thing would happen soon in the St. Gregory Hotel.

Sometimes Hall, who was a thoughtful young man with a Quaker upbringing, wondered about his own part in all these affairs. Despite his newness as an O'Keefe executive, he had already watched several hotels, with pleasantly individual characters, engulfed by chain-management conformity. In a remote way the process saddened him. He had uneasy moments, too, about the ethics by which some ends were accomplished.

But always, weighed against such feelings were personal ambition and the fact that Curtis O'Keefe paid generously for services rendered. Sean Hall's monthly salary check and a growing bank account were cause for satisfaction, even in moments of disquiet.

There were also other possibilities which, even in extravagant daydreaming, he allowed himself to consider only vaguely. Ever since entering this suite this morning he had been acutely aware of Dodo, though at this moment he avoided looking at her directly. Her blond and blatant sexuality, seeming to pervade the room like an aura, did things to Sean Hall that, at home, his pretty brunette wife —a delight on the tennis courts, and recording secretary of the P.T.A.—had never achieved. In considering the presumed good fortune of Curtis O'Keefe, it was a speculative, fanciful thought that in the great man's own early days, he too had been a young, ambitious accountant.

The musings were interrupted by a question from O'Keefe. "Does your impression of poor management apply right down the line?"

"Not entirely, sir." Sean Hall consulted his notes, concentrating on the subject which, in the past two weeks, had become familiar ground. "There is one man—the assistant general manager, McDermott—who seems extremely competent. He's thirty-two, a Cornell-Statler graduate. Unfortunately there's a flaw in his record. The home office ran a check. I have their report here."

O'Keefe perused the single sheet which the young accountant handed him. It contained the essential facts of Peter McDermott's dismissal from the Waldorf and his subsequent attempts—unsuccessful until the St. Gregory —to find new employment.

The hotel magnate returned the sheet without comment. A decision about McDermott would be the business of the wrecking crew. Its members, however, would be familiar with Curtis O'Keefe's insistence that all O'Keefe employees be of unblemished moral character. No matter how competent McDermott might be, it was unlikely that he would continue under a new regime.

"There are also a few other good people," Sean Hall continued, "in lesser posts."

For fifteen minutes more the talk continued. At the end Curtis O'Keefe announced, "Thank you, gentlemen. Call me if there's anything new that's important. Otherwise I'll be in touch with you."

Dodo showed them out.

When she returned, Curtis O'Keefe was stretched full length on the settee which the two accountants had vacated. His eyes were closed. Since his early days in business he had cultivated the ability to catnap at odd moments during a day, renewing the energy which subordinates sometimes thought of as inexhaustible.

Dodo kissed him gently on the lips. He felt their moistness, and the fullness of her body touching his own lightly. Her long fingers sought the base of his skull, massaging gently at the hairline. A strand of soft silken hair fell caressingly beside his face. He looked up, smiling. "I'm charging my batteries." Then, contentedly, "What you're doing helps."

Her fingers moved on. At the end of ten minutes he was rested and refreshed. He stretched, opened his eyes once more, and swung upright. Then, standing, he held out his arms to Dodo.

She came to him with abandon, pressing closely, shaping her body eagerly to his own. Already, he sensed, her ever-smoldering sensuality had become a fierce, demanding flame.

With rising excitement, he led her to the adjoining bedroom.

119

11

The chief house officer, Ogilvie, who had declared he would appear at the Croydons' suite an hour after his cryptic telephone call, actually took twice that time. As a result the nerves of both the Duke and Duchess were excessively frayed when the muted buzzer of the outer door eventually sounded.

The Duchess went to the door herself. Earlier she had dispatched her maid on an invented errand and, cruelly, instructed the moon-faced male secretary—who was terrified of dogs—to exercise the Bedlington terriers. Her own tension was not lessened by the knowledge that both might return at any moment.

A wave of cigar smoke accompanied Ogilvie in. When he had followed her to the living room, the Duchess looked pointedly at the half-burned cigar in the fat man's mouth. "My husband and I find strong smoke offensive. Would you kindly put that out."

The house detective's piggy eyes surveyed her sardonically from his gross jowled face. His gaze moved on to sweep the spacious, well-appointed room, encompassing the Duke who faced them uncertainly, his back to a window.

"Pretty neat set-up you folks got." Taking his time, Ogilvie removed the offending cigar, knocked off the ash and flipped the butt toward an ornamental fireplace on his right. He missed, and the butt fell upon the carpet where he ignored it.

The Duchess's lips tightened. She said sharply, "I imagine you did not come here to discuss décor."

The obese body shook in an appreciative chuckle. "No, ma'am; can't say I did. I like nice things, though." He lowered the level of his incongruous falsetto voice. "Like that car of yours. The one you keep here in the hotel. Jaguar, ain't it?"

"Aah!" It was not a spoken word, but an emission of breath from the Duke of Croydon. His wife shot him a swift, warning glance.

"In what conceivable way does our car concern you?"

As if the question from the Duchess had been a signal, the house detective's manner changed. He inquired abruptly, "Who else is in this place?"

It was the Duke who answered, "No one. We sent them out."

"There's things it pays to check." Moving with surprising speed, the fat man walked around the suite, opening doors and inspecting the space behind them. Obviously he knew the room arrangement well. After reopening and closing the outer door, he returned, apparently satisfied, to the living room.

The Duchess had seated herself in a straight-backed chair. Ogilvie remained standing.

"Now then," he said. "You two was in that hit-'n-run."

She met his eyes directly. "What are you talking about?"

"Don't play games, lady. This is for real." He took out a fresh cigar and bit off the end. "You saw the papers. There's been plenty on radio, too."

Two high points of color appeared in the paleness of the Duchess of Croydon's cheeks. "What you are suggesting is the most disgusting, ridiculous . . ."

"I told you—cut it out!" The words spat forth with sudden savagery, all pretense of blandness gone. Ignoring the Duke, Ogilvie waved the unlighted cigar under his adversary's nose. "You listen to me, your high-an'-mightiness. This city's burnin' mad—cops, mayor, everybody else. They find who done that last night, who killed that kid an' its mother, then high-tailed it, they'll throw the book, and never mind who it hits, or whether they got fancy titles neither. Now I know what I know, and if I do what by rights I should, there'll be a squad of cops in here so fast you'll hardly see 'em. But I come to you first, in fairness, so's you could tell your side of it to me." The piggy eyes blinked, then hardened. " 'F you want it the other way, just say so."

The Duchess of Croydon—three centuries and a half of inbred arrogance behind her—did not yield easily. Springing to her feet, her face wrathful, gray-green eyes blazing, she faced the grossness of the house detective squarely. Her tone would have withered anyone who knew her well. "You unspeakable blackguard! How dare you!"

Even the self-assurance of Ogilvie flickered for an instant. But it was the Duke of Croydon who interjected, "It's no go, old girl, I'm afraid. It was a good try." Facing Ogilvie, he said, "What you accuse us of is true. I am to blame. I was driving the car and killed the little girl."

"That's more like it," Ogilvie said. He lit the fresh cigar. "Now we're getting somewhere."

Wearily, in a gesture of surrender, the Duchess of Croydon sank back into her chair. Clasping her hands to conceal their trembling, she asked. "What is it you know?"

"Well now, I'll spell it out." The house detective took his time, leisurely puffing a cloud of blue cigar smoke, his eyes sardonically on the Duchess as if challenging her objection. But beyond wrinkling her nose in distaste, she made no comment.

Ogilvie pointed to the Duke. "Last night, early on, you went to Lindy's Place in Irish Bayou. You drove there in your fancy Jaguar, and you took a lady friend. Leastways, I guess you'd call her that if you're not too fussy."

As Ogilvie glanced, grinning, at the Duchess, the Duke said sharply, "Get on with it!"

"Well"—the smug fat face swung back—"the way I hear it, you won a hundred at the tables, then lost it at the bar. You were into a second hundred—with a real swinging party—when your wife here got there in a taxi."

"How do you know all this?"

"I'll tell you, Duke—I've been in this town and this hotel a long time. I got friends all over. I oblige them; they do the same for me, like letting me know what gives, an' where. There ain't much, out of the way, which people who stay in this hotel do, I don't get to hear about. Most of 'em never know I know, or know me. They think they got their little secrets tucked away, and so they have—except like now."

The Duke said coldly, "I see."

"One thing I'd like to know. I got a curious nature, ma'am. How'd you figure where he was?"

The Duchess said, "You know so much . . . I suppose it doesn't matter. My husband has a habit of making notes while he is telephoning. Afterward he often forgets to destroy them."

The house detective clucked his tongue reprovingly. "A

little careless habit like that, Duke—look at the mess it gets you in. Well, here's what I figure about the rest. You an' your wife took off home, you drivin', though the way things turned out it might have been better if she'd have drove."

"My wife doesn't drive."

Ogilvie nodded understandingly. "Explains that one. Anyway, I reckon you were lickered up, but good . . ."

The Duchess interrupted. "Then you don't *know!* You don't know anything for sure! You can't possibly prove . . ."

"Lady, I can prove all I need to."

The Duke cautioned, "Better let him finish, old girl."

"That's right," Ogilvie said. "Just set an' listen. Last night I seen you come in—through the basement, so's not to use the lobby. Looked right shaken, too, the pair of you. Just come in myself, an' I got to wondering why. Like I said, I got a curious nature."

The Duchess breathed, "Go on."

"Late last night the word was out about the hit-'n-run. On a hunch I went over the garage and took a quiet look-see at your car. You maybe don't know—it's away in a corner, behind a pillar where the jockeys don't see it when they're comin' by."

The Duke licked his lips. "I suppose that doesn't matter now."

"You might have something there," Ogilvie conceded. "Anyway, what I found made me do some scouting— across at police headquarters where they know me too." He paused to puff again at the cigar as his listeners waited silently. When the cigar tip was glowing he inspected it, then continued. "Over there they got three things to go on. They got a headlight trim ring which musta come off when the kid an' the woman was hit. They got some headlight glass, and lookin' at the kid's clothin', they reckon there'll be a brush trace."

"A what?"

"You rub clothes against something hard, Duchess, specially if it's shiny like a car fender, say, an' it leaves a mark the same way as fingerprints. The police lab kin pick it up like they do prints—dust it, an' it shows."

"That's interesting," the Duke said, as if speaking of

123

something unconnected with himself. "I didn't know that."

"Not many do. In this case, though, I reckon it don't make a lot o' difference. On your car you got a busted headlight, and the trim ring's gone. Ain't any doubt they'd match up, even without the brush trace *an'* the blood. Oh yeah, I shoulda told you. There's plenty of blood, though it don't show too much on the black paint."

"Oh, my God!" A hand to her face, the Duchess turned away.

Her husband asked, "What do you propose to do?"

The fat man rubbed his hands together, looking down at his thick, fleshy fingers. "Like I said, I come to hear your side of it."

The Duke said despairingly, "What can I possibly say? You know what happened." He made an attempt to square his shoulders which did not succeed. "You'd better call the police and get it over."

"Well now, there's no call for being hasty." The incongruous falsetto voice took on a musing note. "What's done's been done. Rushin' any place ain't gonna bring back the kid nor its mother neither. Besides, what they'd do to you across at headquarters, Duke, you wouldn't like. No sir, you wouldn't like it at all."

The other two slowly raised their eyes.

"I was hoping," Ogilvie said, "that you folks could suggest something."

The Duke said uncertainly, "I don't understand."

"I understand," the Duchess of Croydon said. "You want money, don't you? You came here to blackmail us."

If she expected her words to shock, they did not succeed. The house detective shrugged. "Whatever names you call things, ma'am, don't matter to me. All I come for was to help you people outa trouble. But I got to live too."

"You'd accept money to keep silent about what you know?"

"I reckon I might."

"But from what you say," the Duchess pointed out, her poise for the moment recovered, "it would do no good. The car would be discovered in any case."

"I guess you'd have to take that chance. But there's

some reasons it might not be. Something I ain't told you yet."

"Tell us now, please."

Ogilvie said, "I ain't figured this out myself completely. But when you hit that kid you was going away from town, not to it."

"We'd made a mistake in the route," the Duchess said. "Somehow we'd become turned around. It's easily done in New Orleans, with the streets winding as they do. Afterward, using side streets, we went back."

"I thought it might be that," Ogilvie nodded understandingly. "But the police ain't figured it that way. They're looking for somebody who was headed out. That's why, right now, they're workin' on the suburbs and the outside towns. They may get around to searchin' downtown, but it won't be yet."

"How long before they do?"

"Maybe three, four days. They got a lot of other places to look first."

"How could that help us—the delay?"

"It might," Ogilvie said. "Providin' nobody twigs the car—an' seein' where it is, you might be lucky there. *An'* if you can get it away."

"You mean out of the state?"

"I mean out o' the South."

"That wouldn't be easy?"

"No, ma'am. Every state around—Texas, Arkansas, Mississippi, Alabama, all the rest'll be watching for a car damaged the way yours is."

The Duchess considered. "Is there any possibility of having repairs made first? If the work were done discreetly we could pay well."

The house detective shook his head emphatically. "You try that, you might as well walk over to headquarters right now an' give up. Every repair shop in Louisiana's been told to holler 'cops' the minute a car needing fixin' like yours comes in. They'd do it, too. You people are hot."

The Duchess of Croydon kept firm, tight rein on her racing mind. It was essential, she knew, that her thinking remain calm and reasoned. In the last few minutes the conversation had become as seemingly casual as if the discussion were of some minor domestic matter and not survival itself. She intended to keep it that way. Once more, she was aware, the role of leadership had fallen to her, her husband now a tense but passive spectator of the exchange between the evil fat man and herself. No matter. What was inevitable must be accepted. The important thing was to consider all eventualities. A thought occurred to her.

"The piece from our car which you say the police have. What is it called?"

"A trim ring."

"Is it traceable?"

Ogilvie nodded affirmatively. "They can figure what kind o' car it's from—make, model, an' maybe the year, or close to it. Same thing with the glass. But with your car being foreign, it'll likely take a few days."

"But after that," she persisted, "the police will know they're looking for a Jaguar?"

"I reckon that's so."

Today was Tuesday. From all that this man said, they had until Friday or Saturday at best. With calculated coolness the Duchess reasoned: the situation came down to one essential. Assuming the hotel man was bought off, their only chance—a slim one—lay in removing the car quickly. If it could be got north, to one of the big cities where the New Orleans tragedy and search would be unknown, repairs could be made quietly, the incriminating evidence removed. Then, even if suspicion settled on the Croydons later, nothing could be proved. But how to get the car away?

Undoubtedly what this oafish detective said was true: As well as Louisiana, the other states through which the car would have to pass would be alert and watchful. Every highway patrol would be on the lookout for a damaged headlight with a missing trim ring. There would probably be roadblocks. It would be hard not to fall victim to some sharp-eyed policeman.

But it *might* be done. If the car could be driven at night and concealed by day. There were plenty of places to pull off the highway and be unobserved. It would be hazardous, but no more than waiting here for certain detection. There

126

would be back roads. They could choose an unlikely route to avoid attention.

But there would be other complications . . . and now was the time to consider them. Traveling by secondary roads would be difficult unless knowing the terrain. The Croydons did not. Nor was either of them adept at using maps. And when they stopped for petrol, as they would have to, their speech and manner would betray them, making them conspicuous. And yet . . . these were risks which had to be taken.

Or had they?

The Duchess faced Ogilvie. "How much do you want?"

The abruptness took him by surprise. "Well . . . I figure you people are pretty well fixed."

She said coldly, "I asked how much."

The piggy eyes blinked. "Ten thousand dollars."

Though it was twice what she had expected, her expression did not change. "Assuming we paid this grotesque amount, what would we receive in return?"

The fat man seemed puzzled. "Like I said, I keep quiet about what I know."

"And the alternative?"

He shrugged. "I go down the lobby. I pick up a phone."

"No." The statement was unequivocal. "We will not pay you."

As the Duke of Croydon shifted uneasily, the house detective's bulbous countenance reddened, "Now listen, lady . . ."

Peremptorily she cut him off. "I will *not* listen. Instead, you will listen to me." Her eyes were riveted on his face, her handsome, high-cheekboned features set in their most imperious mold. "We would achieve nothing by paying you, except possibly a few days' respite. You have made that abundantly clear."

"That's a chance you gotta . . ."

"Silence!" Her voice was a whiplash. Eyes bored into him. Swallowing, sullenly, he complied.

What came next, the Duchess of Croydon knew, could be the most significant thing she had ever done. There must be no mistake, no vacillation or dallying because of her own smallness of mind. When you were playing for the

127

highest stakes, you made the highest bid. She intended to gamble on the fat man's greed. She must do so in such a way as to place the outcome beyond any doubt.

She declared decisively, "We will not pay you ten thousand dollars. But we will pay you twenty-five thousand dollars."

The house detective's eyes bulged.

"In return for that," she continued evenly, "*you* will drive our car north."

Ogilvie continued to stare.

"Twenty-five thousand dollars," she repeated. "Ten thousand now. Fifteen thousand more when you meet us in Chicago."

Still without speaking, the fat man licked his lips. His beady eyes, as if unbelieving, were focused upon her own. The silence hung.

Then, as she watched intently, he gave the slightest of nods.

The silence remained. At length Ogilvie spoke. "This cigar botherin' you, Duchess?"

As she nodded, he put it out.

12

"It's a funny thing." Christine put down the immense multicolored menu. "I've had a feeling this week that something momentous is going to happen."

Peter McDermott smiled across their candlelit table, its silver and starched white napery gleaming. "Maybe it has already."

"No," Christine said. "At least, not in the way you mean. It's an uneasy kind of thing. I wish I could throw it off."

"Food and drink do wonders."

She laughed, responding to his mood, and closed the menu. "You order for both of us."

They were in Brennan's Restaurant in the French Quarter. An hour earlier, driving a car he rented from the Hertz desk in the St. Gregory lobby, Peter had collected Christine from her apartment. They parked the car at Iberville, just inside the Quarter, and strolled the length of Royal Street, browsing at windows of the antique shops, with their strange mixture of *objets d'art,* imported bric-a-brac and Confederate weaponry—*Any sword in this box, ten dollars.* It was a warm, sultry night, with the sounds of New Orleans surrounding them—a deep growl from buses in narrow streets, the clop and jingle of a horse-drawn fiacre, and from the Mississippi the melancholy wail of an outbound freighter.

Brennan's—as befitting the city's finest restaurant—had been crowded with diners. While waiting for their table, Peter and Christine sipped a leisurely Old Fashioned, herbsaint flavored, in the quiet, softly lighted patio.

Peter had a sense of well being and a delight in Christine's company. It continued as they were ushered to a table in the cool, main floor dining room. Now, accepting Christine's suggestion, he beckoned their waiter.

He ordered for them both: 2-2-2 huîtres—the house's specialty combining Oysters Rockefeller, Bienville and Roffignac—flounder Nouvelle Orleans, stuffed with seasoned crabmeat, choux fleur Polonaise, pommes au four, and—from the hovering wine steward—a bottle of Montrachet.

"It's nice," Christine said appreciatively, "not to have to make decisions." She would be firm, she decided, in throwing off the sense of unease she had mentioned a moment ago. It was, after all, no more than intuition, perhaps simply explained by the fact that she had had less sleep than usual the previous night.

"With a well-run kitchen, as they have here," Peter said, "decisions about food ought not to matter much. It's a question of choice between equal qualities."

She chided him: "Your hotelship's showing."

"Sorry. I guess it does too often."

"Not really. And if you must know, I like it. I've sometimes wondered, though, what got you started to begin with."

"In the hotel business? I was a bellhop who became ambitious."

"It wasn't really that simple?"

"Probably not. I had some luck along with other things.

129

I lived in Brooklyn and in summers, between school, got a job as a bellboy in Manhattan. One night, the second summer, I put a drunk to bed—helped him upstairs, got him in pajamas and tucked him in."

"Did everyone get that kind of service?"

"No. It happened to be a quiet night and, besides, I'd had a lot of practice. I'd been doing the same thing at home—for my old man—for years." For an instant a flicker of sadness touched Peter's eyes, then he continued, "Anyway, it turned out that the one I'd put to bed was a writer for *The New Yorker*. A week or two after, he wrote about what happened. I think he called us 'the hotel that's gentler than mother's milk.' We took a lot of kidding, but it made the hotel look good."

"And you were promoted?"

"In a way. But mostly I got noticed."

"Here come the oysters," Christine said. Two aromatic, heated plates, with the baked half shells in their underlayer of rock salt, were placed dextrously in front of them.

As Peter tasted and approved the Montrachet, Christine said, "Why is it that in Louisiana you can eat oysters all year round—'r' in the month or not?"

He answered emphatically, "You can eat oysters anywhere, at any time. The 'r'-in-the-month idea is an old canard started four hundred years ago by an English country vicar. Name of Butler, I think. Scientists have ridiculed it, the U.S. Government says the rule is silly, but people still believe."

Christine nibbled an Oyster Bienville. "I always thought it was because they spawned in summer."

"So oysters do—some seasons—in New England and New York. But not in Chesapeake Bay, which is the largest oyster source in the world. There and in the South spawning can happen at any time of year. So there isn't a single good reason why northerners can't eat oysters around the calendar, just as in Louisiana."

There was a silence, then Christine said, "When you learn something, do you always remember it?"

"Mostly, I guess. I've a queer sort of mind that things stick to—a bit like an old-fashioned flypaper. In a way it's been lucky for me." He speared an Oyster Rockefeller, savoring its subtle absinthe flavoring.

"How lucky?"

"Well, that same summer—the one we were talking about—they let me try other jobs in the hotel, including helping out at the bar. I was getting interested by then and had borrowed some books. One was about mixing drinks." Peter paused, his mind leafing over events he had half-forgotten. "I happened to be at the bar alone when a customer came in. I didn't know who he was, but he said, 'I hear you're the bright boy *The New Yorker* wrote about. Can you mix me a Rusty Nail?' "

"He was kidding?"

"No. But I'd have thought so if I hadn't read the ingredients—Drambuie and Scotch—a couple of hours earlier. That's what I mean by luck. Anyway, I mixed it and afterward he said, 'That's good, but you won't learn the hotel business this way. Things have changed since *Work of Art.*' I told him I didn't fancy myself as Myron Weagle, but wouldn't mind being Evelyn Orcham. He laughed at that; I guess he'd read Arnold Bennett too. Then he gave me his card and told me to see him next day."

"He owned fifty hotels, I suppose."

"As it turned out, he didn't own anything. His name was Herb Fischer and he was a salesman—bulk canned goods, that kind of stuff. He was also pushy and a braggart, and all the time had a way of talking you down. But he knew the hotel business, and most people in it, because it was there he did his selling."

The oyster plates were removed. Now their waiter, backstopped by a red-coated captain, placed the steaming flounder before them.

"I'm afraid to eat," Christine said. "Nothing can possibly taste as heavenly as that." She sampled the succulent, superbly seasoned fish. "Um! Incredibly, it's even better."

It was several minutes before she said, "Tell me about Mr. Fischer."

"Well, at first I thought he was just a big talker—you get a million of 'em in bars. What changed my mind was a letter from Cornell. It told me to report at Statler Hall—the School of Hotel Admin—for a selection interview. The way things turned out, they offered me a scholarship and I went there from high school. Afterward I discovered it happened because Herb badgered some hotel people into recommending me. I guess he was a good salesman."

"You only guess!"

Peter said thoughtfully, "I've never been quite sure. I owe a lot to Herb Fischer, but sometimes I wonder if people didn't do things, including giving him business, just to get rid of him. After it was fixed about Cornell I only saw him once again. I tried to thank him—the same way I tried to like him. But he wouldn't let me do either; just kept boasting, talking about deals he'd made, or would. Then he said I needed some clothes for college—he was right—and insisted on lending me two hundred dollars. It must have meant a lot, because I found out afterward his commissions weren't big. I paid him back by sending checks for small amounts. Most were never cashed."

"I think it's a wonderful story." Christine had listened raptly. "Why don't you see him any more?"

"He died," Peter said. "I'd tried to reach him several times, but we never seemed to make it. Then about a year ago I got a phone call from a lawyer—Herb didn't have any family, apparently. I went to the funeral. And I found there were eight of us there—whom he'd all helped in the same kind of way. The funny thing was, with all his boasting he'd never told any of us about the others."

"I could cry," Christine said.

He nodded. "I know. I felt I wanted to then. I suppose it should have taught me something, though I've never been quite sure what. Maybe it's that some people raise a great big barrier, all the while wishing you'd tear it down, and if you don't you never really know them."

Christine was quiet through coffee—by agreement they had both ruled out dessert. At length she asked, "Do any of us really know what we want for ourselves?"

Peter considered. "Not entirely, I suppose. Though I know one thing I want to achieve—or at least something like it." He beckoned a waiter for their bill.

"Tell me."

"I'll do better than that," he said. "I'll show you."

Outside Brennan's they paused, adjusting from interior coolness to the warm night air. The city seemed quieter than an hour earlier. A few lights around were darkening, the Quarter's night life moving on to other cantons. Taking Christine's arm, Peter piloted her diagonally across Royal Street. They stopped at the southwest corner of St. Louis, looking directly ahead. "That's what I'd like to create," he said. "Something at least as good, or maybe better."

Beneath graceful grilled balconies and fluted iron columns, flickering gas lanterns cast light and shadow on the white-gray classical façade of the Royal Orleans Hotel. Through arched and mullioned windows amber light streamed outward. On the promenade sidewalk a doorman paced, in rich gold uniform and visored pillbox cap. High above, in a sudden breeze, flags and halliards snapped upon their staffs. A taxi drew up. The doorman moved swiftly to open its door. Women's heels clicked and men's laughter echoed as they moved inside. A door slammed. The taxi pulled away.

"There are some people," Peter said, "who believe the Royal Orleans is the finest hotel in North America. Whether you agree or not doesn't much matter. The point is: it shows how good a hotel can be."

They crossed St. Louis, toward the site which had once been traditional hotel, a center of Creole society; then slave mart, Civil War hospital, state capitol, and now hotel again. Peter's voice took on enthusiasm. "They've everything going for them—history, style, a modern plant and imagination. For the new building there were two firms of New Orleans architects—one tradition steeped, the other modern. They proved you can build freshly yet retain old character."

The doorman, who had ceased pacing, held the main door open as they strolled inside. Directly ahead two giant blackamoor statues guarded white marble stairs to the lobby promenade. "The funny thing is," Peter said, "that with all that's individual, the Royal Orleans is a chain hotel." He added tersely, "But not Curtis O'Keefe's kind."

"More like Peter McDermott's?"

"There's a long way to go for that. And I took a step backward. I guess you know."

"Yes," Christine said, "I know. But you'll still do it. I'd bet a thousand dollars that some day you will."

He squeezed her arm. "If you've that kind of money, better buy some O'Keefe Hotels stock."

They strolled the length of the Royal Orleans lobby— white marbled with antique white, citron and persimmon tapestries—leaving by the Royal Street doors.

For an hour and a half they sauntered through the Quarter, stopping at Preservation Hall to endure its stifling heat and crowded benches for the joy of Dixieland jazz at its purest; enjoying the comparative coolness of Jackson Square, with coffee at the French market on the river side, inspecting critically some of the bad art with which New Orleans abounded; and later, at the Court of the Two Sisters, sipping cool mint juleps under stars, subdued lights and lacy trees.

"It's been wonderful," Christine said. "Now I'm ready to go home."

Strolling toward Iberville and the parked car, a small Negro boy, with cardboard box and brushes, accosted them.

"Shoe shine, mister?"

Peter shook his head. "Too late, son."

The boy, bright eyed, stood squarely in their path, surveying Peter's feet. "Ah bet yo' twenty-five cents ah kin tell you where yo' got those shoes. Ah kin tell you th' city and th' state; and if ah kin—you give me twenty-five cents. But if ah cain't, ah'll give yo' twenty-five cents."

A year ago Peter had bought the shoes in Tenafly, New Jersey. He hesitated, with a feeling of taking advantage, then nodded. "Okay."

The boy's bright eyes flicked upward. "Mister, yo' got those shoes on yo' feet on the concrete sidewalk of New Orleans, in th' State o' Louisiana. Now remember—ah said ah'd tell yo' where yo' got those shoes, not where yo' bought them."

They laughed, and Christine slipped her arm through Peter's as he paid the quarter. They were still laughing during the drive northward to Christine's apartment.

In the dining room of Warren Trent's private suite, Curtis O'Keefe puffed appraisingly at a cigar. He had selected it from a cherry-wood humidor proffered him by Aloysius Royce, and its richness mingled agreeably on his palate with the Louis XIII cognac which had accompanied coffee. To O'Keefe's left, at the head of the oak refectory table at which Royce had deftly served their superb five-course dinner, Warren Trent presided with patriarchal benevolence. Directly across, Dodo, in a clinging black gown, inhaled agreeably on a Turkish cigarette which Royce had also produced and lighted.

"Gee," Dodo said, "I feel like I ate a whole pig."

O'Keefe smiled indulgently. "A fine meal, Warren. Please compliment your chef."

The St. Gregory's proprietor inclined his head graciously. "He'll be gratified at the source of the compliment. By the way, you may like to know that precisely the same meal was available tonight in my main dining room."

O'Keefe nodded, though unimpressed. In his opinion a large elaborate menu was as out of place in a hotel dining room as *paté de foie gras* in a lunch pail. Even more to the point—earlier in the evening he had glanced into the St. Gregory's main restaurant at what should have been its peak service hour, to find the cavernous expanse barely a third occupied.

In the O'Keefe empire, dining was standard and simplified, with the choice of fare limited to a few popular, pedestrian items. Behind this policy was Curtis O'Keefe's conviction—buttressed by experience—that public taste and preferences about eating were equal, and largely unimaginative. In any O'Keefe establishment, though food was precisely prepared and served with antiseptic cleanliness, there was seldom provision for gourmets, who were regarded as an unprofitable minority.

The hotel magnate observed, "There aren't many hotels nowadays offering that kind of cuisine. Most that did have had to change their ways."

"Most but not all. Why should everyone be as docile?"

"Because our entire business has changed, Warren, since you and I were young in it—whether we like the fact or not. The days of 'mine host' and personal service are over. Maybe people cared once about such things. They don't any more."

There was a directness in both men's voices, implying that with the meal's ending the time for mere politeness had gone. As each spoke, Dodo's baby blue eyes shifted curiously between them as if following some action, though barely understood, upon a stage. Aloysius Royce, his back turned, was busy at a sideboard.

Warren Trent said sharply, "There are some who'd disagree."

O'Keefe regarded his glowing cigar tip. "For any who do, the answer's in my balance sheets compared with others. For example, yours."

The other flushed, his lips tightening. "What's happening here is temporary; a phase. I've seen them before. This one will pass, the same as others."

"No. If you think that, you're fashioning a hangman's noose. And you deserve better, Warren—after all these years."

There was an obstinate pause before the growled reply. "I haven't spent my life building an institution to see it become a cheap-run joint."

"If you're referring to my houses, none of them are that." It was O'Keefe's turn to redden angrily. "Nor am I so sure about this one being an institution."

In the cold, ensuing silence Dodo asked, "Will it be a real fight or just a words one?"

Both men laughed, though Warren Trent less heartily. It was Curtis O'Keefe who raised his hands placatingly.

"She's right, Warren. It's pointless for us to quarrel. If we're to continue our separate ways, at least we should remain friends."

More tractably, Warren Trent nodded. In part, his acerbity of a moment earlier had been prompted by a twinge of sciatica which for the time being had passed. Though even allowing for this, he thought bitterly, it was hard not to be resentful of this smooth successful man whose financial conquests so greatly contrasted with his own.

"You can sum up in three words," Curtis O'Keefe declared, "what the public expects nowadays from a hotel: an 'efficient, economic package.' But we can only provide it if we have effective cost accounting of every move—our guests' and our own; an efficient plant; and above all a minimum wage bill, which means automation, eliminating people and old-style hospitality wherever possible."

"And that's all? You'd discount everything else that used to make a fine hotel? You'd deny that a good innkeeper can stamp his personal imprint on any house?" The St. Gregory's proprietor snorted. "A visitor to your kind of hotel doesn't have a sense of belonging, of being someone significant to whom a little more is given—in feeling and hospitality—than is charged for on his bill."

"It's a delusion he doesn't need," O'Keefe said incisively. "If a hotel's hospitable it's because it's paid to be, so in the end it doesn't count. People see through falseness in a way they didn't used to. But they respect fairness—a fair profit for the hotel; a fair price to the guest, which is what my houses give. Oh, I grant you there'll always be a few Tuscanys for those who want special treatment and are willing to pay. But they're small places and for the few. The big houses like yours—if they want to survive my kind of competition—have to think as I do."

Warren Trent growled, "You'll not object if I continue to think for myself for a while."

O'Keefe shook his head impatiently. "There was nothing personal. I was speaking of trends, not particulars."

"The devil with trends! I've an instinct tells me plenty of people still like to travel first class. They're the ones who expect something more than boxes with beds."

"You're misquoting me, but I won't complain." Curtis O'Keefe smiled coolly. "I'll challenge your simile, though. Except for the very few, first class is finished, dead."

"Why?"

"Because jet airplanes killed first-class travel, and an entire state of mind along with it. Before then, first class had an aura of distinction. But jet travel showed everyone how silly and wasteful the old ways were. Air journeys became swift and short, to the point where first class simply wasn't worth it. So people squeezed into their tourist seats

137

and stopped worrying about status—the price was too high. Pretty soon there was a reverse kind of status in traveling tourist. The best people did it. First class, they told each other over their box lunches, was for fools and profligates. And what people realize they get from jets—the efficient, economic package—they require from the hotel business too."

Unsuccessfully Dodo attempted to conceal a yawn behind her hand, then butted her Turkish cigarette. Instantly Aloysius Royce was beside her, proffering a fresh one and deftly lighting it. She smiled warmly, and the young Negro returned the smile, managing to convey a discreet but friendly sympathy. Unobtrusively he replaced used ash trays on the table with fresh, and refilled Dodo's coffee cup, then the others. As Royce slipped out quietly, O'Keefe observed, "A good man you have there, Warren."

Warren Trent responded absently, "He's been with me a long time." Watching Royce himself, he had been wondering how Aloysius's father might have reacted to the news that control of the hotel might soon pass on to other hands. Probably with a shrug. Possessions and money had meant little to the old man. Warren Trent could almost hear him now, asserting in his cracked, sprightly voice, "Yo' had yo' own way so long, could be a passel o' bad times'll be fo' yo' own goodness. God bends our backs an' humbles us, remindin' us we ain't nothin' but His wayward children, 'spite our fancy notions other ways." But then, with calculated contrariness the old man might have added, "All th' same, 'f yo' b'lieve in somethin', yo' fight fo' it shore. After yo' dead yo' won't shoot nobody, cos yo' cain't hardly take aim."

Taking aim—he suspected, waveringly—Warren Trent insisted, "Your way, you make everything to do with a hotel sound so damnably antiseptic. Your kind of hotel lacks warmth or humanity. It's for automatons, with punch-card minds, and lubricant instead of blood."

O'Keefe shrugged. "It's the kind that pays dividends."

"Financial maybe, not human."

Ignoring the last remark, O'Keefe said, "I've talked about our business the way it is now. Let's carry things a shade further. In my organization I've had a blueprint developed for the future. Some might call it a vision, I suppose, though it's more an informed projection of what hotels—certainly O'Keefe hotels—are going to be like a few years ahead.

"The first thing we'll have simplified is Reception, where checking in will take a few seconds at the most. The majority of our people will arrive directly from air terminals by helicopter, so a main reception point will be a private roof heliport. Secondarily there'll be lower-floor receiving points where cars and limousines can drive directly in, eliminating transfer to a lobby, the way we do it now. At all these places there'll be a kind of instant sorting office, masterminded by an IBM brain that, incidentally, is ready now.

"Guests with reservations will have been sent a key-coded card. They'll insert it in a frame and immediately be on their way by individual escalator section to a room which may have been cleared for use only seconds earlier. If a room isn't ready—and it'll happen," Curtis O'Keefe conceded, "just as it does now—we'll have small portable way stations. These will be cubicles with a couple of chairs, wash basin and space for baggage, just enough to freshen up after a journey and give some privacy right away. People can come and go, as they do with a regular room, and my engineers are working on a scheme for making the way stations mobile so that later they can latch on directly to the allocated space. That way, the guest will merely open an IBM cleared door, and walk on through.

"For those driving their own cars there'll be parallel arrangements, with coded, moving lights to guide them into personal parking stalls, from where other individual escalators will take them directly to their rooms. In all cases we'll curtail baggage handling, using high-speed sorters and conveyors, and baggage will be routed into rooms, actually arriving ahead of the guests.

"Similarly, all other services will have automated room delivery systems—valet, beverages, food, florist, drugstore, newsstand; even the final bill can be received and paid by room conveyor. And incidentally, apart from other benefits, I'll have broken the tipping system, a tyranny we've suffered—along with our guests—for years too long."

139

There was a silence in the paneled dining room as the hotel magnate, still commanding the stage, sipped coffee before resuming.

"My building design and automation will keep to a minimum the need for any guest room to be entered by a hotel employee. Beds, recessing into walls, are to be serviced by machine from outside. Air filtration is already improved to the point where dust and dirt have ceased to be problems. Rugs, for example, can be laid on floors of fine steel mesh, with air space beneath, suctioned once a day when a timed relay cuts in.

"All this, and more, can be accomplished now. Our remaining problems, which naturally will be solved"—Curtis O'Keefe waved a hand in his familiar dismissing gesture—"our remaining problems are principally of co-ordination, construction, and investment."

"I hope," Warren Trent said firmly, "that I never live to see it happen in my house."

"You won't," O'Keefe informed him. "Before it can happen here we'll have to tear down your house and build again."

"You'd do that!" It was a shocked rejoinder.

O'Keefe shrugged. "I can't reveal long-range plans, naturally. But I'd say that would be our policy before too long. If you're concerned about your name surviving, I could promise you that a tablet, commemorating the original hotel and possibly your own connection with it, would be incorporated in the new structure."

"A tablet!" The St. Gregory's proprietor snorted. "Where would you put it—in the men's washroom?"

Abruptly Dodo giggled. As the two men turned their heads involuntarily, she remarked, "Maybe they won't have one. I mean, all those conveyor things, who needs it?"

Curtis O'Keefe glanced at her sharply. There were moments occasionally when he wondered if Dodo were perhaps a little brighter than generally she allowed herself to seem.

At Dodo's reaction Warren Trent had flushed with embarrassment. Now he assured her in his most courtly manner, "I apologize, my dear lady, for an unfortunate choice of words."

140

"Gee, don't mind me." Dodo seemed surprised. "Anyway, I think this is a swell hotel." She turned her wide and seemingly innocent eyes toward O'Keefe. "Curtie, why'll you have to pull it down?"

He answered testily, "I was merely reviewing a possibility. In any event, Warren, it's time you were out of the hotel business."

Surprisingly, the response was mild compared with the asperity of a few minutes earlier. "Even if I was willing to be, there are others to consider beside myself. A good many of my old employees rely on me in the same way I've relied on them. You tell me your plan is to replace people with automation. I couldn't walk out realizing that. I owe my staff that much, at least, in return for the loyalty they've given me."

"Do you? Is any hotel staff loyal? Wouldn't all or most of them sell you out this instant if it meant an advantage to themselves?"

"I assure you no. I've run this house for more than thirty years and in that time loyalty builds. Or possibly you've had less experience in that direction."

"I've formed some opinions about loyalty." O'Keefe spoke absently. Mentally he was leafing through the report of Ogden Bailey and the younger assistant Sean Hall which he had read earlier. It was Hall whom he had cautioned against reporting too many details, but one detail which might now prove useful had been included in the written summary. The hotelier concentrated. At length he said, "You've an old employee, haven't you, who runs your Pontalba Bar?"

"Yes—Tom Earlshore. He's been working here almost as long as I have myself." In a way, Warren Trent thought, Tom Earlshore epitomized the older St. Gregory employees whom he could not abandon. He himself had hired Earlshore when they were both young men, and nowadays, though the elderly head barman was stooped, and slowing in his work, he was one of those in the hotel whom Warren Trent counted as a personal friend. As one would a friend, he had helped Tom Earlshore too. There had been the time when the Earlshores' baby daughter, born with a deformed hip, had been sent north to Mayo Clinic for suc-

HOTEL

cessful corrective surgery through arrangements made by
Warren Trent. And afterward he had quietly paid the bills,
for which Tom Earlshore had long ago declared undying
gratitude and devotion. The Earlshore girl was now a married woman with children of her own, but the bond between her father and the hotel operator still remained. "If
there's one man I'd trust with anything," he told Curtis
O'Keefe now, "it's Tom."

"You'd be a fool if you did," O'Keefe said crisply. "I've
information that he's bleeding you white."

In the shocked silence O'Keefe recited the facts. There
were a multiplicity of ways in which a dishonest bartender
could steal from his employer—by pouring short measure
to obtain an extra drink or two from each bottle used; by
failing to ring every sale into the cash register; by introducing his own privately purchased liquor into the bar, so
that an inventory check would show no shortage, but the
proceeds—with substantial profit—would be taken by the
bartender himself. Tom Earlshore appeared to be using all
three methods. As well, according to Sean Hall's informed
observations over several weeks, Earlshore's two assistants
were in collusion with him. "A high percentage of your bar
profit is being skimmed off," O'Keefe declared, "and from
the look of things generally, I'd say it's been going on a
long time."

Throughout the recital Warren Trent had sat immobile,
his face expressionless, though behind it his thoughts were
deep and bitter. Despite his long-standing trust of Tom
Earlshore, and the friendship he had believed existed, he
had not the least doubt that the information provided was
true. He had learned too much of chain hotel espionage
methods to believe otherwise, nor would Curtis O'Keefe
have made the charge without assurance of his facts. Warren Trent had long ago assumed that O'Keefe undercover
men had infiltrated the St. Gregory in advance of their
chief's arrival. But what he had not expected was this searing and personal humiliation. Now he said, "You spoke of
'other things generally.' What did it mean?"

"Your supposedly loyal staff is riddled with corruption.
There's scarcely a department in which you aren't being
robbed and cheated. Naturally, I haven't all the details,

142

but those I have you're welcome to. If you wish I'll have a report prepared."

"Thank you." The words were whispered and barely audible.

"You've too many fat people working for you. It was the first thing I noticed when I arrived. I've always found it a warning sign. Their bellies are full of hotel food, and here they've battened on you every other way."

There was a stillness in the small, intimate dining room, broken only by the subdued ticking of a Dutch canopy clock upon the wall. At last, slowly and with a trace of weariness, Warren Trent announced, "What you have told me may make a difference to my own position."

"I thought it might." Curtis O'Keefe seemed about to rub his hands together, then restrained himself. "In any case, now we've reached that point I'd like to have you consider a proposal."

Warren Trent said drily, "I imagined you'd get to it."

"It's a fair proposition, particularly in the circumstances. Incidentally, I should tell you that I'm familiar with your current financial picture."

"I'd have been surprised if you were not."

"Let me summarize: Your personal holdings in this hotel amount to fifty-one per cent of all shares, giving you control."

"Correct."

"You refinanced the hotel in '39—a four-million-dollar mortgage. Two million dollars of the loan is still outstanding and due in its entirety this coming Friday. If you fail to make repayment the mortgagees take over."

"Correct again."

"Four months ago you attempted to renew the mortgage. You were turned down. You offered the mortgagees better terms which were still rejected. Ever since you've been looking for other financing. You haven't found it. In the short time remaining there is no chance whatever that you will."

Warren Trent growled, "I can't accept that. Plenty of refinancings are arranged at short notice."

"Not this kind. And not with operating deficits as large as yours."

143

Apart from a tightening of the lips, there was no rejoinder.

"My proposal," Curtis O'Keefe said, "is a purchase price for this hotel of four million dollars. Of this, two millions will be obtained by renewing your present mortgage, which I assure you I shall have no difficulty in arranging."

Warren Trent nodded, sourly aware of the other's complacency.

"The balance will be a million dollars cash, enabling you to pay off your minority stockholders, and one million dollars in O'Keefe Hotels stock—a new issue to be arranged. Additionally, as a personal consideration you will have the privilege of retaining your apartment here for as long as you live, with my assurance that should rebuilding be undertaken we will make other and mutually satisfactory arrangements."

Warren Trent sat motionless, his face neither revealing his thoughts nor his surprise. The terms were better than he had expected. If accepted, they would leave him personally with a million dollars, more or less—no small achievement with which to walk away from a lifetime's work. And yet it *would* mean walking away; walking away from all he had built and cared about, or at least—he reflected grimly—that he thought he cared about until a moment or two ago.

"I should imagine," O'Keefe said, with an attempt at joviality, "that living here, with no worries, and your man to take care of you, would be moderately endurable."

There seemed no point in explaining that Aloysius Royce would shortly graduate from law school and presumably have other ideas affecting his own future. It was a reminder, though, that life in this eyrie, atop a hotel he no longer controlled, would be a lonely one.

Warren Trent said abruptly, "Suppose I refuse to sell. What are your plans?"

"I shall look for other property and build. Actually, I think you'll have lost your hotel long before that happens. But even if you don't, the competition we'll provide will force you out of business."

The tone was studiedly indifferent, but the mind behind it astute and calculating. The truth was: the O'Keefe Hotel

Corporation wanted the St. Gregory very much, and urgently. The lack of an O'Keefe affiliate in New Orleans was like a missing tooth in the company's otherwise solid bite on the traveling public. It had already entailed a costly loss of referral business to and from other cities—the sustaining oxygen of a successful hotel chain. Disquietingly too, competitive chains were exploiting the gap. The Sheraton-Charles was long established. Hilton, as well as having its airport inn, was building in the Vieux Carré. Hotel Corporation of America had the Royal Orleans.

Nor were the terms which Curtis O'Keefe had offered Warren Trent other than realistic. The St. Gregory mortgagees had already been sounded out by an O'Keefe emissary and were unco-operative. Their intention, it quickly became evident, was first to obtain control of the hotel and later hold out for a big killing. If the St. Gregory was to be bought reasonably, the crucial moment was now.

"How much time," Warren Trent asked, "are you willing to allow me?"

"I'd prefer your answer at once."

"I'm not prepared to give it."

"Very well." O'Keefe considered. "I've an appointment in Naples, Saturday. I'd like to leave here no later than Thursday night. Suppose we set a deadline of noon Thursday."

"That's less than forty-eight hours!"

"I see no reason to wait longer."

Obstinacy inclined Warren Trent to hold out for more time. Reason reminded him: he would merely advance by a day the Friday deadline he already faced. He conceded, "I suppose if you insist . . ."

"Splendid!" Smiling expansively, O'Keefe pushed back his chair and rose, nodding to Dodo who had been watching Warren Trent with an expression close to sympathy. "It's time for us to go, my dear. Warren, we've enjoyed your hospitality." Waiting another day and a half, he decided, was merely a minor nuisance. After all, there could be no doubt of the eventual result.

At the outer doorway Dodo turned her wide blue eyes upon her host. "Thanks a lot, Mr. Trent."

He took her hand and bowed over it. "I don't recall when these old rooms have been more graced."

O'Keefe glanced sharply sideways, suspecting the compliment's sincerity, then realized it was genuinely meant. That was another strange thing about Dodo: a rapport she achieved at times, as if instinctively, with the most unlikely people.

In the corridor, her fingers resting lightly on his arm, he felt his own senses quicken.

But before anything else, he reminded himself, he must pray to God, giving appropriate thanks for the way the evening had gone.

14

"There's something downright exciting," Peter McDermott observed, "about a girl fumbling in her handbag for the key to her apartment."

"It's a dual symbol," Christine said, still searching. "The apartment shows woman's independence, but losing the key proves she's still feminine. Here!—I've found it."

"Hang on!" Peter took Christine's shoulders, then kissed her. It was a long kiss and in course of it his arms moved, holding her tightly.

At length, a shade breathlessly, she said, "My rent's paid up. If we *are* going to do this, it might as well be in private."

Taking the key, Peter opened the apartment door.

Christine put her bag on a side table and subsided into a deep settee. With relief she eased her feet from the constriction of her patent-leather pumps.

He sat beside her. "Cigarette?"

"Yes, please."

Peter held a match flame for them both.

He had a sense of elation and lightheadedness; an awareness of the here and now. It included a conviction that what was logical between them could happen if he chose to make it.

"This is nice," Christine said. "Just sitting, talking."

He took her hand. "We're not talking."

"Then let's."

"Talking wasn't exactly . . ."

"I know. But there's a question of where we're going, and if, and why."

"Couldn't we just spin the wheel . . ."

"If we did, there'd be no gamble. Just a certainty." She stopped, considering. "What happened just now was for the second time, and there was some chemistry involved."

"Chemically, I thought we were doing fine."

"So in the course of things, there'd be a natural progression."

"I'm not only with you; I'm ahead."

"In bed, I imagine."

He said dreamily, "I've taken the left side—as you face the headboard."

"I've a disappointment for you."

"Don't tell me! I'll guess. You forgot to brush your teeth. Never mind, I'll wait."

She laughed. "You're hard to talk . . ."

"Talking wasn't exactly . . ."

"That's where we started."

Peter leaned back and blew a smoke ring. He followed it with a second and a third.

"I've always wanted to do that," Christine said. "I never could."

He asked, "What kind of disappointment?"

"A notion. That if what could happen . . . happens, it ought to mean something for both of us."

"And would it for you?"

"It could, I think. I'm not sure." She was even less sure of her own reaction to what might come next.

He stubbed out his cigarette, then took Christine's and did the same. As he clasped her hands she felt her assurance crumble.

"We need to get to know each other." His eyes searched her face. "Words aren't always the best way."

His arms reached out and she came to him, at first pliantly, then with mounting, fierce excitement. Her lips formed eager, incoherent sounds and discretion fled, the reservations of a moment earlier dissolved. Trembling, and to the pounding of her heart, she told herself: whatever was to happen must take its course; neither doubt nor reasoning would divert it now. She could hear Peter's quickened breathing. She closed her eyes.

A pause. Then, unexpectedly, they were no longer close together.

"Sometimes," Peter said, "there are things you remember. They crop up at the damnedest times." His arms went around her, but now more tenderly. He whispered, "You were right. Let's give it time."

She felt herself kissed gently, then heard footsteps recede. She heard the unlatching of the outer door and, a moment later, its closing.

She opened her eyes. "Peter dearest," she breathed. "There's no need to go. Please don't go!"

But there was only silence and, from outside, the faint whirr of a descending elevator.

15

A few minutes only remained of Tuesday.

In a Bourbon Street strip joint the big-hipped blonde leaned closer to her male companion, one hand resting on his thigh, the fingers of the other fondling the base of his neck. "Sure," she said. "Sure I want to go to bed with you, honey."

Stan somebody, he had said he was, from a hick town in Iowa she had never heard of. And if he breathes at me any more, she thought, I'll puke. That's not bad breath in his mouth; it's a direct line from a sewer.

"Wadda we waitin' for, then?" the man asked thickly. He took her hand, moving it higher on the inside of his thigh. "I got something special for you there, baby."

She thought contemptuously: they were all the same, the loud-mouth chawbacons who came here—convinced that what they had between their legs was something exceptional which women panted for, and as irrationally proud as if they had grown it themselves like a prize cucumber. Probably, if put to a real white-hot test, this one would wind up incapable and whimpering, like others.

But she had no intention of finding out. *God!—that stinking breath.*

A few feet from their table the discordant jazz combo, too inexpert to get work at one of the better Bourbon Street places like the *Famous Door* or *Paddock,* was raggedly finishing a number. It had been danced—if you chose to call untutored shuffling a dance—by one Jane Mansfield. (A Bourbon Street gimmick was to take the name of a celebrated performer, misspell it slightly, and allocate it to an unknown with the hope that the public passing by might mistake it for the real thing.)

"Listen," the man from Iowa said impatiently, "whyn't we blow?"

"I already told you, sugar. I work here. I can't leave yet. I got my act to do."

"Piss on your act!"

"Now, honey, that's not nice." As if with sudden inspiration, the hippy blonde said, "What hotel you staying at?"

"St. Gregory."

"That's not far from here."

"Can have your pants off in five minutes."

She chided: "Won't I get a drink first?"

"You bet you will! Let's go!"

"Wait, Stanley darling! I've an idea."

The lines were going exactly right, she thought, like a smoothly running playlet. And why not? It was the thousandth performance, give or take a few hundred either way. For the past hour and a half Stan whoever-he-was from somewhere had docilely followed the tired old routine: the first drink—a try-on at four times the price he would have paid in an honest bar. Then the waiter had brought her over to join him. They had been served a succession of drinks, though, like the other girls who worked on bar commission, she had had cold tea instead of cheap whiskey which the customers got. And later she had tipped off the waiter to hustle the full treatment—a split bottle of domestic champagne for which the bill, though Stanley Sucker didn't know it yet, would be forty dollars—and just let him try to get out without paying!

So all that remained was to ditch him, though maybe in doing so—if the lines kept going right—she could earn another small commission. After all, she was entitled to some sort of bonus for enduring that stinking breath.

He was asking, "Wha' idea, baby?"

"Leave me your hotel key. You can get another at the desk; they always have spares. Soon as I'm through here I'll come and join you." She squeezed where he had placed her hand. "You just make sure you're ready for me."

"I'll be ready."

"All right, then. Give me the key."

It was in his hand. But held tightly.

He said doubtfully, "Hey, you sure you'll . . ."

"Honey, I promise I'll fly." Her fingers moved again. *The sickening slob would probably wet his pants in a minute.* "After all, Stan, what girl wouldn't?"

He pressed the key upon her.

Before he could change his mind she had left the table. The waiter would handle the rest, helped by a muscle man if Bad Breath made trouble about the bill. He probably wouldn't, though; just as he wouldn't come back. The suckers never did.

She wondered how long he would lie hopefully awake in his hotel room, and how long it would take him to realize she wasn't coming, and never would, even if he stayed there the rest of his useless life.

Some two hours later, at the end of a day as dreary as most—though at least, she consoled herself, a little more productive—the big-hipped blonde sold the key for ten dollars.

The buyer was Keycase Milne.

WEDNESDAY

1

As the first gray streaks of a new dawn filtered tenuously above New Orleans, Keycase—sitting on the bed of his room at the St. Gregory—was refreshed, alert, and ready for work.

Through the previous afternoon and early evening he had slept soundly. Then he had made an excursion from the hotel, returning at two A.M. For an hour and a half he had slept again, waking promptly at the time he intended. Getting up, he shaved, showered, and at the end turned the shower control to cold. The icy rivulets set his body, first tingling, then glowing as he toweled himself vigorously.

One of his rituals before a professional foray was to put on fresh underwear and a clean, starched shirt. Now he could feel the pleasant crispness of the linen. supplementing the fine edge of tension to which he had honed himself. If momentarily a brief, uneasy doubt obtruded—a shadow of fear concerning the awful possibility of being sent down for fifteen years if he was caught once more—he dismissed it summarily.

Much more satisfying was the smoothness with which his preparations had gone.

Since arriving yesterday he had enlarged his collection of hotel keys from three to five.

One of the extra two keys had been obtained last evening in the simplest way possible—by asking for it at the hotel front desk. His own room number was 830. He had asked for the key of 803.

Before doing so he had taken some elementary precautions. He had made sure that an 803 key was in the rack, and that the slot beneath it contained no mail or messages. If there had been, he would have waited. When handing over mail or messages, desk clerks had a habit of asking key claimants for their names. As it was, he had loitered until the desk was busy, then joined a line of several other guests. He was handed the key without question. If there had been any awkwardness, he would have given the believable explanation that he had confused the number with his own.

The ease of it all, he told himself, was a good omen. Later today—making sure that different clerks were on duty—he would get the keys of 380 and 930 the same way.

A second bet had paid off too. Two nights earlier, through a reliable contact, he had made certain arrangements with a Bourbon Street B-girl. It was she who had provided the fifth key, with a promise of more to come.

Only the rail terminal—after a tedious vigil covering several train departures—had failed to yield results. The same thing had happened on other occasions elsewhere, and Keycase decided to profit from experience. Train travelers were obviously more conservative than air passengers and perhaps for that reason took greater care with hotel keys. So in future he would eliminate railway terminals from his plans.

He checked his watch. There was no longer any cause to delay, even though he was aware of a curious reluctance to stir from the bed where he was sitting. But, overcoming it, he made his last two preparations.

In the bathroom he had already poured a third of a tumbler of Scotch. Going in, he gargled with the whiskey thoroughly, though drinking none, and eventually spitting it out into the wash basin.

Next he took a folded newspaper—an early edition of today's *Times-Picayune,* bought last night—and placed it under his arm.

Finally, checking his pockets where his collection of keys was disposed systematically, he let himself out of the room.

His crepe-soled shoes were silent on the service stairs.

He went two floors down to the sixth, moving easily, not hurrying. Entering the sixth-floor corridor he managed to take a swift, comprehensive look in both directions, though —in case he should be observed—without appearing to.

The corridor was deserted and silent.

Keycase had already studied the hotel layout and the system of numbering rooms. Taking the key of 641 from an inside pocket, he held it casually in his hand and walked unhurriedly to where he knew the room to be.

The key was the first he had obtained at Moisant Airport. Keycase, above all else, had an orderly mind.

The door of 641 was in front of him. He stopped. No light from beneath. No sound from within. He produced gloves and slipped them on.

He felt his senses sharpen. Making no sound, he inserted the key. The key turned. The door opened noiselessly. Removing the key, he went in, gently closing the door behind him.

Faint shadows of dawn relieved the inside darkness. Keycase stood still, orienting himself as his eyes became accustomed to the partial light. The grayness was one reason why skilled hotel thieves chose this time of day to operate. The light was sufficient to see and avoid obstacles but, with luck, not to be observed. There were other reasons. It was a low-point in the life of any hotel—the night staff still on duty were less alert as the end of their shift approached. Day workers had not yet come on. Guests— even party-ers and stay-out-lates—were back in their rooms and most likely to be sleeping. Dawn, too, gave people a sense of security, as if the perils of the night were over.

Keycase could see the shape of a dressing table directly ahead. To the right was the shadow of a bed. From the sound of even breathing, its occupant was well asleep.

The dressing table was the place to look for money first.

He moved cautiously, his feet exploring in an arc ahead for anything which might cause him to trip. He reached out, touching the dressing table as he came to it. Finger tips explored the top.

His gloved fingers encountered a small pile of coins. Forget it!—pocketing loose change meant noise. But where there were coins there was likely to be a wallet. Ah!—he had found it. It was interestingly bulky.

A bright light in the room snapped on.

It happened so suddenly, without any warning sound, that Keycase's quick thinking—on which he prided himself—failed him entirely.

Reaction was instinctive. He dropped the wallet and spun around guiltily, facing the light.

The man who had switched on the bedside lamp was in pajamas, sitting up in bed. He was youngish, muscular, and angry.

He said explosively, "What the devil do you think you're doing?"

Keycase stood, foolishly gaping, unable to speak.

Probably, Keycase reasoned afterward, the awakened sleeper needed a second or two himself to collect his wits, which was why he failed to perceive the initial guilty response of his visitor. But for the moment, conscious of having lost a precious advantage, Keycase swung belatedly into action.

Swaying as if drunkenly, he declaimed, "Wadya mean, wha'm I doin'? Wha' you doin' in my bed?" Unobtrusively, he slipped off the gloves.

"Damn you!—this is my bed. And my room!"

Moving closer, Keycase loosed a blast of breath, whiskey laden from his gargling. He saw the other recoil. Keycase's mind was working quickly now, icily, as it always had. He had bluffed his way out of dangerous situations like this before.

It was important at this point, he knew, to become defensive, not continuing an aggressive tone, otherwise the legitimate room owner might become frightened and summon help. Though this one looked as if he could handle any contingency himself.

Keycase said stupidly, "Your room? You sure?"

The man in bed was angrier than ever. "You lousy drunk! Of course I'm sure it's my room!"

"This 's 614?"

"You stupid jerk! It's 641."

"Sorry ol' man. Guess 's my mistake." From under his arm Keycase took the newspaper, carried to convey the impression of having come in from the street. "Here'sa mornin' paper. Special 'livery."

"I don't want your goddam newspaper. Take it and get out!"

It had worked! Once more the well-planned escape route had paid off.

Already he was on the way to the door. "Said I'm sorry ol' man. No need to get upset. I'm goin'."

He was almost out, the man in bed still glaring. He used a folded glove to turn the doorknob. Then he had made it. Keycase closed the door behind him.

Listening intently, he heard the man inside get out of bed, footsteps pad to the door, the door rattle, the protective chain go on. Keycase continued to wait.

For fully five minutes he stood in the corridor, not stirring, waiting to hear if the man in the room telephoned downstairs. It was essential to know. If he did, Keycase must return to his own room at once, before a hue and cry. But there was no sound, no telephone call. The immediate danger was removed.

Later, though, it might be a different story.

When Mr. 641 awoke again in the full light of morning he would remember what had occurred. Thinking about it, he might ask himself some questions. For example: Why was it that even if someone arrived at the wrong room, their key fitted and they were able to get in? And once in, why stand in darkness instead of switching on a light? There was also Keycase's initial guilty reaction. An intelligent man, wide awake, might reconstruct that part of the scene and perhaps reassess it. In any case there would be reason enough for an indignant telephone call to the hotel management.

Management—probably represented by a house detective—would recognize the signs instantly. A routine check would follow. Whoever was in room 614 would be contacted and, if possible, the occupants of both rooms brought face to face. Each would affirm that neither had ever seen the other previously. The house dick would not be surprised, but it would confirm his suspicion that a professional hotel thief was at large in the building. Word would spread quickly. At the outset of Keycase's campaign, the entire hotel staff would be alert and watchful.

It was likely, too, that the hotel would contact the local police. They, in turn, would ask the FBI for information about known hotel thieves who might be moving around the country. Whenever such a list came, it was a certainty that the name of Julius Keycase Milne would be on it. There would be photographs—police mug shots for showing around the hotel to desk clerks and others.

What he ought to do was pack up and run. If he hurried, he could be clear of the city in less than an hour.

Except that it wasn't quite that simple. He had invested money—the car, the motel, his hotel room, the B-girl. Now, funds were running low. He must show a profit—a good one—out of New Orleans. Think again, Keycase told himself. Think hard.

So far he had considered the worst that could happen. Look at it the other way.

Even if the sequence of events he had thought of occurred, it might take several days. The New Orleans police were busy. According to the morning paper, all available detectives were working overtime on an unsolved hit-and-run case—a double killing the whole city was excited about. It was unlikely the police would take time out from that when, in the hotel, no crime had actually been committed. They'd get around to it eventually, though. They always did.

So how long did he have? Being conservative, another clear day; probably two. He considered carefully. It would be enough.

By Friday morning he could have cleaned up and be clear of the city, covering his tracks behind him.

The decision was made. Now, what next—at this moment? Return to his own room on the eighth floor, leaving further action until tomorrow, or carry on? The temptation not to continue was strong. The incident of a moment ago had shaken him far more—if he was honest with himself—than the same kind of thing ever used to. His own room seemed a safe and comfortable haven.

Then he decided grimly: he must go on. He had once read that when a military airplane pilot crashed through no fault of his own, he was at once sent up again before he could lose his nerve. He must follow the same principle.

The very first key he had obtained had failed him. Perhaps it was an omen, indicating that he should reverse the order and try the last. The Bourbon Street B-girl had given him 1062. Another omen!—his lucky two. Counting the flights as he went, Keycase ascended the service stairs.

The man named Stanley, from Iowa, who had fallen for the oldest sucker routine on Bourbon Street, was at last asleep. He had waited for the big-hipped blonde, hopefully at first, then, as the hours passed, with diminishing confidence plus a discomfiting awareness that he had been taken, but good. Finally, when his eyes would stay open no longer, he rolled over into a deep, alcoholic sleep.

He neither heard Keycase enter, nor move carefully and methodically around the room. He continued to sleep soundly as Keycase extracted the money from his wallet, then pocketed his watch, signet ring, gold cigarette case, matching lighter and diamond cuff links. He did not stir as Keycase, just as quietly, left.

It was mid-morning before Stanley from Iowa awoke, and another hour before he was aware—through the miasma of a whopping hangover—of having been robbed. When at length the extent of this new disaster penetrated, adding itself to his present wretchedness plus the costly and unproductive experience of the night before, he sat in a chair and blubbered like a child.

Long before then, Keycase cached his gains.

Leaving 1062, Keycase had decided it was becoming too light to risk another entry elsewhere, and returned to his own room, 830. He counted the money. It amounted to a satisfactory ninety-four dollars, mostly fives and tens, and all used bills which meant they could not be identified. Happily he added the cash to his own wallet.

The watch and other items were more complex. He had hesitated at first about the wisdom of taking them, but had given in to greed and opportunity. It meant, of course, that an alarm would be raised sometime today. People might lose money and not be certain how or where, but the absence of jewelry pointed conclusively to theft. The possibility of prompt police attention was now much more

157

likely, and the time he had allowed himself might be lessened, though perhaps not. He found his confidence increasing, along with more willingness now to take risks if needed.

Among his effects was a small businessman's valise—the kind you could carry in and out of a hotel without attracting attention. Keycase packed the stolen items in it, observing that they would undoubtedly bring him a hundred dollars from a reliable fence, though in real value they were worth much more.

He waited, allowing time for the hotel to awaken and the lobby to become reasonably occupied. Then he took the elevator down and walked out with the bag to the Canal Street parking lot where he had left his car the night before. From there he drove carefully to his rented room in the motel on Chef Menteur Highway. He made one stop en route, raising the hood of the Ford and pretending engine trouble while he retrieved the motel key hidden in the carburetor air filter. At the motel he stayed only long enough to transfer the valuables to another locked bag. On the way back to town he repeated the pantomime with the car, replacing the key. When he had parked the car—on a different parking lot this time—there was nothing, either on his person or in his hotel room, to connect him with the stolen loot.

He now felt so good about everything, he stopped for breakfast in the St. Gregory coffee shop.

It was afterward, coming out, that he saw the Duchess of Croydon.

She had emerged, a moment earlier, from an elevator into the hotel lobby. The Bedlington terriers—three on one side, two on the other—frisked ahead like spirited outriders. The Duchess held their leashes firmly and with authority, though her thoughts were clearly elsewhere, her eyes focused forward, as if seeing through the hotel walls and far beyond. The superb hauteur, her hallmark, was as evident as always. Only the observant might have noticed lines of strain and weariness in her face which cosmetics and an effort of will power had not obscured entirely.

Keycase stopped, at first startled and unbelieving. His eyes reassured him: it *was* the Duchess of Croydon. Keycase, an avid reader of magazines and newspapers, had

158

seen too many photographs not to be sure. And the Duchess was staying, presumably, in this hotel.

His mind raced. The Duchess of Croydon's gem collection was among the world's most fabulous. Whatever the occasion, she never appeared anywhere without being resplendently jeweled. Even now his eyes narrowed at the sight of her rings and a sapphire clip, worn casually, which must be priceless. The Duchess's habit meant that, despite precautions, there would always be a part of her collection close at hand.

A half-formed idea—reckless, audacious, impossible . . . or was it? . . . was taking shape in Keycase's mind.

He continued watching as, the terriers preceding, the Duchess of Croydon swept through the St. Gregory lobby and into the sunlit street.

2

Herbie Chandler arrived early at the hotel, but for his own advantage, not the St. Gregory's.

Among the bell captain's sideline rackets was one referred to—in the many hotels where it existed—as "the liquor butt hustle."

Hotel guests who entertained in their rooms, or even drank alone, often had an inch or two of liquor left in bottles at the time of their departure. When packing their bags, most of these guests refrained from including the liquor ends, either through fear of leakage or to avoid airline excess baggage charges. But human psychology made them balk at pouring good liquor away and usually it was left, intact, on dressing tables of the vacated rooms.

If a bellboy observed such a residue when summoned to carry a guest's bags at checkout time, he was usually back within a few minutes to collect it. Where guests carried their own bags, as many preferred to do nowadays, the floor maid would usually notify a bellboy, who would cut her in on his eventual share of profit.

The dribs and drabs of liquor found their way to the corner of a basement storeroom, the private domain of Herbie Chandler. It was preserved as such through the agency of a storekeeper who, in turn, received help from Chandler with certain larcenies of his own.

The bottles were brought here, usually in laundry bags which bellboys could carry within the hotel without arousing comment. In the course of a day or two the amount collected was surprisingly large.

Every two or three days—more frequently if the hotel was busy with conventions—the bell captain consolidated his hoard, as he was doing now.

Herbie sorted the bottles containing gin into a single group. Selecting two of the more expensive labels, and employing a small well-worn funnel, he emptied the other miscellaneous brands into them. He ended with the first bottle full and the second three quarters full. He capped them both, putting the second bottle aside for topping up at the next consolidation. He repeated the process with bourbon, Scotch, and rye. In all, there were seven full bottles and several partial ones. A lonely few ounces of vodka he emptied, after a moment's hesitation, into the gin.

Later in the day the seven full bottles would be delivered to a bar a few blocks from the St. Gregory. The bar owner, only mildly concerned with scruples about quality, served the liquor to customers, paying Herbie half the going price of regularly bottled supplies. Periodically, for those involved within the hotel, Herbie would declare a dividend—usually as small as he dared make it.

Recently the liquor butt hustle had been doing well, and today's accumulation would have pleased Herbie if he had not been preoccupied with other thoughts. Late last night there had been a telephone call from Stanley Dixon. The young man had relayed his own version of the conversation between himself and Peter McDermott. He had also reported the appointment—for himself and his cronies— in McDermott's office at four P.M. the following afternoon, which was now today. What Dixon wanted to find out was: Just how much did McDermott know?

Herbie Chandler had been unable to supply an answer, except to warn Dixon to be discreet and admit nothing. But, ever since, he had been wondering what exactly happened in rooms 1126–7 two nights earlier, and just how well informed—concerning the bell captain's own part in it—the assistant general manager was.

It was another nine hours until four o'clock. They would, Herbie expected, pass slowly.

3

As he did most mornings, Curtis O'Keefe showered first and prayed afterward. The procedure was typically efficient since he came clean to God and also dried off thoroughly in a towel robe during the twenty minutes or so he was on his knees.

Bright sunshine, entering the comfortable air-conditioned suite, gave the hotelier a sense of well being. The feeling transferred itself to his loquacious prayers which took on the air of an intimate man-to-man chat. Curtis O'Keefe did not forget, however, to remind God of his own continuing interest in the St. Gregory Hotel.

Breakfast was in Dodo's suite. She ordered for them both, after frowning at length over a menu, followed by a protracted conversation with room service during which she changed the entire order several times. Today the choice of juice seemed to be causing her the most uncertainty and she vacillated—through an exchange with the unseen order taker lasting several minutes—over the comparative merits of pineapple, grapefruit, and orange. Curtis O'Keefe amusedly pictured the havoc which the prolonged call was causing at the busy room-service order desk eleven floors below.

Waiting for the meal to arrive, he leafed through the morning newspapers—the New Orleans *Times-Picayune* and an airmailed New York *Times*. Locally, he observed, there had been no fresh developments in the hit-and-run case that had eclipsed most other Crescent City news. In New York, he saw, on the Big Board, O'Keefe Hotels stock had slipped three quarters of a point. The decline was not significant—merely a normal fluctuation, and there was sure to be an offsetting rise when word of the chain's new acquisition in New Orleans leaked out, as it probably would before too long.

161

The thought reminded him of the annoying two days he would have to wait for confirmation. He regretted that he had not insisted on a decision last night; but now, having given his word, there was nothing to do but bide his time patiently. He had not the least doubt of a favorable decision from Warren Trent. There could, in fact, be no possible alternative.

Near the end of breakfast there was a telephone call—which Dodo answered first—from Hank Lemnitzer, Curtis O'Keefe's personal representative on the West Coast. Half-suspecting the nature of the call, he took it in his own suite, closing the communicating door behind him.

The subject he had expected to be raised came up after a routine report on various financial interests—outside the hotel business—on which Lemnitzer astutely rode herd.

"There's one thing, Mr. O'Keefe"—the nasal Californian drawl came down the telephone. "It's about Jenny La-Marsh, the doll . . . er, the young lady you kindly expressed interest in that time at the Beverly Hills Hotel. You remember her?"

O'Keefe remembered well: a striking, rangy brunette with a superb figure, coolly amused smile, and a quick mischievous wit. He had been impressed both with her obvious potential as a woman and the range of her conversation. Someone had said, he seemed to recall, that she was a Vassar graduate. She had a contract of sorts with one of the smaller movie studios.

"Yes, I do."

"I've talked with her, Mr. O'Keefe—quite a few times. Anyway, she'd be pleased to go along with you on a trip. Or two."

There was no need to ask if Miss LaMarsh knew the kind of relationship her trip would entail. Hank Lemnitzer would have taken care of that. The possibilities, Curtis O'Keefe admitted to himself, were interesting. Conversation, as well as other things with Jenny LaMarsh, would be highly stimulating. Certainly she would have no trouble holding her own with people they met together. Nor would she be torn by indecisions about things as simple as choosing fruit juice.

But, surprising himself, he hesitated.

"There's one thing I'd like to ensure, and that's Miss Lash's future."

Hank Lemnitzer's voice came confidently across the continent. "Don't give it a thought. I'll take care of Dodo, same's I did all the others."

Curtis O'Keefe said sharply, "That isn't the point." Despite Lemnitzer's usefulness, at times there were certain subtleties he lacked.

"Just what is the point, Mr. O'Keefe?"

"I'd like you to line up something for Miss Lash specifically. Something good. And I want to know about it before she leaves."

The voice sounded doubtful. "I guess I could. Of course, Dodo isn't the brightest . . ."

O'Keefe insisted, "Not just anything, you understand. And take your time if necessary."

"What about Jenny LaMarsh?"

"She doesn't have anything else . . . ?"

"I guess not." There was the grudging sense of concession to a whim, then, breezily once more: "Okay, Mr. O'Keefe, whatever you say. You'll be hearing from me."

When he returned to the sitting room of the other suite, Dodo was stacking their used breakfast dishes on the room-service trolley. He snapped irritably, "Don't do that! There are hotel staff paid for that kind of work."

"But I like doing it, Curtie." She turned her eloquent eyes upon him and momentarily, he saw, there was a bewildered hurt. But she stopped all the same.

Unsure of the reason for his own ill humor, he informed her, "I'm going to take a walk through the hotel." Later today, he decided, he would make amends to Dodo by taking her on an inspection of the city. There was a harbor tour, he recalled, on an ungainly old stern-wheeler called the S.S. *President*. It was usually packed with sightseers and was the kind of thing she would enjoy.

At the outer doorway, on impulse, he told her about it. She responded by flinging her arms around his neck. "Curtie, it'll be endsville! I'll fix my hair so it doesn't blow in the wind. Like this!"

She removed one lissome arm and with it pulled the flowing ash-blond hair back from her face, twisting it into a tight, profiling skein. The effect—her face tilted upward, her unaffected joy—was of such breathtaking, simple beauty that he had an impulse to change his immediate plans and stay. Instead, he grunted something about returning soon and abruptly closed the suite door behind him.

He rode an elevator down to the main mezzanine and from there took the stairway to the lobby where he resolutely put Dodo out of his mind. Strolling with apparent casualness, he was aware of covert glances from passing hotel employees who, at the sight of him, seemed affected with sudden energy. Ignoring them, he continued to observe the physical condition of the hotel, comparing his own reactions with those in Ogden Bailey's undercover report. His opinion of yesterday that the St. Gregory required a firm directing hand was confirmed by what he saw. He also shared Bailey's view about potential new sources of revenue.

Experience told him, for example, that the massive pillars in the lobby were probably not holding anything up. Providing they weren't, it would be a simple matter to hollow out a section of each and rent the derived space as showcases for local merchants.

In the arcade beneath the lobby he observed a choice area occupied by a florist shop. The rent which the hotel received was probably around three hundred dollars monthly. But the same space, developed imaginatively as a modern cocktail lounge (a riverboat theme!—why not?) might easily gross fifteen thousand dollars in the same period. The florist could be relocated handily.

Returning to the lobby, he could see more space that should be put to work. By eliminating part of the existing public area, another half-dozen sales counters—air lines, car rental, tours, jewelry, a drugstore perhaps—could be profitably squeezed in. It would entail a change in character, naturally; the present air of leisurely comfort would have to go, along with the shrubbery and thick pile rugs. But nowadays, brightly lighted lobbies with advertising everywhere you looked were what helped to make hotel balance sheets more cheerful.

Another thing: most of the chairs should be taken away. If people wanted to sit down, it was more profitable that they be obliged to do so in one of the hotel's bars or restaurants.

He had learned a lesson about free seating years ago. It was in his very first hotel—a jerry-built, false-fronted fire trap in a small Southwestern city. The hotel had one distinction: a dozen pay toilets which at various times were used—or seemed to be—by every farmer and ranch hand for a hundred miles around. To the surprise of young Curtis O'Keefe, the revenue from this source was substantial, but one thing prevented it becoming greater: a state law which required one of the twelve toilets to be operated free of charge, and the habit, which thrifty minded farm hands had acquired, of lining up to use the free one. He solved the problem by hiring the town drunk. For twenty cents an hour and a bottle of cheap wine the man had sat on the free toilet stoically through every busy day. Receipts from the others had soared immediately.

Curtis O'Keefe smiled, remembering.

The lobby, he noticed, was becoming busier. A group of new arrivals had just come in and were registering, preceding others still checking baggage that was being unloaded from an airport limousine. A small line had formed at the reception counter. O'Keefe stood watching.

It was then he observed what apparently no one else, so far, had seen.

A middle-aged, well-dressed Negro, valise in hand, had entered the hotel. He came toward Reception, walking unconcernedly as if for an afternoon stroll. At the counter he put down his bag and stood waiting, third in line.

The exchange, when it came, was clearly audible.

"Good morning," the Negro said. His voice—a Midwestern accent—was amiable and cultured. "I'm Dr. Nicholas; you have a reservation for me." While waiting he had removed a black Homburg hat revealing carefully brushed iron-gray hair.

"Yes, sir; if you'll register, please." The words were spoken before the clerk looked up. As he did, his features stiffened. A hand went out, withdrawing the registration pad he had pushed forward a moment earlier.

"I'm sorry," he said firmly, "the hotel is full."

Unperturbed, the Negro responded smilingly. "I have a

reservation. The hotel sent a letter confirming it." His hand went to an inside pocket, producing a wallet with papers protruding, from which he selected one.

"There must have been a mistake. I'm sorry." The clerk barely glanced at the letter placed in front of him. "We have a convention here."

"I know." The other nodded, his smile a shade thinner than before. "It's a convention of dentists. I happen to be one."

The room clerk shook his head. "There's nothing I can do for you."

The Negro put away his papers. "In that case I'd like to talk with someone else."

While they had been speaking still more new arrivals had joined the line in front of the counter. A man in a belted raincoat inquired impatiently, "What's the hold-up here?" O'Keefe remained still. He had a sense that in the now crowded lobby a time bomb was ticking, ready to explode.

"You can talk to the assistant manager." Leaning forward across the counter, the room clerk called sharply, "Mr. Bailey!"

Across the lobby an elderly man at an alcove desk looked up.

"Mr. Bailey, would you come here, please?"

The assistant manager nodded and, with a suggestion of tiredness, eased himself upright. As he walked deliberately across, his lined, pouched face assumed a professional greeter's smile.

An old-timer, Curtis O'Keefe thought; after years of room clerking he had been given a chair and desk in the lobby with authority to handle minor problems posed by guests. The title of assistant manager, as in most hotels, was mainly a sop to the public's vanity, allowing them to believe they were dealing with a higher personage than in reality. The real authority of the hotel was in the executive offices, out of sight.

"Mr. Bailey," the room clerk said, "I've explained to this gentleman that the hotel is full."

"And I've explained," the Negro countered, "that I have a confirmed reservation."

166

The assistant manager beamed benevolently, his manifest good-will encompassing the line of waiting guests. "Well," he acknowledged, "we'll just have to see what we can do." He placed a pudgy, nicotine-stained hand on the sleeve of Dr. Nicholas's expensively tailored suit. "Won't you come and sit down over here?" As the other allowed himself to be steered toward the alcove: "Occasionally these things happen, I'm afraid. When they do, we try to make amends."

Mentally Curtis O'Keefe acknowledged that the elderly man knew his job. Smoothly and without fuss, a potentially embarrassing scene had been eased from center stage into the wings. Meanwhile the other arrivals were being quickly checked in with the aid of a second room clerk who had joined the first. Only a youthful, broad-shouldered man, owlish behind heavy glasses, had left the line-up and was watching the new development. Well, O'Keefe thought, perhaps there might be no explosion after all. He waited to see.

The assistant manager gestured his companion to a chair beside the desk and eased into his own. He listened carefully, his expression noncommittal, as the other repeated the information he had given the room clerk.

At the end the older man nodded. "Well, doctor"—the tone was briskly businesslike—"I apologize for the misunderstanding, but I'm sure we can find you other accommodation in the city." With one hand he pulled a telephone toward him and lifted the receiver. The other hand slid out a leaf from the desk, revealing a list of phone numbers.

"Just a moment." For the first time the visitor's soft voice had taken on an edge. "You tell me the hotel is full, but your clerks are checking people in. Do *they* have some special kind of reservation?"

"I guess you could say that." The professional smile had disappeared.

"Jim Nicholas!" The boisterously cheerful greeting resounded across the lobby. Behind the voice a small elderly man with a sprightly rubicund face surmounted by a coxcomb of unruly white hair took short hurried strides toward the alcove.

The Negro stood. "Dr. Ingram! How good to see you!" He extended his hand which the older man grasped.

"How are you, Jim, my boy? No, don't answer! I can see for myself you're fine. Prosperous too, from the look of you. I assume your practice is going well."

"It is, thank you." Dr. Nicholas smiled. "Of course my university work still takes a good deal of time."

"Don't I know it! Don't I know it! I spend all my life teaching fellows like you, and then you all go out and get the big-paying practices." As the other grinned broadly: "Anyway you seem to have gotten the best of both—with a fine reputation. That paper of yours on malignant mouth tumors has caused a lot of discussion and we're all looking forward to a first-hand report. By the way, I shall have the pleasure of introducing you to the convention. You know they made me president this year?"

"Yes, I'd heard. I can't think of a finer choice."

As the two talked, the assistant manager rose slowly from his chair. His eyes moved uncertainly between their faces.

The small, white-haired man, Dr. Ingram, was laughing. He patted his colleague jovially on the shoulder. "Give me your room number, Jim. A few of us will be getting together for drinks later on. I'd like to have you join us."

"Unfortunately," Dr. Nicholas said, "I've been told I won't be getting a room. It seems to have something to do with my color."

There was a shocked silence in which the dentists' president flushed deep red. Then, his face muscles hardening, he asserted, "Jim, I'll deal with this. I promise you there'll be an apology *and* a room. If there isn't, I guarantee every other dentist will walk out of this hotel."

A moment earlier the assistant manager had beckoned a bellboy. Now he instructed urgently, "Get Mr. McDermott—fast!"

4

For Peter McDermott the day began with a minor piece of organization. Among his morning mail was a memo from Reservations, informing him that Mr. and Mrs. Justin

Kubek of Tuscaloosa were due to check into the St. Gregory the following day. What made the Kubeks special was an accompanying note from Mrs. Kubek, advising that her husband's height was seven foot one.

Seated behind his office desk, Peter wished all hotel problems were that simple.

"Tell the carpenters' shop," he instructed his secretary, Flora Yates. "They probably still have that bed and mattress we used for General de Gaulle; if not, they'll have to put something else together. Tomorrow have a room allocated early and the bed made up before the Kubeks get here. Tell Housekeeping too; they'll need special sheets and blankets."

Seated composedly on the opposite side of the desk, Flora made her notes, as usual without fuss or question. The instructions would be relayed correctly, Peter knew, and tomorrow—without his needing to remind her—Flora would check to make sure that they had been carried out.

He inherited Flora on first coming to the St. Gregory and had long since decided she was everything a secretary should be—competent, reliable, nudging forty, contentedly married, and plain as a cement block wall. One of the handy things about Flora, Peter thought, was that he could like her immensely—as he did—without it proving a distraction. Now, if Christine had been working for him, he reflected, instead of for Warren Trent, the effect would have been far different.

Since his impetuous departure from Christine's apartment last night, she had been out of his mind only briefly. Even sleeping, he had dreamed about her. The dream was an odyssey in which they floated serenely down a green-banked river (he was not sure aboard what) to an accompaniment of heady music in which harps, he seemed to recall, were featured strongly. He had told Christine this on telephoning her early this morning and she had asked, "Were we going upstream or down?—that ought to be significant." But he could not remember—only that he had enjoyed the whole thing tremendously and hoped (he informed Christine) to pick up later where he had left off last night.

Before that, however—sometime this evening—they

were to meet again. Just when and where would be arranged later, they agreed. "It'll give me an excuse to call you," Peter said.

"Who needs a reason?" she had responded. "Besides, this morning I intend to find some terribly unimportant piece of paper that suddenly has to be delivered to you personally." She sounded happy, almost breathless, as if the excitement they had found in each other last night had spilled over into the new day.

Hoping Christine would come soon, he returned his attention to Flora and the morning mail.

It was a normal mixed batch, including several queries about conventions, which he dealt with first. As usual, Peter assumed his favorite position for dictating—feet elevated on a high leather wastebasket, and his padded swivel chair tilted precariously back, so that his body was almost horizontal. He found he could think incisively in that position, which he had refined through experimentation, so that now the chair was poised at the outer limits of balance, with only a hairsbreadth between equilibrium and disaster. As she often did, Flora watched expectantly during pauses in note taking. She just sat watching, making no comment.

There was another letter today—which he answered next —from a New Orleans resident whose wife had attended a private wedding reception in the hotel some five weeks earlier. During the reception she placed her wild mink jacket on a piano, along with clothes and belongings of other guests. Subsequently she had discovered a bad cigarette burn, necessitating a one-hundred-dollar repair to the coat. The husband was attempting to collect from the hotel, and his latest letter contained a strongly worded threat to sue.

Peter's reply was polite but firm. He pointed out—as he had previously—that the hotel provided checking facilities which the letter writer's wife had chosen not to use. Had she used the check room, the hotel would have considered a claim. As it was, the St. Gregory was not responsible.

The husband's letter, Peter suspected, was probably just a try-on, though it could develop into a lawsuit; there had been plenty of equally silly ones in the past. Usually the courts dismissed such claims with costs for the hotel, but they were annoying because of time and effort they consumed. It sometimes seemed, Peter thought, as if the public considered a hotel a convenient milch cow with a cornucopian udder.

He had selected another letter when there was a light tap on the door from the outer office. He looked up, expecting to see Christine.

"It's just me," Marsha Preyscott said. "There wasn't anyone outside, so I . . ." She caught sight of Peter. "Oh, my goodness!—won't you fall over backwards?"

"I haven't yet," he said—and promptly did.

The resounding crash was followed by a second's startled silence.

From the floor behind his desk, looking upward, he assessed the damage. His left ankle stung painfully where it had struck a leg of the overturning chair on the way down. The back of his head ached as he fingered it, though fortunately the rug had cushioned most of the impact. And there was his vanished dignity—attested to by Marsha's rippling laughter and Flora's more discreet smile.

They came around the desk to help him up. Despite his discomfiture, he was aware once more of Marsha's fresh, breathtaking radiance. Today she had on a simple blue linen dress which somehow emphasized the half-woman, half-child quality he had been conscious of yesterday. Her long black hair, as it had the day before, hung lustrously about her shoulders.

"You should use a safety net," Marsha said. "Like they do in a circus."

Peter grinned ruefully. "Maybe I could get a clown outfit too."

Flora restored the heavy swivel chair to its upright position. As he clambered up, Marsha and Flora taking an elbow each, Christine came in. She stopped at the doorway, a sheaf of papers in her hand. Her eyebrows went up. "Am I intruding?"

"No," Peter said. "I . . . well, I fell out of my chair."

Christine's eyes moved to the solidly standing chair.

He said, "It went over backwards."

"They do that, don't they? All the time." Christine glanced toward Marsha. Flora had quietly left.

Peter introduced them.

"How do you do, Miss Preyscott," Christine said. "I've heard of you."

Marsha had glanced appraisingly from Peter to Christine. She answered coolly, "I expect, working in a hotel, you hear all kinds of gossip, Miss Francis. You do work here, don't you?"

"Gossip wasn't what I meant," Christine acknowledged. "But you're right, I work here. So I can come back any old time, when things aren't so hectic or private."

Peter sensed an instant antagonism between Marsha and Christine. He wondered what had caused it.

As if interpreting his thoughts, Marsha smiled sweetly. "Please don't go on my account, Miss Francis. I just came in for a minute to remind Peter about dinner tonight." She turned toward him. "You hadn't forgotten, had you?"

Peter had a hollow feeling in his stomach. "No," he lied, "I hadn't forgotten."

Christine broke the ensuing silence. "Tonight?"

"Oh dear," Marsha said. "Does he have to work or something?"

Christine shook her head decisively. "He won't have a thing to do. I'll see to it myself."

"That's terribly sweet of you." Marsha flashed the smile again. "Well, I'd better be off. Oh, yes—seven o'clock," she told Peter, "and it's on Prytania Street—the house with four big pillars. Goodbye, Miss Francis." With a wave of her hand she went out, closing the door.

Her expression guileless, Christine inquired, "Would you like me to write that down?—the house with four big pillars. So you won't forget."

He raised his hands in a gesture of helplessness. "I know—you and I had a date. When I made it, I'd forgotten about the other arrangement because last night . . . with you . . . drove everything else out of my mind. When we talked this morning. I guess I was confused."

Christine said brightly, "Well, I can understand that. Who wouldn't be confused with so many women under foot?"

172

She was determined—even though with an effort—to be lighthearted and, if necessary, understanding. She reminded herself: despite last night, she had no lien on Peter's time, and what he said about confusion was probably true. She added, "I hope you have a delightful evening."

He shifted uncomfortably. "Marsha's just a child."

There were limits, Christine decided, even to patient understanding. Her eyes searched his face. "I suppose you really believe that. But speaking as a woman, let me advise you that little Miss Preyscott bears as much resemblance to a child as a kitten to a tiger. But it would be fun I should think—for a man—to be eaten up."

He shook his head impatiently. "You couldn't be more wrong. It's simply that she went through a trying experience two nights ago and . . ."

"And needed a friend."

"That's right."

"And there you were!"

"We got talking. And I said I'd go to a dinner party at her house tonight. There'll be other people."

"Are you sure?"

Before he could reply, the telephone shrilled. With a gesture of annoyance, he answered it.

"Mr. McDermott," a voice said urgently, "there's trouble in the lobby and the assistant manager says will you please come quickly."

When he replaced the telephone, Christine had gone.

5

There were moments of decision, Peter McDermott thought grimly, which you hoped you would never have to face. When and if you did, it was like a dreaded nightmare come to reality. Even worse, your conscience, conviction, integrity, and loyalties were torn asunder.

It had taken him less than a minute to size up the situation in the lobby, even though explanations were still continuing. The dignified, middle-aged Negro, now seated quietly by the alcove desk, the indignant Dr. Ingram—respected president of the dentists' congress, and the assistant manager's bland indifference now that responsibility had been shifted from his shoulders—these alone told Peter all he needed to know.

It was distressingly plain that a crisis had abruptly appeared which, if badly handled, might set off a major explosion.

He was aware of two spectators—Curtis O'Keefe, the familiar, much-photographed face watching intently from a discreet distance. The second spectator was a youthful, broad-shouldered man with heavy rimmed glasses, wearing gray flannel trousers with a tweed jacket. He was standing, a well-traveled suitcase beside him, seemingly surveying the lobby casually, yet missing nothing of the dramatic scene beside the assistant manager's desk.

The dentists' president drew himself to his full five feet six height, his round rubicund face flushed and tight lipped beneath the unruly white hair. "McDermott, if you and your hotel persist in this incredible insult, I'm giving you fair warning you've bought yourself a pile of trouble." The diminutive doctor's eyes flashed angrily, his voice rising. "Dr. Nicholas is a highly distinguished member of our profession. When you refuse to accommodate him, let me inform you it's a personal affront to me and to every member of our congress."

If I were on the sidelines, Peter thought, and not involved, I'd probably be cheering for that. Reality cautioned him: I *am* involved. My job is to get this scene out of the lobby, somehow. He suggested, "Perhaps you and Dr. Nicholas"—his eyes took in the Negro courteously—"would come to my office where we can discuss this quietly."

"No, sir!—we'll damn well discuss it right here. There'll be no hiding this in some dark corner." The fiery little doctor had his feet set firmly. "Now then!—will you register my friend and colleague Dr. Nicholas, or not?"

Heads were turning now. Several people had paused in their progress through the lobby. The man in the tweed jacket, still feigning disinterest, had moved closer.

What quirk of fate was it, Peter McDermott wondered dismally, that placed him in opposition to a man like Dr. Ingram, whom instinctively he admired? It was ironic, too, that only yesterday Peter had argued against the policies of Warren Trent which had created this very incident. The impatiently waiting doctor had demanded: *Will you register my friend?* For a moment Peter was tempted to say yes, and hang the consequences. But it was useless, he knew.

There were certain orders he could give the room clerks, but to admit a Negro as a guest was not among them. On that point there was a firm, standing instruction which could be countermanded only by the hotel proprietor. To dispute this with the room clerks would merely prolong the scene and, in the end, gain nothing.

"I'm as sorry as you, Dr. Ingram," he said, "about having to do this. Unfortunately there *is* a house rule and it prevents me offering Dr. Nicholas accommodation. I wish I could change it, but I don't have authority."

"Then a confirmed reservation means nothing at all?"

"It means a great deal. But there are certain things we should have made clear when your convention was booked. It's our fault we didn't."

"If you had," the little doctor snapped, "you wouldn't have got the convention. What's more, you may lose it yet."

The assistant manager interjected, "I did offer to find other accommodation, Mr. McDermott."

"We're not interested!" Dr. Ingram swung back to Peter. "McDermott, you're a young man, and intelligent I should imagine. How do you feel about what you're doing at this moment?"

Peter thought: Why evade? He replied, "Frankly, Doctor, I've seldom been more ashamed." He added to himself, silently: If I had the courage of conviction, I'd walk out of this hotel and quit. But reason argued: If he did, would anything be achieved? It would not get Dr. Nicholas a room and would effectively silence Peter's own right of protest to Warren Trent, a right he had exercised yesterday and intended to do again. For that reason alone wasn't it better to stay, to do—in the long run—what you could? He wished, though, he could be more sure.

"Goddam, Jim." There was anguish in the older doctor's voice. "I'm not going to settle for this."

The Negro shook his head. "I won't pretend it doesn't

175

hurt, and I suppose my militant friends would tell me I should make more of a fight." He shrugged. "On the whole, I prefer research. There's an afternoon flight north. I'll try to be on it."

Dr. Ingram faced Peter. "Don't you *understand?* This man is a respected teacher and researcher. He's to present one of our most important papers."

Peter thought miserably: there must be some way.

"I wonder," he said, "if you'd consider a suggestion. If Dr. Nicholas will accept accommodation at another hotel, I'll arrange for his attendance at the meetings here." He was being reckless, Peter realized. It would be hard to ensure and would involve a showdown with Warren Trent. But that much he would accomplish—or go himself.

"And the social events—the dinner and luncheons?" The Negro's eyes were directly on his own.

Slowly Peter shook his head. It was useless to make a promise he could not fulfill.

Dr. Nicholas shrugged; his face hardened. "There would be no point. Dr. Ingram, I'll mail my paper so it can be circulated. I think there are some things in it that will interest you."

"Jim." The diminutive, white-haired man was deeply troubled. "Jim, I don't know what to tell you, except you haven't heard the last of this."

Dr. Nicholas looked around for his bag. Peter said, "I'll get a bellboy."

"No!" Dr. Ingram brushed him aside. "Carrying that bag is a privilege I'll reserve for myself."

"Excuse me, gentlemen." It was the voice of the man in the tweed jacket and glasses. As they turned, a camera shutter clicked. "That's good," he said. "Let's try it once more." He squinted through a Rolleiflex viewfinder and the shutter clicked again. Lowering the camera he remarked, "These fast films are great. Not long ago I'd have needed flash for that."

Peter McDermott inquired sharply, "Who are you?"

"Do you mean who or what?"

"Whichever it is, this is private property. The hotel . . ."

"Oh, come on! Let's not go through that old routine." The picture taker was adjusting his camera settings. He

176

looked up as Peter took a step toward him. "And I wouldn't try anything, buster. Your hotel's going to stink when I'm through with it, and if you want to add roughhousing a photog, go ahead." He grinned, as Peter hesitated. "You think fast, I'll say that for you."

Dr. Ingram asked, "Are you a newspaperman?"

"Good question, Doctor." The man with the glasses grinned. "Sometimes my editor says no, though I guess he won't today. Not when I send him this little gem from my vacation."

"What paper?" Peter asked. He hoped it was an obscure one.

"New York *Herald Trib*."

"Good!" The dentists' president nodded approvingly. "They'll make the most of this. I hope you saw what happened."

"You might say I got the picture," the newspaperman said. "I'll need a few details from you, so I can spell the names right. First, though, I'd like another shot outside— you and the other doctor together."

Dr. Ingram seized his Negro colleague's arm. "It's the way to fight this thing, Jim. We'll drag the name of this hotel through every newspaper in the country."

"You're right there," the newspaperman agreed. "The wire services'll go for this; my pictures too, I shouldn't wonder."

Dr. Nicholas nodded slowly.

There was nothing to do, Peter thought glumly. Nothing at all.

Curtis O'Keefe, he noticed, had disappeared.

As the others moved away, "I'd like to do this fairly quickly," Dr. Ingram was saying. "As soon as you have your pictures I intend to start pulling our convention out of this hotel. The only way to hit these people is where they feel it most—financially." His forthright voice receded from the lobby.

6

"Has there been any change," the Duchess of Croydon demanded, "in what the police know?"

It was nearing eleven A.M. Once more, in the privacy of the Presidential Suite, the Duchess and her husband anxiously faced the chief house officer. Ogilvie's great obese body overflowed the cane-seated chair he had chosen to sit on. It creaked protestingly as he moved.

They were in the spacious, sunlit living room of the suite, with the doors closed. As on the previous day, the Duchess had dispatched the secretary and maid on invented errands.

Ogilvie considered before answering. "They know a lotta places the car they're lookin' for ain't. 'S far's I can find out, they been workin' the out o' town an' suburbs, usin' all the men they got. There's still more ground to cover, though I reckon by tomorrow they'll start thinkin' about closer in."

There had been a subtle change since yesterday in the relationship between the Croydons and Ogilvie. Before, they had been antagonists. Now they were conspirators, though still uncertainly, and as if feeling their way toward an alliance, as yet not quite defined.

"If there's so little time," the Duchess said, "why are we wasting it?"

The house detective's mean eyes hardened. "You figure I should pull the car out now? Right in daylight? Maybe park it on Canal Street?"

Unexpectedly, the Duke of Croydon spoke for the first time. "My wife has been under considerable strain. It isn't necessary to be rude to her."

Ogilvie's facial expression—a brooding skepticism—remained unchanged. He took a cigar from the pocket of his coat, regarded it, then abruptly put it back. "Reckon we're all a bit strained. Will be, too, till it's all over."

The Duchess said impatiently, "It doesn't matter. I'm more interested in what's happening. Do the police have any idea yet they're looking for a Jaguar?"

The immense head with its layered jowls moved slowly from side to side. "They do, we'll hear fast enough. Like I said, yours bein' a foreign car, it may take a few days to pin it down for sure."

"There isn't any sign of . . . well, their not being so concerned? Sometimes when a lot of attention is given to something, after a day or two with nothing happening, people lose interest."

"You crazy?" There was astonishment on the fat man's face. "You seen the mornin' paper?"

"Yes," the Duchess said. "I saw it. I suppose my question was a kind of wishful thinking."

"Ain't nothin' changed," Ogilvie declared. " 'Cept maybe the police are keener. There's a lot of reputations ridin' on solvin' that hit-'n-run, an' the cops know if they don't come through there'll be a shake-down, startin' at the top. Mayor's as good as said so, so now there's politics in it too."

"So that getting the car clear of the city will be harder than ever?"

"Put it this way, Duchess. Every last cop on the beat knows if he spots the car they're lookin' for—your car—he'll be sewin' stripes on his sleeve within the hour. They got their eyeballs polished. That's how tough it is."

There was a silence in which Ogilvie's heavy breathing was the only sound. It was obvious what the next question would have to be, but there seemed a reluctance to ask it, as if the answer might mean deliverance or the diminution of hope.

At length the Duchess of Croydon said, "When do you propose to leave? When will you drive the car north?"

"Tonight," Ogilvie answered. "That's why I come to see you folks."

There was an audible emission of breath from the Duke.

"How will you get away?" the Duchess asked. "Without being seen?"

"Ain't no guarantee I can. But I done some figuring."

"Go on."

"I reckon the best time to pull out's around one."

"One in the morning?"

Ogilvie nodded. "Not much doin' then. Traffic's quiet. Not too quiet."

"But you might still be seen?"

"Could be seen any time. We got to take a chance on bein' lucky."

"If you get away—clear of New Orleans—how far will you go?"

"Be light by six. Figure I'll be in Miss'sippa. Most likely 'round Macon."

"That isn't far," the Duchess protested. "Only halfway up Mississippi. Not a quarter of the way to Chicago."

The fat man shifted in his chair, which creaked in protest. "You reckon I should go speedin'? Break a few records? Maybe get some ticket-happy cop tailin' me?"

"No, I don't think so. I'm merely concerned to have the car as far from New Orleans as possible. What will you do during the day?"

"Pull off. Lie low. Plenty places in Miss'sippa."

"And then?"

"Soon's it's dark, I hi' tail it. Up through Alabama, Tennessee, Kentucky, Indiana."

"When will it be safe? Really safe."

"Indiana, I reckon."

"And you'll stop in Indiana Friday?"

"I guess."

"So that you'll reach Chicago Saturday?"

"Sat'day mornin'."

"Very well," the Duchess said. "My husband and I will fly to Chicago Friday night. We shall register at the Drake Hotel and wait there until we hear from you."

The Duke was looking at his hands, avoiding Ogilvie's eyes.

The house detective said flatly, "You'll hear."

"Is there anything you need?"

"I best have a note to the garage. Case I need it. Sayin' I kin take your car."

"I'll write it now." The Duchess crossed the room to a *secretaire*. She wrote quickly and a moment later returned with a sheet of hotel stationery, folded. "This should do."

Without looking at the paper, Ogilvie placed it in an inside pocket. His eyes remained fixed on the Duchess's face.

There was an awkward silence. She said uncertainly, "It isn't what you wanted?"

The Duke of Croydon rose and walked stiffly away. Turning his back, he said testily, "It's the money. He wants money."

Ogilvie's fleshy features shaped themselves into a smirk.

"That's it, Duchess. Ten thousan' now, like we said. Fifteen more in Chicago, Sat'day."

The Duchess's jeweled fingers went swiftly to her temples in a distracted gesture. "I don't know how . . . I'd forgotten. There's been so much else."

"Don't matter none. I woulda remembered."

"It will have to be this afternoon. Our bank must arrange . . ."

"In cash," the fat man said. "Nothing bigger'n twenties, an' not new bills."

She looked at him sharply. "Why?"

"Ain't traceable that way."

"You don't trust us?"

He shook his head. "In somethin' like this, it ain't smart to trust anybody."

"Then why should we trust you?"

"I got another fifteen grand ridin'." The odd falsetto voice held an undertone of impatience. "An' remember—that's to be cash too, an' banks don't open Sat'day."

"Suppose," the Duchess said, "that in Chicago we didn't pay you."

There was no longer a smile, or even an imitation of one. "I'm sure glad you brought that up," Ogilvie said. "Just so's we understand each other."

"I think I understand, but tell me."

"What'll happen in Chicago, Duchess, is this. I'll stash the car some place, though you won't know where. I come to the hotel, collect the fifteen g's. When I done that, you get the keys 'n I tell you where the car is."

"You haven't answered my question."

"I'm gettin' to it." The little pig's eyes gleamed. "Anythin' goes wrong—like f'rinstance you say there's no cash 'cos you forgot the banks wasn't open, I holler cops—right there in Chicago."

"You'd have a good deal of explaining to do yourself. For example, how you came to drive the car north."

"No mystery about that. All I'd say is, you paid me a couple hundred—I'd have it on me—to bring the car up. You said it was too far. You and the Duke here wanted to fly. Weren't until I got to Chicago an' took a good look

181

at the car, I figured things out. So . . ." The enormous shoulders shrugged.

"We have no intention," the Duchess of Croydon assured him, "of failing to keep our part of the bargain. But like you, I wanted to be sure we understood each other."

Ogilvie nodded. "I reckon we do."

"Come back at five," the Duchess said. "The money will be ready."

When Ogilvie had gone, the Duke of Croydon returned from his self-imposed isolation across the room. There was a tray of glasses and bottles on a sideboard, replenished since last night. Pouring a stiff Scotch, he splashed in soda and tossed the drink down.

The Duchess said acidly, "You're begining early again, I see."

"It's a cleansing agent." He poured himself a second drink, though this time sipping it more slowly. "Being in the same room with that man makes me feel dirty."

"Obviously he's less particular," his wife said. "Otherwise *he* might object to the company of a drunken child killer."

The Duke's face was white. His hands trembled as he put the drink down. "That's below the belt, old girl."

She added, "Who also ran away."

"By God—you shan't get away with that." It was an angry shout. His hands clenched and for an instant it seemed as if he might strike out. "You were the one!— the one who pleaded to drive on, and afterward not go back. But for you, I would have! It would do no good, you said; what was done was done. Even yesterday I'd have gone to the police. You were against it! So now we have *him*, that . . . that leper who'll rob us of every last vestige . . ." The voice tailed off.

"Am I to assume," the Duchess inquired, "that you've completed your hysterical outburst?" There was no answer, and she continued, "May I remind you that you've needed remarkably little persuasion to act precisely as you have. Had you wished or intended to do otherwise, no opinion of mine need have mattered in the least. As for leprosy, I doubt you'll contract it since you've carefully stood aside, leaving all that had to be done with that man, to be done by me."

Her husband sighed. "I should have known better than to argue. I'm sorry."

"If argument's necessary to straighten your thinking," she said indifferently, "I've no objection."

The Duke had retrieved his drink and turned the glass idly in his hand. "It's a funny thing," he said. "I had the feeling for a while that all this, bad as it was, had brought us together."

The words were so obviously an appeal that the Duchess hesitated. For her, too, the session with Ogilvie had been humiliating and exhausting. She had a longing, deep within, for a moment's tranquillity.

Yet, perversely, the effort of conciliation was beyond her. She answered, "If it has, I'm not aware of it." Then, more astringently: "In any case, we've scarcely time for sentimentality."

"Right!" As if his wife's words were a signal, the Duke downed his drink and poured another.

She observed scathingly, "I'd be obliged if you'd at least retain consciousness. I assume I shall have to deal with the bank, but there may be papers they'll require you to sign."

7

Two self-imposed tasks faced Warren Trent, and neither was palatable.

The first was to confront Tom Earlshore with Curtis O'Keefe's accusation of the night before. "He's bleeding you white," O'Keefe had declared of the elderly head barman. And: "From the look of things it's been going on a long time."

As promised, O'Keefe had documented his charge. Shortly after ten A.M., a report—with specific details of observations, dates and times—was delivered to Warren Trent by a young man who introduced himself as Sean Hall of the O'Keefe Hotels Corporation. The young man, who had come directly to Warren Trent's fifteenth-floor suite, seemed embarrassed. The hotel proprietor thanked him and settled down to read the seven-page report.

He began grimly, a mood which deepened as he read on. Not only Tom Earlshore's, but other names of trusted employees appeared in the investigators' findings. It was distressingly apparent to Warren Trent that he was being cheated by the very men and women whom he had relied on most, including some who, like Tom Earlshore, he had considered personal friends. It was obvious, too, that throughout the hotel the depredation must be even more extensive than was documented here.

Folding the typewritten sheets carefully, he placed them in an inside pocket of his suit.

He knew that if he allowed himself, he could become enraged, and would expose and castigate, one by one, those who had betrayed his trust. There might even be a melancholy satisfaction in doing so.

But excessive anger was an emotion which nowadays left him drained. He would personally confront Tom Earlshore, he decided, but no one else.

The report, however, Warren Trent reflected, had had one useful effect. It released him from an obligation.

Until last night a good deal of his thinking about the St. Gregory had been conditioned by a loyalty which he assumed he owed to the hotel's employees. Now, by the revealed disloyalty to himself, he was freed from this restraint.

The effect was to open up a possibility, which earlier he had shunned, for maintaining his own control of the hotel. Even now the prospect was still distasteful, which was why he decided to take the lesser of the two unpleasant steps and seek out Tom Earlshore first.

The Pontalba Lounge was on the hotel's main floor, accessible from the lobby through double swing doors ornamented in leather and bronze. Inside, three carpeted steps led down to an L-shaped area containing tables and booths with comfortable, upholstered seating.

Unlike most cocktail lounges, the Pontalba was brightly lighted. This meant that patrons could observe each other as well as the bar itself, which extended across the junction of the L. In front of the bar were a half-dozen padded stools for unaccompanied drinkers who could, if they chose, pivot their seats around to survey the field.

It was twenty-five minutes before noon when Warren Trent entered from the lobby. The lounge was quiet, with only a youth and a girl in one of the booths and two men with lapel convention badges talking in low voices at a table nearby. The usual press of lunchtime drinkers would begin arriving in another fifteen minutes, after which the opportunity to speak quietly to anyone would be gone. But ten minutes, the hotel proprietor reasoned, should be sufficient for what he had come to do.

Observing him, a waiter hurried forward but was waved away. Tom Earlshore, Warren Trent observed, was behind the bar with his back to the room and intent upon a tabloid newspaper he had spread out on the cash register. Warren Trent walked stiffly across and occupied one of the bar stools. He could see now that what the elderly bartender was studying was a *Racing Form.*

He said, "Is that the way you've been using my money?"

Earlshore wheeled, his expression startled. It changed to mild surprise, then apparent pleasure as he realized the identity of his visitor.

"Why, Mr. Trent, you sure give a fellow the jumps." Tom Earlshore deftly folded the *Racing Form,* stuffing it into a rear pants pocket. Beneath his domed bald head, with its Santa Claus fringe of white hair, the seamed leathery face creased into a smile. Warren Trent wondered why he had never before suspected it was an ingratiating smile.

"It's been a long time since we've seen you in here, Mr. Trent. Too long."

"You're not complaining, are you?"

Earlshore hesitated. "Well, no."

"I should have thought that being left alone has given you a lot of opportunities."

A fleeting shadow of doubt crossed the head barman's face. He laughed as if to reassure himself. "You always liked your little joke, Mr. Trent. Oh, while you're in there's something I've got to show you. Been meaning to come in to your office, but never got around to it." Earlshore opened a drawer beneath the bar and took out an envelope

185

from which he extracted a colored snapshot. "This is one of Derek—that's my third grandchild. Healthy young tyke —like his mother, thanks to what you did for her a long time ago. Ethel—that's my daughter, you remember— often asks after you; always sends her best wishes, same as the rest of us at home." He put the photograph on the bar.

Warren Trent picked it up and deliberately, without looking down, handed it back.

Tom Earlshore said uncomfortably, "Is anything wrong, Mr. Trent?" When there was no answer: "Can I mix you something?"

About to refuse, he changed his mind. "A Ramos gin fizz."

"Yessir! Coming right up!" Tom Earlshore reached swiftly for the ingredients. It had always been a pleasure to watch him at work. Sometimes in the past, when Warren Trent entertained guests in his suite, he would have Tom come up to handle drinks, mostly because his bartending was a performance which matched the quality of his potions. He had an organized economy of movement and the swift dexterity of a juggler. He exercised his skill now, placing the drink before the hotel proprietor with a final flourish.

Warren Trent sipped and nodded.

Earlshore asked, "It's all right?"

"Yes," Warren Trent said. "It's as good as any you've ever made." His eyes met Earlshore's. "I'm glad of that because it's the last drink you'll ever mix in my hotel."

The uneasiness had changed to apprehension. Earlshore's tongue touched his lips nervously. "You don't mean that, Mr. Trent. You couldn't mean it."

Ignoring the remark, the hotel proprietor pushed his glass away. "Why did you do it, Tom? Of all people why did it have to be you?"

"I swear to God I don't know . . ."

"Don't con me, Tom. You've done that long enough."

"I tell you, Mr. Trent . . ."

"Stop lying!" The snapped command cut sharply through the quietness.

Within the lounge the peaceful hum of conversation stopped. Watching the alarm in the barman's shifting eyes,

Warren Trent guessed that behind him heads were turning. He was conscious of a rising anger he had intended to control.

Earlshore swallowed. "Please, Mr. Trent. I've worked here thirty years. You've never talked to me like this." His voice was barely audible.

From the inside jacket pocket where he had placed it earlier, Warren Trent produced the O'Keefe investigators' report. He turned two pages and folded back a third, covering a portion with his hand. He instructed, "Read!"

Earlshore fumbled with glasses and put them on. His hands were trembling. He read a few lines then stopped. He looked up. There was no denial now. Only the instinctive fear of a cornered animal.

"You can't prove anything."

Warren Trent slammed his hand upon the surface of the bar. Uncaring of his own raised voice, he let his rage erupt. "If I choose to, I can. Make no mistake of that. You've cheated and you've stolen, and like all cheats and thieves you've left a trail behind you."

In an agony of apprehension Tom Earlshore sweated. It was as if suddenly, with explosive violence, his world which he had believed secure had split apart. For more years than he could remember he had defrauded his employer—to a point where he had long ago become convinced of his own invulnerability. In his worst forebodings he had never believed this day could come. Now he wondered fearfully if the hotel owner had any idea how large the accumulated loot had been.

Warren Trent's forefinger stabbed the document between them on the bar. "These people smelled out the corruption because they didn't make the mistake—my mistake—of trusting you, believing you a friend." Momentarily emotion stopped him. He continued, "But if I dug, I'd find evidence. There's plenty more besides what's here. Isn't there?"

Abjectly Tom Earlshore nodded.

"Well, you needn't worry; I don't intend to prosecute. If I did, I'd feel I was destroying something of myself."

A flicker of relief crossed the elderly barman's face; he tried, as quickly, to conceal it. He pleaded, "I swear if

187

you'll give me another chance it'll never happen again."

"You mean that now you've been caught—after years of thievery and deceit—you'll kindly stop stealing."

"It'll be hard for me, Mr. Trent—to get another job at my time. I've a family . . ."

Warren Trent said quietly, "Yes, Tom. I remember that."

Earlshore had the grace to blush. He said awkwardly, "The money I earned here—this job by itself was never enough. There were always bills; things for the children . . ."

"And the bookmakers, Tom. Let's not forget them. The bookmakers were always after you, weren't they?—wanting to be paid." It was a random shot but Earlshore's silence showed it had found a target.

Warren Trent said brusquely, "There's been enough said. Now get out of the hotel and don't ever come here again."

More people were entering the Pontalba Lounge now, coming in through the doorway from the lobby. The hum of conversation had resumed, its volume rising. A young assistant bartender had arrived behind the bar and was dispensing drinks which waiters were collecting. He studiedly avoided looking at his employer and former superior.

Tom Earlshore blinked. Unbelievingly he protested, "The lunchtime trade . . ."

"It's no concern of yours. You don't work here any more."

Slowly, as the inevitability penetrated, the ex-head barman's expression changed. His earlier mask of deference slipped away. A twisted grin took its place as he declared, "All right, I'll go. But you won't be far behind, Mr. High-and-Mighty Trent, because you're getting thrown out too, and everybody around here knows it."

"Just what do they know?"

Earlshore's eyes gleamed. "They know you're a useless, washed-up old half-wit who couldn't manage the inside of a paper bag, never mind a hotel. It's the reason you'll lose this place for dead damned sure, and when you do I'm one of a good many who'll laugh their guts out." He hesitated, breathing heavily, his mind weighing the consequences of caution and recklessness. The urge to retaliate won out.

"For more years'n I remember, you acted like you owned everybody in this place. Well, maybe you did pay a few more cents in wages than some others, and hand out bits of charity the way you did to me, making like Jesus Christ and Moses rolled in one. But you didn't fool any of us. You paid the wages to keep out the unions, and the charity made *you* feel great, so people knew it was more for you than for them. That's when they laughed at you, and took care of themselves the way I did. Believe me, there's been plenty going on—stuff you'll never learn about." Earlshore stopped, his face revealing a suspicion he had gone too far.

Behind them the lounge was filling rapidly. Alongside, two of the adjoining bar stools were already occupied. To a growing tempo of sound Warren Trent drummed his fingers thoughtfully upon the leather-topped bar. Strangely, the anger of a few moments ago had left him. In its place was a steely resolution—to hesitate no longer about the second step he had considered earlier.

He raised his eyes to the man who, for thirty years, he believed he had known, but never had. "Tom, you'll not know the why or how, but the last thing you've done for me has been a favor. Now go—before I change my mind about sending you to jail."

Tom Earlshore turned and, looking neither to right nor left, walked out.

Passing through the lobby on his way to the Carondelet Street door, Warren Trent coldly avoided glances from employees who observed him. He was in no mood for pleasantries, having learned this morning that betrayal wore a smile and cordiality could be a sheathing for contempt. The remark that he had been laughed at for his attempts to treat employees well had cut deeply—the more, because it had a ring of truth. Well, he thought; wait a day or two. We'll see who's laughing then.

As he reached the busy, sunlit street outside, a uniformed doorman saw him and stepped forward deferentially. Warren Trent instructed, "Get me a taxi." He had intended to walk a block or two, but a twinge of sciatica, knifing sharply as he came down the hotel steps, made him change his mind.

The doorman blew a whistle and from the press of traffic a cab nosed to the curb. Warren Trent climbed in stiffly, the man holding the door open, then touching his cap respectfully as he slammed it closed. The respect was another empty gesture, Warren Trent supposed. From now on, he knew, he would look suspiciously on a good many things he once accepted at face value.

The cab pulled away, and aware of the driver's scrutiny through the rear-view mirror, he instructed, "Just drive me a few blocks. I want a telephone."

The man said, "Lotsa those in the hotel, boss."

"Never mind that. Take me to a pay phone." He felt disinclined to explain that the call he was about to make was far too secret to risk the use of any hotel line.

The driver shrugged. After two blocks he turned south on Canal Street, once more inspecting his fare through the mirror. " 'S a nice day. There's phones down by the harbor."

Warren Trent nodded, glad of a moment or two's respite.

The traffic thinned as they crossed Tchoupitoulas Street. A minute later the cab stopped at the parking area in front of the Port Commissioner's building. A telephone booth was a few paces away.

He gave the driver a dollar, dismissing the change. Then, about to head for the booth, he changed his mind and crossed Eads Plaza to stand beside the river. The midday heat bore down upon him from above and seeped up comfortingly through his feet from the concrete walkway. The sun, the friend of old men's bones, he thought.

Across the half-mile width of Mississippi, Algiers on the far bank shimmered in the heat. The river was smelly today, though that was not unusual. Odor, sluggishness, and mud were part of the Father of Waters' moods. Like life, he thought; the silt and sludge unchangingly about you.

A freighter slipped by, heading seaward, its siren wailing at an inbound barge train. The barge train changed course; the freighter moved on without slackening speed. Soon the ship would exchange the river's loneliness for the greater loneliness of the ocean. He wondered if those aboard were aware, or cared. Perhaps not. Or perhaps, like himself, they had come to learn there is no place in the world where a man is not alone.

He retraced his steps to the telephone and closed the booth door carefully. "A credit card call," he informed the operator. "To Washington, D.C."

It took several minutes, which included questioning about the nature of his business, before he was connected with the individual he sought. At length the bluff, blunt voice of the nation's most powerful labor leader—and, some said, among the most corrupt—came on the line.

"Go ahead. Talk."

"Good morning," Warren Trent said. "I was hoping you wouldn't be at lunch."

"You get three minutes," the voice said shortly. "You've already wasted fifteen seconds."

Warren Trent said hurriedly, "Some time ago, when we met, you made a tentative proposal. Possibly you don't remember . . ."

"I always remember. Some people wish I didn't."

"On that occasion I regret that I was somewhat curt."

"I've a stop watch going here. That was half a minute."

"I'm willing to make a deal."

"I make deals. Others accept them."

"If time's so all-fired important," Warren Trent shot back, "let's not waste it hair-splitting. For years you've been trying to get a foot in the hotel business. You also want to strengthen your union's position in New Orleans. I'm offering you a chance for both."

"How high's the price?"

"Two million dollars—in a secured first mortgage. In return you get a union shop and write your own contract. I presume it would be reasonable since your own money would be involved."

"Well," the voice mused. "Well, well, well."

"Now," Warren Trent demanded, "will you turn off that damned stop watch?"

A chuckle down the line. "Never was one. Be surprised, though, how the idea gets people moving. When do you need the money?"

"The money by Friday. A decision before tomorrow midday."

"Came to me last, eh? When everybody'd turned you down?"

There was no point in lying. He answered shortly, "Yes."

"You been losing money?"

"Not so much that the trend can't be changed. The O'Keefe people believe it can. They've made an offer to buy."

"Might be smart to take it."

"If I do, you'll never get this chance from them."

There was a silence which Warren Trent did not disturb. He could sense the other man thinking, calculating. He had not the least doubt that his proposal was being considered seriously. For a decade the International Brotherhood of Journeymen had attempted to infiltrate the hotel industry. So far, however, unlike most of the Journeymen's intensive membership campaigns, they had failed dismally. The reason had been a unity—on this one issue—between hotel operators, who feared the Journeymen, and more honest unions who despised them. For the Journeymen, a contract with the St. Gregory—until now a nonunion hotel—could be a crack in this massive dam of organized resistance.

As to the money, a two-million-dollar investment—if the Journeymen chose to make it—would be a small bite from the union's massive treasury. Over the years they had spent a good deal more on the abortive hotel membership campaign.

Within the hotel industry, Warren Trent realized, he would be reviled and branded a traitor if the arrangement he was suggesting went through. And among his own employees he would be heatedly condemned, at least by those informed enough to know they had been betrayed.

It was the employees who stood to lose most. If a union contract was signed there would have to be a small wage increase, he supposed, as was usual in such circumstances, as a token gesture. But the increase was due anyway—in fact, overdue—and he had intended to award it himself if the hotel refinancing had been arranged some other way. The existing employees' pension plan would be abandoned in favor of the union's, but the only advantage would be to the Journeymen's treasury. Most significant, union dues —probably six to ten dollars monthly—would become compulsory. Thus, not only would any immediate wage increase be wiped out, but employees' take-home pay would be decreased.

Well, Warren Trent reflected, the opprobrium of his colleagues in the hotel industry would have to be endured. As to the rest, he stifled his conscience by reminding himself of Tom Earlshore and the others like him.

The blunt voice on the telephone broke in on his thoughts.

"I'll send two of my financial people. They'll fly down this afternoon. Overnight they'll take your books apart. I really mean apart, so don't figure on holding back anything we should know." The unmistakable threat was a reminder that only the brave or foolhardy ever attempted to trifle with the Journeymen's Union.

The hotel proprietor said huffily, "I've nothing to conceal. You'll have access to all the information there is."

"If tomorrow morning my people report okay to me, you'll sign a three-year union shop contract." It was a statement, not a question.

"Naturally, I'll be glad to sign. Of course, there'll have to be an employees' vote, though I'm certain I can guarantee the outcome." Warren Trent had a moment's uneasiness, wondering if he really could. There would be opposition to an alliance with the Journeymen; that much was certain. A good many employees, though, would go along with his personal recommendation if he made it strong enough. The question was: Would they provide the needed majority?

The Journeymen's president said, "There won't be a vote."

"But surely the law . . ."

The telephone rasped angrily. "Don't try teaching me labor law! I know more of it, and better'n you ever will." There was a pause, then the growled explanation, "This will be a Voluntary Recognition Agreement. Nothing in law says it has to be voted on. There will be no vote."

193

It could, Warren Trent conceded, be done in just that way.

The procedure would be unethical, immoral, but unquestionably legal. His own signature on a union contract would, in the circumstances, be binding on every hotel employee, whether they liked it or not. Well, he thought grimly, so be it. It would make everything a great deal simpler, with the end result the same.

He asked, "How will you handle the mortgage?" It was a ticklish area, he knew. In the past, Senate investigating committees had scathingly censured the Journeymen for investing heavily in companies with whom the union had labor contracts.

"You will give a note, payable to the Journeymen's Pension Fund, for two million dollars at eight per cent. The note to be secured by a first mortgage on the hotel. The mortgage will be held by the Southern Conference of Journeymen, in trust for the pension fund."

The arrangement, Warren Trent realized, was diabolically clever. It contravened the spirit of every law affecting use of union funds, while remaining technically inside them.

"The note will be due in three years, forfeited if you fail to meet two successive interest payments."

Warren Trent demurred, "I'll agree to the rest, but I want five years."

"You're getting three."

It was a hard bargain, but three years would at least give him time to restore the hotel's competitive position.

He said reluctantly, "Very well."

There was a click as, at the other end, the line went dead.

Emerging from the telephone booth, despite a renewed onset of sciatic pain, Warren Trent was smiling.

8

After the angry scene in the lobby, culminating in the departure of Dr. Nicholas, Peter McDermott wondered disconsolately what came next. On reflection he decided there was nothing to be gained by hasty intervention with officials of the Congress of American Dentistry. If the dentists' president, Dr. Ingram, persisted in his threat to pull the entire convention out of the hotel, it was not likely to be accomplished before tomorrow morning at the earliest. That meant it would be both safe and prudent to wait an hour or two, until this afternoon, for tempers to cool. Then he would approach Dr. Ingram, and others in the congress if necessary.

As for the presence of the newspaperman during the unhappy scene, obviously it was too late to change whatever damage had been done. For the hotel's sake, Peter hoped that whoever made decisions about the importance of news stories would see the incident as a minor item only.

Returning to his office on the main mezzanine, he occupied himself with routine business for the remainder of the morning. He resisted a temptation to seek out Christine, instinct telling him that here, too, a cooling-off period might help. Sometime soon, though, he realized, he would have to make amends for his monumental gaffe of earlier today.

He decided to drop in on Christine shortly before noon, but the intention was eclipsed by a telephone call from the duty assistant manager who informed Peter that a guest room, occupied by Mr. Stanley Kilbrick of Marshalltown, Iowa, had been robbed. Though reported only a short time earlier, the robbery apparently occurred during the night. A long list of valuables and cash was alleged to be missing, and the guest, according to the assistant manager, seemed extremely upset. A house detective was already on the scene.

Peter placed a call for the chief house officer. He had no idea whether Ogilvie was in the hotel or not, the fat man's hours of duty being a mystery known only to himself. Shortly afterward, however, a message advised that Ogilvie had taken over the inquiry and would report as soon as possible. Some twenty minutes later he arrived in Peter McDermott's office.

The chief house officer lowered his bulk carefully into the deep leather chair facing the desk.

Trying to subdue his instinctive dislike, Peter asked, "How does it all look?"

"The guy who was robbed's a sucker. He got hooked. Here's what's missin'." Ogilvie laid a handwritten list on Peter's desk. "I kept one o' these myself."

"Thanks. I'll get it to our insurers. How about the room —is there any sign of forced entry?"

The detective shook his head. "Key job sure. It all figures. Kilbrick admits he was on the loose in the Quarter last night. I guess he shoulda had his mother with him. Claims he lost his key. Won't change his story. More'n likely, though, he fell for a B-girl routine."

"Doesn't he realize that if he levels with us we stand a better chance of recovering what was stolen?"

"I told him that. Didn't do no good. For one thing, right now he feels plenty stupid. For another, he's already figured the hotel's insurance is good for what he lost. Maybe a bit more; he says there was four hundred dollars cash in his wallet."

"Do you believe him?"

"No."

Well, Peter thought, the guest was due for an awakening. Hotel insurance covered the loss of goods up to a hundred dollars' value, but not cash in any amount. "What's your feeling about the rest? Do you think it was a once-only job?"

"No, I don't," Ogilvie said. "I reckon we got ourselves a professional hotel thief, an' he's workin' inside the house."

"What makes you think so?"

"Somethin' that happened this mornin'—complaint from room 641. Guess it ain't come up to you yet."

"If it has," Peter said, "I don't recall it."

"Early on—near dawn's far's I can make out—some character let himself in 641 with a key. The man in the room woke up. The other guy made like he was drunk and said he'd mistook it for 614. The man in the room went back to sleep, but when he woke up started wondering how the key of 614 would fit 641. That's when I heard about it."

"The desk could have given out a wrong key."

"Could have, but didn't. I checked. Night-room clerk

swears neither of them keys went out. And 614's a married couple; they went to bed early last night an' stayed put."

"Do you have a description of the man who entered 641?"

"Not enough so's it's any good. Just to be sure, I got the two men—641 and 614—together. It wasn't 614 who went in 641's room. Tried the keys too; neither one'll fit the other room."

Peter said thoughtfully, "It looks as if you're right about a professional thief. In which case we should start planning a campaign."

"I done some things," Ogilvie said. "I already told the desk clerks for the next few days to ask names when they hand out keys. If they smell anything funny, they're to let the key go, but get a good look at whoever takes it, then tell one of my people fast. The word's bein' passed around to maids and bellhops to watch for prowlers, an' anything else that don't sit right. My men'll be doin' extra time, with patrols round every floor all night."

Peter nodded approvingly. "That sounds good. Have you considered moving into the hotel yourself for a day or two? I'll arrange a room if you wish."

Fleetingly, Peter thought, a worried expression crossed the fat man's face. Then he shook his head. "Won't need it."

"But you'll be around—available?"

"Sure I'll be around." The words were emphatic but, peculiarly, lacked conviction. As if aware of the deficiency, Ogilvie added, "Even if I ain't right here all the time, my men know what to do."

Still doubtfully, Peter asked, "What's our arrangement with the police?"

"There'll be a couple of plain-clothes men over. I'll tell 'em about the other thing, an' I guess they'll do some checkin' to see who might be in town. If it's some joe with a record, we could get lucky'n pick him up."

"In the meantime, of course, our friend—whoever he is —won't sit still."

"That's for sure. An' if he's smart as I think, he'll figure

197

by now we're on to him. So likely he'll try to work fast, then get clear."

"Which is one more reason," Peter pointed out, "why we need you close at hand."

Ogilvie protested, "I reckon I thought of everythin'."

"I believe you did, too. In fact I can't think of anything you've left out. What I'm concerned about is that when you're not here someone else may not be as thorough or as quick."

Whatever else might be said of the chief house officer, Peter reasoned, he knew his business when he chose to do it. But it was infuriating that their relationship made it necessary to plead about something as obvious as this.

"You don't hafta worry," Ogilvie said. But Peter's instinct told him that for some reason the fat man was worried himself as he heaved his great body upward and lumbered out.

After a moment or two Peter followed, stopping only to give instructions about notifying the hotel's insurers of the robbery, along with the inventory of stolen items which Ogilvie had supplied.

Peter walked the short distance to Christine's office. He was disappointed to discover that she was not there. He would come back, he decided, immediately after lunch.

He descended to the lobby and strolled to the main dining room. As he entered he observed that today's luncheon business was brisk, reflecting the hotel's present high occupancy.

Peter nodded agreeably to Max, the head waiter, who hurried forward.

"Good day, Mr. McDermott. A table by yourself?"

"No, I'll join the penal colony." Peter seldom exercised his privilege, as assistant general manager, of occupying a table of his own in the dining room. Most days he preferred to join other executive staff members at the large circular table reserved for their use near the kitchen door.

The St. Gregory's comptroller, Royall Edwards, and Sam Jakubiec, the stocky, balding credit manager, were already at lunch as Peter joined them. Doc Vickery, the chief engineer, who had arrived a few minutes earlier, was studying a menu. Slipping into the chair which Max held out, Peter inquired, "What looks good?"

"Try the watercress soup," Jakubiec advised between sips of his own. "It's not like any mother made; it's a damn sight better."

Royall Edwards added in his precise accountant's voice, "The special today is fried chicken. We have that coming."

As the head waiter left, a young table waiter appeared swiftly beside them. Despite standing instructions to the contrary, the executives' self-styled penal colony invariably received the best service in the dining room. It was hard—as Peter and others had discovered in the past—to persuade employees that the hotel's paying customers were more important than the executives who ran the hotel.

The chief engineer closed his menu, peering over his thick-rimmed spectacles which had slipped, as usual, to the tip of his nose. "The same'll do for me, sonny."

"I'll make it unanimous." Peter handed back the menu which he had not opened.

The waiter hesitated. "I'm not sure about the fried chicken, sir. You might prefer something else."

"Well," Jakubiec said, "now's a fine time to tell us that."

"I can change your order easily, Mr. Jakubiec. Yours too, Mr. Edwards."

Peter asked, "What's wrong with the fried chicken?"

"Maybe I shouldn't have said." The waiter shifted uncomfortably. "Fact is, we've been getting complaints. People don't seem to like it." Momentarily he turned his head, eyes ranging the busy dining room.

"In that case," Peter told him, "I'm curious to know why. So leave my order the way it is." A shade reluctantly, the others nodded agreement.

When the waiter had gone, Jakubiec asked, "What's this rumor I hear—that our dentists' convention may walk out?"

"Your hearing's good, Sam. This afternoon I'll know whether it remains a rumor." Peter began his soup, which had appeared like magic, then described the lobby fracas of an hour earlier. The faces of the others grew serious as they listened.

Royall Edwards remarked, "It has been my observation on disasters that they seldom occur singly. Judging by our financial results lately—which you gentlemen are aware of —this could merely be one more."

"If it turns out that way," the chief engineer observed, "nae doubt the first thing ye'll do is lop some muir from engineering's budget."

"Either that," the comptroller rejoined, "or eliminate it entirely."

The chief grunted, unamused.

"Maybe we'll all be eliminated," Sam Jakubiec said. "If the O'Keefe crowd takes over." He looked inquiringly at Peter, but Royall Edwards gave a cautioning nod as their waiter returned. The group remained silent as the young man deftly served the comptroller and credit manager while, around them, the hum of the dining room, a sub-dued clatter of plates and the passage of waiters through the kitchen door, continued.

When the waiter had gone, Jakubiec asked pointedly, "Well, what *is* the news?"

Peter shook his head. "Don't know a thing, Sam. Except that was darn good soup."

"If you remember," Royall Edwards said, "we recom-mended it, and I will now offer you some more well-founded advice—quit while you're ahead." He had been sampling the fried chicken served to himself and Jakubiec a moment earlier. Now he put down his knife and fork. "Another time I suggest we listen more respectfully to our waiter."

Peter asked, "Is it really that bad?"

"I suppose not," the comptroller said. "If you happen to be partial to rancid food."

Dubiously, Jakubiec sampled his own serving as the others watched. At length he informed them: "Put it this way. If I were paying for this meal—I wouldn't."

Half-rising in his chair, Peter caught sight of the head waiter across the dining room and beckoned him over. "Max, is Chef Hèbrand on duty?"

"No, Mr. McDermott, I understand he's ill. Sous-chef Lemieux is in charge." The head waiter said anxiously, "If it's about the fried chicken, I assure you everything is taken care of. We've stopped serving that dish and where there have been complaints the entire meal has been replaced." His glance went to the table. "We'll do the same thing here at once."

"At the moment," Peter said, "I'm more concerned about finding out what happened. Would you ask Chef Lemieux if he'd care to join us?"

With the kitchen door so close, Peter thought, it was a temptation to stride through and inquire directly what had gone so amiss with the luncheon special. But to do so would be unwise.

In dealing with their senior chefs, hotel executives followed a protocol as proscribed and traditional as that of any royal household. Within the kitchen the chef de cuisine —or, in the chef's absence, the sous-chef—was undisputed king. For a hotel manager to enter the kitchen without invitation was unthinkable.

Chefs might be fired, and sometimes were. But unless and until that happened, their kingdoms were inviolate.

To invite a chef outside the kitchen—in this case to a table in the dining room—was in order. In fact, it was close to a command since, in Warren Trent's absence, Peter McDermott was the hotel's senior officer. It would also have been permissible for Peter to stand in the kitchen doorway and wait to be asked in. But in the circumstance—with an obvious crisis in the kitchen—Peter knew that the first course was the more correct.

"If you ask me," Sam Jakubiec observed as they waited, "it's long past bedtime for old Chef Hèbrand."

Royall Edwards asked, "If he did retire, would anyone notice the difference?" It was a reference, as they all knew, to the chef de cuisine's frequent absences from duty, another of which had apparently occurred today.

"The end comes soon enough for all of us," the chief engineer growled. "It's natural nae one wants to hurry it himsel'." It was no great secret that the comptroller's cool astringency grated at times on the normally good-natured chief.

"I haven't met our new sous-chef," Jakubiec said. "I guess he's been keeping his nose in the kitchen."

Royall Edwards' eyes went down to his barely touched

plate. "If he has, it must be a remarkably insensitive organ."

As the comptroller spoke, the kitchen door swung open once more. A busboy, about to pass through, stood back deferentially as Max the head waiter emerged. He preceded, by several measured paces, a tall slim figure in starched whites, with high chef's hat and, beneath it, a facial expression of abject misery.

"Gentlemen," Peter announced to the executives' table, "in case you haven't met, this is Chef André Lemieux."

"Messieurs!" The young Frenchman halted, spreading his hands in a gesture of helplessness. "To 'ave this happen . . . I am desolate." His voice was choked.

Peter McDermott had encountered the new sous-chef several times since the latter's arrival at the St. Gregory six weeks earlier. At each meeting Peter found himself liking the newcomer more.

André Lemieux's appointment had followed the abrupt departure of his predecessor. The former sous-chef, after months of frustrations and inward seething, had erupted in an angry outburst against his superior, the aging M. Hèbrand. In the ordinary way nothing might have happened after the scene, since emotional outbursts among chefs and cooks occurred—as in any large kitchen—with predictable frequency. What marked the occasion as different was the late sous-chef's action in hurling a tureen of soup at the chef de cuisine. Fortunately the soup was Vichyssoise, or consequences might have been even more serious. In a memorable scene the chef de cuisine, shrouded in liquid white and dripping messily, escorted his late assistant to the street staff door and there—with surprising energy for an old man—had thrown him through it. A week later André Lemieux was hired.

His qualifications were excellent. He had trained in Paris, worked in London—at Prunier's and the Savoy—then briefly at New York's Le Pavillon before attaining the more senior post in New Orleans. But already in his short time at the St. Gregory, Peter suspected, the young sous-chef had encountered the same frustration which demented his predecessor. This was the adamant refusal of M. Hèbrand to allow procedural changes in the kitchen, despite the chef de cuisine's own frequent absences from duty, leaving his sous-chef in charge. In many ways, Peter thought sympathetically, the situation paralleled his own relationship with Warren Trent.

Peter indicated a vacant seat at the executives' table. "Won't you join us?"

"Thank you, monsieur." The young Frenchman seated himself gravely as the head waiter held out a chair.

His arrival was followed by the table waiter who, without bothering with instructions, had amended all four luncheon orders to Veal Scallopini. He removed the two offending portions of chicken, which a hovering busboy banished hastily to the kitchen. All four executives received the substitute meal, the sous-chef ordering merely a black coffee.

"That's more like it," Sam Jakubiec said approvingly.

"Have you discovered," Peter asked, "what caused the trouble?"

The sous-chef glanced unhappily toward the kitchen. "The troubles they have many causes. In this, the fault was frying fat badly tasting. But it is I who must blame myself —that the fat was not changed, as I believed. And I, André Lemieux, I allowed such food to leave the kitchen." He shook his head unbelievingly.

"It's hard for one person to be everywhere," the chief engineer said. "All of us who ha' departments know that."

Royall Edwards voiced the thought which had occurred first to Peter. "Unfortunately we'll never know how many didn't complain about what they had, but won't come back again."

André Lemieux nodded glumly. He put down his coffee cup. "Messieurs, you will excuse me. Monsieur McDermott, when you 'ave finished, perhaps we could talk together, yes?"

Fifteen minutes later Peter entered the kitchen through the dining-room door. André Lemieux hurried forward to meet him.

"It is good of you to come, monsieur."

Peter shook his head. "I enjoy kitchens." Looking around, he observed that the activity of lunchtime was tapering off. A few meals were still going out, past the two middle-aged women checkers seated primly, like suspicious schoolmistresses, at elevated billing registers. But more dishes were coming in from the dining room as busboys and waiters cleared tables while the assemblage of guests thinned out. At the big dishwashing station at the rear of the kitchen, where chrome countertops and waste containers resembled a cafeteria in reverse, six rubber-aproned kitchen helpers worked concertedly, barely keeping pace with the flow of dishes arriving from the hotel's several restaurants and the convention floor above. As usual, Peter noticed, an extra helper was intercepting unused butter, scraping it into a large chrome container. Later, as happened in most commercial kitchens—though few admitted to it—the retrieved butter would be used for cooking.

"I wished to speak with you alone, monsieur. With others present, you understand, there are things that are hard to say."

Peter said thoughtfully, "There's one point I'm not clear about. Did I understand that you gave instructions for the deep fryer fat to be changed, but that it was not?"

"That is true."

"Just what happened?"

The young chef's face was troubled. "This morning I give the order. My nose it informed me the fat is not good. But M. Hèbrand—without telling—he countermanded. Then M. Hèbrand he has gone 'ome and I am left, without knowing, 'olding the bad fat."

Involuntarily Peter smiled. "What was the reason for changing the order?"

"Fat is high cost—very 'igh; that I agree with M. Hèbrand. Lately we have changed it many times. Too many."

"Have you tried to find the reason for that?"

André Lemieux raised his hands in a despairing gesture. "I have proposed, each day, a chemical test—for free fatty acid. It could be done in a laboratory, even here. Then, intelligently, we would look for the cause the fat has failed. M. Hèbrand does not agree—with that or other things."

"You believe there's a good deal wrong here?"

"Many things." It was a short, almost sullen answer, and for a moment it appeared as if the discussion would end. Then abruptly, as if a dam had burst, words tumbled out. "Monsieur McDermott, I tell you there is much wrong. This is not a kitchen to work with pride. It is a how-you-say . . . 'odge-podge—poor food, some old ways that are bad, some new ways that are bad, and all around much waste. I am a good chef; others would tell you. But it must be that a good chef is happy at what he does or he is no longer good. Yes, monsieur, I would make changes, many changes, better for the hotel, for M. Hèbrand, for others. But I am told—as if an infant—to change nothing."

"It's possible," Peter said, "there may be large changes around here generally. Quite soon."

André Lemieux drew himself up haughtily. "If you refer to Monsieur O'Keefe, whatever changes he may make, I shall not be 'ere to see. I have no intent to be an instant cook for a chain 'otel."

Peter asked curiously, "If the St. Gregory stayed independent, what kind of changes would you have in mind?"

They had strolled almost the length of the kitchen—an elongated rectangle extending the entire width of the hotel. At each side of the rectangle, like outlets from a control center, doorways gave access to the several hotel restaurants, service elevators and food preparation rooms on the same floor and below. Skirting a double line of soup cauldrons, bubbling like monstrous crucibles, they approached the glass paneled office where, in theory, the two principal chefs—the chef de cuisine and the sous-chef—divided their responsibilities. Nearby, Peter observed, was the big quadruple-unit deep fryer, cause of today's dissatisfaction. A kitchen helper was draining the entire assembly of fat; considering the quantity, it was easy to see why too frequent replacement would be costly. They stopped as André Lemieux considered Peter's question.

"What changes, you say, monsieur? Most important it is the food. For some who prepare food, the façade, how a dish looks, it is more important than how it tastes. In this hotel we waste much money on the décor. The parsley, it is all around. But not enough in the sauce. The watercress it is on the plate, when more is needed in the soup. And those arrangements of color in gelatine!" Young Lemieux threw both arms upward in despair. Peter smiled sympathetically.

"As for the wines, monsieur! *Dieu merci,* the wines they are not my province."

"Yes," Peter said. He had been critical himself of the St. Gregory's inadequately stocked wine bins.

"In a word, monsieur, all the horrors of a low-grade table d'hôte. Such disrespect colossal for food, such abandon of money for the appearance, it is to make one weep. Weep, monsieur!" He paused, shrugged, and continued. "With less throw-away we could have a cuisine that invites the taste and honors the palate. Now it is dull, extravagantly ordinary."

Peter wondered if André Lemieux was being sufficiently realistic where the St. Gregory was concerned. As if sensing this doubt, the sous-chef insisted, "It is true that a hotel it has special problems. Here it is not a gourmet house. It cannot be. We must cook fast many meals, serve many people who are too much in an American hurry. But in these limitations there can be excellence of a kind. Of a kind one can live with. Yet, Monsieur Hèbrand, he tells me that my ideas they are too 'igh cost. It is not so, as I 'ave proved."

"How have you proved?"

"Come, please."

The young Frenchman led the way into the glass-paneled office. It was a small, crowded cubicle with two desks, file cabinets, and cupboards tightly packed around three walls. André Lemieux went to the smaller desk. Opening a drawer he took out a large Manila envelope and, from this, a folder. He handed it to Peter. "You ask what changes. It is all here."

Peter McDermott opened the folder curiously. There were many pages, each filled with a fine, precise handwriting. Several larger, folded sheets proved to be charts, hand-drawn and lettered in the same careful style. It was, he realized, a master catering plan for the entire hotel. On successive pages were estimated costs, menus, a plan of quality control and an outlined staff reorganization. Merely leafing through quickly, the entire concept and its author's grasp of detail were impressive.

Peter looked up, catching his companion's eyes upon him. "If I may, I'd like to study this."

"Take it. There is no haste." The young sous-chef smiled dourly. "I am told it is unlikely any of my 'orses will come 'ome."

"The thing that surprises me is how you could develop something like this so quickly."

André Lemieux shrugged. "To perceive what is wrong, it does not take long."

"Maybe we could apply the same idea in finding what went wrong with the deep fryer."

There was a responsive gleam of humor, then chagrin. "Touché! It is true—I had eyes for this, but not the 'ot fat under my nose."

"No," Peter objected. "From what you've told me, you did detect the bad fat but it wasn't changed as you instructed."

"I should have found the cause the fat went bad. There is always a cause. Greater trouble there may be if we do not find it soon."

"What kind of trouble?"

"Today—through much good fortune—we have used the frying fat a little only. Tomorrow, monsieur, there are six hundred fryings for convention luncheons."

Peter whistled softly.

"Just so." They had walked together from the office to stand beside the deep fryer from which the last vestiges of the recently offending fat were being cleaned.

"The fat will be fresh tomorrow, of course. When was it changed previously?"

"Yesterday."

"That recently!"

André Lemieux nodded. "M. Hèbrand he was making no joke when he complained of the 'igh cost. But what is wrong it is a mystery."

Peter said slowly, "I'm trying to remember some bits of food chemistry. The smoke-point of new, good fat is . . ."

"Four 'undred and twenty-five degrees. It should never be heated more, or it will break down."

"And as fat deteriorates its smoke-point drops slowly."

"Very slowly—if all is well."

"Here you fry at . . ."

"Three 'undred and sixty degrees; the best temperature —for kitchens and the 'ousewives too."

"So while the smoke-point remains about three hundred and sixty, the fat will do its job. Below that, it ceases to."

"That is true, monsieur. And the fat it will give food a bad flavor, tasting rancid, as today."

Facts, once memorized but rusty with disuse, stirred in Peter's brain. At Cornell there had been a course in food chemistry for Hotel Administration students. He remembered a lecture dimly . . . in Statler Hall on a darkening afternoon, the whiteness of frost on window panes. He had come in from the biting, wintry air outside. Inside was warmth and the drone of information . . . *fats and catalyzing agents*.

"There are certain substances," Peter said reminiscently, "which, in contact with fat, will act as catalysts and break it down quite quickly."

"Yes, monsieur." André Lemieux checked them off on his fingers. "They are the moisture, the salt, the brass or the copper couplings in a fryer, too much 'eat, the oil of the olive. All these things I have checked. This is not the cause."

A word had clicked in Peter's brain. It connected with what he had observed, subconsciously, in watching the deep fryer being cleaned a moment earlier.

"What metal are your fry baskets?"

"They are chrome." The tone was puzzled. Chromium, as both men knew, was harmless to fat.

"I wonder," Peter said, "how good the plating job is. If it isn't good, what's under the chrome and is it—in any places—worn?"

Lemieux hesitated, his eyes widening slightly. Silently he lifted one of the baskets down and wiped it carefully with a cloth. Moving under a light, they inspected the metal surface.

The chrome was scratched from long and constant use. In small spots it had worn away entirely. Beneath scratches and worn spots was a gleam of yellow.

"It is brass!" The young Frenchman clapped a hand to his forehead. "Without doubt it 'as caused the bad fat. I have been a great fool."

"I don't see how you can blame yourself," Peter pointed out. "Obviously, long before you came, someone economized and bought cheap fry baskets. Unfortunately it's cost more in the end."

"But I should have discovered this—as you have done, monsieur." André Lemieux seemed close to tears. "Instead, you, monsieur, you come to the kitchen—from your *paperasserie*—to tell *me* what is 'aywire here. It will be a laughing joke."

"If it is," Peter said, "it will be because you talked about it yourself. No one will hear from me."

André Lemieux said slowly, "Others they have said to me you are a good man, and intelligent. Now, myself, I know this is true."

Peter touched the folder in his hand. "I'll read your report and tell you what I think."

"Thank you, monsieur. And I shall demand new fry baskets. Of stainless steel. Tonight they will be here if I have to 'ammer someone's 'ead."

Peter smiled.

"Monsieur, there is something else that I am thinking."

"Yes?"

The young sous-chef hesitated. "You will think it, how you say, presumptuous. But you and I, Monsieur McDermott—with the hands free—we could make this a 'ot-shot hotel."

Though he laughed impulsively, it was a statement which Peter McDermott thought about all the way to his office on the main mezzanine.

9

A second after knocking at the door of room 1410, Christine Francis wondered why she had come. Yesterday, of course, it had been perfectly natural for her to visit Albert Wells, after his brush with death the night before and her own involvement. But now Mr. Wells was being adequately cared for and, with recovery, had reverted to his role as an ordinary guest among more than a thousand and a half others in the hotel. Therefore, Christine told herself, there was no real reason to make another personal call.

Yet there was something about the little elderly man which drew her to him. Was it, she wondered, because of his fatherliness and her perception, perhaps, of some of the traits of her own father to whose loss she had never quite adjusted, even after five long years. But no! The relationship with her father had been one of her reliance on him. With Albert Wells she found herself protective, just as yesterday she had wanted to shield him from the consequences of his own action in choosing the private nursing arrangement.

Or maybe, Christine reflected, she was, at this moment, just plain lonely, wanting to offset her disappointment in learning she would not meet Peter this evening, as they had both planned. And as to that—*had* it been disappointment, or some stronger emotion on discovering that he would be dining, instead, with Marsha Preyscott?

If she was honest with herself, Christine admitted, she had been angry this morning, though she hoped she had concealed it, covering up with mild annoyance and the slight acidity of comment she had been unable to resist. It would have been a big mistake, either to have shown a possessiveness about Peter or to have given little Miss Marshmallow the satisfaction of believing she had won a feminine victory even though, in fact, she had.

There was still no response to her knock. Remembering that the nurse should be on duty, Christine knocked again, more sharply. This time there was the sound of a chair moving and footsteps approaching from inside.

The door opened to reveal Albert Wells. He was fully dressed. He looked well and there was color in his face, which brightened as he saw Christine. "I was hoping you'd come, miss. If you hadn't, I was going to look for you."

She said, surprised, "I thought . . ."

The little birdlike man chuckled. "You thought they'd keep me pinned down; well, they didn't. I felt good, so I made your hotel doctor send for that specialist—the one from Illinois, Dr. Uxbridge. He's got a lot of sense; said if people feel well, they mostly are. So we bundled the nurse home, and here I am." He beamed. "Well, miss, come on in."

Christine's reaction was of relief that the considerable expense of the private nursing had ended. She suspected that a realization of its cost had had a good deal to do with Albert Wells' decision.

As she followed him into the room, he asked, "Did you knock before?"

She admitted that she had.

"Had an idea I'd heard something. I guess my mind was on this." He pointed to a table near the window. On it was a large and intricate jigsaw puzzle, of which about two thirds was completed. "Or maybe," he added, "I thought it was Bailey."

Christine asked curiously, "Who's Bailey?"

The old man's eyes twinkled. "If you stay a minute, you'll meet him. Leastways, either him or Barnum."

She shook her head, not understanding. Walking toward the window, she leaned over the jigsaw puzzle, inspecting it. There were sufficient pieces in place to recognize the scene depicted as New Orleans—the city at dusk, viewed from high above, with the shining river winding through. She said, "I used to do these once, a long time ago. My father helped me."

Beside her, Albert Wells observed, "There are some who'd say it isn't much of a pastime for a grown man. Mostly, though, I set out one of these when I want to think. Sometimes I discover the key piece, and the answer to what I'm thinking about, around the same time."

"A key piece? I've never heard of that."

"It's just an idea of mine, miss. I reckon there's always one—to this, and most other problems you can name. Sometimes you think you've found it, and you haven't. When you do, though, all of a sudden you can see a whole lot clearer, including how other things fit in around."

Abruptly there was a sharp, authoritative knock at the outer door. Albert Wells' lips formed the word, "Bailey!"

She was surprised, when the door opened, to see a uniformed hotel valet. He had a collection of suits on hangers over one shoulder; in front he held a pressed blue serge suit which, from its old-fashioned cut, undoubtedly belonged to Albert Wells. With practiced speed the valet hung the suit in a closet and returned to the door where the little man was waiting. The valet's left hand held the suits on his shoulder; his right came up automatically, palm outstretched.

"I already took care of you," Albert Wells said. His eyes betrayed amusement. "When the suit was picked up this morning."

"Not me, you didn't, sir." The valet shook his head decisively.

"No, but your friend. It's the same thing."

The man said stoically, "I wouldn't know anything about that."

"You mean he holds out on you?"

The outstretched hand went down. "I don't know what you're talking about."

"Come on now!" Albert Wells was grinning broadly. "You're Bailey. I tipped Barnum."

The valet's eyes flickered to Christine. As he recognized her, a trace of doubt crossed his face. Then he grinned sheepishly. "Yes, sir." He went out, closing the door behind him.

"Now what in the world was all that about?"

The little man chuckled. "You work in a hotel, and don't know the Barnum and Bailey dodge?"

Christine shook her head.

"It's a simple thing, miss. Hotel valets work in pairs, but the one who picks up a suit is never the one who delivers it back. They figure it that way, so mostly they get tipped twice. Afterward they pool the tips and divvy up."

"I can see how it works," Christine said. "But I've never thought about it."

"Nor do most others. Which is why it costs them a double tip for the same service." Albert Wells rubbed his sparrow-beak nose ruminatively. "With me it's a kind of game—to see how many hotels there are where the same thing happens."

She laughed. "How did you find out?"

"A valet told me once—after I let him know I'd rumbled. He told me another thing. You know in hotels with dial telephones, from some phones you can dial rooms directly. So Barnum or Bailey—whichever one's which for that day—will dial the rooms he has deliveries for. If there's no answer, he waits and calls again later. If there is an answer—which means someone's in—he'll hang up without saying anything. Then a few minutes later he'll deliver your suit and pick up the second tip."

"You don't like tipping, Mr. Wells?"

"It isn't so much that, miss. Tipping's like dying; it's here to stay, so what good's worrying? Anyway I tipped Barnum well this morning—sort of paying in advance for the bit of fun I had with Bailey just now. What I don't like, though, is to be taken for a fool."

"I shouldn't imagine that happens often." Christine was beginning to suspect that Albert Wells needed a good deal less protection than she had at first supposed. She found him, though, as likeable as ever.

He acknowledged: "That's as may be. There's one thing, though, I'll tell you. There's more of that kind of malarkey goes on in this hotel than most."

"Why do you think so?"

"Because mostly I keep my eyes open, miss, and I talk to people. They tell me things they maybe wouldn't you."

"What kind of things?"

"Well, for one, a good many figure they can get away with anything. It's because you don't have good management, I reckon. It could be good, but it isn't, and maybe that's why your Mr. Trent is in trouble right now."

"It's almost uncanny," Christine said. "Peter McDermott told me exactly the same thing—almost in those words." Her eyes searched the little man's face. For all his lack of worldliness, he seemed to have a homespun instinct for getting at the truth.

Albert Wells nodded approvingly. "Now there's a smart young man. We had a talk yesterday."

This disclosure surprised her. "Peter came here?"

"That's right."

"I didn't know." But it was the kind of thing, she reasoned, that Peter McDermott would do—an efficient follow-up to whatever it was he was concerned with personally. She had observed before, his capacity for thinking largely, yet seldom omitting detail.

"Are you going to marry him, miss?"

The abrupt question startled her. She protested, "Whatever gave you that idea?" But to her embarrassment she felt her face was flushing.

Albert Wells chuckled. There were moments, Christine thought, when he had the mien of a mischieveous elf.

"I sort of guessed—by the way you said his name just now. Besides, I'd figured the two of you must see a lot of each other, both working where you do; and if that young man has the kind of sense I think, he'll find out he doesn't have to look much further."

"Mr. Wells, you're outrageous! You . . . you read people's minds, then you make them feel terrible." But the warmth of her smile belied the reproof. "And please stop calling me 'miss.' My name is Christine."

He said quietly, "That's a special name for me. It was my wife's, too."

"Was?"

He nodded. "She died, Christine. So long ago, sometimes I get to thinking the times we had together never really happened. Not the good ones or the hard, and there were plenty of both. But then, once in a while, it seems as if all that happened was only yesterday. It's then I get weary, mostly of being so much alone. We didn't have children." He stopped, his eyes reflective. "You never know how much you share with someone until the sharing ends. So you and your young man—grab on to every minute there is. Don't waste a lot of time; you never get it back."

She laughed. "I keep telling you he isn't my young man. At least, not yet."

"If you handle things right, he can be."

"Perhaps." Her eyes went to the partially completed jigsaw puzzle. She said slowly, "I wonder if there *is* a key piece to everything—the way you say. And when you've found it, if you really know, or only guess, and hope." Then, almost before she knew it, she found herself confiding in the little man, relating the happenings of the past —the tragedy in Wisconsin, her aloneness, the move to New Orleans, the adjusting years, and now for the first time the possibility of a full and fruitful life. She revealed, too, the breakdown of this evening's arrangements and her disappointment at the cause.

At the end Albert Wells nodded sagely. "Things work themselves out a lot of times. Other times, though, you need to push a bit so's to start people moving."

She asked lightly, "Any ideas?"

He shook his head. "Being a woman, you'll know plenty more'n me. There's one thing, though. Because of what happened, I shouldn't wonder if that young man'll ask you out tomorrow."

Christine smiled. "He might."

"Then get yourself another date before he does. He'll appreciate you more, having to wait an extra day."

"I'd have to invent something."

"No need for that, unless you want. I was going to ask anyway, miss . . . excuse me, Christine. I'd like us to have dinner, you and me—a kind of thank you for what you did the other night. If you can bear an old man's company, I'd be glad to be a stand-in."

She answered, "I'd love to have dinner, but I promise you won't be any stand-in."

"Good!" The little man beamed. "We'd best make it here in the hotel, I reckon. I told that doctor I'd not go outdoors for a couple of days."

Briefly, Christine hesitated. She wondered if Albert Wells knew just how high were the evening prices in the St. Gregory's main dining room. Though the nursing expense had ended, she had no wish to deplete still further whatever funds he had remaining. Suddenly she thought of a way to prevent that happening.

Putting the idea aside to be dealt with later, she assured him, "The hotel will be fine. It's a special occasion, though. You'll have to give me time to go home and change into something really glamorous. Let's make it eight o'clock—tomorrow night."

On the fourteenth floor, after leaving Albert Wells, Christine noticed that number four elevator was out of service. Maintenance work, she observed, was being done both on the landing doors and the elevator cage.

She took another elevator to the main mezzanine.

10

The dentists' president, Dr. Ingram, glared at the visitor to his suite on the seventh floor. "McDermott, if you've come here with some idea of smoothing things over, I'll tell you right now you're wasting time. *Is* that why you came?"

"Yes," Peter admitted. "I'm afraid it is."

The older man said grudgingly, "At least you don't lie."

"There's no reason I should. I'm an employee of the hotel, Dr. Ingram. While I work here I've an obligation to do the best I can for it."

"And what happened to Dr. Nicholas was the best you could do?"

"No, sir. I happen to believe it's the worst thing we could have done. The fact that I had no authority to change a hotel standing order doesn't make it any better."

The dentists' president snorted. "If you really felt that way, you'd have the guts to quit and get a job some other place. Maybe where the pay is poorer but the ethics higher."

Peter flushed, refraining from a quick retort. He reminded himself that this morning in the lobby he had admired the elderly dentist for his forthright stand. Nothing had changed since then.

"Well?" The alert, unyielding eyes were focused on his own.

"Suppose I did quit," Peter said. "Whoever took my job might be perfectly satisfied with the way things are. At least I'm not. I intend to do what I can to change the ground rules here."

"Rules! Rationalization! Damned excuses!" The doctor's rubicund face grew redder. "In my time I've heard them all! They make me sick! Disgusted, ashamed, and sick of the human race!"

Between them there was a silence.

"All right." Dr. Ingram's voice dropped, his immediate anger spent. "I'll concede you're not as bigoted as some, McDermott. You've a problem yourself, and I guess my bawling you out doesn't solve anything. But don't you see, son?—half the time it's the damned reasonableness of people like you and me which adds up to the sort of treatment Jim Nicholas got today."

"I do see, Doctor. Though I think the whole business isn't quite so simple as you'd make it."

"Plenty of things aren't simple," the older man growled. "You heard what I told Nicholas. I said if he didn't get an apology and a room, I'd pull the entire convention out of this hotel."

Peter said guardedly, "In the ordinary way aren't there events at your convention—medical discussions, demonstrations, that kind of thing—that benefit a lot of people?"

"Naturally."

"Then would it help? I mean, if you wiped out everything, what could anyone gain? Not Dr. Nicholas . . ." He stopped, aware of renewed hostility as his words progressed.

Dr. Ingram snapped, "Don't give me a snow job, McDermott. And credit me with intelligence to have thought of that already."

"I'm sorry."

"There are always reasons for *not* doing something; plenty of times they're good reasons. That's why so few people ever take a stand for what they believe in, or say they do. In a couple of hours, when some of my well-meaning colleagues hear what I'm planning, I predict they'll offer the same kind of argument." Breathing heavily, the older man paused. He faced Peter squarely, "Let me ask *you* something. This morning you admitted you were ashamed of turning Jim Nicholas away. If you were me, here and now, what would you do?"

"Doctor, that's a hypothetical . . ."

"Never mind the horse-shit! I'm asking you a simple, direct question."

Peter considered. As far as the hotel was concerned, he supposed whatever he said now would make little difference to the outcome. Why not answer honestly?

He said, "I think I'd do exactly as you intended—cancel out."

"Well!" Stepping back a pace, the dentists' president regarded him appraisingly. "Beneath all that hotel crap lies an honest man."

"Who may shortly be unemployed."

"Hang onto that black suit, son! You can get a job helping out at funerals." For the first time Dr. Ingram chuckled. "Despite everything, McDermott, I like you. Got any teeth need fixing?"

Peter shook his head. "If you don't mind, I'd sooner know what your plans are. As soon as possible." There would be immediate things to do, once the cancellation was confirmed. The loss to the hotel was going to be disastrous, as Royall Edwards had pointed out at lunch. But at least some of the preparations for tomorrow and the next day could be halted at once.

Dr. Ingram said crisply, "You've leveled with me; I'll do the same for you. I've called an emergency executive session for five this afternoon." He glanced at his watch. "That's in two and a half hours. Most of our senior officers will have arrived by then."

"No doubt we'll be in touch."

Dr. Ingram nodded. His grimness had returned. "Because we've relaxed a minute, McDermott, don't let it fool you. Nothing has changed since this morning, and I intend to kick you people where it hurts."

Surprisingly, Warren Trent reacted almost with indifference to the news that the Congress of American Dentistry might abandon its convention and stage a protest withdrawal from the hotel.

Peter McDermott had gone immediately to the main mezzanine executive suite after leaving Dr. Ingram. Christine—a trifle coolly, he thought—had told him the hotel proprietor was in.

Warren Trent, Peter sensed, was noticeably less tense than on other occasions recently. At ease behind the black marble-topped desk in the sumptuous managing director's office, he betrayed none of the irascibility so apparent the previous day. There were moments, while listening to Peter's report, that a slight smile played around his lips, though

218

it seemed to have little to do with events on hand. It was rather, Peter thought, as if his employer were savoring some private pleasure known only to himself.

At the end, the hotel proprietor shook his head decisively. "They won't go. They'll talk, but that will be the end of it."

"Dr. Ingram seems quite serious."

"He may be, but others won't. You say there's a meeting this afternoon; I can tell you what will happen. They'll debate around for a while, then there'll be a committee formed to draft a resolution. Later—tomorrow probably —the committee will report back to the executive. They may accept the report, they may amend it; either way they'll talk some more. Later still—perhaps the next day —the resolution will be debated on the convention floor. I've seen it all before—the great democratic process. They'll still be talking when the convention's over."

"I suppose you could be right," Peter said. "Though I'd say it's a pretty sick point of view."

He had spoken recklessly and braced himself for an explosive response. It failed to occur. Instead Warren Trent growled, "I'm practical, that's all. People will cluck about so-called principles till their tongues dry out. But they won't inconvenience themselves if they can avoid it."

Peter said doggedly, "It might still be simpler if we changed our policy. I can't believe that Dr. Nicholas, if we'd admitted him, would have undermined the hotel."

"*He* might not. But the riff-raff who'd follow would. Then we'd be in trouble."

"It's been my understanding we're that way already." Perversely, Peter was conscious of indulging in verbal brinksmanship. He speculated on just how far he could go. And why—today—he wondered, was his employer in such comparative good humor?

Warren Trent's patrician features creased sardonically. "We may have been in trouble for a while. In a day or two, however, that will not be true." Abruptly he asked: "Is Curtis O'Keefe still in the hotel?"

"So far as I know. I'd have heard if he'd checked out."

"Good!" The hovering smile remained. "I've some information that may interest you. Tomorrow I shall tell O'Keefe and his entire hotel chain to go jump in Lake Pontchartrain."

11

From his vantage point at the bell captain's upright desk, Herbie Chandler watched covertly as the four young men entered the St. Gregory from the street outside. It was a few minutes before four P.M.

Two of the group Herbie recognized as Lyle Dumaire and Stanley Dixon, the latter scowling as he led the way toward the elevators. A few seconds later they were out of sight.

On the telephone yesterday, Dixon had assured Herbie that the bell captain's part in the previous night's embroilment would not be divulged. But Dixon, Herbie realized uneasily, was merely one of four. How the others—and perhaps Dixon too—would react under questioning, possibly threats, was something else again.

As he had for the past twenty-four hours, the bell captain continued to brood with growing apprehension.

On the main mezzanine, Stanley Dixon again led the way as the four youths left the elevator. They stopped outside a paneled doorway with a softly illumined sign, EXECUTIVE OFFICES, while Dixon morosely repeated an earlier warning. "Remember!—leave the talking to me."

Flora Yates showed them into Peter McDermott's office. Looking up coldly, he motioned them to chairs and inquired, "Which of you is Dixon?"

"I am."

"Dumaire?"

Less confidently, Lyle Dumaire nodded.

"I don't have the other two names."

"That's too bad," Dixon said. "If we'd known, we could have all brought calling cards."

The third youth interjected, "I'm Gladwin. This is Joe Waloski." Dixon shot him an irritated glance.

"All of you," Peter stated, "are undoubtedly aware that I've listened to Miss Marsha Preyscott's report of what occurred Monday night. If you wish, I'm willing to hear your version."

Dixon spoke quickly, before anyone else could intervene. "Listen!—coming here was your idea, not ours. There's nothing we want to say to you. So if you've got any talking, get on with it."

Peter's face muscles tightened. With an effort he controlled his temper.

"Very well. I suggest we deal with the least important matter first." He shuffled papers, then addressed Dixon. "Suite 1126-7 was registered in your name. When you ran away"—he emphasized the last two words—"I assumed you had overlooked checking out, so I did it for you. There is an unpaid bill of seventy-five dollars and some cents. There is a further bill, for damage to the suite, of one hundred and ten dollars."

The one who had introduced himself as Gladwin whistled softly.

"We'll pay the seventy-five," Dixon said. "That's all."

"If you dispute the other account, that's your privilege," Peter informed him. "But I'll tell you we don't intend to drop the matter. If necessary, we'll sue."

"Listen, Stan . . ." It was the fourth youth, Joe Waloski. Dixon waved him to silence.

Beside him, Lyle Dumaire shifted uneasily. He said softly, "Stan, whatever happens they can make a lot of fuss. If we have to, we can split it four ways." He addressed Peter: "If we do pay—the hundred and ten—we might have trouble getting it all at once. Could we pay a little at a time?"

"Certainly." There was no reason, Peter decided, not to extend the normal amenities of the hotel. "One or all of you can see our credit manager and he'll make the arrangements." He glanced around the group. "Are we to regard that part as settled?"

One by one the quartet nodded.

"That leaves the matter of the attempted rape—four so-called men against one girl." Peter made no effort to keep the contempt from his voice.

Waloski and Gladwin flushed. Lyle Dumaire uncomfortably avoided Peter's eyes.

Only Dixon maintained his self-assurance. "That's her story. Could be, we'd tell a different one."

"I already said I'm willing to listen to your version."

"Nuts!"

"Then I've no alternative but to accept Miss Preyscott's."

Dixon sniggered. "Don't you wish you'd been there, buster? Or maybe you had your piece after."

Waloski muttered, "Take it easy, Stan."

Peter gripped the arms of his chair tightly. He fought back an impulse to rush out from behind the desk and strike the smugly leering face in front of him. But he knew that if he did he would give Dixon an advantage which the youth was probably, and astutely, trying to gain. He would not, he told himself, be goaded into losing control.

"I assume," he said icily, "you are all aware that criminal charges can be laid."

"If they were going to be," Dixon countered, "somebody'd have done it by now. So don't feed us that old line."

"Would you be willing to repeat that statement to Mr. Mark Preyscott? If he's brought back from Rome after being told what happened to his daughter?"

Lyle Dumaire looked up sharply, his expression alarmed. For the first time there was a flicker of disquiet in Dixon's eyes.

Gladwin inquired anxiously, "Is he being told?"

"Shut up!" Dixon enjoined. "It's a trick. Don't fall for it!" But there was a shade less confidence than a moment earlier.

"You can judge for yourself whether it's a trick or not." Peter opened a drawer of his desk and took out a folder which he opened. "I have here a signed statement, made by me, of exactly what I was informed by Miss Preyscott, and what I observed myself on arrival at suite 1126–7, Monday night. It has not been attested to by Miss Preyscott, but it can be, along with any other details she may see fit to add. There is a further statement made and signed by Aloysius Royce, the hotel employee you assaulted, confirming my report and describing what happened immediately after his arrival."

The idea of obtaining a statement from Royce had

occurred to Peter late yesterday. In response to a telephoned request the young Negro had delivered it early
this morning. The neatly typed document was clear and
carefully phrased, reflecting Royce's legal training. At the
same time Aloysius Royce had cautioned Peter, "I still say
no Louisiana court will take a nigger boy's word in a white
rape case." Though irritated by Royce's continued abra-
siveness, Peter assured him, "I'm sure it will never come
to court, but I need the ammunition."

Stan Jakubiec had been helpful also. At Peter's request
the credit manager had made discreet inquiries about the
two youths, Stanley Dixon and Lyle Dumaire. He reported:
"Dumaire's father, as you know, is the bank president;
Dixon's father is a car dealer—good business, big home.
Both kids seemingly get a lot of freedom—parental in-
dulgence, I guess—and a fair amount of money, though
not unlimited. From all I hear, both fathers wouldn't exactly disapprove of their kids laying a girl or two; more
likely to say 'I did the same when I was young.' But attempted rape is something else again, particularly involving
the Preyscott girl. Mark Preyscott has as much influence
as anyone in this town. He and the other two men move
in the same circle, though Preyscott probably rates higher
socially. Certainly if Mark Preyscott got after the older
Dixon and Dumaire, accusing their sons of raping his
daughter, or trying to, the roof would fall in and the Dixon
and Dumaire kids know it." Peter had thanked Jakubiec,
storing the information for use if necessary.

"All that statement stuff," Dixon said, "ain't worth as
much as you make it out. You weren't there until after, so
yours is hearsay."

"That may be true," Peter said. "I'm not a lawyer, so
I wouldn't know. But I wouldn't discount it entirely. Also,
whether you won or lost you would not come out of court
smelling sweetly, and I imagine your families might give
some of you a hard time." From a glance between Dixon
and Dumaire he knew the last thrust had gone home.

"Christ!" Gladwin urged the others, "we don't want to
go in any court."

Lyle Dumaire asked sullenly, "What are you going to
do?"

"Providing you cooperate, I intend to do nothing more, at least so far as you are concerned. On the other hand, if you continue making things difficult I intend, later to-day, to cable Mr. Preyscott in Rome and deliver these papers to his lawyers here."

It was Dixon who asked disagreeably, "What's 'cooper-ate' supposed to mean?"

"It means that here and now you will each write a full account of what took place Monday night, including what-ever occurred in the early part of the evening and who, if anyone, was involved from the hotel."

"Like hell!" Dixon said. "You can stuff that . . ."

Gladwin cut in impatiently. "Can it, Stan!" He inquired of Peter, "Suppose we do make statements. What will you do then?"

"Much as I'd like to see them used otherwise, you have my word they will be seen by no one, other than internally within the hotel."

"How do we know we can trust you?"

"You don't. You'll have to take that chance."

There was a silence in the room, the only sounds the creaking of a chair and the muffled clatter of a typewriter outside.

Abruptly Waloski said, "I'll take a chance. Give me something to write on."

"I guess I will too." It was Gladwin.

Lyle Dumaire, unhappily, nodded his assent.

Dixon scowled, then shrugged. "So everybody's on a writing kick. What's the difference?" He told Peter, "I like a pen with a broad nib. It suits my style."

A half hour later Peter McDermott reread, more care-fully, the several pages he had skimmed over quickly be-fore the youths filed out.

The four versions of Monday's evening events, though differing in a few details, corroborated each other in essen-tial facts. All of them filled in earlier gaps in information, and Peter's instructions that hotel staff be identified had been specifically followed.

The bell captain, Herbie Chandler, was firmly and un-erringly impaled.

12

The original, half-formed idea in the mind of Keycase Milne had taken shape.

Unquestionably, his instinct told him, the appearance of the Duchess of Croydon at the same time he himself was passing through the lobby, had been more than coincidence. It was an omen among omens, pointing a path for him to tread, at the end of which lay the Duchess's glistering jewels.

Admittedly, the fabled Croydon gem collection was not likely to be—in its entirety—in New Orleans. On her travels, as was known, the Duchess carried only portions of her Aladdin's treasure trove. Even so, the potential loot was likely to be large and, though some jewels might be safeguarded in the hotel's vault, it was a certainty there would be others immediately at hand.

The key to the situation, as always, lay in a key to the Croydons' suite. Systematically, Keycase Milne set out to obtain it.

He rode elevators several times, choosing different cars so as not to make himself conspicuous. Eventually, finding himself alone with an elevator operator, he asked the seemingly casual question, "Is it true the Duke and Duchess of Croydon are staying in the hotel?"

"That's right, sir."

"I suppose the hotel keeps special rooms for visitors like that." Keycase smiled genially. "Not like us ordinary people."

"Well, sir, the Duke and Duchess have the Presidential Suite."

"Oh, really! What floor's that?"

"Ninth."

Mentally, Keycase ticked off "point one" and left the elevator at his own floor, the eighth.

Point two was to establish the precise room number. It proved simple. Up one flight by the service stairs, then a short walk! Double padded-leather doors with gold fleur-de-lis proclaimed the Presidential Suite. Keycase noted the number: 973–7.

Down to the lobby once more, this time for a stroll—apparently casual—past the reception desk. A quick, keen-eyed inspection showed that 973-7, like more plebian rooms, had a conventional mail slot. A room key was in the slot.

It would be a mistake to ask for the key at once. Keycase sat down to watch and wait. The precaution proved wise.

After a few minutes' observation it became obvious that the hotel had been alerted. Compared with the normal easy-going method of handing out room keys, today the desk clerks were being cautious. As guests requested keys, the clerks asked names, then checked the answer against a registration list. Undoubtedly, Keycase reasoned, his coup of early this morning had been reported, with security tightened as a result.

A cold stab of fear was a reminder of an equally predictable effect: the New Orleans police would by now be alerted and, within hours, might be seeking Keycase Milne by name. True, if the morning paper was to be believed, the hit-and-run fatalities of two nights earlier still commanded the bulk of police attention. But it was a certainty that someone at police headquarters would still find time to teletype the FBI. Once again, remembering the awful price of one more conviction, Keycase was tempted to play safe, check out and run. Irresolution held him. Then, forcing doubts aside, he comforted himself with the memory of this morning's omen in his favor.

After a time the waiting proved worth while. One desk clerk, a young man with light wavy hair, appeared unsure of himself and at moments nervous. Keycase judged him to be new to his job.

The presence of the young man provided a possible opportunity, though to utilize it would be a gamble, Keycase reasoned, and a long shot at that. But perhaps the opportunity—like other events today—was an omen in itself. He resolved to take it, employing a technique he had used before.

Preparations would occupy at least an hour. Since it was now mid-afternoon, they must be completed before the young man went off duty. Hurriedly, Keycase left the hotel. His destination was the Maison Blanche department store on Canal Street.

Using his money frugally, Keycase shopped for inexpensive but bulky items—mainly children's toys—waiting while each was enclosed in a distinctive Maison Blanche box or wrapping paper. At the end, carrying an armful of packages he could scarcely hold, he left the store. He made one additional stop—at a florist's, topping off his purchases with a large azalea plant in bloom, after which he returned to the hotel.

At the Carondelet Street entrance a uniformed doorman hurried to hold the doorway wide. The man smiled at Keycase, largely hidden behind his burden of parcels and the flowering azalea.

Inside the hotel, Keycase loitered, ostensibly inspecting a series of showcases, but actually waiting for two things to happen. One was a convergence of several people on the reception and mail desk; the second, the reappearance of the young man he had observed earlier. Both events occurred almost at once.

Tensely, his heart pounding, Keycase approached the Reception area.

He was third in line in front of the young man with light wavy hair. A moment later there was only a middle-aged woman immediately ahead, who secured a room key after identifying herself. Then, about to leave, the woman remembered a query concerning readdressed mail. Her questions seemed interminable, the young desk clerk's answers hesitant. Impatiently, Keycase was aware that around him the knot of people at the desk was thinning. Already one of the other room clerks was free, and he glanced across. Keycase avoided his eye, praying silently for the colloquy ahead to finish.

At length the woman moved away. The young clerk turned to Keycase, then—as the doorman had done— smiled involuntarily at the awkward profusion of packages topped by the blooms.

Speaking acidly, Keycase used a line already rehearsed. "I'm sure it's very funny. But if it isn't too much trouble I'd like the key of 973."

The young man reddened, his smile dissolving instantly.

227

"Certainly, sir." Flustered, as Keycase intended, he wheeled and selected the key from its place in the rack.

At the mention of the room number, Keycase had seen one of the other clerks glance sideways. It was a crucial moment. Obviously the number of the Presidential Suite would be well known, and intervention by a more experienced clerk could mean exposure. Keycase sweated.

"Your name, sir?"

Keycase snapped, "What is this—an interrogation?" Simultaneously he allowed two parcels to drop. One stayed on the counter, the other rebounded to the floor behind the desk. Increasingly flustered, the young clerk retrieved both. His more senior colleague, with an indulgent smile, looked away.

"I beg your pardon, sir."

"Never mind." Accepting the parcels and rearranging the others, Keycase held out his hand for the key.

For a hairsbreadth of time the young man hesitated. Then the image Keycase had hoped to create won out: a tired, frustrated shopper; absurdly burdened; the epitome of respectability as attested by the familiar Maison Blanche wrappings; an already irritated guest, not to be trifled with further . . .

Deferentially the desk clerk handed over the key of 973.

As Keycase walked unhurriedly toward the elevators, activity at the reception desk resumed. A fleeting backward glance showed him the desk clerks were once more busy. Good! It lessened the likelihood of discussion and possible second thoughts about what had just occurred. All the same, he must return the key as quickly as possible. Its absence might be noticed, leading to questions and suspicion—especially dangerous since the hotel was already partially alert.

He instructed the elevator operator, "Nine"—a precaution in case anyone had heard him demand a ninth-floor key. Stepping out as the elevator stopped, he loitered, adjusting parcels until the doors closed behind him, then hurried to the service stairs. It was a single flight down to his own floor. On a landing, halfway, was a garbage can. Opening it, he stuffed in the plant which had served its purpose. A few seconds later he was in his own room, 830.

He shoved the parcels hurriedly into a closet. Tomorrow he would return them to the store and claim refunds. The cost was not important compared with the prize he hoped to win, but they would be awkward to take along, and to abandon them would leave a conspicuous trail.

Still moving swiftly, he unzipped a suitcase, taking out a small leather-covered box. It contained a number of white cards, some finely sharpened pencils, calipers, and a micrometer. Selecting one of the cards, Keycase laid the Presidential Suite key upon it. Then, holding the key still, he painstakingly drew an outline around the edge. Next, with micrometer and calipers, he measured the thickness of the key and the exact dimensions of each horizontal groove and vertical cut, jotting the results beside the outline on the card. A manufacturer's letter-number code was stamped on the metal. He copied it; the code might help in selecting a suitable blank. Finally, holding the key to the light, he drew a careful free-hand sketch of its end view.

He now had an expertly detailed specification which a skilled locksmith could follow unerringly. The procedure, Keycase often reflected amusedly, was a long way from the wax impression gambit beloved by detective fiction writers, but a good deal more effective.

He put the leather-covered box away, the card in his pocket. Moments later he was back in the main lobby.

Precisely as before, he waited until the desk clerks were busy. Then, walking casually across, he laid the 973 key unnoticed upon the counter.

Again he watched. At the next lull a room clerk observed the key. Disinterestedly, he lifted it, glanced at the number and returned it to its slot.

Keycase felt a warming glow of professional achievement. Through a combination of inventiveness and skill, and overcoming the hotel's precautions, his first objective had been won.

Selecting a dark blue Schiaparelli tie from several in his clothes closet, Peter McDermott knotted it pensively. He was in his small downtown apartment, not far from the hotel, which he had left an hour earlier. In another twenty minutes he was due at Marsha Preyscott's dinner party. He wondered who the other guests would be. Presumably, as well as Marsha's friends—who, he hoped, would be of a different caliber from the Dixon-Dumaire quartet—there would be one or two older people, accounting for his own inclusion.

Now that the time had come, he found himself resenting the commitment, wishing instead that he had remained free to meet Christine. He was tempted to telephone Christine before leaving, then decided it would be more discreet to wait until tomorrow.

He had an unsettled sense tonight, of being suspended in time between the past and future. So much he was concerned with seemed indefinite, with decisions delayed until outcomes should be known. There was the question of the St. Gregory itself. Would Curtis O'Keefe take over? If so, other affairs seemed minor by comparison—even the dentists' convention, whose officers were still debating whether or not to march protestingly from the St. Gregory. An hour ago the executive session called by the fiery dentists' president, Dr. Ingram, was still in progress and looked like continuing, according to the head waiter of room service, whose staff had made several trips into the meeting to replenish ice and mixes. Although Peter had confined his behind-scenes inquiry as to whether the meeting showed signs of breaking up, the head waiter informed him there appeared to be a good deal of heated discussion. Before leaving the hotel Peter left word with the duty assistant manager that if any decision from the dentists became known, he was to be telephoned immediately. So far there had been no word. He wondered now whether Dr. Ingram's forthright viewpoint would prevail or if Warren Trent's more cynical prediction about nothing happening would prove true.

The same uncertainty had caused Peter to defer—at least until tomorrow—any action concerning Herbie Chandler. What ought to be done, he knew, was immediate dismissal of the sleazy bell captain, which would be like purging the hotel of an unclean spirit. Specifically, of course, Chandler would not be dismissed for running a call girl system—which someone else would organize if Chandler didn't—but for allowing greed to overcome good sense.

With Chandler gone, a good many other abuses could be curbed, though whether Warren Trent would agree to such summary action was an open question. However, remembering the accumulated evidence and Warren Trent's concern with the hotel's good name, Peter had an idea he might.

Either way, Peter reminded himself, he must ensure that the Dixon-Dumaire group statements were safeguarded and used within the hotel only. He would keep his promise on that point. Also he had been bluffing this afternoon in threatening to inform Mark Preyscott about the attempted rape of his daughter. Then, as now, Peter remembered Marsha's entreaty: *My father's in Rome. Don't tell him, please—ever!*

The thought of Marsha was a reminder to hurry. A few minutes later he left the apartment and hailed a cruising cab.

Peter asked, "This is the house?"

"Sure is." The cab driver looked speculatively at his passenger. "Leastways, if you got the address right."

"It was right." Peter's eyes followed the driver's to the immense, white-fronted mansion. The façade alone was breathtaking. Behind a yew hedge and towering magnolia trees, graceful fluted columns rose from a terrace to a high railed gallery. Above the gallery the columns soared on to a crowning, classically proportioned pediment. At either end of the main building two wings repeated the details in miniature. The entire façade was in superb repair, its wood surfaces preserved and paintwork fresh. Around the house the scent of sweet olive blossoms hung in the early evening air.

Paying off the cab, Peter approached an iron grilled gate which opened smoothly. A curving pathway of old red brick led between trees and lawns. Though barely dusk, two elevated flare pots had been lighted at either side of the pathway as it neared the house. He had reached the terrace steps when a latch clicked solidly and the double doors to the house swung open. The wide doorway framed Marsha. She waited until he reached the head of the steps, then walked toward him.

She was in white—a slim, sheath gown, her raven black hair startling by contrast. He was aware, more than ever, of the provoking woman-child quality.

Marsha said gaily, "Welcome!"

"Thank you." He gestured about him. "At the moment I'm a little overwhelmed."

"So's everybody." She entwined her arm in his. "I'll give you the Preyscott official tour before it's dark."

Returning down the terrace steps, they crossed the lawn, soft underfoot. Marsha remained close. Through his coat sleeve he could feel the warm firmness of her flesh. Her finger tips touched his wrist lightly. There was an added gentle fragrance to the scent of olive blossoms.

"There!" Abruptly Marsha wheeled. "This is where you see it all best. It's from here they always take the pictures."

From this side of the lawn the view was even more impressive.

"A fun-lovin' French nobleman built the house," Marsha said. "In the 1840s. He liked Greek Revival architecture, happy laughing slaves, and also having his mistress handy, which was the reason for an extra wing. My father added the other wing. He prefers things balanced—like accounts and houses."

"This is the new guide style—philosophy with fact?"

"Oh, I'm brimming with both. You want facts?—look at the roof." Their eyes went up together. "You'll see it overhangs the upper gallery. The Louisiana-Greek style— most old big houses here were built that way—makes sense because in this climate it gave shade and air. Lots of times the gallery was the most lived-in place. It became a family center, a place of talk and sharing."

He quoted, "Households and families, a sharing of the

good life, in a form at once complete and self-sufficient."

"Who said that?"

"Aristotle."

Marsha nodded. "He'd dig galleries." She stopped, considering. "My father did a lot of restoration. The house is better now, but not our use of it."

"You must love all this very much."

"I hate it," Marsha said. "I've hated this place as long as I remember."

He looked at her inquiringly.

"Oh, I wouldn't if I came to see it—as a visitor, lined up with others who'd paid fifty cents to be shown around, the way we open the house for Spring Fiesta. I'd admire it because I love old things. But not to live with always, especially alone and after dark."

He reminded her, "It's getting dark now."

"I know," she said. "But you're here. That makes it different."

They had begun to return across the lawn. For the first time he was conscious of the quiet.

"Won't your other guests be missing you?"

She glanced sideways, mischievously. "What other guests?"

"You told me . . ."

"I said I was giving a dinner party; so I am. For you. If it's chaperonage you're worried about, Anna's here." They had passed into the house. It was shadowy and cool, with ceilings high above. In the background a small elderly woman in black silk nodded, smiling. "I told Anna about you," Marsha said, "and she approves. My father trusts her absolutely, so everything's all right. Then there's Ben."

A Negro manservant followed them, soft footed, to a small booklined study. From a sideboard he brought a tray with decanter and sherry glasses. Marsha shook her head. Peter accepted a sherry and sipped it thoughtfully. From a settee Marsha motioned him to sit beside her.

He asked, "You spend a lot of time alone here?"

"My father comes home between trips. It's just that the trips get longer and the time between shorter. What I'd prefer to live in is an ugly modern bungalow. Just so long as it was alive."

233

"I wonder if you really would."

"I know I would," Marsha said firmly. "If I shared it with someone I really cared about. Or maybe a hotel would be as good. Don't hotel managers get an apartment to live in—at the top of their hotel?"

Startled, he looked up to find her smiling.

A moment later the manservant announced quietly that dinner was served.

In an adjoining room a small circular table was set for two. Candlelight gleamed on the dinner setting and paneled walls. Above a black marble mantel the portrait of a stern-faced patriarch gazed down, giving Peter an impression of being studied critically.

"Don't let great-grandfather bother you," Marsha said when they were seated. "It's me he's frowning at. You see, he once wrote in his diary that he wanted to found a dynasty and I'm his last forlorn hope."

They chatted through dinner—with lessening restraint—as the manservant served them unobtrusively. The fare was exquisite—the main course a superbly seasoned Jambalaya, followed by a delicately flavored Crème Brûlée. In a situation he had approached with misgiving, Peter discovered he was enjoying himself genuinely. Marsha seemed more vivacious and charming as the minutes passed, and he himself more relaxed in her company. Which was less than surprising, he reminded himself, since the gap in their ages was by no means great. And in the glow of candlelight, the old room shadowed around them, he was reminded how exceedingly beautiful she was.

He wondered if long ago the French nobleman who built the great house, and his mistress, had dined as intimately here. Or was the thought the product of a spell which the surroundings and the occasion had cast on him?

At the end of dinner Marsha said, "We'll have coffee on the gallery."

He held out her chair and she got up quickly, impulsively taking his arm as she had earlier. Amused, he allowed himself to be guided to a hallway and up a broad curving staircase. At the top, a wide corridor, its frescoed walls dimly lighted, led to the open gallery they had viewed from the now darkened garden below.

Demitasse cups and a silver coffee service were on a wicker table. A flickering gas lantern burned above. They took their coffee to a cushioned porch glider which swung lazily as they sat down. The nighttime air was comfortably cool, with the faintest stirring of a breeze. From the garden, the hum of insects sounded sonorously; the muted sounds of traffic came over from St. Charles Avenue, two blocks distant. He was conscious of Marsha, quite still beside him.

Peter chided, "You've suddenly become quiet."

"I know. I was wondering how to say something."

"You might try directly. It often works."

"All right." There was a breathlessness to her voice. "I've decided I want to marry you."

For what seemed like long minutes but were, he suspected, seconds only, Peter remained unmoving, with even the gentle motion of the glider stopped. At last, with careful precision, he put down his coffee cup.

Marsha coughed, then changed the cough to a nervous laugh. "If you want to run, the stairs are thataway."

"No," he said. "If I did that I'd never know why you said what you did just now."

"I'm not sure myself." She was looking directly ahead, out into the night, her face turned half away. He sensed that she was trembling. "Except I suddenly wanted to say it. And quite sure I should."

It was important, he knew, that whatever he next said to this impulsive girl should be with gentleness and consideration. He was also uncomfortably aware of a nervous constriction in his throat. Irrationally, he remembered something Christine had said this morning: *Little Miss Preyscott bears as much resemblance to a child as a kitten to a tiger. But it would be fun I should think—for a man —to be eaten up.* The comment was unfair of course, even harsh. But it was true that Marsha was not a child, nor should she be treated like one.

"Marsha, you scarcely know me, or I you."

"Do you believe in instinct?"

"To a point, yes."

"I had an instinct about you. From the very first moment." Initially her voice had faltered; now she steadied it. "Most times my instincts have been right."

He reminded her gently, "About Stanley Dixon, Lyle Dumaire?"

"I had the right instincts. I didn't follow them, that's all. This time I have."

"But instinct may still be wrong."

"You can always be wrong, even when you wait a long time." Marsha turned, facing him directly. As her eyes searched his own, he was aware of a strength of character he had not observed before. "My father and mother knew each other fifteen years before they married. My mother once told me that everyone they knew said it would be the perfect match. As it turned out, it was the worst. I know; I was in the middle."

He was silent, not knowing what to say.

"It taught me some things. So did something else. You saw Anna tonight?"

"Yes."

"When she was seventeen she was forced to marry a man she'd met just once before. It was a kind of family contract; in those days they did that kind of thing."

Watching Marsha's face, he said, "Go on."

"The day before the wedding, Anna wept all night. But she was married just the same, and stayed married for forty-six years. Her husband died last year; they lived with us here. He was the kindest, sweetest man I've ever known. If ever there was a perfect marriage it belonged to them."

He hesitated, not wishing to score a debater's point, but objected, "Anna didn't follow her instinct. If she had, she'd not have married."

"I know. I'm simply saying there isn't any guaranteed way, and instinct can be as good a guide as any." There was a pause, then Marsha said, "I know I could make you love me, in time."

Absurdly, unexpectedly, he felt a sense of excitement. The idea was preposterous, of course; a romantic product of a girlish imagery. He, who had suffered from his own romantic notions in the past, was qualified to know. Yet was he? Was every situation an aftermath of what had gone before? Was Marsha's proposal so fantastic really? He had a sudden, irrational conviction that what she said might well be true.

He wondered what the reaction of the absent Mark Preyscott would be.

"If you're thinking about my father . . ."

Startled, he said, "How did you know?"

"Because I'm beginning to know *you*."

He breathed deeply, with a sense of inhaling rarefied air. "What about your father?"

"I expect he'd be worried to begin with, and he'd probably fly home in a hurry. I wouldn't mind that." Marsha smiled. "But he always listens to reason and I know I could convince him. Besides, he'd like you. I know the kind of people he admires most, and you're one."

"Well," he said, not knowing whether to be amused or serious, "at least that's a relief."

"There's something else. It isn't important to me, but it would be to him. You see, I know—and my father would too—that someday you'll be a big success with hotels, and maybe own your own. Not that *I* care about that. It's you I want." She finished breathlessly.

"Marsha," Peter said gently, "I don't . . . I simply don't know what to say."

There was a pause in which he could sense Marsha's confidence leave her. It was as if, earlier, she had bolstered her self-assurance with a reserve of will, but now the reserve was gone and boldness with it. In a small, uncertain voice she said, "You think I've been silly. You'd better say so and get it over."

He assured her, "I don't believe you've been silly. If more people, including me, were honest like you . . ."

"You mean you don't mind?"

"Far from minding, I'm moved and overwhelmed."

"Then don't say any more!" Marsha leaped to her feet, her hands held out toward him. He took them and stood facing her, their fingers interlaced. She had a way, he realized, of bounding back after uncertainty, even if her doubts were only partially resolved. She urged him, "Just go away and think! Think, think, think! Especially about me."

He said—and meant it—"It will be difficult not to."

She put up her face to be kissed and he leaned toward her. He intended to brush her cheek, but she put up her

237

lips to his and, as they touched, her arms wound tightly around him. Dimly in his mind an alarm bell jangled. Her body pressed against him; the sense of contact was electric. Her slim fragrance was immediate and breathtaking. Her perfume filled his nostrils. It was impossible, at this moment, to think of Marsha as anything but a woman. He felt his body awaken excitedly, his senses swim. The alarm bell was silenced. He could remember only: *Little Miss Preyscott . . . would be fun . . . for a man—to be eaten up.*

Resolutely, he forced himself away. Taking Marsha's hands gently, he told her, "I must go."

She came with him to the terrace. His hand caressed her hair. She whispered, "Peter, darling."

He went down the terrace steps, scarcely knowing they were there.

14

At 10:30 P.M., Ogilvie, the chief house officer, used a staff sub-basement tunnel to walk lumberingly from the main portion of the St. Gregory to the adjoining hotel garage.

He chose the tunnel instead of the more convenient main floor walkway for the same reason he had carefully picked the time—to be as inconspicuous as possible. At 10:30, guests taking their cars out for the evening had already done so, but it was too early yet for many to be returning. Nor, at that hour, were there likely to be new arrivals at the hotel, at least by road.

Ogilvie's original plan to drive the Duke and Duchess of Croydon's Jaguar north at one A.M.—now less than three hours away—had not changed. Before departure, however, the fat man had work to do and it was important that he be unobserved.

The materials for the work were in a paper bag he carried in his hand. They represented an omission in the Duchess of Croydon's elaborate scheming. Ogilvie had been aware of the omission from the beginning, but preferred to keep his own counsel.

In the double fatality of Monday night, one of the

Jaguar's headlights had been shattered. Additionally, because of the loss of the trim ring, now in possession of the police, the headlight mounting had been loosened. To drive the car in darkness as planned, the headlight would have to be replaced and its mounting repaired temporarily. Yet obviously it was too dangerous to take the car to a service garage in the city and equally out of the question to have the work done by the hotel's own mechanic.

Yesterday, also choosing a time when the garage was quiet, Ogilvie had inspected the car in its out-of-the-way stall behind a pillar. He had decided that if he could obtain the right type of headlight, he could effect a temporary repair himself.

He weighed the risk of buying a replacement headlight from New Orleans' solitary Jaguar dealer, and rejected the idea. Even though the police were not yet aware—so far as Ogilvie knew—of the make of the car they were seeking, they would know in a day or two when the shattered glass fragments were identified. If he bought a Jaguar headlight now, it might easily be remembered when inquiries were made, and the purchase traced. He had compromised by buying a standard, double-filament North American sealed-beam lamp at a self-serve auto parts store. His visual inspection had shown this might be usable. Now he was ready to try it.

Getting the lamp had been one more item in a tightly-crammed day, which had left the chief house officer feeling both satisfaction and an edgy unease. He was also physically tired, a poor beginning to the long drive north which faced him. He consoled himself with remembering the twenty-five thousand dollars, ten thousand of which, as arranged, he had received this afternoon from the Duchess of Croydon. It had been a tense, cold scene, the Duchess tight-lipped and formal, Ogilvie, not caring, greedily stuffed the piled bills into a brief case. Beside them the Duke swayed drunkenly, blear-eyed, and scarcely aware of what was happening.

The thought of the money gave the fat man a pleasant glow. It was safely hidden now, with only two hundred dollars on his person—a precaution in case anything went wrong during the journey to come.

His contrasting unease had two causes. One was awareness of the consequences to himself if he failed to get the Jaguar clear of New Orleans and later Louisiana, Mississippi, Tennessee, and Kentucky. The second was Peter McDermott's emphasis on the need for Ogilvie to remain close to the hotel.

The robbery last night, and the likelihood that a professional thief was at work in the St. Gregory, could not have occurred at a worse time. Ogilvie had done as much as he could. He had advised the city police, and detectives had interviewed the robbed guest. Hotel staff, including the other house officers, had been alerted and Ogilvie's second-in-command had received instructions about what to do in various contingencies. Nonetheless, Ogilvie was well aware that he should be on hand to direct operations personally. When his absence came to McDermott's attention, as it would tomorrow, there was bound to be a first-class row. In the long run the row would not matter because McDermott and others like him would come and go while Ogilvie, for reasons known only to himself and Warren Trent, would still retain his job. But it would have the effect—which the chief house officer wanted to avoid above all else—of drawing attention to his movements in the next few days.

Only in one way had the robbery and its aftermath been useful. It provided a valid reason for a further visit to police headquarters where he inquired casually about progress of the hit-and-run investigation. Police attention, he learned, was still concentrated on the case, with the entire force alert for any break. In this afternoon's *States-Item* the police had issued a new appeal for the public to report any car with fender or headlight damage. It had been as well to have the information, but it also made the chances less of getting the Jaguar out of town without detection. Ogilvie sweated a little when he thought of it.

He had reached the end of the tunnel and was in the garage sub-basement.

The austerely lighted garage was quiet. Ogilvie hesitated, torn between going directly to the Croydons' car several floors above or to the garage office where the night checker was on duty. He decided it would be prudent to visit the office first.

Laboriously, breathing heavily, he climbed two flights of metal stairs. The checker, an elderly officious man named Kulgmer, was alone in his brightly lighted cubicle near the street entry-exit ramp. He put down an evening paper as the chief house officer came in.

"Wanted to let you know," Ogilvie said. "I'll be taking the Duke of Croydon's car out soon. It's stall 371. I'm doin' a favor for him."

Kulgmer frowned. "Don't know as I can let you do that, Mr. O. Not without proper authority."

Ogilvie produced the Duchess of Croydon's note, written this morning at his request. "I guess this is all the authority you'll need."

The night checker read the wording carefully, then turned the paper over. "It seems all right."

The chief house officer put out a pudgy hand to take the note back.

Kulgmer shook his head. "I'll have to keep this. To cover me."

The fat man shrugged. He would have preferred to have the note, but to insist would raise an issue, emphasizing the incident, which otherwise might be forgotten. He motioned to the paper bag. "Just goin' up to leave this. I'll be takin' the car out, couple of hours from now."

"Suit yourself, Mr. O." The checker nodded, returning to his paper.

A few minutes later, approaching stall 371, Ogilvie glanced with apparent casualness around him. The low-ceilinged, concrete parking area, about fifty per cent occupied by cars, was otherwise silent and deserted. The night-duty car jockeys were undoubtedly in their locker room on the main floor, taking advantage of the lull to nap or play cards. But it was necessary to work fast.

In the far corner, sheltered by the Jaguar and its partially screening pillar, Ogilvie emptied the paper bag of the headlight, a screwdriver, pliers, insulated wire, and black electrician's tape.

His fingers, for all their seeming awkwardness, moved with surprising dexterity. Using gloves to protect his hands, he removed the remnants of the shattered headlight. It took only a moment to discover that the replacement headlight would fit the Jaguar, but the electrical connections would not. He had anticipated this. Working swiftly, using the pliers, wire, and tape, he fashioned a rough but effective connection. With additional wire he secured the light in place, stuffing cardboard from his pockets into the gap left by the missing trim ring. He covered this with black tape, passing the tape through and securing it behind. It was a patch job which would be easily detectable in light, but adequate in darkness. It had taken almost fifteen minutes. Opening the car door on the driver's side, he turned the headlight switch to "on." Both headlights worked.

He gave a grunt of relief. At the same instant, from below, came the sharp staccato of a horn and the roar of an accelerating car. Ogilvie froze. The motor roared nearer, its sound magnified by concrete walls and low ceilings. Then, abruptly, headlights flashed by, sweeping up the ramp to the floor above. There was a squeal of tires, the motor stopped, a car door slammed. Ogilvie relaxed. The car jockey, he knew, would use the manlift to return below.

When he heard footsteps receding, he put the tools and supplies back into the paper bag, along with a few larger fragments of the original headlight. He put the bag aside to take with him later.

On the way up he had observed a cleaners' closet on the floor below. Using the downward ramp, he walked to it now.

As he had hoped, there was cleaning equipment inside and he selected a broom, dustpan, and a bucket. He partly filled the bucket with warm water and added a washcloth. Listening cautiously for sounds from below, he waited until two cars had passed, then hurried back to the Jaguar on the floor above.

With the broom and dustpan, Ogilvie swept carefully around the car. There must be no identifiable glass fragments left for police to compare with those from the accident scene.

There was little time left. The cars coming in to be parked were increasing in number. Twice during the sweep-

242

ing he had stopped for fear of being seen, holding his breath as one car swung into a stall on the same floor, a few yards only from the Jaguar. Luckily, the car jockey had not bothered to look around, but it was a warning to hurry. If a jock observed him and came across, it would mean curiosity and questions, which would be repeated downstairs. The explanation for his presence which Ogilvie had given the night checker would seem unconvincing. Not only that, the chances of an undetected run north depended on leaving as scant a trail as possible behind.

One more thing remained. Taking the warm water and cloth, he carefully wiped the damaged portion of the Jaguar's fender and the area around it. As he wrung out the cloth, the water, which had been clear, became brown. He inspected his handiwork carefully, then grunted approval. Now, whatever else might happen, there was no dried blood on the car.

Ten minutes later, sweating from his exertions, he was back in the main building of the hotel. He went directly to his office where he intended to snatch an hour's sleep before setting out on the long drive to Chicago. He checked the time. It was 11:15 P.M.

15

"I might be able to help more," Royall Edwards observed pointedly, "if someone told me what this is all about."

The St. Gregory's comptroller addressed himself to the two men facing him across the long, accounting office table. Between them, ledgers and files were spread open and the entire office, normally shrouded in darkness at this time of night, was brightly lit. Edwards himself had switched on the lights an hour ago on bringing the two visitors here, directly from Warren Trent's fifteenth-floor suite.

The hotel proprietor's instructions had been explicit. "These gentlemen will examine our books. They will probably work through until tomorrow morning. I'd like you

243

to stay with them. Give them everything they ask for. Hold no information back."

In issuing the instructions, Royall Edwards reflected, his employer had seemed more cheerful than for a long time. The cheerfulness, however, did not appease the comptroller, already piqued at being summoned from his home where he had been working on his stamp collection, and further irritated by not being taken into confidence concerning whatever was afoot. He also resented—as one of the hotel's most consistent nine-to-fivers—the idea of working all night.

The comptroller knew, of course, about the mortgage deadline of Friday and the presence of Curtis O'Keefe in the hotel, with its obvious implications. Presumably this latest visitation was related to both, though in what way was hard to guess. A possible clue was luggage tags on both visitors' bags, indicating they had flown to New Orleans from Washington, D.C. Yet instinct told him that the two accountants—which obviously they were—had no connection with government. Well, he would probably know all the answers eventually. Meanwhile it was annoying to be treated like some minor clerk.

There had been no response to his remark that he might be able to help more if better informed, and he repeated it.

The older of the two visitors, a heavy-set middle-aged man with an immobile face, lifted the coffee cup beside him and drained it. "One thing I always say, Mr. Edwards, there's nothing quite like a good cup of coffee. Now you take most hotels, they just don't brew coffee the right way. This one does. So I reckon there can't be much wrong with a hotel that serves coffee like that. What do you say, Frank?"

"I'd say if we're to get through this job by morning, we'd better have less chit-chat." The second man answered dourly, without looking up from a trial balance sheet he was studying intently.

The first made a placating gesture with his hands. "You see how it is, Mr. Edwards? I guess Frank's right; he often is. So, much as I'd like to explain the whole thing, maybe we'd better keep right on."

Aware of being rebuffed, Royall Edwards said stiffly, "Very well."

"Thank you, Mr. Edwards. Now I'd like to go over your inventory system—purchasing, card control, present stocks, your last supply check, all the rest. Say, that *was* good coffee. Could we have some more?"

The comptroller said, "I'll telephone down." He observed dispiritedly that it was already close to midnight. Obviously they were going to be here for hours more.

THURSDAY

1

If he expected to be alert for a new day's work, Peter McDermott supposed he had better head home and get some sleep.

It was a half hour past midnight. He had walked, he thought, for a couple of hours, perhaps longer. He felt refreshed and agreeably tired.

Walking at length was an old habit, especially when he had something on his mind or a problem which defied solution.

Earlier tonight, after leaving Marsha, he had returned to his downtown apartment. But he had been restless in the cramped quarters and disinclined for sleep, so he had gone out walking, toward the river. He had strolled the length of the Poydras and Julia Street Wharves, past moored ships, some dimly lighted and silent, others active and preparing for departure. Then he had taken the Canal Street ferry across the Mississippi and on the far side walked the lonely levees, watching the city lights against the darkness of the river. Returning, he made his way to the Vieux Carré and now sat, sipping *café au lait,* in the old French market.

A few minutes earlier, remembering hotel affairs for the first time in several hours, he had telephoned the St. Gregory. He inquired if there was any more news concerning the threatened walkout of the Congress of American Dentistry convention. Yes, the night assistant manager informed him, a message had been left shortly before midnight by the convention floor head waiter. So far as the head waiter could learn, the dentists' executive board, after a six-hour session, had reached no firm conclusion. However, an emergency general meeting of all convention delegates was to be held at 9:30 A.M. in the Dauphine Salon. About three hundred were expected to attend. The meeting would be *in camera*, with elaborate security precautions, and the hotel had been asked to assist in assuring privacy.

Peter left instructions that whatever was asked should be done, and put the matter from his mind until the morning.

Apart from this brief diversion, most of his thoughts had been of Marsha and the night's events. Questions buzzed in his head like pertinacious bees. How to handle the situation with fairness, yet not clumsily or hurting Marsha in doing so? One thing, of course, was clear: her proposal was impossible. And yet it would be the worst kind of churlishness to dismiss offhandedly an honest declaration. He had told her: *"If more people were honest like you . . ."*

There was something else—and why be afraid of it if honesty was to be served both ways? He had been drawn to Marsha tonight, not as a young girl but as a woman. If he closed his eyes he could see her as she had been. The effect was still like heady wine.

But he had tasted heady wine before, and the taste had turned to bitterness he had vowed would never come his way again. Did that kind of experience temper judgment, make a man wiser in his choice of women? He doubted it.

And yet he *was* a man, breathing, feeling. No self-imposed seclusion could, or should, last forever. The question: When and how to end it?

In any case, what next? Would he see Marsha again? He supposed—unless he severed their connection decisively, at once—it was inevitable he should. Then on what terms? And what, too, of their differences in age?

Marsha was nineteen. He was thirty-two. The gap between seemed wide, yet was it? Certainly if they were both ten years older, an affair—or marriage—would not be thought of as extraordinary. Also, he doubted very much if Marsha would find close rapport with a boy her own age.

The questions were endless. But a decision as to whether, and in what circumstances, he would see Marsha again had yet to be made.

In all his reasoning, too, there remained the thought of Christine. Within the space of a few days he and Christine seemed to have drawn closer together than at any time before. He remembered that his last thought before leaving for the Preyscott house last evening had been of Christine. Even now, he found himself anticipating keenly the sight and sound of her again.

Strange, he reflected, that he, who a week ago had been resolutely unattached, should feel torn at this moment between two women!

Peter grinned ruefully as he paid for the coffee and rose to go home.

The St. Gregory was more or less on the way and instinctively his footsteps took him past it. When he reached the hotel it was a few minutes after one A.M.

There was still activity, he could see, within the lobby. Outside, St. Charles Avenue was quiet, with only a cruising cab and a pedestrian or two in sight. He crossed the street to take a short cut around the rear of the hotel. Here it was quieter still. He was about to pass the entry to the hotel garage when he halted, warned by the sound of a motor and the reflection of headlight beams approaching down the inside ramp. A moment later a low-slung black car swung into sight. It was moving fast and braked sharply, tires squealing, at the street. As the car stopped it was directly in a pool of light. It was a Jaguar, Peter noticed, and it looked as if a fender had been dented; on the same side there was something odd about the headlight too. He hoped the damage had not occurred through negligence in the hotel garage. If it had, he would hear about it soon enough.

Automatically he glanced toward the driver. He was startled to see it was Ogilvie. The chief house officer, meeting Peter's eyes, seemed equally surprised. Then abruptly the car pulled out of the garage and continued on.

Peter wondered why and where Ogilvie was driving; and why a Jaguar instead of the house officer's usual battered

Chevrolet? Then, deciding that what employees did away from the hotel was their own business, Peter continued on to his apartment.

Later, he slept soundly.

2

Unlike Peter McDermott, Keycase Milne did not sleep well.

The speed and efficiency with which he obtained precise details of the Presidential Suite key had not been followed by equal success in having a duplicate made for his own use. The connections which Keycase established on arriving in New Orleans had proved less helpful than he expected. Eventually a locksmith on a slum street near the Irish Channel—whom Keycase was assured could be trusted—agreed to do the job, though grumbling at having to follow specifications instead of copying an existing key. But the new key would not be ready until midday Thursday, and the price demanded was exorbitant.

Keycase had agreed to the price, as he had agreed to wait, realizing there was no alternative. But the waiting was especially trying since he was aware that the passage of every hour increased his chances of being traced and apprehended.

Tonight before going to bed he had debated whether to make a new foray through the hotel in the early morning. There were still two room keys in his collection which he had not utilized—449, the second key obtained at the airport Tuesday morning, and 803 which he had asked for and received at the desk instead of his own key 830. But he decided against the idea, arguing with himself that it was wiser to wait and concentrate on the larger project involving the Duchess of Croydon. Yet Keycase knew, even while reaching the decision, that its major motivation was fear.

In the night, as sleep eluded him, the fear grew stronger, so that he no longer attempted to conceal it from himself with even the thinnest veil of self-deception. But tomorrow, he determined, he would somehow beat fear down and become his own lion-hearted self once more.

He fell at length into an uneasy slumber in which he dreamed that a great iron door, shutting out air and daylight, was inching closed upon him. He tried to run while a gap remained, but was powerless to move. When the door had closed, he wept, knowing it would never open again.

He awoke shivering, in darkness. His face was wet with tears.

3

Some seventy miles north of New Orleans, Ogilvie was still speculating on his encounter with Peter McDermott. The initial shock had had an almost physical impact. For more than an hour afterward, Ogilvie had driven tensely, yet at times scarcely conscious of the Jaguar's progress, first through the city, then across the Pontchartrain Causeway, and eventually northward on Interstate 59.

His eyes moved constantly to the rear-view mirror. He watched each set of headlights which appeared behind, expecting them to overtake swiftly, with the sound of a pursuing siren. Ahead, around each turn of the road, he prepared to brake at imagined police roadblocks.

His immediate assumption had been that the only possible reason for Peter McDermott's presence was to witness his own incriminating departure. How McDermott might have learned of the plan, Ogilvie had no idea. But apparently he had, and the house detective, like the greenest amateur, had ambled into a trap.

It was only later, as the countryside sped by in the lonely darkness of early morning, that he began to wonder: Could it have been coincidence after all?

Surely, if McDermott had been there with some intent, the Jaguar would have been pursued or halted at a roadblock long before now. The absence of any such attempt made coincidence more likely, in fact almost certain. At the thought, Ogilvie's spirits rose. He began to think gloatingly of the twenty-five thousand dollars which would be his at the journey's end.

He debated: Since everything had turned out so well thus far, would it be wiser to keep going? In just over an hour it would be daylight. His original plan had been to pull off the road and wait for darkness again before continuing. But there could be danger in a day of inaction. He was only halfway across Mississippi, still relatively close to New Orleans. Going on, of course, would involve the risk of being spotted, but he wondered just how great the risk was. Against the idea was his own physical strain from the previous day. Already he was tiring, the urge to sleep strong.

It was then it happened. Behind him, appearing as if magically, was a flashing red light. A siren shrieked imperiously.

It was the very thing which for the past several hours he had expected to happen. When it failed to, he had relaxed. Now, the reality was a double shock.

Instinctively, his accelerator foot slammed to the floor. Like a superbly powered arrow, the Jaguar surged forward. The speedometer needle swung sharply . . . to 70, 80, 85. At ninety, Ogilvie slowed for a bend. As he did, the flashing red light drew close behind. The siren, which had stopped briefly, wailed again. Then the red light moved sideways as the driver behind pulled out to pass.

It was useless, Ogilvie knew. Even if he outdistanced pursuit now, he could not avoid others forewarned ahead. Resignedly, he let his speed fall off.

He had a momentary impression of the other vehicle flashing by: a long limousine body, light colored, a dim interior light and a figure bending over another. Then the ambulance was gone, its flashing red beacon diminishing down the road ahead.

The incident left him shaken and convinced of his own tiredness. He decided that no matter how the alternate risks compared, he must pull off and remain there for the day. He was now past Macon, a small Mississippi community which had been his objective for the first night's driving. A glimmer of dawn was beginning to light the sky. He stopped to consult a map and shortly afterward turned off the highway onto a complex of minor roads.

Soon the road surface had deteriorated to a rutted,

grassy track. It was rapidly becoming light. Getting out of the car, Ogilvie surveyed the surrounding countryside.

It was sparsely wooded and desolate, with no habitation in sight. The nearest main road was more than a mile away. Not far ahead was a cluster of trees. Reconnoitering on foot, he discovered that the track went into the trees and ended.

The fat man gave one of his approving grunts. Returning to the Jaguar, he drove it forward carefully until foliage concealed it. He then made several checks, satisfying himself that the car could not be seen except at close quarters. When he had finished, he climbed into the back seat and slept.

4

For several minutes after coming awake, shortly before eight A.M., Warren Trent was puzzled to know why his spirits were instinctively buoyant. Then he remembered: this morning he would consummate the deal made yesterday with the Journeymen's Union. Defying pressures, glum predictions and sundry assorted obstacles, he had saved the St. Gregory—with only hours to spare—from engorgement by the O'Keefe hotel chain. It was a personal triumph. He pushed to the back of his mind a thought that the bizarre alliance between himself and the union might lead to even greater problems later on. If that happened, he would worry at the proper time; most important was removal of the immediate threat.

Getting out of bed, he looked down on the city from a window of his fifteenth-floor suite atop the hotel. Outside, it was another beautiful day, the sun—already high—shining from a near-cloudless sky.

He hummed softly to himself as he showered and afterward was shaved by Aloysius Royce. His employer's obvious cheerfulness was sufficiently unusual for Royce to raise his eyebrows in surprise, though Warren Trent—not yet far enough into the day for conversation—offered no enlightenment.

When he was dressed, on entering the living room he

immediately telephoned Royall Edwards. The comptroller, whom a switchboard operator located at his home, managed to convey both that he had worked all night and that his employer's telephone call had brought him from a well-earned breakfast. Ignoring the undertone of grievance, Warren Trent sought to discover what reaction had come from the two visiting accountants during the night. According to the comptroller's report, the visitors, though briefed on the hotel's current financial crisis, had uncovered nothing else extraordinary and seemed satisfied by Edwards' responses to their queries.

Reassured, Warren Trent left the comptroller to his breakfast. Perhaps even at this moment, he reflected, a report confirming his own representation of the St. Gregory's position was being telephoned north to Washington. He supposed he would receive direct word soon.

Almost at once the telephone rang.

Royce was about to serve breakfast from the room-service trolley which had arrived a few minutes earlier. Warren Trent motioned him to wait.

An operator's voice announced that the call was long distance. When he had identified himself, a second operator asked him to wait. At length the Journeymen's Union president came brusquely on the line.

"Trent?"

"Yes. Good morning!"

"I goddam well warned you yesterday not to hold back on information. You were stupid enough to try. Now I'm telling you: people who work trickery on me finish up wishing they hadn't been born. You're lucky this time that the whistle blew before a deal was closed. But this is a warning: don't ever try that game again!"

The unexpectedness, the harsh chilling voice, momentarily robbed Warren Trent of speech. Recovering, he protested, "In God's name, I've not the least idea what this is about."

"No idea, when there'd been a race riot in your goddamned hotel! When the story's spewed over every New York and Washington newspaper!"

It took several seconds to connect the angry harangue with Peter McDermott's report of the previous day.

"There was an incident yesterday morning, a small one. It was certainly not a race riot or anything near. At the time we talked I was unaware that it had happened. Even if I had known, it would not have occurred to me as important enough to mention. As to the New York newspapers, I haven't seen them."

"My members'll see them. If not those papers, then others across the country that'll carry the story by tonight. What's more, if I put money into a hotel that turns away nigs, they'd scream bloody murder along with every two-bit congressman who wants the colored vote."

"It's not the principle you care about, then. You don't mind what we do as long as it isn't noticed."

"What I care about is my business. So is where I invest union funds."

"Our transaction could be kept confidential."

"If you believe that, you're an even bigger fool than I thought."

It was true, Warren Trent conceded glumly: sooner or later news of an alliance would leak out. He tried another approach. "What occurred here yesterday is not unique. It's happened to Southern hotels before; it will happen again. A day or two afterward, attention moves on to something else."

"Maybe it does. But if your hotel got Journeymen's financing—after today—attention would damn soon switch back. And it's the kind I can do without."

"I'd like to be clear about this. Am I to understand that despite your accountants' inspection of our affairs last night, our arrangement of yesterday no longer stands?"

The voice from Washington said, "The trouble isn't with your books. The report my people made was affirmative. It's for the other reason all bets are off."

So after all, Warren Trent thought bitterly, through an incident which yesterday he had dismissed as trifling, the nectar of victory had been snatched away. Aware that whatever was said would make no difference now, he commented acidly, "You haven't always been so particular about using union funds."

There was a silence. Then the Journeymen's president said softly, "Someday you may be sorry for that."

Slowly, Warren Trent replaced the telephone. On a table nearby Aloysius Royce had spread open the airmailed New York newspapers. He indicated the *Herald Tribune*. "It's mostly in here. I don't see anything in the *Times*."

"They've later editions in Washington." Warren Trent skimmed the *Herald Tribune* headline and glanced briefly at the accompanying picture. It showed yesterday's scene in the St. Gregory lobby with Dr. Nicholas and Dr. Ingram as central figures. He supposed that later he would have to read the report in full. At the moment he had no stomach for it.

"Would you like me to serve breakfast now?"

Warren Trent shook his head. "I'm not hungry." His eyes flickered upward, meeting the young Negro's steady gaze. "I suppose you think I got what I deserved."

Royce considered. "Something like that, I guess. Mostly, I'd say, you don't accept the times we live in."

"If it's true, that needn't trouble you any more. From tomorrow I doubt if my opinion will count for much around here."

"I'm sorry for that part."

"What this means is that O'Keefe will take over." The older man walked to a window and stood looking out. He was silent, then said abruptly, "I imagine you heard the terms I was offered—among them that I'd continue to live here."

"Yes."

"Since it's to be that way, I suppose that when you graduate from law school next month, I'll still have to put up with you around the place. Instead of booting you out the way I should."

Aloysius Royce hesitated. Ordinarily, he would have tossed back a quick, barbed rejoinder. But he knew that what he was hearing was the plea of a defeated, lonely man for him to stay.

The decision troubled Royce; all the same, it would have to be made soon. For almost twelve years Warren Trent had treated him in many ways like a son. If he remained, he knew, his duties could become negligible outside of being a companion and confidant in the hours free from his own legal work. The life would be far from unpleasant. And yet there were other, conflicting pressures affecting the choice to go or stay.

"I haven't thought about it much," he lied. "Maybe I'd better."

Warren Trent reflected: all things, large and small, were changing, most of them abruptly. In his mind he had not the least doubt that Royce would leave him soon, just as control of the St. Gregory had finally eluded him. His sense of aloneness, and now of exclusion from the mainstream of events, was probably typical of people who had lived too long.

He informed Royce, "You can go, Aloysius. I'd like to be alone for a while."

In a few minutes, he decided, he would call Curtis O'Keefe and officially surrender.

5

Time magazine, whose editors recognized a newsy story when they read it in their morning papers, had hopped nimbly onto the St. Gregory civil rights incident. Their local stringer—a staffer on the New Orleans *States-Item*—was alerted and told to file everything he could get on local background. *Time*'s Houston bureau chief had been telephoned the previous night, soon after an early edition of the *Herald Tribune* broke the story in New York, and had flown in on an early flight.

Now both men were closeted with Herbie Chandler, the bell captain, in a cramped, main floor cubbyhole. Loosely known as a press room, it was sparsely furnished with a desk, telephone, and hat stand. The Houston man, as became his status, had the solitary chair.

Chandler, respectfully aware of *Time*'s liberality to those who smoothed its way, was reporting on a reconnaissance from which he had just returned.

"I checked about the dentists' meeting. They're closing it up tighter'n a drum. They've told the head floor waiter no one's to get in except members, not even wives, and they'll have their own people at the door checking names.

Before the meeting starts all the hotel help has to leave and doors'll be locked."

The bureau chief nodded. An eager, crewcut young man named Quaratone, he had already interviewed the dentists' president, Dr. Ingram. The bell captain's report confirmed what he had been told.

"Sure we're having an emergency general meeting," Dr. Ingram had said. "It was decided by our executive board last night, but it's to be a closed-door deal. If it was my say-so, son, you and anybody else could come in, and welcome. But some of my colleagues see it the other way. They think people'll speak more freely if they know the press isn't there. So I guess you'll have to sit that one out."

Quaratone, with no intention of sitting anything out, had thanked Dr. Ingram politely. With Herbie Chandler already purchased as an ally, Quaratone's immediate idea had been to employ an old ruse and attend the meeting in a borrowed bellboy's uniform. Chandler's latest report showed the need for a change of scheme.

"The room where the meeting will be held," Quaratone queried; "is at a good size convention hall?"

Chandler nodded. "The Dauphine Salon, sir. Seats three hundred. That's about how many they're expecting."

The *Time* man considered. Any meeting involving three hundred people would obviously cease to be secret the instant it finished. Afterward he could easily mingle with the emerging delegates and, by posing as one of them, learn what happened. That way, though, he would miss most of the minutiae of human interest which *Time* and its readers thrived on.

"Does the wotsit saloon have a balcony?"

"There's a small one, but they've already thought of it. I checked. There'll be a couple of convention people up there. Also, the p.a. microphones are being disconnected."

"Hell!" the local newspaperman objected. "What's this outfit afraid of—saboteurs?"

Quaratone said, thinking aloud, "Some of them want to speak their piece but avoid getting it on the record. Professional people—on racial issues anyway—don't usually take strong stands. Here they've already got themselves in a box by admitting to a choice between the drastic action of walking out or making a token gesture, just for appearance sake. To that extent I'd say the situation's unique." It was also, he thought, why there might be a better story here than he had supposed at first. More than ever he was determined to find a way of getting into the meeting.

Abruptly, he told Herbie Chandler, "I want a plan of the convention floor and the floor above. Not just a room layout, you understand, but a technical plan showing walls, ducts, ceiling spaces, all the rest. I want it fast because if we're to do any good we've less than an hour."

"I really don't know if there is such a thing, sir. In any case . . ." The bell captain stopped, watching Quaratone who was peeling off a succession of twenty-dollar bills.

The *Time* man handed five of the bills to Chandler. "Get to somebody in maintenance, engineering or whatever. Use that for now. I'll take care of you later. Meet me back here in half an hour, earlier if possible."

"Yessir!" Chandler's weasel face screwed into an obsequious smile.

Quaratone instructed the New Orleans reporter, "Carry on with the local angles, will you? Statements from city hall, leading citizens; better talk to the N.A.A.C.P. You know the kind of thing."

"I could write it in my sleep."

"Don't. And watch for human interest. Might be an idea if you could catch the mayor in the washroom. Washing his hands while he gave you a statement. Symbolic. Make a good lead."

"I'll try hiding in a toilet." The reporter went off cheerfully, aware that he too would be generously paid for his spare-time work.

Quaratone himself waited in the St. Gregory coffee shop. He ordered iced tea and sipped it absently, his mind on the developing story. It would not be a major one, but providing he could find some refreshing angles, it might rate a column and a half in next week's issue. Which would please him because in recent weeks a dozen or more of his carefully nurtured stories had either been rejected by New York or squeezed out during makeup of the magazine. This was not unusual and writing in a vacuum was a frustration which *Time-Life* staffers learned to live with. But Quaratone liked to get into print and be noticed where it counted.

He returned to the undersized press room. Within a few minutes Herbie Chandler arrived, shepherding a youngish, sharp-featured man in coveralls. The bell captain introduced him as Ches Ellis, a hotel maintenance worker. The newcomer shook hands diffidently with Quaratone, then, touching a roll of whiteprints under his arm, said uneasily, "I have to get these back."

"What I want won't take long." Quaratone helped Ellis roll out the plans, weighting the edges down. "Now, where's the Dauphine Salon?"

"Right here."

Chandler interjected, "I told him about the meeting, sir. How you want to hear what's happening without being in."

The *Time* man asked Ellis, "What's in the walls and ceilings?"

"Walls are solid. There's a gap between the ceiling and the next floor above, but if you're thinking of getting in there, it wouldn't work. You'd fall through the plaster."

"Check," said Quaratone, who had been considering just that. His finger stubbed the plan. "What are these lines?"

"Hot air outlet from the kitchen. Anywhere near that you'd roast."

"And this?"

Ellis stooped, studying the whiteprint. He consulted a second sheet. "Cold-air duct. Runs through the Dauphine Salon ceiling."

"Are there outlets to the room?"

"Three. Center and each end. You can see them marked."

"How big is the duct?"

The maintenance man considered. "I reckon about three feet square."

Quaratone said decisively, "I'd like you to get me in that duct. I want to get in it, and crawl out so I can hear and see what's going on below."

It took surprisingly little time. Ellis, at first reluctant, was prodded by Chandler into obtaining a second set of coveralls and a tool kit. The *Time* man changed quickly into coveralls and hoisted the tools. Then nervously, but without incident, Ellis shepherded him to an annex off the convention floor kitchen. The bell captain hovered discreetly out of sight. Quaratone had no idea how much of the hundred dollars Chandler had passed over to Ellis—he suspected not all—but it was evidently enough.

The progress through the kitchen—ostensibly of two hotel maintenance workers—went unnoticed. In the annex a metal grille, high on the wall, had been removed by Ellis in advance. A tall stepladder stood in front of an opening which the grille had covered. Without conversation, Quaratone ascended the stepladder and eased himself upward and in. There was, he discovered, room to crawl forward, using his elbows—but only just. Darkness, except for stray glimmers from the kitchen, was complete. He felt a breath of cool air on his face; the air pressure increased as his body filled more of the metal duct.

Ellis whispered after him, "Count four outlets! The fourth, fifth, and sixth are the Dauphine Salon. Keep the noise down, sir, or you'll be heard. I'll come back in half an hour; if you're not ready, half an hour after that."

Quaratone tried to turn his head and failed. It was a reminder that getting out would be harder than getting in. Calling back a low-voiced "Roger!" he began to move.

The metallic surface was hard on knees and elbows. It also had agonizingly sharp projections. Quaratone winced as the business end of a screw ripped the coveralls and cut painfully into his leg. Reaching back, he disengaged himself and moved forward cagily.

The air duct outlets were easy to spot because of light filtering upward. He eased over three, hoping grilles and duct were securely anchored. Nearing the fourth he could hear voices. The meeting, it seemed, had begun. To Quaratone's delight the voices came up clearly and, by craning, he could see a portion of the room below. The view, he thought, might be even better from the next outlet. It was. Now he could see more than half the crowded assemblage below, including a raised platform where the dentists' president, Dr. Ingram, was speaking. Reaching around, the *Time* man brought out a notebook and a ball-point pen, the latter with a tiny light in its tip.

". . . urge you," Dr. Ingram was asserting, "to take the strongest possible stand."

He paused, then continued, "Professional people like us who are by nature middle-of-the-roaders, have dilly-dallied too long on issues of human rights. Among ourselves we do not discriminate—at least most of the time—and in the past we have considered that to be enough. Generally, we've ignored events and pressures outside our own ranks. Our reasoning has been that we are professional, medical men with time for little else. Well, maybe that's true, even if convenient. But here and now—like it or not—we *are* involved up to our wisdom teeth."

The little doctor paused, his eyes searching the faces of his audience. "You have already heard of the unpardonable insult by this hotel to our distinguished colleague, Dr. Nicholas—an insult in direct defiance of civil rights law. In retaliation, as your president, I have recommended drastic action. It is that we should cancel our convention and walk from this hotel en masse."

There was a gasp of surprise from several sections of the room. Dr. Ingram continued, "Most of you have already learned of this proposal. To others, who arrived this morning, it is new. Let me say to both groups that the step I have proposed involves inconvenience, disappointment— to me, no less than to you—and a professional as well as a public loss. But there are occasions, involving matters of great conscience, when nothing less than the most forceful action will suffice. I believe this to be one. It is also the only way in which the strength of our feelings will be demonstrated and by which we shall prove, unmistakably, that in matters of human rights this profession is not to be trifled with again."

From the floor came several cries of "hear, hear!" but, as well, a rumble of dissent.

Near the center of the room a burly figure lumbered to his feet. Quaratone, leaning forward from his vantage point, had an impression of jowls, a thick-lipped smile and heavy-rimmed glasses. The burly man announced, "I'm from Kansas City." There was a good-natured cheer which was acknowledged with the wave of a pudgy hand. "I've just one question for the doctor. Will he be the one who'll explain to my little woman—who's been counting on this trip like a lot of other wives, I reckon—why it is that having just got here we're to turn tail and go home?"

An outraged voice protested, "That isn't the point!" It was drowned out by ironic cheers and laughter from others in the hall.

"Yessir," the burly man said, "I'd like him to be the one to tell my wife." Looking pleased with himself, he sat down.

Dr. Ingram was on his feet, red faced, indignant. "Gentlemen, this is an urgent, serious matter. We have already delayed action for twenty-four hours which in my opinion is at least half a day too long."

There was applause, but brief and scattered. A number of other voices spoke at once. Beside Dr. Ingram, the meeting's chairman pounded with a gavel.

Several speakers followed, deploring the expulsion of Dr. Nicholas, but leaving unanswered the question of reprisal. Then, as if by assent, attention focused on a slim, dapper figure standing with a suggestion of authority near the front of the hall. Quaratone missed the name which the chairman announced, but caught ". . . second vice-president and member of our executive board."

The new speaker began in a dry crisp voice, "It was at my urging, supported by several fellow executive members, that this meeting is being held *in camera*. As a result, we may speak freely, knowing that whatever we say will not be recorded, and perhaps misrepresented, outside this room. This arrangement, I may add, was strongly opposed by our esteemed president, Dr. Ingram."

From the platform, Dr. Ingram growled, "What are you afraid of—involvement?"

Ignoring the question, the dapper man continued, "I yield to no one in my personal distaste for discrimination. Some of my best . . ."—he hesitated—". . . my best-liked associates are those of other creeds and races. Furthermore, I deplore with Dr. Ingram the incident of yesterday. It is merely on the question of procedure at this moment that we disagree. Dr. Ingram—if I may emulate his choice of metaphor—favors extraction. My own view is to treat

more mildly for an unpleasant but localized infection."
There was a ripple of laughter at which the speaker smiled.

"I cannot believe that our unfortunately absent colleague, Dr. Nicholas, would gain in the least from cancellation of our convention. Certainly, as a profession, we would lose. Furthermore—and since we are in private session I say this frankly—I do not believe that as an organization the broad issue of race relations is any of our concern."

A single voice near the rear protested, "Of course it's our concern! Isn't it everybody's?" But through most of the room there was merely attentive silence.

The speaker shook his head. "Whatever stands we take or fail to, should be as individuals. Naturally we must support our own people where necessary, and in a moment I shall suggest certain steps in the case of Dr. Nicholas. But otherwise I agree with Dr. Ingram that we are professional medical men with time for little else."

Dr. Ingram sprang to his feet. "I did not say that! I pointed out that it's a view which has been held in the past. I happen to disagree strongly."

The dapper man shrugged. "Nevertheless the statement was made."

"But not with that kind of implication. I will not have my words twisted!" The little doctor's eyes flashed angrily. "Mr. Chairman, we're talking here glibly, using words like 'unfortunate,' 'regrettable.' Can't all of you see that this is more than just that; that we are considering a question of human rights and decency? If you had been here yesterday and witnessed, as I witnessed, the indignity to a colleague, a friend, a good man . . ."

There were cries of "Order! order!" As the chairman pounded with his gavel, reluctantly, his face flushed, Dr. Ingram subsided.

The dapper man inquired politely, "May I continue?" The chairman nodded.

"Thank you. Gentlemen, I will make my suggestions briefly. First, I propose that our future conventions shall be held in locales where Dr. Nicholas and others of his race will be accepted without question or embarrassment. There are plenty of places which the remainder of us, I am sure, will find acceptable. Secondly, I propose that we pass a resolution disapproving the action of this hotel in rejecting Dr. Nicholas, after which we should continue with our convention as planned."

On the platform, Dr. Ingram shook his head in disbelief.

The speaker consulted a single sheet of paper in his hand. "In conjunction with several other members of your executive board, I have drafted a resolution . . ."

In his eyrie Quaratone had ceased to listen. The resolution itself was unimportant. Its substance was predictable; if necessary he could obtain a text later. He was watching, instead, the faces of the listeners below. They were average faces, he decided, of reasonably educated men. They mirrored relief. Relief, Quaratone thought, from the need for the kind of action—uncomfortable, unaccustomed— which Dr. Ingram had proposed. The salve of words, paraded primly in democratic style, offered a way out. Conscience would be relieved, convenience intact. There had been some mild protest—a single speaker supporting Dr. Ingram—but it was short-lived. Already the meeting had settled down to what looked like becoming a prolix discussion of the resolution's wording.

The *Time* man shivered—a reminder that as well as other discomforts, he had been close to an hour in a cold air duct. But the effort had been worth while. He had a live story which the stylists in New York could rewrite searingly. He also had a notion that this week his work would not be squeezed out.

6

Peter McDermott heard of the Dentistry Congress decision to continue with its convention almost as soon as the *in-camera* meeting ended. Because of the obvious importance of the meeting to the hotel, he had stationed a convention department clerk outside the Dauphine Salon with instructions to report promptly whatever could be learned. A moment or two ago the clerk telephoned to say that from the conversation of emerging delegates it was obvious that the proposal to cancel the convention had been overruled.

Peter supposed that for the hotel's sake he should be pleased. Instead, he had a feeling of depression. He wondered about the effect on Dr. Ingram whose strong motivation and forthrightness had clearly been repudiated.

Peter reflected wryly that Warren Trent's cynical assessment of the situation yesterday had proven accurate after all. He supposed he should let the hotel proprietor know.

As Peter entered the managing director's section of the executive suite, Christine looked up from her desk. She smiled warmly, reminding him how much he had wanted to talk with her last evening.

She inquired, "Was it a nice party?" When he hesitated, Christine seemed amused. "You haven't forgotten already?"

He shook his head. "Everything was fine. I missed you, though—and still feel badly about getting the arrangements mixed."

"We're twenty-four hours older. You can stop now."

"If you're free, perhaps I could make up for it tonight."

"It's snowing invitations!" Christine said. "Tonight I'm having dinner with Mr. Wells."

Peter's eyebrows went up. "He *has* recovered."

"Not enough to leave the hotel, which is why we're dining here. If you work late, why not join us afterward?"

"If I can, I will." He indicated the closed double doors of the hotel proprietor's office. "Is W.T. available?"

"You can go in. I hope it isn't problems, though. He seems depressed this morning."

"I've some news may cheer him. The dentists just voted against canceling out." He said more soberly, "I suppose you saw the New York papers."

"Yes, I did. I'd say we got what we deserved."

He nodded agreement.

"I also saw the local papers," Christine said. "There's nothing new on that awful hit-and-run. I keep thinking about it."

Peter said sympathetically, "I have too." Once more the scene of three nights earlier—the roped-off, floodlighted road, with police searching grimly for clues—came sharply back into focus. He wondered if the police investigation would uncover the offending car and driver. Perhaps by now both were safely clear and past detection, though he

265

hoped not. The thought of one crime was a reminder of another. He must remember to ask Ogilvie if there had been any developments overnight in the hotel robbery investigation. He was surprised, come to think of it, that he had not heard from the chief house officer before now.

With a final smile for Christine, he knocked at the door of Warren Trent's office and went in.

The news which Peter brought seemed to make little impression. The hotel proprietor nodded absently, as if reluctant to switch his thoughts from whatever private reverie he had been immersed in. He seemed about to speak—on another subject, Peter sensed—then, as abruptly, changed his mind. After only the briefest of conversation, Peter left.

Albert Wells had been right, Christine thought, in predicting Peter McDermott's invitation for tonight. She had a momentary regret at having arranged—deliberately—to be unavailable.

The exchange reminded her of the stratagem she had thought of yesterday to make the evening inexpensive for Albert Wells. She telephoned Max, head waiter of the main dining room.

"Max," Christine said, "your evening dinner prices are outrageous."

"I don't set them, Miss Francis. Sometimes I wish I did."

"You haven't been crowded lately?"

"Some nights," the head waiter replied, "I feel like I'm Livingstone waiting for Stanley. I'll tell you, Miss Francis, people are getting smarter. They know that hotels like this have one central kitchen, and whichever of our restaurants they eat in, they'll get the same kind of food, cooked the same way by the same chefs. So why not sit where prices are lower, even if the service isn't as fancy?"

"I've a friend," Christine said, "who likes dining-room service—an elderly gentleman named Mr. Wells. We'll be in for dinner tonight. I want you to make sure that his bill is light, though not so small that he'll notice. The difference you can put on my account."

The head waiter chuckled. "Say! You're the kind of girl I'd like to know myself."

She retorted, "With you I wouldn't do it, Max. Everybody knows you're one of the two wealthiest people in the hotel."

"Who's supposed to be the other?"

"Isn't it Herbie Chandler?"

"You do me no favor in linking my name with that one."

"But you'll take care of Mr. Wells?"

"Miss Francis, when we present his bill he'll think he ate in the automat."

She hung up, laughing, aware that Max would handle the situation with tact and good sense.

With incredulous, seething anger, Peter McDermott read Ogilvie's memo, slowly, for the second time.

The memo had been waiting on his desk when he returned from the brief meeting with Warren Trent.

Dated and time-stamped last night, it had presumably been left in Ogilvie's office for collection with this morning's interoffice mail. Equally clear was that both the timing and method of delivery were planned so that when he received the memo it would be impossible to take any action—at least for the time being—concerning its contents.

It read:

Mr. P. McDermott

Subject: Vacation

The undersigned begs to report I am taking four days leave commencing immediately. From the seven that is due, for personal urgent reasons.

W. Finegan, dep. chief house officer, is advised re robbery, steps taken, etc. etc. Also can act with all other matters.

Undersigned will return to duty Monday next.

> *Yours truly,*
> T. I. Ogilvie
> Chief House Officer.

Peter remembered indignantly that it was less than twenty-four hours since Ogilvie conceded that a professional hotel thief was most likely operating within the St. Gregory. At the time, Peter had urged the house officer to move into the hotel for a few days, a suggestion the fat man had rejected. Even then, Ogilvie must have known of his intention to leave within a few hours, but had kept silent. Why? Obviously, because he realized Peter would object strongly, and he had no stomach for argument and perhaps delay.

The memo said *"personal urgent reasons."* Well, Peter theorized, that much was probably true. Even Ogilvie, despite his vaunted intimacy with Warren Trent, would realize that his absence at this time, without warning, would precipitate a major showdown on return.

But what kind of personal reason was involved? Clearly nothing straightforward, to be brought out in the open and discussed. Or it would not have been handled this way. Hotel business notwithstanding, a genuine personal crisis of an employee would be dealt with sympathetically. It always was.

So it had to be something else which Ogilvie could not disclose.

Even that, Peter thought, was no concern of his except to the extent that it obstructed efficient running of the hotel. Since it did, however, he was entitled to be curious. He decided he would make an effort to learn where the chief house officer had gone and why.

He buzzed for Flora, holding up the memo as she came in.

She made a doleful face. "I read it. I thought you'd be annoyed."

"If you can," Peter said, "I want you to find out where he is. Try his home telephone, then any other places we happen to know about. Find out if anyone's seen him today or if he's expected. Leave messages. If you locate Ogilvie, I'll talk to him myself."

Flora wrote on her note pad.

"Another thing—call the garage. I happened to be walking by the hotel last night. Our friend drove out around one o'clock—in a Jaguar. It's possible he told someone where he was going."

When Flora left, he sent for the deputy chief house officer, Finegan, a gaunt, slow-speaking New Englander who deliberated before answering Peter's impatient questions.

No, he had no idea where Mr. Ogilvie had gone. It was only late yesterday that Finegan was informed by his superior that he would be in charge for the next few days. Yes, last night there had been continuous patrols through the hotel, but no suspicious activity was observed. Nor was there any report this morning of illicit entry into rooms. No, there had been no further word from the New Orleans police department. Yes, Finegan would personally follow up with the police as Mr. McDermott suggested. Certainly, if Finegan heard from Mr. Ogilvie, Mr. McDermott would be informed at once.

Peter dismissed Finegan. At the moment there was nothing more to be done, though Peter's anger with Ogilvie was still intense.

It had not moderated a few minutes later when Flora announced on the office intercom, "Miss Marsha Preyscott on line two."

"Tell her I'm busy, I'll call later." Peter checked himself. "Never mind, I'll talk."

He picked up the telephone. Marsha's voice said brightly, "I heard that."

Irritably he resolved to remind Flora that the telephone "hold" button should be down when the intercom was open. "I'm sorry," he said. "It's a low-grade morning in contrast to a great night before."

"I'll bet the first thing hotel managers learn is to make fast recoveries like that."

"Some may. But this is me."

He sensed her hesitate. Then she said, "Was it all great —the evening?"

"All of it."

"Good! Then I'm ready to keep my promise."

"My impression was you had."

"No," Marsha said, "I promised some New Orleans history. We could start this afternoon."

He was about to say no; that it was impossible to leave the hotel, then realized he wanted to go. Why not? He seldom took the two full days off duty he was entitled to each week and lately had worked plenty of extra hours as well. A brief absence could easily be managed.

"All right," he said. "Let's see how many centuries we can cover between two o'clock and four."

7

Twice during the twenty-minute prayer session before breakfast in his suite, Curtis O'Keefe found his thoughts wandering. It was a familiar sign of restlessness for which he apologized briefly to God, though not belaboring the point since an instinct to be ever moving on was a part of the hotel magnate's nature, and presumably divinely shaped.

It was a relief, however, to remember that this was his final day in New Orleans. He would leave for New York tonight and Italy tomorrow. The destination there, for himself and Dodo, was the Naples-O'Keefe Hotel. Besides the change of scene, it would be satisfying to be in one of his own houses once more. Curtis O'Keefe had never understood the point, which his critics made, that it was possible to travel around the world, staying at O'Keefe Hotels without ever leaving the U.S.A. Despite his attachment to foreign travel, he liked familiar things about him—American décor, with only minor concessions to local color; American plumbing; American food and—most of the time—American people. O'Keefe establishments provided them all.

Nor was it important that a week from now he would be as impatient to leave Italy as he was, at this moment, to depart from New Orleans. There were plenty of places within his own empire—the Taj Mahal O'Keefe, O'Keefe Lisbon, Adelaide O'Keefe, O'Keefe Copenhagen, and others—where a visit from the panjandrum, although nowadays not essential to the chain's efficient running, would stimulate business as a cathedral's might quicken from the sojourn of a pope.

Later, of course, he would return to New Orleans, probably in a month or two when the St. Gregory—by then the O'Keefe-St. Gregory—was overhauled and molded to the conformity of an O'Keefe hotel. His arrival for the inaugural ceremonies would be triumphal, with fanfare, a civic welcome and coverage by press, radio, and television. As usual on such occasions, he would bring a retinue of celebrities, including Hollywood stars, not difficult to recruit for a lavish free-loading junket.

Thinking about it, Curtis O'Keefe was impatient for these things to happen soon. He was also mildly frustrated at not having received, so far, Warren Trent's official acceptance of the proffered terms of two nights earlier. It was now mid-morning of Thursday. The noon deadline agreed to was less than ninety minutes away. Obviously, for reasons of his own, the St. Gregory's proprietor intended to wait until the last possible moment before acceptance.

O'Keefe prowled restlessly around the suite. Half an hour earlier Dodo had left on a shopping expedition for which he had given her several hundred dollars in large bills. Her purchases, he suggested, should include some lightweight clothes since Naples was likely to be even hotter than New Orleans, and there would be no time for shopping in New York. Dodo thanked him appreciatively, as she always did, though strangely without the glowing enthusiasm she had shown yesterday during their boat trip around the harbor which cost a mere six dollars. Women, he thought, were perplexing creatures.

He stopped at a window, looking out, when across the living room the telephone rang. He reached it in half a dozen strides.

"Yes?"

He expected to hear the voice of Warren Trent. Instead, an operator announced that the call was long distance. A moment later the nasal Californian drawl of Hank Lemnitzer came on the line.

"That you, Mr. O'Keefe?"

"Yes, it is." Irrationally, Curtis O'Keefe wished that his West Coast representative had not found it necessary to telephone twice within twenty-four hours.

"Got some great news for you."

"What kind of news?"

"I inked a deal for Dodo."

"I thought I made it clear yesterday that I insist on something special for Miss Lash."

"How special can you get, Mr. O'Keefe? This is the greatest; a real break. Dodo's a lucky kid."

"Tell me."

"Walt Curzon's shooting a remake of *You Can't Take It With You*. Remember?—we put money in his pot."

"I remember."

"Yesterday I found out Walt needed a girl to play the old Ann Miller role. It's a good supporting part. Fits Dodo like a tight brassiere."

Curtis O'Keefe wished peevishly once again that Lemnitzer would be subtler in his choice of words.

"I assume there'll be a screen test."

"Sure will."

"Then how do we know Curzon will agree to the casting?"

"Are you kidding? Don't underrate your influence, Mr. O'Keefe. Dodo's in. Besides, I've lined up Sandra Straughan to work with her. You know Sandra?"

"Yes." O'Keefe was well aware of Sandra Straughan. She had a reputation as one of filmdom's most accomplished dramatic coaches. Among other achievements, she possessed a remarkable record of accepting unknown girls with influential sponsors and shaping them into box office princesses.

"I'm real glad for Dodo," Lemnitzer said. "She's a kid I've always liked. Only thing is, we have to move fast."

"How fast?"

"They need her yesterday, Mr. O'Keefe. It all fits, though, with the rest I've arranged."

"The rest of what?"

"Jenny LaMarsh." Hank Lemnitzer sounded puzzled. "You hadn't forgotten?"

"No." O'Keefe had certainly not forgotten the witty and beautiful Vassar brunette who had so impressed him a month or two ago. But after yesterday's talk with Lemnitzer he had shelved thoughts of Jenny LaMarsh for the time being.

"Everything's fixed, Mr. O'Keefe. Jenny flies to New York tonight; she'll join you there tomorrow. We'll switch Dodo's Naples reservations to Jenny, then Dodo can fly here direct from New Orleans. Simple, eh?"

It was indeed simple. So simple, in fact, that O'Keefe could find no flaw in the plan. He wondered why he wanted to.

"You assure me positively that Miss Lash will get the part?"

"Mr. O'Keefe, I swear it on my mother's grave."

"Your mother isn't dead."

"Then my grandmother's." There was a pause, then, as if with sudden perception, Lemnitzer said, "If you're worried about telling Dodo, why don't I do it? You just go out for a couple of hours. I'll call her, fix everything. That way—no fuss, no farewells."

"Thank you. I'm quite capable of handling the matter personally."

"Suit yourself, Mr. O'Keefe. Just trying to help."

"Miss Lash will telegraph you the time of her arrival in Los Angeles. You'll meet the flight?"

"Sure thing. It'll be great to see Dodo. Well, Mr. O'Keefe, have a swell time in Naples. I envy you having Jenny."

Without acknowledgment, O'Keefe hung up.

Dodo returned breathlessly, loaded with packages and followed by a grinning bellboy, similarly burdened.

"I have to go back, Curtie. There's more."

O'Keefe said gruffly, "You could have had all this delivered."

"Oh, this is more exciting! Like Christmas." She told the bellboy, "We're going to Naples. That's in Italy."

O'Keefe gave the bellboy a dollar and waited until he had gone.

Disentangling herself from packages, Dodo flung her arms impulsively around O'Keefe's neck. She kissed him on both cheeks. "Did you miss me? Gee, Curtie, I'm happy!"

273

O'Keefe disengaged her arms gently. "Let's sit down. I want to tell you about some changes in plan. I also have some good news."

"We're going sooner!"

He shook his head. "It concerns you more than me. The fact is, my dear, you're being given a movie role. It's something I've been working on. I heard this morning—it's all arranged."

He was aware of Dodo's innocent blue eyes regarding him.

"I'm assured it's a very good part; in fact, I insisted that it should be. If things go well, as I expect them to, it could be the beginning of something very big for you." Curtis O'Keefe stopped, conscious of a hollowness to his own words.

Dodo said slowly, "I guess it means . . . I have to go away."

"Unfortunately, my dear, it does."

"Soon?"

"I'm afraid—tomorrow morning. You'll fly directly to Los Angeles. Hank Lemnitzer will meet you."

Dodo moved her head slowly in assent. The slim fingers of one hand went absently to her face, brushing back a strand of ash-blond hair. It was a simple movement yet, like so many of Dodo's, profoundly sensuous. Unreasonably, O'Keefe experienced a jealous twinge at the thought of Hank Lemnitzer with Dodo. Lemnitzer, who had managed the ground work for most of his employer's liaisons in the past, would never dare to trifle with a chosen favorite in advance. But afterward . . . Afterward was something else again. He thrust the thought away.

"I want you to know, my dear, that losing you is a great blow to me. But we have to think of your future."

"Curtie, it's all right." Dodo's eyes were still upon him. Despite their innocence, he had an absurd notion they had penetrated to the truth. "It's all right. You don't have to worry."

"I'd hoped—about the movie role—you might be more pleased."

"I am, Curtie! Gee, I really am! I think it's swell the way you always do the sweetest things."

The reaction bolstered his own confidence. "It's really a tremendous opportunity. I'm sure you'll do well, and of course I shall follow your career closely." He resolved to concentrate his thoughts on Jenny LaMarsh.

"I guess . . ." There was the slightest catch in Dodo's voice. "I guess you'll go tonight. Before me."

Making an instantaneous decision, he answered, "No, I'll cancel my flight and leave tomorrow morning. Tonight will be a special evening for us both."

As Dodo looked up gratefully, the telephone rang. With a sense of relief for something else to do, he answered it.

"Mr. O'Keefe?" a pleasant woman's voice inquired.

"Yes."

"This is Christine Francis—Mr. Warren Trent's assistant. Mr. Trent wondered if it would be convenient for him to come to see you now."

O'Keefe glanced at his watch. It showed a few minutes before noon.

"Yes," he acknowledged. "I'll see Mr. Trent. Tell him to come."

Replacing the telephone, he smiled at Dodo. "It seems, my dear, we each have something to celebrate—you a glittering future, and me, a new hotel."

8

An hour or so earlier Warren Trent sat brooding behind the closed double doors of his office in the executive suite. Several times already this morning he had reached out for the telephone with the intention of calling Curtis O'Keefe, accepting the latter's terms for take-over of the hotel. There no longer seemed any cause for delay. The Journeymen's Union had been the final hope of alternate financing. The brusque rejection from that source had crumbled Warren Trent's last resistance against absorption by the O'Keefe behemoth.

Yet on each occasion, after the initial motion of his hand, Warren Trent held back. He was like a prisoner, he mused, condemned to death at a specific hour but with the choice of suicide beforehand. He accepted the inevitable. He realized that he would end his own tenure because there was no alternative. Yet human nature urged him to cling to each remaining moment until all were gone and the need for decision ended.

He had been closest to capitulation when the arrival of Peter McDermott forestalled him. McDermott reported the decision of the Congress of American Dentistry to continue its convention, a fact which did not surprise Warren Trent since he had predicted it the day before. But now the entire affair seemed remote and unimportant. He was glad when McDermott left.

Afterward, for a while, he fell into a reverie, remembering past triumphs and the satisfactions they had brought. That had been the time—not so long ago, really—when his house was sought by the great and near-great—presidents, crowned heads, nobility, resplendent women and distinguished men, the nabobs of power and wealth, famous and infamous—all with one distinction: they commanded attention and received it. And where these élite led, others followed, until the St. Gregory was both a mecca and a machine for making gold.

When memories were all one had—or seemed likely to have—it was wise to savor them. Warren Trent hoped that for the hour or so which remained of his proprietorship he would be undisturbed.

The hope proved vain.

Christine Francis came in quietly, as usual sensing his mood. "Mr. Emile Dumaire would like to speak with you. I wouldn't have disturbed you, but he insisted it's urgent."

Trent grunted. The vultures were gathering, he thought. Though on second thoughts, perhaps the simile was hardly fair. A good deal of money from the Industrial Merchants Bank, of which Emile Dumaire was president, was tied up in the St. Gregory Hotel. It was also Industrial Merchants which, months earlier, had refused an extension of credit as well as a larger loan for refinancing. Well, Dumaire and his fellow directors had nothing to worry about now. With the impending deal their money would be forthcoming. Warren Trent supposed he should give that reassurance.

He reached for the telephone.

"No," Christine said. "Mr. Dumaire is here, waiting outside."

Warren Trent stopped, surprised. It was highly unusual for Emile Dumaire to leave the fastness of his bank to make a personal call on anyone.

A moment later Christine ushered the visitor in, closing the door as she left.

Emile Dumaire, short, portly and with a fringe of curly white hair, had an unbroken line of Creole ancestry. Yet he looked—perversely—as if he had stepped from the pages of *Pickwick Papers*. His manner had a pompous fussiness to match.

"I apologize, Warren, for the abrupt intrusion without an appointment. However, the nature of my business left little time for niceties."

They shook hands perfunctorily. The hotel proprietor waved his visitor to a chair.

"What business?"

"If you don't object, I'd prefer to take things in order. First, permit me to say how sorry I was that it was not feasible to accede to your loan request. Unfortunately, the sum and terms were far beyond our resources or established policy."

Warren Trent nodded noncommittally. He had little liking for the banker, though he had never made the mistake of underrating him. Beneath the bumbling affectations —which lulled and deceived many—was a capable, shrewd mind.

"However, I am here today with a purpose which I hope may offset some of the unfortunate aspects of that earlier occasion."

"That," Warren Trent asserted, "is extremely unlikely."

"We'll see." From a slim briefcase the banker extracted several sheets of ruled paper covered with penciled notes. "It is my understanding that you have received an offer for this hotel from the O'Keefe Corporation."

"You don't need the FBI to tell you that."

The banker smiled. "You wouldn't care to inform me of the terms?"

"Why should I?"

"Because," Emile Dumaire said carefully, "I am here to make a counter-offer."

"If that's the case, I'd have even less reason to speak out. What I will tell you is that I've agreed to give the O'Keefe people an answer by noon today."

"Quite so. My information was to that effect, which is the reason for my abrupt appearance here. Incidentally, I apologize for not being earlier, but my information and instructions have taken some time to assemble."

The news of an eleventh-hour offer—at least, from the present source—did not excite Warren Trent. He supposed that a local group of investors, for whom Dumaire was spokesman, had combined in an attempt to buy in cheaply now and sell out later with a capital gain. Whatever the suggested terms, they could hardly match the offer of O'Keefe. Nor was Warren Trent's own position likely to be improved.

The banker consulted his penciled notes. "It is my understanding that the terms offered by O'Keefe Corporation are a purchase price of four millions. Of this, two millions would be applied to renewal of the present mortgage, the balance to be a million cash and a million dollars in a new issue of O'Keefe stock. There's an additional rumor that you personally would be given some kind of life tenancy of your quarters in the hotel."

Warren Trent's face reddened with anger. He slammed a clenched fist hard upon the surface of his desk. "Goddam, Emile! Don't play cat and mouse with me!"

"If I appeared to, I'm sorry."

"For God's sake! If you know the details already, why ask?"

"Frankly," Dumaire said, "I was hoping for the confirmation that you just gave me. Also, the offer I am authorized to make is somewhat better."

He had fallen, Warren Trent realized, for an ancient, elementary gambit. But he was indignant that Dumaire should have seen fit to play it on him.

It was also obvious that Curtis O'Keefe had a defector in his own organization, possibly someone at O'Keefe headquarters who was privy to high-level policy. In a way, there was ironic justice in the fact that Curtis O'Keefe, who used espionage as a business tool, should be spied upon himself.

"Just how are the terms better? And by whom are they offered?"

"To reply to the second question first—at present I am not at liberty to say."

Warren Trent snorted, "I do business with people I can see, not ghosts."

"I am no ghost," Dumaire reminded him. "Moreover you have the bank's assurance that the offer I am empowered to make is bona fide, and that the parties whom the bank represents have unimpeachable credentials."

Still irked by the stratagem of a few moments earlier, the hotel proprietor said, "Let's get to the point."

"I was about to do so." The banker shuffled his notes. "Basically, the valuation which my principals place upon this hotel is identical with that of the O'Keefe Corporation."

"That's hardly surprising, since you had O'Keefe's figures."

"In other respects, however, there are several significant differences."

For the first time since the beginning of the interview, Warren Trent was conscious of a mounting interest in what the banker had to say.

"First, my principals have no wish that you should sever your personal connection with the St. Gregory Hotel or divorce yourself from its financial structure. Second, it would be their intention—insofar as is commercially feasible—to maintain the hotel's independence and existing character."

Warren Trent gripped the arms of his chair tightly. He glanced at a wall clock to his right. It showed a quarter to twelve.

"They would, however, insist on acquiring a majority of the outstanding common shares—a reasonable requirement in the circumstances—to provide effective management control. You yourself would thus revert to the status of largest minority stock holder. A further requirement would be your immediate resignation as president and managing director. Could I trouble you for a glass of water?"

Warren Trent filled a single glass from the Thermos jug on his desk. "What do you have in mind—that I become a busboy? Or perhaps assistant doorman?"

"Scarcely that." Emile Dumaire sipped from the glass, then regarded it. "It has always struck me as quite remarkable how our muddy Mississippi can become such pleasant tasting water."

"Get on with it!"

The banker smiled. "My principals propose that immediately following your resignation you be appointed chairman of the board, initially for a two-year term."

"A mere figurehead, I suppose!"

"Perhaps. But it would seem to me that there are worse things. Or perhaps you'd prefer the figurehead to be Mr. Curtis O'Keefe."

The hotel proprietor was silent.

"I am further instructed to inform you that my principals will match any offer of a personal nature concerning accommodation here which you may have received from the O'Keefe Corporation. Now, as to the question of stock transference and refinancing. I'd like to go into that in some detail."

As the banker talked on, closely consulting his notes, Warren Trent had a sense of weariness and unreality. Out of memory an incident came to him from long ago. Once, as a small boy, he had attended a country fair, clutching a few hoarded pennies to spend on the mechanical rides. There had been one that he had ventured on—a cake walk. It was a form of amusement, he supposed, which had long since passed into limbo. He remembered it as a platform with a multiple-hinged floor which moved continually—now up, now down, now tilting forward, backward, forward . . . so that perspective was never level, and for the cost of a penny one had an imminent chance of falling before attaining the far end. Beforehand it had seemed exciting, but he remembered that nearing the finish of the cake walk he had wanted, more than anything else, merely to get off.

The past weeks had been like a cake walk too. At the

beginning he had been confident, then abruptly the floor had canted away beneath him. It had risen, as hope revived, then slanted away again. Near the end the Journeymen's Union held a promise of stability, then abruptly that too had collapsed on lunatic hinges.

Now, unexpectedly, the cake walk had stabilized once more and all he wanted to do was get off.

Later on, Warren Trent knew, his feelings would change, his personal interest in the hotel reviving, as it always had. But for the moment he was conscious only of relief that, one way or another, the burden of responsibility was shifting on. Along with relief was curiosity.

Who, among the city's business leaders, was behind Emile Dumaire? Who might care enough to run the financial risk of maintaining the St. Gregory as a traditionally independent house? Mark Preyscott, perhaps? Could the department-store chieftain be seeking to augment his already widespread interests? Warren Trent recalled having heard from someone, during the past few days, that Mark Preyscott was in Rome. That might account for the indirect approach. Well, whoever it was, he supposed he would learn soon enough.

The stock transaction which the banker was spelling out was fair. Compared with the offer from O'Keefe, Warren Trent's personal cash settlement would be smaller, but offset by a retained equity in the hotel. In contrast, the O'Keefe terms would cast him adrift from the St. Gregory's affairs entirely.

As to an appointment as chairman of the board, while it might be a token post only, devoid of power, he would at least be an inside, privileged spectator to whatever might ensue. Nor was the prestige to be dismissed lightly.

"That," Emile Dumaire concluded, "is the sum and substance. As to the offer's integrity, I have already stated that it is guaranteed by the bank. Furthermore, I am prepared to give you a notarized letter of intention, this afternoon, to that effect."

"And completion, if I agree?"

The banker pursed his lips, considering. "There is no reason why papers could not be drawn quickly, besides which the matter of the impending mortgage expiry lends some urgency. I would say completion tomorrow at this time."

"And also at that time, no doubt, I would be told the purchaser's identity."

"That," Emile Dumaire conceded, "would be essential to the transaction."

"If tomorrow, why not now?"

The banker shook his head. "I am bound by my instructions."

Briefly, in Warren Trent's mind, his old ill temper flared. He was tempted to insist on revelation as a condition of assent. Then reason argued: Did it matter, providing the stipulations pledged were met? Disputation, too, would involve effort to which he felt unequal. Once more, the weariness of a few minutes earlier engulfed him.

He sighed, then said simply, "I accept."

9

Incredulously, wrathfully, Curtis O'Keefe faced Warren Trent.

"You have the effrontery to stand there telling me you've sold elsewhere!"

They were in the living room of O'Keefe's suite. Immediately following the departure of Emile Dumaire, Christine Francis had telephoned to make the appointment which Warren Trent was keeping now. Dodo, her expression uncertain, hovered behind O'Keefe.

"You may call it effrontery," Warren Trent replied. "As far as I'm concerned it's information. You may also be interested to know that I have not sold entirely, but have retained a substantial interest in the hotel."

"Then you'll lose it!" O'Keefe's face flushed with rage. It had been many years since anything he wished to buy had been denied him. Even now, obsessed with bitterness and disappointment, he could not believe the rejection to be true. "By God! I swear I'll break you."

Dodo reached out. Her hand touched O'Keefe's sleeve. "Curtie!"

He wrenched the arm free. "Shut up!" A vein pulsed visibly across his temples. His hands were clenched.

"You're excited, Curtie. You shouldn't . . ."

"Damn you! Keep out of this!"

Dodo's eyes went appealingly to Warren Trent. They had the effect of curbing Trent's own temper which had been about to erupt.

He told O'Keefe, "You may do what you please. But I'd remind you you have no divine right of purchase. Also, you came here of your own accord with no invitation from me."

"You'll rue this day! You and the others, whoever they are. I'll build! I'll drive this hotel down, and out of business. Every vestige of my planning will be directed at smashing this place and you with it."

"If either of us lives so long." Having contained himself already, Warren Trent felt his own self-control increase as O'Keefe's diminished. "We may not see it happen, of course, because what you intend will take time. Also, the new people here may give you a run for your money." It was an uninformed prediction, but he hoped it would prove true.

O'Keefe raged, "Get out!"

Warren Trent said, "This is my house still. While you are my guest you have certain privileges in your own rooms. I'd suggest, though, you don't abuse them." With a slight, courteous bow to Dodo, he went out.

"Curtie," Dodo said.

O'Keefe did not appear to hear. He was breathing heavily.

"Curtie, are you all right?"

"Must you ask stupid questions? Of course I'm all right!" He stormed the length of the room and back.

"It's only a hotel, Curtie. You got so many others."

"I want this one!"

"That old man—it's the only one he's got . . ."

"Oh yes! Of course you'd see it that way. Disloyally! Stupidly!" His voice was high, hysterical. Dodo, frightened, had never known him in a mood so uncontrolled before.

"Please, Curtie!"

"I'm surrounded by fools! Fools, fools, fools! You're a

283

fool! It's why I'm getting rid of you. Replacing you with someone else."

He regretted the words the instant they were out. Their impact, even upon himself, was of shock, snuffing out his anger like a suddenly doused flame. There was a second of silence before he mumbled, "I'm sorry. I shouldn't have said that."

Dodo's eyes were misty. She touched her hair abstractedly in the gesture he had noticed earlier.

"I guess I knew, Curtie. You didn't have to tell me."

She went into the adjoining suite, closing the door behind her.

10

An unexpected bonus had revived the spirits of Keycase Milne.

During the morning, Keycase had returned his strategic purchases of yesterday to the Maison Blanche department store. There was no difficulty and he received prompt, courteous refunds. This, at the same time, relieved him of an encumbrance and filled an otherwise empty hour. There were still several more hours to wait, however, until the specially made key, ordered yesterday from the Irish Channel locksmith, would be ready for collection.

He was on the point of leaving the Maison Blanche store when his good fortune occurred.

At a main floor counter, a well-dressed woman shopper, fumbling for a credit card, dropped a ring of keys. Neither she nor anyone else but Keycase, it seemed, observed the loss. Keycase loitered, inspecting neckties at a neighboring counter, until the woman moved on.

He walked the length of the other counter, then, as if seeing the keys for the first time, stopped to pick them up. He observed at once that as well as car keys there were several others which looked as if they fitted house locks. Even more significant was something else which his experienced eyes had spotted initially—a miniature auto license tag. It was the kind mailed to car owners by disabled veterans, providing a return service for lost keys. The tag showed a Louisiana license number.

Holding the keys plainly in sight, Keycase hurried after the woman, who was leaving the store. If his action of a moment earlier had been observed, it was now obvious that he was hastening to restore the keys to their owner.

But on joining the press of pedestrians on Canal Street, he palmed the keys and transferred them to a pocket.

The woman was still in sight. Keycase followed her at a cautious distance. After two blocks she crossed Canal Street and entered a beauty parlor. From outside, Keycase saw her approach a receptionist who consulted an appointment book, after which the woman sat down to wait. With a sense of elation, Keycase hurried to a telephone.

A local telephone call established that the information he sought was obtainable from the state capital at Baton Rouge. Keycase made the long distance call, asking for the Motor Vehicle Division. The operator answering knew at once the extension he required.

Holding the keys in front of him, Keycase read out the license number from the miniature tag. A bored clerk informed him that the car was registered to one, F. R. Drummond, with an address in the Lakeview district of New Orleans.

In Louisiana, as in other states and provinces of North America, motor vehicle ownership was a matter of public record, obtainable in most instances by no greater effort than a telephone call. It was a nugget of knowledge which Keycase had used advantageously before.

He made one more telephone call, dialing the listed number for F. R. Drummond. As he had hoped, after prolonged ringing there was no answer.

It was necessary to move speedily. Keycase calculated that he had an hour, perhaps a little more. He hailed a taxi which took him quickly to where his car was parked. From there, with the aid of a street map, he drove to Lakeview, locating without difficulty the address he had jotted down.

He surveyed the house from half a block away. It was a well-cared-for two-story residence with a double garage and spacious garden. The driveway was sheltered by a large cypress tree, fortuitously blocking the view from neighboring houses on either side.

Keycase drove his car boldly under the tree and walked to the front door. It opened easily to the first key he tried.

Inside, the house was silent. He called out loudly, "Anybody home?" If there had been an answer, he was ready with a prepared excuse about the door being ajar and having come to the wrong address. There was none.

He scouted the main floor rooms quickly, then went upstairs. There were four bedrooms, all unoccupied. In a closet of the largest were two fur coats. He pulled them out, piling them on the bed. Another closet revealed suitcases. Keycase selected a large one and bundled the furs in. A dressing-table drawer yielded a jewelry box which he emptied into the suitcase, adding a movie camera, binoculars and a portable radio. He closed the case and carried it downstairs, then reopened it to add a silver bowl and salver. A tape recorder, which he noticed at the last moment, he carried out to the car in one hand, the larger case in the other.

In all, Keycase had been inside the house barely ten minutes. He stowed the case and recorder in the trunk of his car and drove away. Just over an hour later he had cached the haul in his motel room on Chef Menteur Highway, parked his car once more in its downtown location, and was walking jauntily back to the St. Gregory Hotel.

On the way, with a gleam of humor, he put the keys into a mail box, as the miniature license tag requested. No doubt the tag organization would fulfill its promise and return them to their owner.

The unexpected booty, Keycase calculated, would net him close to a thousand dollars.

He had a coffee and sandwich in the St. Gregory coffee shop, then walked to the Irish Channel locksmith's. The duplicate key to the Presidential Suite was ready and, despite the extortionate price demanded, he paid cheerfully.

Returning, he was conscious of the sun shining benevolently from a cloudless sky. That, and the morning's unexpected bounty, were plainly omens, portents of success for the major mission soon to come. His old assurance, Keycase found, plus a conviction of invincibility, had seeped quietly back.

Across the city, in leisurely disorder, the chimes of New Orleans were ringing the noon hour. Their melodies in counterpoint came dimly through the ninth-floor window —closed and sealed for effective air conditioning—of the Presidential Suite. The Duke of Croydon, unsteadily pouring a Scotch and soda, his fourth since mid-morning, heard the bells and glanced at his watch for confirmation of their message. He shook his head unbelievingly and muttered, "That's all? . . . Longest day . . . ever remember living."

"Eventually it will end." From a sofa where she had been attempting unsuccessfully to concentrate on W. H. Auden's *Poems,* his wife's rejoinder was less severe than most of her responses of the past several days. The waiting period since the previous night, with the awareness that Ogilvie and the incriminating car were somewhere to the north—but where?—had been a strain on the Duchess too. It was now nineteen hours since the Croydons' last contact with the chief house officer and there had been no word of a development of any kind.

"For God's sake!—couldn't the fellow telephone?" The Duke paced the living room agitatedly as he had, off and on, since early morning.

"We agreed there should be no communication," the Duchess reminded him, still mildly. "It's a good deal safer that way. Besides, if the car is hidden for the daytime, as we hoped, he's probably remaining out of sight."

The Duke of Croydon pored over an opened Esso road map, examining it as he had countless times already. His finger traced a circle around the area surrounding Macon, Mississippi. He said, half to himself, "It's close, still so infernally close. And all of today . . . just waiting . . . waiting!" Moving away from the map, he muttered, "Fellow could be discovered."

"Obviously he hasn't been, or we would have heard one way or another." Beside the Duchess was a copy of the afternoon *States-Item;* she had sent their secretary down to the lobby for an early edition. As well, they had listened to hourly radio news broadcasts throughout the morning. A radio was turned on softly now, but the announcer was describing damage from a summer storm in Massachusetts and the preceding item had been a White House statement on Vietnam. Both the newspaper and earlier broadcasts had referred to the hit-and-run investigation, but merely to note that it was continuing and nothing new had come to light.

"There were only a few hours for driving last night," the Duchess continued, as if to reassure herself. "Tonight it will be different. He can start immediately it's dark and by tomorrow morning everything should be safe."

"Safe!" Her husband returned morosely to his drink. "I suppose it's the sensible thing to care about. Not what happened. That woman . . . the child. There were pictures . . . suppose you saw."

"We've been over that. It won't do any good again."

He appeared not to have heard. "Funeral today . . . this afternoon . . . at least could go."

"You can't, and you know you won't."

There was a heavy silence in the elegant, spacious room.

It was broken abruptly by the jangle of the telephone. They faced each other, neither attempting to answer. The muscles of the Duke's face jerked spasmodically.

The bell sounded again, then stopped. Through intervening doors they heard the voice of the secretary indistinctly, answering on an extension.

A moment later the secretary knocked and came in diffidently. He glanced toward the Duke. "Your Grace, it's one of the local newspapers. They say that they have had" —he hesitated at an unfamiliar term—"a flash bulletin which appears to concern you."

With an effort the Duchess recovered her poise. "I will take the call. Hang up the extension." She picked up the telephone near her. Only a close observer would have noticed that her hands were trembling.

She waited for the click as the extension was replaced, then announced, "The Duchess of Croydon speaking."

A man's crisp voice responded, "Ma'am, this is the *States-Item* city desk. We've a flash from Associated Press and there's just been a follow-up . . ." The voice stopped.

"Pardon me." She heard the speaker say irritably, "Where in hell is that . . . Hey, toss over that flimsy, Andy."

There was a rustle of paper, then the voice resuming. "Sorry, ma'am. I'll read this to you.

"LONDON (AP)—Parliamentary sources here today name the Duke of Croydon, noted British government trouble shooter, as Britain's next ambassador to Washington. Initial reaction is favorable. An official announcement is expected soon.

There's more, ma'am. I won't bother you with it. Why we called was to see if your husband has a statement, then with your permission we'd like to send a photographer to the hotel."

Momentarily the Duchess closed her eyes, letting waves of relief, like soothing anodynes, wash over her.

The voice on the telephone cut in, "Ma'am, are you still there?"

"Yes." She forced her mind to function.

"About a statement, what we'd like . . ."

"At the moment," the Duchess injected, "my husband has no statement, nor will he have unless and until the appointment is officially confirmed."

"In that case . . ."

"The same applies to photography."

The voice sounded disappointed. "We'll run what we have, of course, in the next edition."

"That is your privilege."

"Meanwhile, if there's an official announcement we'd like to be in touch."

"Should that occur, I'm sure my husband will be glad to meet the press."

"Then we may telephone again?"

"Please do."

After replacing the telephone, the Duchess of Croydon sat upright and unmoving. At length, a slight smile hovering around her lips, she said, "It's happened. Geoffrey has succeeded."

Her husband stared incredulously. He moistened his lips. "Washington?"

289

She repeated the gist of the AP bulletin. "The leak was probably deliberate, to test reaction. It's favorable."

"I wouldn't have believed that even your brother . . ."

"His influence helped. Undoubtedly there were other reasons. Timing. Someone with your kind of background was needed. Politics fitted. Don't forget either that we knew the possibility existed. Fortunately, everything chanced to fall together."

"Now that it's happened . . ." He stopped, unwilling to complete the thought.

"Now that it's happened—what?"

"I wonder . . . can I carry it through?"

"You can and you will. *We* will."

He moved his head doubtfully. "There was a time . . ."

"There is still a time." The Duchess's voice sharpened with authority. "Later today you will be obliged to meet the press. There will be other things. It will be necessary for you to be coherent and remain so."

He nodded slowly. ". . . Do best I can." He lifted his glass to sip.

"No!" The Duchess rose. She removed the tumbler from her husband's fingers and walked to the bathroom. He heard the contents of the glass being poured into the sink. Returning, she announced, "There will be no more. You understand? No more whatever."

He seemed about to protest, then acknowledged, "Suppose . . . only way."

"If you'd like me to take away the bottles, pour out this one . . ."

He shook his head. "I'll manage." Perceptibly, with an effort of will, he brought his thoughts to focus. With the same chameleon quality he had exhibited the day before, there seemed more strength in his features than a moment earlier. His voice was steady as he observed, "It's very good news."

"Yes," the Duchess said. "It can mean a new beginning."

He took a half step toward her, then changed his mind. Whatever the new beginning, he was well aware it would not include that.

His wife was already reasoning aloud. "It will be necessary to revise our plans about Chicago. From now on your movements will be the subject of close attention. If we go there together it will be reported prominently in the Chicago press. It could arouse curiosity when the car is taken for repair."

"One of us must go."

The Duchess said decisively, "I shall go alone. I can change my appearance a little, wear glasses. If I'm careful I can escape attention." Her eyes went to a small attaché case beside the *secrétaire*. "I will take the remainder of the money and do whatever else is needed."

"You're assuming . . . that man will get to Chicago safely. He hasn't yet."

Her eyes widened as if remembering a forgotten nightmare. She whispered, "Oh God! Now . . . above all else . . . he must! He must!"

12

Shortly after lunch, Peter McDermott managed to slip away to his apartment where he changed, from the formal business suit he wore most of the time in the hotel, to linen slacks and a lightweight jacket. He returned briefly to his office to sign letters which, on the way out, he deposited on Flora's desk.

"I'll be back late this afternoon," he told her. Then, as an afterthought: "Did you discover anything about Ogilvie?"

His secretary shook her head. "Not really. You asked me to find out if Mr. Ogilvie told anyone where he was going. Well, he didn't."

Peter grunted. "I didn't really expect he would."

"There's just one thing." Flora hesitated. "It's probably not important, but it seemed a little strange."

"What?"

"The car Mr. Ogilvie used—you said it was a Jaguar?"

"Yes."

"It belongs to the Duke and Duchess of Croydon."

"Are you sure someone hasn't made a mistake?"

"I wondered about that," Flora said, "so I asked the

291

garage to double check. They told me to talk to a man named Kulgmer who's the garage night checker."

"Yes, I know him."

"He was on duty last night and I phoned him at home. He says Mr. Ogilvie had written authority from the Duchess of Croydon to take the car."

Peter shrugged. "Then I guess there's nothing wrong." It was strange, though, to think of Ogilvie using the Croydons' car; even stranger that there should be any kind of rapport between the Duke and Duchess and the uncouth house officer. Obviously, Flora had been considering the same thing.

He inquired, "Has the car come back?"

Flora shook her head negatively. "I wondered if I should check with the Duchess of Croydon. Then I thought I'd ask you first."

"I'm glad you did." He supposed it would be simple enough to ask the Croydons if they knew Ogilvie's destination. Since Ogilvie had their car, it seemed probable they would. All the same, he hesitated. After his own skirmish with the Duchess on Monday night, Peter was reluctant to risk another misunderstanding, especially since any kind of inquiry might be resented as a personal intrusion. There was also the embarrassing admission to be made that the hotel had no knowledge of the whereabouts of its chief house officer.

He told Flora, "Let's leave it for the time being."

There was another piece of unfinished business, Peter remembered—Herbie Chandler. This morning he had intended to inform Warren Trent of the statements made yesterday by Dixon, Dumaire, and the others, implicating the bell captain in events leading up to Monday night's attempted rape. However, the hotel owner's obvious preoccupation made him decide against it. Now Peter supposed he had better see Chandler himself.

"Find out if Herbie Chandler's on duty this evening," he instructed Flora. "If he is, tell him I'd like to see him here at six o'clock. If not, tomorrow morning."

Leaving the executive suite, Peter descended to the lobby. A few minutes later, from the comparative gloom

292

of the hotel, he stepped out into the brilliant, early afternoon sunlight of St. Charles Street.

"Peter! I'm here."

Turning his head, he saw Marsha waving from the driver's seat of a white convertible, the car wedged into a line
of waiting cabs. An alert hotel doorman briskly preceded
Peter and opened the car door. As Peter slid into the seat
beside Marsha, he saw a trio of cab drivers grin, and one
gave a long wolf whistle.

"Hi!" Marsha said. "If you hadn't come I was going to
have to pick up a fare." In a light summer dress, she appeared as delectable as ever, but for all the lighthearted
greeting he sensed a shyness, perhaps because of what had
passed between them the night before. Impulsively, he
took her hand and squeezed it.

"I like that," she assured him, "even though I promised
my father I'd use both hands to drive." With help from
the taxi drivers, who moved forward and back to create a
space, she eased the convertible out into traffic.

It seemed, Peter reflected as they waited for a green light
at Canal Street, that he was constantly being driven about
New Orleans by attractive women. Was it only three days
ago that he had ridden with Christine in the Volkswagen
to her apartment? That was the same night he had met
Marsha for the first time. It seemed longer than three days,
perhaps because a proposal of marriage by Marsha had
occurred in the meantime. In the reality of daylight he
wondered if she had had more rational second thoughts,
though either way, he decided, he would say nothing unless
she revived the subject herself.

There was an excitement, just the same, in being close
together, especially remembering their parting moments of
the night before—the kiss, tender, then with mounting
passion as restraint dissolved; the breathless moment when
he had thought of Marsha not as a girl, but as a woman;
had held her, tightly, sensing the urgent promise of her
body. He watched her covertly now; her eager youthfulness, the lissome movements of her limbs; the slightness
of her figure beneath the thin dress. If he reached out . . .

He checked the impulse, though reluctantly. In the same
self-chastening vein, he reminded himself that all his adult

life, so far, the immediacy of women had clouded his own judgment, precipitating indiscretions.

Marsha glanced sideways, diverting her attention from the traffic ahead. "What were you thinking about just then?"

"History," he lied. "Where do we start?"

"The old St. Louis Cemetery. You haven't been there?"

Peter shook his head. "I've never put cemeteries high on my list of things to do."

"In New Orleans you should."

It was a short drive to Basin Street. Marsha parked neatly on the south side and they crossed the boulevard to the walled cemetery—St. Louis number one—with its ancient pillared entrance.

"A lot of history begins here," Marsha said, taking Peter's arm. "In the early 1700s, when New Orleans was founded by the French, the land was mostly swamp. It would still be swamp, even now, if it weren't for the levees which keep the river out."

"I know it's a wet city underneath," he agreed. "In the hotel basement, twenty-four hours a day, we pump our waste water up, not down, to meet the city sewers."

"It used to be a whole lot wetter. Even in dry places water was just three feet down, so when a grave was dug it flooded before anyone could put a coffin in. There are stories that gravediggers used to stand on coffins to force them down. Sometimes they punched holes in the wood to make the coffin sink. People used to say, if you weren't really dead, you'd drown."

"Sounds like a horror movie."

"Some books say the smell of dead bodies used to seep into the drinking water." She made a grimace of distaste. "Anyway, later on there was a law that all burials had to be above the ground."

They began to walk between rows of uniquely constructed tombs. The cemetery was unlike any other Peter had ever seen. Marsha gestured around them. "This is what happened after the law was passed. In New Orleans we call these places cities of the dead."

"I can understand why."

It *was* like a city, he thought. The streets irregular, with

294

tombs in the style of miniature houses, brick and stuccoed, some with ironwork balconies and narrow sidewalks. The houses had several floors or levels. An absence of windows was the only consistent feature, but in their place were countless tiny doorways. He pointed. "They're like apartment entrances."

"They are apartments, really. And most on short leases."

He looked at her curiously.

"The tombs are divided into sections," Marsha explained. "The ordinary family tombs have two to six sections, the bigger ones more. Each section has its own little door. When there's to be a funeral, ahead of time one of the doorways is opened up. The coffin already inside is emptied, and the remains from it pushed to the back where they fall through a slot into the ground. The old coffin is burned and the new one put in. It's left for a year, then the same thing happens."

"Just a year?"

A voice behind said, " 'S all it needs. 'Times, though, it's longer—if the next to go ain't in a hurry. Cockroaches help some."

They turned. An elderly, barrel-shaped man in stained denim coveralls regarded them cheerfully. Removing an ancient straw hat, he mopped his bald head with a red silk handkerchief. "Hot, ain't it? Lot cooler in there." He slapped his hand familiarly against a tomb.

"If it's all one to you," Peter said, "I'll settle for the heat."

The other chuckled. "Git y' anyhow in th' end. Howdy, Miss Preyscott."

"Hullo, Mr. Collodi," Marsha said. "This is Mr. McDermott."

The sexton nodded agreeably. "Takin' a look at the family snuggery?"

"We were going to," Marsha said.

"This way, then." Over his shoulder he called out. "We cleaned 'er up, week or two back. Lookin' mighty good now."

As they threaded their way through the narrow, make-believe streets, Peter had an impression of ancient dates and names. Their guide pointed to a smoldering pile of rubble in an open space. "Havin' a bit of a burn-up." Peter could see portions of coffin amid the smoke.

They stopped before a six-sectioned tomb, built like a traditional Creole house. It was painted white and in better repair than most around it. On weathered marble tablets were many names, mostly of Preyscotts. "We're an old family," Marsha said. "It must be getting crowded down among the dust."

Sunshine slanted brightly on the tomb.

"Purty, ain't it?" The sexton stood back admiringly, then pointed to a doorway near the top. "That's the next one for opening, Miss Preyscott. Your daddy'll go in there." He touched another in a second tier. "That'n 'll be fer you. Doubt, though, I'll be the one to put you in." He stopped, then added contemplatively, "Comes sooner than we want for all of us. Don't do, neither, to waste no time; no sir!" Mopping his head once more, he ambled off.

Despite the heat of the day, Peter shivered. The thought of earmarking a place of death for someone so young as Marsha troubled him.

"It's not as morbid as it seems." Marsha's eyes were on his face and he was aware once more of her ability to understand his thoughts. "It's simply that here we're brought up to see all this as part of us."

He nodded. Just the same, he had had enough of this place of death.

They were on the way out, near the Basin Street gate, when Marsha put a hand on his arm restrainingly.

A line of cars had stopped immediately outside. As their doors opened, people emerged and were gathering on the sidewalk. From their appearance it was obvious that a funeral procession was about to come in.

Marsha whispered, "Peter, we'll have to wait." They moved away, still within sight of the gates, but less conspicuously.

Now the group on the sidewalk parted, making way for a small cortege. A sallow man with the unctuous bearing of an undertaker came first. He was followed by a priest.

Behind the priest was a group of six pallbearers, moving slowly, a heavy coffin on their shoulders. Behind them,

296

four others carried a tiny white coffin. On it was a single spray of oleanders.

"Oh no!" Marsha said.

Peter gripped her hand tightly.

The priest intoned, "May the angels take you into paradise: may the martyrs come to welcome you on your way, and lead you into the holy city, Jerusalem."

A group of mourners followed the second coffin. In front, walking alone, was a youngish man. He wore an ill-fitting black suit and carried a hat awkwardly. His eyes seemed riveted on the tiny coffin. Tears coursed his cheeks. In the group behind, an older woman sobbed, supported by another.

". . . May the choir of angels welcome you, and with Lazarus who was once poor, may you have everlasting rest . . ."

Marsha whispered, "It's the people who were killed in that hit-and-run. There was a mother, a little girl. It was in the newspapers." He saw that she was crying.

"I know." Peter had a sense of being part of this scene, of sharing its grief. The earlier chance encounter of Monday night had been grim and stark. Now the sense of tragedy seemed closer, more intimately real. He felt his own eyes moisten as the cortege moved on.

Behind the family mourners were others. To his surprise, Peter recognized a face. At first he was unable to identify its owner, then realized it was Sol Natchez, the elderly room-service waiter suspended from duty after the dispute with the Duke and Duchess of Croydon on Monday night. Peter had sent for Natchez on Tuesday morning and conveyed Warren Trent's edict to spend the rest of the week away from the hotel, with pay. Natchez looked across now to where Peter and Marsha were standing but gave no sign of recognition.

The funeral procession moved farther into the cemetery and out of sight. They waited until all the mourners and spectators had followed it.

"We can go now," Marsha said.

Unexpectedly a hand touched Peter's arm. Turning, he saw it was Sol Natchez. So he had observed them, after all.

"I saw you watching, Mr. McDermott. Did you know the family?"

"No," Peter said. "We were here by chance." He introduced Marsha.

She asked, "You didn't wait for the end of the service?"

The old man shook his head. "Sometimes there's just so much you can bear to watch."

"You knew the family, then?"

"Very well. It's a sad, sad thing."

Peter nodded. There seemed nothing else to say.

Natchez said, "I didn't get to say it Tuesday, Mr. McDermott, but I appreciate what you did. In speaking up for me, I mean."

"It's all right, Sol. I didn't think you were to blame."

"It's a funny thing when you think about it." The old man looked at Marsha, then Peter. He seemed reluctant to leave.

"What's funny?" Peter asked.

"All this. The accident." Natchez gestured in the direction the cortege had gone. "It must have happened just before I had that bit of trouble Monday night. Just think, while you and me were talking . . ."

"Yes," Peter said. He felt disinclined to explain his own experience later at the accident scene.

"I meant to ask, Mr. McDermott—was anything more said about that business with the Duke and Duchess?"

"Nothing at all."

Peter supposed that Natchez found it a relief, as he himself did, to consider something other than the funeral.

The waiter ruminated, "I thought about it a lot after. Seemed almost as if they went out of their way to make a fuss. Couldn't figure it out. Still can't."

Natchez, Peter remembered, had said much the same thing on Monday night. The waiter's exact words came back to him. Natchez had been speaking of the Duchess of Croydon. *She jogged my arm. If I didn't know better, I'd say it was deliberate.* And later Peter had had the same general impression: that the Duchess wanted the incident remembered. What was it she had said? Something about spending a quiet evening in the suite, then taking a walk around the block. They had just come back, she said. Peter recalled wondering at the time why she had made such a point of it.

Then the Duke of Croydon had mumbled something about leaving his cigarettes in the car, and the Duchess had snapped back at him.

The Duke had left his cigarettes in the car.

But if the Croydons had stayed in the suite, then merely walked around the block . . .

Of course, the cigarettes might have been left earlier in the day.

Somehow Peter didn't think so.

Oblivious of the other two, he concentrated.

Why did the Croydons wish to conceal the use of their car on Monday night? Why create an appearance—apparently false—of having spent the evening in the hotel? Was the complaint about spilled shrimp Creole a staged device —deliberately involving Natchez, then Peter—intended to uphold this fiction? Except for the Duke's chance remark, *which angered the Duchess,* Peter would have accepted it as true.

Why conceal the use of their car?

Natchez had said a moment ago: *It's a funny thing . . . the accident . . . must have happened just before I had that bit of trouble.*

The Croydons' car was a Jaguar.

Ogilvie.

He had a sudden memory of the Jaguar emerging from the garage last night. As it stopped, momentarily under a light, there had been something strange. He recalled noticing. But what? With an awful coldness he remembered: *it was the fender and headlight; both were damaged.* For the first time the significance of police bulletins of the past few days struck home.

"Peter," Marsha said, "you've suddenly gone white."

He scarcely heard.

It was essential to get away, to be somewhere alone where he could think. He must reason carefully, logically, unhurriedly. Above all, there must be no hasty, ready-made conclusions.

There were pieces of a puzzle. Superficially, they appeared to relate. But they must be considered, reconsidered, arranged, and rearranged. Perhaps discarded.

The idea was impossible. It was simply too fantastic to be true. And yet . . .

As if from a distance, he heard Marsha's voice. "Peter! Something's wrong. What is it?"

Sol Natchez, too, was looking at him strangely.

"Marsha," Peter said, "I can't tell you now. But I have to go."

"Go where?"

"Back to the hotel. I'm sorry. I'll try to explain later."

Her voice showed disappointment. "I'd planned we'd have tea."

"Please believe me! It's important."

"If you must go, I'll drive you."

"No." Driving with Marsha would involve talking, explanations. "Please. I'll call you later."

He left them standing, bewildered, looking after him.

Outside, on Basin Street, he hailed a cruising cab. He had told Marsha that he was going to the hotel but, changing his mind, he gave the driver the address of his apartment.

It would be quieter there.

To think. To decide what he should do.

It was approaching late afternoon when Peter McDermott summarized his reasoning.

He told himself: When you added something twenty, thirty, forty times; when every time the conclusion you arrived at was the same; when the issue was the kind of issue you were facing now; with all of this, your own responsibility was inescapable.

Since leaving Marsha an hour and a half ago, he had remained in his apartment. He had forced himself—subduing agitation and an impulse for haste—to think rationally, carefully, unexcitedly. He had reviewed, point by point, the accumulated incidents since Monday night. He had searched for alternatives of explanation, both for single happenings and the accumulation of them all. He found none that offered either consistency or sense, save the

300

awful conclusion he had reached so suddenly this afternoon.

Now the reasoning had ended. A decision must be made.

He contemplated placing all that he knew and conjec-
tured before Warren Trent. Then he dismissed the idea as
being cowardly, a shirking of his own responsibility. Whatever was to be done, he must do alone.

There was a sense of the fitness of things to be served.
He changed quickly from his light suit to a darker one.
Leaving, he took a taxi the few blocks to the hotel.

From the lobby he walked, acknowledging salutations,
to his office on the main mezzanine. Flora had left for the
day. There was a pile of messages on his desk which he
ignored.

He sat quietly for a moment in the silent office, contemplating what he must do. Then he lifted the telephone,
waited for a line, and dialed the number of the city police.

13

The persistent buzzing of a mosquito, which had somehow found its way into the Jaguar's interior, woke Ogilvie
during the afternoon. He came awake slowly and at first
had difficulty remembering where he was. Then the sequence of events came back: the departure from the hotel,
the drive in early morning darkness, the alarm—unfounded,
his decision to wait out the day before resuming the journey north; and finally the rutted, grassy track with a cluster
of trees at its end where he had concealed the car.

The hideaway had apparently been well chosen. A glance
at his watch showed that he had slept, uninterrupted, for
almost eight hours.

With consciousness also came intense discomfort. The
car was stifling, his body stiff and aching from confinement
in the cramped rear seat. His mouth was dry and tasted
foully. He was thirsty and ravenously hungry.

With grunts of anguish Ogilvie eased his bulk to a sitting position and opened the car door. Immediately, he
was surrounded by a dozen more mosquitoes. He brushed
them away, then glanced around, taking time to reorient

himself, comparing what he saw now with his impressions of the place this morning. Then it had been barely light, and cool; now the sun was high and, even under the shade of the trees, the heat intense.

Moving to the edge of the trees he could see the distant main road with heat waves shimmering above it. Early this morning there had been no traffic. Now there were several cars and trucks, moving swiftly in both directions, the sound of their motors faintly audible.

Closer at hand, apart from a steady hum of insects, there was no sign of activity. Between himself and the main road were only drowsy meadows, the quiet path and the secluded clump of trees. Beneath the latter the Jaguar remained hidden.

Ogilvie relieved himself, then opened a package he had stowed in the trunk of the car before leaving the hotel. It included a Thermos of coffee, several cans of beer, sandwiches, a salami sausage, a jar of pickles, and an apple pie. He ate voraciously, washing down the meal with copious draughts of beer and, later, coffee. The coffee had cooled since the night before but was strong and satisfying.

While eating, he listened to the car radio, waiting for a newscast from New Orleans. When it came there was only a brief reference to the hit-and-run investigation, to the effect that no new developments had been reported.

Afterward, he decided to explore. A few hundred yards away, on the crest of a knoll, was a second clump of trees, somewhat larger than the first. He crossed an open field toward it and, on the other side of the trees, found a mossy bank and a sluggish, muddy stream. Kneeling beside the stream, he made a rough toilet and afterward felt refreshed. The grass was greener and more inviting than where the car was sheltered and he lay down gratefully, using his suit coat for a pillow.

When he was comfortably settled, Ogilvie reviewed the events of the night and the prospect ahead. Reflection confirmed his earlier conclusion that the encounter with Peter McDermott outside the hotel had been accidental and could now be dismissed. It was predictable that McDermott's reaction, on learning of the chief house officer's absence, would be explosive. But that in itself would not reveal either Ogilvie's destination or his reason for departure.

Of course, it was possible that through some other cause an alarm had been raised since last night, and that even now Ogilvie and the Jaguar were being actively sought. But in light of the radio report it seemed unlikely.

On the whole, the outlook appeared bright, especially when he thought of the money already in safe keeping, and the remainder he would collect tomorrow in Chicago.

Now he had only to wait for darkness.

14

The exhilarated mood of Keycase Milne persisted through the afternoon. It bolstered his confidence as, shortly after five P.M., he cautiously approached the Presidential Suite.

Once more he had used the service stairs from the eighth floor to the ninth. The duplicate key, manufactured by the Irish Channel locksmith, was in his pocket.

The corridor outside the Presidential Suite was empty. He stopped at the double leather-padded doors, listening intently, but could hear no sound.

He glanced both ways down the corridor then, with a single movement, produced the key and tried it in the lock. Beforehand he had brushed the key with powdered graphite, as a lubricant. It went in, caught momentarily, then turned. Keycase opened one of the double doors an inch. There was still no sound from inside. He closed the door carefully and removed the key.

It was not his purpose now to enter the suite. That would come later. Tonight.

His intention had been to reconnoiter and ensure that the key was a good fit, ready for instant use whenever he chose. Later he would begin a vigil, watching for an opportunity his planning had foreseen.

For now, he returned to his room on the eighth floor and there, after setting an alarm clock, slept.

Outside it was growing dusk and, excusing himself, Peter McDermott got up from his desk to switch on the office lights. He returned to face, once more, the quietly spoken man in gray flannel, seated opposite. Captain Yolles of the Detective Bureau, New Orleans Police, looked less like a policeman than anyone Peter had ever seen. He continued to listen politely, as a bank manager might consider an application for a loan, to Peter's recital of fact and surmise. Only once during the lengthy discourse had the detective interrupted, to inquire if he could make a telephone call. Informed that he could, he used an extension on the far side of the office and spoke in a voice so low that Peter heard nothing of what was said.

The absence of any measurable response had the effect of reviving Peter's doubts. At the end, he observed, "I'm not sure all this, or even any of it, makes sense. In fact I'm already beginning to feel a little foolish."

"If more people took a chance on that, Mr. McDermott, it would make police work a lot easier." For the first time Captain Yolles produced pencil and notebook. "If anything should come of this, naturally we'll need a full statement. Meanwhile, there are a couple of details I'd like to have. One is the license number of the car."

The information was in a memo from Flora, confirming her earlier report. Peter read it aloud and the detective copied the number down.

"Thank you. The other thing is a physical description of your man Ogilvie. I know him, but I'd like to have it from you."

For the first time Peter smiled. "That's easy."

As he concluded the description, the telephone rang. Peter answered, then pushed the phone across. "For you."

This time he could hear the detective's end of the conversation which consisted largely of repeating "yes, sir" and "I understand."

At one point the detective looked up, his eyes appraisingly on Peter. He said into the telephone, "I'd say he's very dependable." A slight smile creased his face. "Worried too."

He repeated the information concerning the car number and Ogilvie's description, then hung up.

Peter said, "You're right about being worried. Do you intend to contact the Duke and Duchess of Croydon?"

"Not yet. We'd like a little more to go on." The detective regarded Peter thoughtfully. "Have you seen tonight's paper?"

"No."

"There's been a rumor—the *States-Item* published it—that the Duke of Croydon is to be British ambassador to Washington."

Peter whistled softly.

"It's just been on the radio, according to my chief, that the appointment is officially confirmed."

"Doesn't that mean there would be some kind of diplomatic immunity?"

The detective shook his head. "Not for something that's already happened. *If* it happened."

"But a false accusation . . ."

"Would be serious in any case, especially so in this one. It's why we're moving warily, Mr. McDermott."

Peter reflected that it would go hard both for the hotel and himself if word of the investigation leaked out, with the Croydons innocent.

"If it'll ease your mind a bit," Captain Yolles said, "I'll let you in on a couple of things. Our people have done some figuring since I phoned them first. They reckon your man Ogilvie may be trying to get the car out of the state, maybe to some place north. How he ties in with the Croydons, of course, we don't know."

Peter said, "I couldn't guess that either."

"Chances are, he drove last night—after you saw him—and holed up somewhere for the day. With the car the way it is, he'd know better than to try and make a run in daylight. Tonight, if he shows, we're ready. A twelve-state alarm is going out right now."

"Then you do take this seriously?"

"I said there were two things." The detective pointed to the telephone. "One reason for that last call was to tell me we've had a State lab report on broken glass and a trim ring our people found at the accident scene last Monday. There was some difficulty about a manufacturer's specification change, which was why it took time. But we know now that the glass and trim ring are from a Jaguar."

"You can really be that certain?"

"We can do even better, Mr. McDermott. If we get to the car that killed the woman and child, we'll prove it beyond the shadow of a doubt."

Captain Yolles rose to go, and Peter walked with him to the outer office. Peter was surprised to find Herbie Chandler waiting, then remembered his own instructions for the bell captain to report here this evening or tomorrow. After the developments of the afternoon, he was tempted to postpone what would most likely be an unpleasant session, then concluded there was nothing to be gained by putting it off.

He saw the detective and Chandler exchange glances.

"Good night, Captain," Peter said, and took a malicious satisfaction in observing a flicker of anxiety cross Chandler's weasel face. When the policeman had gone, Peter beckoned the bell captain into the inner office.

He unlocked a drawer of his desk and took out a folder containing the statements made yesterday by Dixon, Dumaire, and the other two youths. He handed them to Chandler.

"I believe these will interest you. In case you should get any ideas, these are copies and I have the originals."

Chandler looked pained, then began reading. As he turned the pages, his lips tightened. Peter heard him suck in breath through his teeth. A moment later he muttered, "Bastards!"

Peter snapped, "You mean because they've identified you as a pimp?"

The bell captain flushed, then put down the papers. "What you gonna do?"

"What I'd like to do is fire you on the spot. Because you've been here so long, I intend to place the whole thing before Mr. Trent."

There was a whine to Chandler's voice as he asked, "Mr. Mac, could we talk around this for a bit?"

When there was no answer, he began, "Mr. Mac, there's a lot of things go on in a place like this . . ."

"If you're telling me the facts of life—about call girls and all the other rackets—I doubt if there's much I don't know already. But there's something else I know, and so do you: at certain things managements draw the line. Supplying women to minors is one."

"Mr. Mac, couldn't you, maybe this time, not go to Mr. Trent? Couldn't you just keep this between you and me?"

"No."

The bell captain's gaze moved shiftily around the room, then returned to Peter. His eyes were calculating. "Mr. Mac, if some people was to live and let live . . ." He stopped.

"Yes?"

"Well, sometimes it can be worth while."

Curiosity kept Peter silent.

Chandler hesitated, then deliberately unfastened the button of a tunic pocket. Reaching inside he removed a folded envelope which he placed on the desk.

Peter said, "Let me see that."

Chandler pushed the envelope nearer. It was unsealed and contained five one-hundred-dollar bills. Peter inspected them curiously.

"Are they real?"

Chandler smirked. "They're real all right."

"I was curious to know how high you thought my price came." Peter tossed the money back. "Take it and get out."

"Mr. Mac, if it's a question of a little more . . ."

"Get out!" Peter's voice was low. He half-rose in his chair. "Get out before I break your dirty little neck."

As he retrieved the money and left, Herbie Chandler's face was a mask of hatred.

When he was alone, Peter McDermott sat slumped, silently, behind his desk. The interviews with the policeman and Chandler had exhausted and depressed him. Of the two, he thought, the second had lowered his spirits most, probably because handling the proffered bribe had left him with a feeling of being unclean.

Or had it? He thought: be honest with yourself. There had been an instant, with the money in his hands, when

307

he was tempted to take it. Five hundred dollars was a useful sum. Peter had no illusion about his own earnings compared with those of the bell captain, who undoubtedly raked in a good deal more. If it had been anyone other than Chandler, he might possibly have succumbed. Or would he? He wished he could be sure. Either way, he would not be the first hotel manager to accept a pay-off from his staff.

The irony, of course, was that despite Peter's insistence that the evidence against Herbie Chandler would be placed before Warren Trent, there was no guarantee that it would happen. If the hotel changed ownership abruptly, as seemed likely, Warren Trent would no longer be concerned. Nor might Peter himself be around. With the advent of new management, the records of senior staff would undoubtedly be examined and, in his own case, the old, unsavory Waldorf scandal disinterred. Had he yet, Peter wondered, lived that down? Well, there was every likelihood he would find out soon.

He returned his attention to the present.

On his desk was a printed form, which Flora had left, with a late-afternoon house count. For the first time since coming in, he studied the figures. They showed that the hotel was filling and tonight, it seemed, there was a certainty of another full house. If the St. Gregory was going down to defeat, at least it was doing so to the sound of trumpets.

As well as the house count and telephone messages, there was a fresh pile of mail and memos. Peter skimmed through them all, deciding that there was nothing which could not be left until tomorrow. Beneath the memos was a Manila folder which he opened. It was the proposed master catering plan which the sous-chef, André Lemieux, had given him yesterday. Peter had begun studying the plan this morning.

Glancing at his watch, he decided to continue his reading before making an evening tour of the hotel. He settled down, the precisely handwritten pages and carefully drawn charts spread out before him.

As he read on, his admiration for the young sous-chef grew. The presentation appeared masterly, revealing a broad grasp both of the hotel's problems and the potentialities of its restaurant business. It angered Peter that the chef de cuisine, M. Hèbrand, had—according to Lemieux —dismissed the proposals entirely.

True, some conclusions were arguable, and Peter disagreed himself with a few of Lemieux's ideas. At first glance, too, a number of estimated costs seemed optimistic. But these were minor. The important thing was that a fresh and clearly competent brain had brooded over present deficiencies in food management and come up with suggested remedies. Equally obvious was that unless the St. Gregory made better use of André Lemieux's considerable talents, he would soon take them elsewhere.

Peter returned the plan and charts to their folder with a sense of pleasure that someone in the hotel should possess the kind of enthusiasm for his work which Lemieux had shown. He decided that he would like to tell André Lemieux his impressions even though—with the hotel in its present uncertain state—there seemed nothing more that Peter could do.

A telephone call elicited the information that, this evening, the chef de cuisine was absent through continued sickness, and that the sous-chef, M. Lemieux, was in charge. Preserving protocol, Peter left a message that he was coming down to the kitchen now.

André Lemieux was waiting at the doorway from the main dining room.

"Come in, monsieur! You are welcome." Leading the way into the noisy, steaming kitchen, the young sous-chef shouted close to Peter's ear, "You find us, as the musicians say, near the crescendo."

In contrast to the comparative quietness of yesterday afternoon, the atmosphere now, in early evening, was pandemonic. With a full shift on duty, chefs in starched whites, their assistant cooks, and juniors, seemed to have sprouted like daisies in a field. Around them, through gusts of steam and waves of heat, sweating kitchen helpers noisily hefted trays, pans, and cauldrons, while others thrust trolleys recklessly, all dodging each other as well as hurrying waiters and waitresses, the latter's serving trays held high. On steam tables the day's dinner menu dishes were being

309

portioned and served for delivery to dining rooms. Special orders—from à la carte menus and for room service—were being prepared by fast-moving cooks whose arms and hands seemed everywhere at once. Waiters hovered, questioning progress of their orders as cooks barked back. Other waiters, with loaded trays, moved quickly past the two austere women checkers at elevated billing registers. From the soup section, vapor rose swirling as giant cauldrons bubbled. Not far away two specialist cooks arranged, with dextrous fingers, canapés and hot hors-d'oeuvres. Beyond them, an anxious pastry chef supervised desserts. Occasionally, as oven doors clanged open, a reflection of flames flashed over concentrating faces, with the ovens' interiors like a glimpse of hell. Over all, assailing ears and nostrils, was the clatter of plates, the inviting odor of food and the sweet, fresh fragrance of brewing coffee.

"When we are busiest, monsieur, we are the proudest. Or should be, if one did not look beneath the cabbage leaf."

"I've read your report." Peter returned the folder to the sous-chef, then followed him into the glass-paneled office where the noise was muted. "I like your ideas. I'd argue a few points, but not many."

"It would be good to argue if, at the end, the action was to follow."

"It won't yet. At least, not the kind you have in mind." Ahead of any reorganization, Peter pointed out, the larger issue of the hotel's ownership would have to be settled.

"Per'aps my plan and I must go elsewhere. No matter." André Lemieux gave a Gallic shrug, then added, "Monsieur, I am about to visit the convention floor. Would you care to accompany me?"

Peter had intended to include the convention dinners, scheduled for tonight, in his evening rounds of the hotel. It would be just as effective to begin his inspection from the convention floor kitchen. "Thank you. I'll come."

They rode a service elevator two floors up, stepping out into what, in most respects, was a duplicate of the main kitchen below. From here some two thousand meals could be served at a single sitting to the St. Gregory's three convention halls and dozen private dining rooms. The tempo at the moment seemed as frenetic as downstairs.

"As you know, monsieur, it is two big banquets that we 'ave tonight. In the Grand Ballroom and the Bienville 'all."

Peter nodded. "Yes, the Dentists' Congress and Gold Crown Cola." From the flow of meals toward opposite ends of the long kitchen, he observed that the dentists' main course was roast turkey, the cola salesmen's, flounder sauté. Teams of cooks and helpers were serving both, apportioning vegetables with machine-like rhythm, then, in a single motion, slapping metal covers on the filled plates and loading the whole onto waiters' trays.

Nine plates to a tray—the number of conventioneers at a single table. Two tables per waiter. Four courses to the meal, plus extra rolls, butter, coffee, and *petits fours*. Peter calculated: there would be twelve heavily loaded trips, at least, for every waiter; most likely more if diners were demanding or, as sometimes happened under pressure, extra tables were assigned. No wonder some waiters looked weary at an evening's end.

Less weary, perhaps, would be the maître d'hôtel, poised and immaculate in white tie and tails. At the moment, like a police chief on point duty, he was stationed centrally in the kitchen directing the flow of waiters in both directions. Seeing André Lemieux and Peter, he moved toward them.

"Good evening, Chef; Mr. McDermott." Though in hotel precedence Peter outranked the other two, in the kitchen the maître d'hôtel deferred, correctly, to the senior chef on duty.

André Lemieux asked, "What are our numbers for dinner, Mr. Dominic?"

The maître d' consulted a slip of paper. "The Gold Crown people estimated two hundred and forty and we've seated that many. It looks as if they're mostly in."

"They're salesmen on salary," Peter said. "They have to be there. The dentists please themselves. They'll probably straggle and a lot won't show."

The maître d' nodded agreement. "I heard there was a good deal of drinking in rooms. Ice consumption is heavy, and room service had a run on mixes. We thought it might cut the meal figure down."

The conundrum was how many convention meals to prepare at any time. It represented a familiar headache to all three men. Convention organizers gave the hotel a minimum guarantee, but in practice the figure was liable to vary a hundred or two either way. A reason was uncertainty about how many delegates would break up into smaller parties and pass up official banquets or, alternatively, might arrive en masse in a last-minute surge.

The final minutes before a big convention banquet were inevitably tense in any hotel kitchen. It was a moment of truth, since all involved were aware that reaction to a crisis would show just how good or bad their organization was.

Peter asked the maître d'hôtel, "What was the original estimate?"

"For the dentists, five hundred. We're close to that and we've begun serving. But they still seem to be coming in."

"Are we getting a fast count of new arrivals?"

"I've a man out now. Here he is." Dodging fellow waiters, a red-coated captain was hastening through the service doors from the Grand Ballroom.

Peter asked André Lemieux, "If we have to, can we produce extra food?"

"When I have the word of requirements, monsieur, then we will do our best."

The maître d' conferred with the captain, then returned to the other two. "It looks like an additional hundred and seventy people. They're flooding in! We're already setting up more tables."

As always, when crisis struck, it was with little warning. In this case it had arrived with major impact. One hundred and seventy extra meals, required at once, would tax the resources of any kitchen. Peter turned to André Lemieux, only to discover that the young Frenchman was no longer there.

The sous-chef had sprung to action as if catapulted. He was already among his staff, issuing orders with the crackle of rapid fire. *A junior cook to the main kitchen, there to seize seven turkeys roasting for tomorrow's cold collation . . . A shouted order to the preparation room: Use the re-*

312

serves! Speed up! Carve everything in sight! . . . More vegetables! Steal some from the second banquet which looked like using less than allowed! . . . A second junior sent running to the main kitchen to round up all vegetables he could find elsewhere . . . And deliver a message: rush up more help! Two carvers, two more cooks . . . Alert the pastry chef! One hundred and seventy more desserts required in minutes . . . Rob Peter for Paul! Juggle! Feed the dentists! Young André Lemieux, quick thinking, confident, good natured, running the show.

Already, waiters were being reassigned: some smoothly withdrawn from the smaller banquet of Gold Crown Cola, where those remaining must do extra work. Diners would never notice; only, perhaps, that their next course would be served by someone with a vaguely different face. Other waiters, already assigned to the Grand Ballroom and the dentists, would handle three tables—twenty-seven place settings—instead of two. A few seasoned hands, known to be fast with feet and fingers, might manage four. There would be some grumbling, though not much. Convention waiters were mostly free-lancers, called in by any hotel as requirements rose. Extra work earned extra money. Four dollars' pay for three hours' work was based on two tables; each extra table brought half as much again. Tips, added to a convention's bill by prior arrangement, would double the entire amount. The fast-feet men would go home with sixteen dollars; if lucky, they might have earned the same at lunch or breakfast.

A trolley with three fresh-cooked turkeys, Peter saw, was already highballing from a service elevator. The preparation-room cooks fell upon it. The assistant cook who had brought the three returned for more.

Fifteen portions from a turkey. Rapid dissection with surgeon's skill. To each diner the same portion: white meat, dark meat, dressing. Twenty portions to a serving tray. Rush the tray to a service counter. Fresh trolleys of vegetables, steaming in like ships converging.

The sous-chef's dispatch of messengers had depleted the serving team. André Lemieux stepped in, replacing the absent two. The team picked up speed, moved faster than it had before.

Plate . . . meat . . . first vegetable . . . second . . . gravy . . . slide the plate . . . cover on! A man for each move; arms, hands, ladles moving together. A meal each second . . . faster still! In front of the serving counter, a line of waiters, becoming long.

Across the kitchen, the pastry chef opening refrigerators; inspecting, selecting, slamming the doors closed. Main kitchen pastry cooks running to help. Draw on reserve desserts. More on the way from basement freezers.

Amid the urgency, a moment of incongruity.

A waiter reported to a captain, the captain to the head waiter, the head waiter to André Lemieux.

"Chef, there's a gentleman says he doesn't like turkey. May he have rare roast beef?"

A shout of laughter went up from the sweating cooks.

But the request had observed protocol correctly, as Peter knew. Only the senior chef could authorize any deviation from a standard menu.

A grinning André Lemieux said, "He may have it, but serve him last at his table."

That, too, was an old kitchen custom. As a matter of public relations, most hotels would change standard fare if asked, even if the substitute meal was costlier. But invariably—as now—the individualist must wait until those seated near him had begun eating, a precaution against others being inspired with the same idea.

Now the line of waiters at the serving counter was shortening. To most guests in the Grand Ballroom—latecomers included—the main course had been served. Already bus boys were appearing with discarded dishes. There was a sense of crisis passed. André Lemieux surrendered his place among the servers, then glanced questioningly at the pastry chef.

The latter, a matchstick of a man who looked as if he seldom sampled his own confections, made a circle with thumb and forefinger. "All set to go, Chef."

André Lemieux, smiling, rejoined Peter. "Monsieur, it seems we 'ave, as you say it, fielded the ball."

"I'd say you've done a good deal better. I'm impressed."

The young Frenchman shrugged. "What you have seen was good. But it is one part only of the work. Elsewhere we do not look so well. Excuse me, monsieur." He moved away.

The dessert was *bombe aux marrons, cherries flambées.* It would be served with ceremony, the ballroom lights dimmed, the flaming trays held high.

Now, waiters were lining up before the service doors. The pastry chef and helpers were checking arrangement of the trays. When touched off, a central dish on each would spring to flame. Two cooks stood by with lighted tapers.

André Lemieux inspected the line.

At the entry to the Grand Ballroom, the head waiter, an arm raised, watched the sous-chef's face.

As André Lemieux nodded, the head waiter's arm swept down.

The cooks with tapers ran down the line of trays, igniting them. The double service doors were flung back and fastened. Outside, on cue, an electrician dimmed the lights. The music of an orchestra diminished, then abruptly stopped. Among guests in the great hall, a hum of conversation died.

Suddenly, beyond the diners, a spotlight sprang on, framing the doorway from the kitchen. There was a second's silence, then a fanfare of trumpets. As it ended, orchestra and organ swung together, *fortissimo,* into the opening bars of *The Saints.* In time to the music, the procession of waiters, with flaming trays, marched out.

Peter McDermott moved into the Grand Ballroom for a better view. He could see the overflow, unexpected crowd of diners, the great room tightly packed.

Oh, when the Saints; Oh, when the Saints; Oh, when the Saints go marching in . . . From the kitchen, waiter after waiter, in trim blue uniform, marched out in step. For this moment, every last man had been impressed. Some, in moments only, would return to complete their work in the other banquet hall. Now, in semidarkness, their flames reared up like beacons . . . *Oh when the Saints; Oh, when the Saints; Oh, when the Saints go marching in* . . . From the diners, a spontaneous burst of applause, changing to handclapping in time with the music as waiters encircled the room. For the hotel, a commitment had been met as planned. No one outside the kitchen could know that minutes earlier a crisis had been encountered and overcome . . . *Lord, I want to be in that number, When the Saints go marching in* . . . As waiters reached their tables, the lights went up to renewed applause and cheers.

André Lemieux had come to stand beside Peter. "That is the all for tonight, monsieur. Unless, perhaps you 'ave a wish for the cognac. In the kitchen I have the small supply."

"No, thank you." Peter smiled. "It was a good show. Congratulations!"

As he turned away, the sous-chef called after him, "Good night, monsieur. And do not forget."

Puzzled, Peter stopped. "Forget what?"

"What I have already said. The 'ot-shot 'otel, monsieur, that you and I could make."

Half amused, half thoughtful, Peter threaded his way through the banquet tables toward the ballroom outer doorway.

He had gone most of the distance when he was aware of something out of place. He stopped, glancing around, uncertain what it was. Then abruptly he realized. Dr. Ingram, the fiery little president of the Dentistry Congress, should have been presiding at this, one of the main events of the convention. But the doctor was neither at the president's position nor anywhere else at the long head table.

Several delegates were table hopping, greeting friends in other sections of the room. A man with a hearing aid stopped beside Peter. "Swell turnout, eh?"

"It certainly is. I hope you enjoyed your dinner."

"Not bad."

"By the way," Peter said. "I was looking for Dr. Ingram. I don't see him anywhere."

"You won't." The tone was curt. Eyes regarded him suspiciously. "You from a newspaper?"

"No, the hotel. I met Dr. Ingram a couple of times . . ."

"He resigned. This afternoon. If you want my opinion, he behaved like a damn fool."

Peter controlled his surprise. "Do you happen to know if the doctor is still in the hotel?"

316

"No idea." The man with the hearing aid moved on.

There was a house phone on the convention mezzanine. Dr. Ingram, the switchboard reported, was still shown as registered, but there was no answer from his room. Peter called the chief cashier. "Has Dr. Ingram of Philadelphia checked out?"

"Yes, Mr. McDermott, just a minute ago. I can see him in the lobby now."

"Send someone to ask if he'll please wait. I'm on my way down."

Dr. Ingram was standing, suitcases beside him, a raincoat over his arm, when Peter arrived.

"What's your trouble now, McDermott? If you want a testimonial to this hotel, you're out of luck. Besides which, I've a plane to catch."

"I heard about your resignation. I came to say I'm sorry."

"I guess they'll make out." From the Grand Ballroom two floors above, the sound of applause and cheering drifted down to where they stood. "It sounds as if they have already."

"Do you mind very much?"

"No." The little doctor shifted his feet, looking down, then growled, "I'm a liar. I mind like hell. I shouldn't, but I do."

Peter said, "I imagine anyone would."

Dr. Ingram's head snapped up. "Understand this, McDermott: I'm no beaten rug. I don't need to feel like one. I've been a teacher all my life, with plenty to show for it: Good people I've brought on—Jim Nicholas for one, and others, procedures carrying my name, books I've written that are standard texts. All that's solid stuff. The other"— he nodded in the direction of the Grand Ballroom—"that's frosting."

"I didn't realize . . ."

"All the same, a little frosting does no harm. A fellow even gets to like it. I wanted to be president. I was glad when they elected me. It's an accolade from people whose opinion you value. If I'm honest, McDermott—and God knows why I'm telling you this—it's eating my heart out, not being up there tonight." He paused, looking up, as the sounds from the ballroom were audible once more.

"Once in a while, though, you have to weigh what you want against what you believe in." The little doctor grunted. "Some of my friends think I've behaved like an idiot."

"It isn't idiotic to stand up for a principle."

Dr. Ingram eyed Peter squarely. "You didn't do it, McDermott, when you had the chance. You were too worried about this hotel, your job."

"I'm afraid that's true."

"Well, you've the grace to admit it, so I'll tell you something, son. You're not alone. There've been times I haven't measured up to everything I believe. It goes for all of us. Sometimes, though, you get a second chance. If it happens to you—take it."

Peter beckoned a bellboy. "I'll come with you to the door."

Dr. Ingram shook his head. "No need for that. Let's not crap around, McDermott. I don't love this hotel or you either."

The bellboy looked at him inquiringly. Dr. Ingram said, "Let's go."

16

In the late afternoon, near the cluster of trees in which the Jaguar was hidden, Ogilvie slept again. He awoke as dusk was settling, the sun an orange ball nudging a ridge of hills toward the west. The heat of the day had changed into a pleasant evening coolness. Ogilvie hurried, realizing it would soon be time to go.

He listened to the car radio first. There appeared to be no fresh news, merely a repetition of what he had heard earlier. Satisfied, he snapped the radio off.

He returned to the stream beyond the small clump of trees and freshened himself, splashing water on his face and head to banish the last vestiges of drowsiness. He made a hasty meal from what was left of his supply of food, then refilled the Thermos flasks with water, leaving them on the rear seat of the car along with some cheese and bread. The makeshift fare would have to sustain him through the night. Until daylight tomorrow he intended to make no unnecessary stops.

His route, which he had planned and memorized before leaving New Orleans, lay northwest through the remainder of Mississippi. Then he would traverse the western shoulder of Alabama, afterward heading due north through Tennessee and Kentucky. From Louisville he would turn diagonally west across Indiana, by way of Indianapolis. He would cross into Illinois near Hammond, thence to Chicago.

The remaining journey spanned seven hundred miles. Its entire distance was too great for a single stint of driving, but Ogilvie estimated he could be close to Indianapolis by daybreak where he believed he would be safe. Once there, only two hundred miles would separate him from Chicago.

Darkness was complete as he backed the Jaguar out of the sheltering trees and steered it gently toward the main highway. He gave a satisfied grunt as he turned northward on U.S. 45.

At Columbus, Mississippi, where the dead from the Battle of Shiloh were brought for burial, Ogilvie stopped for gas. He was careful to choose a small general store on the outskirts of town, with a pair of old-fashioned gas pumps illumined by a single light. He pulled the car forward as far as possible from the light, so that its front was in shadow.

He discouraged conversation by ignoring the storekeeper's "Nice night," and "Going far?" He paid cash for the gas and a half-dozen chocolate bars, then drove on.

Nine miles to the north he crossed the Alabama state line.

A succession of small towns came and went. Vernon, Sulligent, Hamilton, Russellville, Florence, the last—so a sign recorded—noted for the manufacture of toilet seats. A few miles farther on, he crossed the border into Tennessee.

Traffic was averagely light and the Jaguar performed superbly. Driving conditions were ideal, helped by a full moon which rose soon after darkness. There was no sign of police activity of any kind.

Ogilvie was contentedly relaxed.

Fifty miles south of Nashville, at Columbia, Tennessee, he turned onto U.S. 31.

Traffic was heavier now. Massive tractor-trailers, their headlights stabbing the night like an endless dazzling chain, thundered south toward Birmingham and northward to the industrial Midwest. Passenger cars, a few taking risks the truck drivers would not, threaded the stream. Occasionally, Ogilvie himself pulled out to pass a slow-moving vehicle, but he was careful not to exceed posted speed limits. He had no wish, by speeding or any other means, to invite attention. After a while, he observed a following car, which remained behind him, driving at approximately his own speed. Ogilvie adjusted the rear-view mirror to reduce the glare, then slowed to let the other car pass. When it failed to, unconcerned, he resumed his original speed.

A few miles farther on, he was aware of the northbound lanes of traffic slowing. Warning taillights of other vehicles were flashing on. Leaning to the left, he could see what appeared to be a group of headlights, with both northbound lanes funneling into one. The scene bore the familiar pattern of a highway accident.

Then, abruptly, rounding a curve, he saw the real reason for the delay. Two lines of Tennessee Highway Patrol cruisers, their red roof lights flashing, were positioned on both sides of the road. A flare-draped barrier was across the center lane. At the same instant, the car which had been following, switched on a police beacon of its own.

As the Jaguar slowed and stopped, State Troopers with drawn guns ran toward it.

Quaking, Ogilvie raised his hands above his head.

A husky sergeant opened the car door. "Keep your hands where they are," he ordered, "and come out slowly. You're under arrest."

17

Christine Francis mused aloud, "There!—you're doing it again. Both times, when the coffee was poured, you've held your hands around the cup. As if it gave you a kind of comfort."

Across the dinner table, Albert Wells gave his perky sparrow's smile. "You notice more things'n most people."

He seemed frail again tonight, she thought. Some of the paleness of three days earlier had returned and occasionally, through the evening, a bronchial cough had been troublesome, though not diminishing his cheerfulness. What he needs, Christine reflected, is someone to take care of him.

They were in the St. Gregory's main dining room. Since their arrival more than an hour ago, most of the other diners had left, though a few still lingered over coffee and liqueurs. Although the hotel was full, attendance in the dining room had been thin all evening.

Max, the head waiter, came discreetly to their table.

"Will there be anything else, sir?"

Albert Wells glanced at Christine who shook her head.

"I reckon not. When you'd like to, you can bring the bill."

"Certainly, sir." Max nodded to Christine, his eyes assuring her that he had not forgotten their arrangement of this morning.

When the head waiter had gone, the little man said, "About the coffee. Prospecting, in the north, you never waste anything if you want to stay alive, not even the heat from a cup you're holding. It's a habit you get into. I could lose the way of it, I guess, though there's things it's wise to remind yourself of once in a while."

"Because they were good times, or because life is better now?"

He considered. "Some of both, I reckon."

"You told me you were a miner," Christine said. "I didn't know about your being a prospector too."

"A lot of the time, one's the other. Especially on the Canadian Shield—that's in the Northwest Territories, Christine, near as far as Canada goes. When you're there alone, just you and the tundra—the arctic desert, they call it—you do everything from driving claim stakes to burning through the permafrost. If you don't, most times there's no one else."

"When you were prospecting, what was it for?"

"Uranium, cobalt. Mostly gold."

"Did you find any? Gold, I mean."

He nodded affirmatively. "Plenty did. Around Yellow-knife, Great Slave Lake. There were discoveries there from the 1890s to a stampede in 1945. Mostly, though, the country was too tough to mine and take it out."

Christine said, "It must have been a hard life."

The little man coughed, then took a sip of water, smiling apologetically. "I was tougher then. Though give the Shield half a chance, it'll kill you." He looked around the pleasantly appointed dining room, lighted by crystal chandeliers. "It seems a long way from here."

"You said that mostly it was too difficult to mine the gold. It wasn't always?"

"Not always. Some were luckier 'n others, though even for them things 'd go wrong. Maybe it's part because the Shield and the Barren Lands do strange things to people. Some you think 'd be strong—and not just in body either —they turn out to be the weak ones. And some you'd trust with your life, you discover you can't. Then there's the other way around. One time I remember . . ." He stopped as the head waiter placed a salver on the table with their bill.

She urged, "Go on."

"It's kind of a long story, Christine." He turned over the bill, inspecting it.

"I'd like to hear," Christine said, and meant it. As time went on, she thought, she liked this modest little man more and more.

He looked up and there seemed to be amusement in his eyes. He glanced across the room at the head waiter, then back toward Christine. Abruptly, he took out a pencil and signed the bill.

"It was in '36," the little man began, "around the time that one of the last Yellowknife stampedes was gettin' started. I was prospecting near the shore of Great Slave Lake. Had a partner then. Name of Hymie Eckstein. Hymie'd come from Ohio. He'd been in the garment trade, a used-car salesman, lot of other things, I guess. He was pushy and a fast talker. But he had a way of making people like him. I guess you'd call it charm. When he got to

Yellowknife he had a little money. I was broke. Hymie grubstaked the two of us."

Albert Wells took a sip of water, pensively.

"Hymie'd never seen a snowshoe, never heard of permafrost, couldn't tell schist from quartz. From the beginning, though, we got along well. And we made out.

"We'd been out a month, maybe two. On the Shield you lose all track of time. Then one day, near the mouth of the Yellowknife River, the two of us sat down to roll our cigarettes. Sitting there, the way prospectors do, I chipped away at some gossam—that's oxidized rock, Christine—and slipped a piece or two in my pocket. Later, by the lakeshore, I panned the rock. You could have shoved me over when it showed good coarse gold."

"When it really happens," Christine said, "it must seem the most exciting thing in the world."

"Maybe there are other things excite you more. If there are, they never came my way. Well, we rushed back to the place I'd chipped the rock and we covered it with moss. Two days later, we found the ground had already been staked. I guess it was the darnedest blow either of us ever had. Turned out, a Toronto prospector 'd done the staking. He'd been out the year before, then gone back east, not knowing what he had. Under Territories law, if he didn't work the claim, his rights'd run out a year from recording."

"How long away was that?"

"We made our find in June. If things stayed the way they were, the land 'd come clear the last day in September."

"Couldn't you keep quiet, and just wait?"

"We aimed at that. Except it wasn't so easy. For one thing, the find we'd made was right in line with a producing mine an' there were other prospectors, like ourselves, working the same country. For another, Hymie and me 'd run clean out of money and food."

Albert Wells beckoned a passing waiter. "I reckon I'll have more coffee after all." He asked Christine, "How about you?"

She shook her head. "No thank you. Don't stop. I want to hear the rest." How strange, she thought, that the kind of epic adventure which people dreamed about should have happened to someone as apparently ordinary as the little man from Montreal.

"Well, Christine, I reckon the next three months were the longest any two men lived. Maybe the hardest. We existed. On fish, some bits of plants. Near the end I was thinner'n a twig and my legs were black with scurvy. Had this bronchitis and phlebitis too. Hymie wasn't a whole lot better, but he never complained and I got to like him more."

The coffee arrived and Christine waited.

"Finally it got to the last day of September. We'd heard through Yellowknife that when the first claim ran out, there'd be others try to move in, so we didn't take chances. We had our stakes ready. Right after midnight we rammed 'em home. I remember—it was a pitch-black night, snowing hard and blowing a gale."

His hands went around the coffee cup as they had before.

"That's about all I do remember because, after that, nature took over 'n the next clear thing I know was being in a hospital in Edmonton, near a thousand miles from where we staked. I found out after, Hymie got me out from the Shield, though I never figured how he did it. And a bush pilot flew me south. Plenty of times, including in the hospital, they gave me up for dead. I didn't die. Though when I got things sorted out, I wished I had." He stopped to drink from the coffee cup.

Christine asked, "Wasn't the claim legal?"

"The claim was fine. The trouble was Hymie." Albert Wells stroked his sparrow-beak nose reflectively. "Maybe I should take the story back a bit. While we were waiting our time out on the Shield, we'd signed two bills of sale. Each of us—on paper—turned over his half of the claim to the other."

"Why would you do that?"

"It was Hymie's idea, in case one of us didn't come through. If that happened, the survivor 'd keep the paper showing that all of the claim was his, and he'd tear up the other. Hymie said it'd save a lot of legal mess. At the time, it seemed to make sense. If we both made it through, the arrangement was, we'd scrap both papers."

Christine prompted, "So while you were in the hospital . . ."

"Hymie 'd taken both papers and registered his. By the time I was in shape to take an interest, Hymie had full title and was already mining with proper machinery and help. I found out there'd been an offer of a quarter million dollars from one of the big smelting companies for him to sell out, and there were other bidders lining up."

"Was there nothing at all you could do?"

The little man shook his head. "I figured I was licked before I started. All the same, soon's I could get out of that hospital, I borrowed enough money to get back up north."

Albert Wells stopped and waved a greeting across the dining room. Christine looked up to see Peter McDermott approaching their table. She had wondered if Peter would remember her suggestion about joining them after dinner. The sight of him brought a delightful quickening of her senses. Then, immediately, she sensed that he was despondent.

The little man welcomed Peter warmly and a waiter hurried forward with an extra chair.

Peter sank into it gratefully. "I'm afraid I left it a little late. There've been a few things happening." It was, he reflected to himself, a monument of understatement.

Hoping there would be an opportunity to talk privately with Peter afterward, Christine said, "Mr. Wells has been telling me a wonderful story. I must hear the end."

Peter sipped his coffee which the waiter had brought. "Go ahead, Mr. Wells. It'll be like coming into a movie part way through. I'll catch the beginning later."

The little man smiled, looking down at his gnarled and toughened hands. "There isn't a whole lot more, though most of what there is has kind of a twist. I went north and found Hymie in Yellowknife, in what passes for a hotel. I called him every foul name I could lay my tongue to. All the while he had a great wide grin, which made me madder, till I was ready to kill him there 'n then. I wouldn't have, though. He knew me well enough for that."

Christine said, "He must have been a hateful man."

"I figured so. Except, when I'd quieted down some, Hymie told me to come with him. We went to a lawyer and there were papers, ready drawn, handing me back my half share, fair 'n square—in fact fairer, 'cos Hymie 'd taken nothing for himself for all the work he'd done those months I'd been away."

Bewildered, Christine shook her head. "I don't understand. Why did he . . ."

"Hymie explained. Said he knew from the beginning there'd be a lot of legal things, papers to sign, especially if we didn't sell, and hung on to work the claim instead, which he knew I wanted to do. There were bank loans—for the machinery, wages, all the rest. With me in hospital, and most of the time not knowing up from down, he couldn't have done any of it—not with my name on the property. So Hymie used my bill of sale and went ahead. He always intended to hand my share back. Only thing was, he wasn't much of a one for writing and never let me know. Right from the beginning, though, he'd fixed things up legally. If he'd died, I'd have got his share as well as mine."

Peter McDermott and Christine were staring across the table.

"Later on," Albert Wells said, "I did the same with my half—made a will so it'd go to Hymie. We had the same arrangement—about that one mine—till the day Hymie died, which was five years ago. I reckon he taught me something: When you believe in somebody, don't be in a rush to change your mind."

Peter McDermott said, "And the mine?"

"Well, we kept right on refusing offers to buy us out, and it turned out we were right in the end. Hymie ran it a good many years. It still goes on—one of the best producers in the north. Now 'n then I go back to take a look, for old times' sake."

Speechless, her mouth agape, Christine stared at the little man. "You . . . *you* . . . own a gold mine."

Albert Wells nodded cheerfully. "That's right. There's a few other things now, besides."

326

"If you'll pardon my curiosity," Peter McDermott said, "other things such as what?"

"I'm not sure of all of it." The little man shifted diffidently in his chair. "There's a couple of newspapers, some ships, an insurance company, buildings, other bits 'n pieces. I bought a food chain last year. I like new things. It keeps me interested."

"Yes," Peter said, "I should imagine it would."

Albert Wells smiled mischievously. "Matter of fact, there's something I was going to tell you tomorrow, but I may as well do it now. I just bought this hotel."

18

"Those are the gentlemen, Mr. McDermott."

Max, the dining-room head waiter, pointed across the lobby where two men—one of them the police detective, Captain Yolles—were waiting quietly beside the hotel newsstand.

A moment or two earlier, Max had summoned Peter from the dining-room table where, with Christine, he was sitting in dazed silence after Albert Wells' announcement. Both Christine and himself, Peter knew, had been too astounded either to grasp the news entirely or assess its implications. It had been a relief to Peter to be informed that he was required urgently outside. Hastily excusing himself, he promised to return later if he could.

Captain Yolles walked toward him. He introduced his companion as Detective-Sergeant Bennett. "Mr. McDermott, is there some place handy we can talk?"

"This way." Peter led the two men past the concierge's counter into the credit manager's office, unused at night. As they went in, Captain Yolles handed Peter a folded newspaper. It was an early edition of tomorrow's *Times-Picayune*. A three-column head read:

CROYDON CONFIRMED U.K. AMBASSADOR NEWS REACHES HIM IN CRESCENT CITY

Captain Yolles closed the office door. "Mr. McDermott, Ogilvie has been arrested. He was stopped an hour ago, with the car, near Nashville. The Tennessee State Police are holding him and we've sent to bring him back. The car is being returned by truck, under wraps. But from an investigation on the spot, there doesn't seem much doubt it's the one we want."

Peter nodded. He was aware of the two policemen watching him curiously.

"If I seem a little slow catching on to all that's happening," Peter said, "I should tell you that I've just had something of a shock."

"Concerning this?"

"No. The hotel."

There was a pause, then Yolles said, "You may be interested to hear that Ogilvie has made a statement. He claims he knew nothing about the car being involved in an accident. All that happened, he says, is that the Duke and Duchess of Croydon paid him two hundred dollars to drive it north. He had that amount of money on him."

"Do you believe that?"

"It might be true. Then again, it might not. We'll know better after we've done some questioning tomorrow."

By tomorrow, Peter thought, a good deal might be clearer. Tonight held a quality of unreality. He inquired, "What happens next?"

"We intend to pay a call on the Duke and Duchess of Croydon. If you don't mind, we'd like you along."

"I suppose . . . if you think it necessary."

"Thank you."

"There is one other thing, Mr. McDermott," the second detective said. "We understand that the Duchess of Croydon gave some sort of written permission for their car to be taken from the hotel garage."

"I was told that, yes."

"It could be important, sir. Do you suppose anyone kept that note?"

Peter considered. "It's possible. If you like, I'll telephone the garage."

"Let's go there," Captain Yolles said.

Kulgmer, the garage night checker, was apologetic and chagrined. "Do you know, sir, I said to myself I might

328

need that piece of paper, just to cover me in case anything got asked. And if you'll believe me, sir, I looked for it tonight before I remembered I must have thrown it out yesterday with the paper from my sandwiches. It isn't really my fault, though, when you look at it fair." He gestured to the glass cubicle from which he had emerged. "There's not much space in there. No wonder things get mixed. I was saying just last week, if that place was only bigger. Now, you take the way I have to do the nightly tally . . ."

Peter McDermott interrupted, "What did the note from the Duchess of Croydon say?"

"Just that Mr. O. had permission to take away the car. I kind of wondered at the time . . ."

"Was the note written on hotel stationery?"

"Yes, sir."

"Do you remember if the paper was embossed and had 'Presidential Suite' at the top?"

"Yes, Mr. McDermott, I do remember that. It was just like you said, and sort of a small size sheet."

Peter told the detectives, "We have special stationery for that particular suite."

The second detective queried Kulgmer, "You say you threw the note out with your sandwich wrappings?"

"Don't see how it could have happened any other way. You see, I'm always very careful. Now, take what happened last year . . ."

"What time would that be?"

"Last year?"

The detective said patiently, "Last night. When you threw out the sandwich wrapping. What time?"

"I'd say around two in the morning. I usually start my lunch around one. Things have quieted down by then and . . ."

"Where did you throw them?"

"Same place as always. Over here." Kulgmer led the way to a cleaners' closet containing a garbage can. He removed the lid.

"Is there a chance of last night's stuff still being in there?"

"No, sir. You see, this is emptied every day. The hotel's fussy about that. That's right, Mr. McDermott, isn't it?"

Peter nodded.

"Besides," Kulgmer said, "I remember the can was almost full last night. You can see there's hardly anything in there now."

"Let's make sure." Captain Yolles glanced at Peter for approval, then turned the garbage can upside down, emptying its contents. Though they searched carefully, there was no sign either of Kulgmer's sandwich wrappings or the missing note from the Duchess of Croydon.

Kulgmer left them to attend to several cars entering and leaving the garage.

Yolles wiped his hands on a paper towel. "What happens to the garbage when it leaves here?"

"It goes to our central incinerator," Peter informed him. "By the time it gets there, it's in big trolleys, with everything from the whole hotel mixed up together. It would be impossible to identify any one source. In any case, what was collected from here is probably burned by now."

"Maybe it doesn't matter," Yolles said. "All the same, I'd like to have had that note."

The elevator stopped at the ninth floor. As the detectives followed him out, Peter observed, "I'm not looking forward to this."

Yolles reassured him, "We'll ask a few questions, that's all. I'd like you to listen carefully. And to the answers. It's possible we might need you as a witness later."

To Peter's surprise, the doors of the Presidential Suite were open. As they approached, a buzz of voices could be heard.

The second detective said, "Sounds like a party."

They stopped at the doorway and Peter depressed the bell push. Through a second, partially opened door inside, he could see into the spacious living room. There was a group of men and women, the Duke and Duchess of Croydon among them. Most of the visitors were holding drinks in one hand, notebooks or paper in another.

The Croydons' male secretary appeared in the interior

hallway. "Good evening," Peter said. "These two gentlemen would like to see the Duke and Duchess."

"Are they from the press?"

Captain Yolles shook his head.

"Then I'm sorry, it's impossible. The Duke is holding a press conference. His appointment as British Ambassador was confirmed this evening."

"So I understand," Yolles said. "All the same, our business is important."

While speaking, they had moved from the corridor into the suite hallway. Now, the Duchess of Croydon detached herself from the group in the living room and came toward them. She smiled agreeably. "Won't you come in?"

The secretary injected, "These gentlemen are not from the press."

"Oh!" Her eyes went to Peter with a glance of recognition, then to the other two.

Captain Yolles said, "We're police officers, madam. I have a badge but perhaps you'd prefer me not to produce it here." He looked toward the living room from where several people were watching curiously.

The Duchess gestured to the secretary who closed the living-room door.

Was it imagination, Peter wondered, or had a flicker of fear crossed the Duchess's face at the word "police?" Imagined or not, she was in command of herself now.

"May I ask why you are here?"

"There are some questions, madam, that we'd like to ask you and your husband."

"This is scarcely a convenient time."

"We'll do our best to be as brief as possible." Yolles' voice was quiet, but its authority unmistakable.

"I'll inquire if my husband will see you. Please wait in there."

The secretary led the way to a room off the hallway, furnished as an office. A moment or two later, as the secretary left, the Duchess re-entered, followed by the Duke. He glanced uncertainly from his wife to the others.

"I have informed our guests," the Duchess announced, "that we shall be away no more than a few minutes."

Captain Yolles made no comment. He produced a notebook. "I wonder if you'd mind telling me when you last used your car. It's a Jaguar, I believe." He repeated the registration number.

"Our car?" The Duchess seemed surprised. "I'm not sure what was the last time we used it. No, just a moment. I do remember. It was Monday morning. It's been in the hotel garage since then. It's there now."

"Please think carefully. Did you or your husband, either separately or together, use the car on Monday evening?"

It was revealing, Peter thought, how, automatically, Yolles addressed his questions to the Duchess and not to the Duke.

Two spots of color appeared on the Duchess of Croydon's cheeks. "I am not accustomed to having my word doubted. I have already said that the last occasion the car was used was on Monday morning. I also think you owe us an explanation as to what this is all about."

Yolles wrote in his notebook.

"Are either of you acquainted with Theodore Ogilvie?"

"The name has a certain familiarity . . ."

"He is the chief house officer of this hotel."

"I remember now. He came here. I'm not sure when. There was some query about a piece of jewelry which had been found. Someone suggested it might be mine. It was not."

"And you, sir?" Yolles addressed the Duke directly. "Do you know, or have you had any dealings with, Theodore Ogilvie?"

Perceptibly, the Duke of Croydon hesitated. His wife's eyes were riveted on his face. "Well . . ." He stopped. "Only as my wife has described."

Yolles closed his notebook. In a quiet, level voice he asked, "Would it, then, surprise you to know that your car is at present in the State of Tennessee, where it was driven by Theodore Ogilvie, who is now under arrest? Furthermore, that Ogilvie has made a statement to the effect that he was paid by you to drive the car from New Orleans to Chicago. And, still further, that preliminary investigation indicates your car to have been involved in a hit-and-run fatality, in this city, last Monday night."

"Since you ask," the Duchess of Croydon said, "I would

be extremely surprised. In fact it's the most ridiculous series of fabrications I ever heard."

"There is no fabrication, madam, in the fact that your car is in Tennessee and Ogilvie drove it there."

"If he did so, it was without the authority or knowledge either of my husband or myself. Furthermore if, as you say, the car was involved in an accident on Monday night, it seems perfectly obvious that the same man took the car and used it for his own purposes on that occasion."

"Then you accuse Theodore Ogilvie . . ."

The Duchess snapped, "Accusations are your business. You appear to specialize in them. I will, however, make one to the effect that this hotel has proved disgracefully incompetent in protecting the property of its guests." The Duchess swung toward Peter McDermott. "I assure you that you will hear a great deal more of this."

Peter protested, "But you wrote an authorization. It specified that Ogilvie could take the car."

The effect was as if he had slapped the Duchess across the face. Her lips moved uncertainly. Visibly, she paled. He had reminded her, he realized, of the single incriminating factor she had overlooked.

The silence seemed endless. Then her head came up. "Show it to me!"

Peter said, "Unfortunately, it's been . . ."

He caught a gleam of mocking triumph in her eyes.

19

At last, after more questions and banalities, the Croydons' press conference had ended.

As the outside door of the Presidential Suite closed behind the last to leave, pent-up words burst from the Duke of Croydon's lips. "My God, you can't do it! You couldn't possibly get away with . . ."

"Be *quiet!*" The Duchess of Croydon glanced around the now silent living room. "Not here. I've come to mistrust this hotel and everything about it."

"Then where? For God's sake, where?"

"We'll go outside. Where no one can overhear. But when we do, please behave less excitably than now."

She opened the connecting door to their bedrooms where the Bedlington terriers had been confined. They tumbled out excitedly, barking as the Duchess fastened their leads, aware of what the sign portended. In the hallway, the secretary dutifully opened the suite door as the terriers led the way out.

In the elevator, the Duke seemed about to speak but his wife shook her head. Only when they were outside, away from the hotel and beyond the hearing of other pedestrians, did she murmur, "Now!"

His voice was strained, intense. "I tell you it's madness! The whole mess is already bad enough. We've compounded and compounded what happened at first. Can you conceive what it will be like now, when the truth finally comes out?"

"Yes, I've some idea. *If* it does."

He persisted, "Apart from everything else—the moral issue, all the rest—you'd never get away with it."

"Why not?"

"Because it's impossible. Inconceivable. We are already worse off than at the beginning. Now, with this . . ." His voice choked.

"We are *not* worse off. For the moment we are better off. May I remind you of the appointment to Washington."

"You don't seriously suppose we have the slightest chance of ever getting there?"

"There is every chance."

Preceded eagerly by the terriers, they had walked along St. Charles Avenue to the busier and brightly lighted expanse of Canal Street. Now, turning southeast toward the river, they affected interest in the colorful store windows as groups of pedestrians passed in both directions.

The Duchess's voice was low. "However distasteful, there are certain facts that I must know about Monday night. The woman you were with at Irish Bayou. Did you drive her there?"

The Duke flushed. "No. She went in a taxi. We met inside. I intended afterward . . ."

"Spare me your intentions. Then, for all she knew, you could have come in a taxi yourself."

"I hadn't thought about it. I suppose so."

"After I arrived—also by taxi, which can be confirmed if necessary—I noticed that when we went to our car, you had parked it well away from that awful club. There was no attendant."

"I put it out of the way deliberately. I suppose I thought there was less chance of your getting to hear."

"So at no point was there any witness to the fact that you were driving the car on Monday night."

"There's the hotel garage. When we came in, someone could have seen us."

"No! I remember you stopped just inside the garage entrance, and you left the car, as we often do. We. saw no one. No one saw us."

"What about taking it out?"

"You couldn't have taken it out. Not from the hotel garage. On Monday *morning* we left it on an outside parking lot."

"That's right," the Duke said. "I got it from there at night."

The Duchess continued, thinking aloud, "We shall say, of course, that we did take the car to the hotel garage after we used it Monday evening. There will be no record of it coming in, but that proves nothing. As far as we are concerned, we have not seen the car since midday Monday."

The Duke was silent as they continued to walk. With a gesture he reached out, relieving his wife of the terriers. Sensing a new hand on their leash, they strained forward more vigorously than before.

At length he said, "It's really quite remarkable how everything fits together."

"It's more than remarkable. It's meant to be that way. From the beginning, everything has worked out. Now . . ."

"Now you propose to send another man to prison instead of me."

"No!"

He shook his head. "I couldn't do it, even to him."

"As far as he is concerned, I promise you that nothing will happen."

"How could you be sure?"

"Because the police would have to prove he was driving

335

the car at the time of the accident. They can't possibly do it, any more than they can prove it was you. Don't you understand? They may *know* that it was one or the other of you. They may believe they know which. But believing is not enough. Not without proof."

"You know," he said, with admiration, "there are times when you are absolutely incredible."

"I'm practical. And speaking of being practical, there's something else you might remember. That man Ogilvie has had ten thousand dollars of our money. At least we should get something for it."

"By the way," the Duke said, "where is the other fifteen thousand?"

"Still in the small suitcase which is locked and in my bedroom. We'll take it with us when we go. I already decided it might attract attention to return it to the bank here."

"You really do think of everything."

"I didn't with that note. When I thought they had it . . . I must have been mad to write what I did."

"You couldn't have foreseen."

They had reached the end of the brightly lighted portion of Canal Street. Now they turned, retracing their steps toward the city center.

"It's diabolical," the Duke of Croydon said. His last drink had been at noon. As a result, his voice was a good deal clearer than in recent days. "It's ingenious, devilish, and diabolical. But it might, it just might work."

20

"That woman is lying," Captain Yolles said. "But it'll be hard to prove, if we ever do." He continued to pace, slowly, the length of Peter McDermott's office. They had come here—the two detectives, with Peter—after an ignominious departure from the Presidential Suite. So far Yolles had done little more than pace and ponder while the other two waited.

"Her husband might break," the second detective suggested. "If we could get him by himself."

Yolles shook his head. "There isn't a chance. For one thing, she's too smart to let it happen. For another, with them being who and what they are, we'd be walking on eggshells." He looked at Peter. "Don't ever kid yourself there isn't one police procedure for the poor and another for the rich and influential."

Across the office, Peter nodded, though with a sense of detachment. Having done what duty and conscience required, what followed now, he felt, was the business of the police. Curiosity, however, prompted a question. "The note that the Duchess wrote to the garage . . ."

"If we had that," the second detective said, "it'd be a clincher."

"Isn't it enough for the night checker—and Ogilvie, I suppose—to swear that the note existed?"

Yolles said, "She'd claim it was a forgery, that Ogilvie wrote it himself." He mused, then added, "You said it was on special stationery. Let me see some."

Peter went outside and in a stationery cupboard found several sheets. They were a heavy bond paper, light blue, with the hotel name and crest embossed. Below, also embossed, were the words *Presidential Suite*.

Peter returned and the policemen examined the sheets.

"Pretty fancy," the second detective said.

Yolles asked, "How many people have access to this?"

"In the ordinary way, just a few. But I suppose a good many others could get hold of a sheet if they really wanted to."

Yolles grunted. "Rules that out."

"There is one possibility," Peter said. For the moment, with a sudden thought, his detachment vanished.

"What?"

"I know you asked me this, and I said that once garbage had been cleared—as it was from the garage—there was no chance of retrieving anything. I really thought . . . it seemed so impossible, the idea of locating one piece of paper. Besides, the note wasn't so important then."

He was aware of the eyes of both detectives intently on his face.

"We do have a man," Peter said. "He's in charge of the

incinerator. A lot of the garbage he sorts by hand. It would be a long shot and it's probably too late . . ."

"For Christ's sake!" Yolles snapped. "Let's get to him."

They walked quickly to the main floor, then used a staff doorway to reach a freight elevator which would take them the rest of the way down. The elevator was busy on a lower level where Peter could hear packages being unloaded. He shouted down for the crew to hurry.

While they were waiting, the second detective, Bennett, said, "I hear you've had some other trouble this week."

"There was a robbery early yesterday. With all this, I'd almost forgotten."

"I was talking with one of our people. He was with your senior house dick . . . what's his name?"

"Finegan. He's acting chief." Despite the seriousness, Peter smiled. "Our regular chief is otherwise engaged."

"About the robbery, there wasn't much to go on. Our people checked your guest list, didn't turn up anything. Today, though, a funny thing happened. There was a break-in in Lakeview—private home. A key job. The woman lost her keys downtown this morning. Whoever found them must have gone straight there. It had all the signs of your robbery here, including the kind of stuff taken, and no prints."

"Has there been an arrest?"

The detective shook his head. "Wasn't discovered till hours after it happened. There is a lead, though. A neighbor saw a car. Couldn't remember anything, except it had license plates that were green and white. Five states use plates with those colors—Michigan, Idaho, Nebraska, Vermont, Washington—and Saskatchewan in Canada."

"How does that help?"

"For the next day or two, all our boys will be watching for cars from those places. They'll stop them and check. It could turn something up. We've been lucky before, with a whole lot less to go on."

Peter nodded, though with lukewarm interest. The robbery had happened two days ago, with no recurrence. At present a good deal else seemed more important.

A moment later the elevator arrived.

The sweat-shining face of Booker T. Graham beamed with pleasure at the sight of Peter McDermott, the only member of the hotel's executive staff who ever bothered visiting the incinerator room, deep within the hotel basement. The visits, though infrequent, were treasured by Booker T. Graham as royal occasions.

Captain Yolles wrinkled his nose at the overpowering odor of garbage, magnified by intense heat. The reflection of flames danced on smoke-grimed walls. Shouting to make himself heard above the roar of the furnace set into one side of the enclosure, Peter cautioned, "Better leave this to me. I'll explain what we want."

Yolles nodded. Like others who had preceded him here, it occurred to him that the first sight of hell might be remarkably like this moment. He wondered how a human being could exist in these surroundings for any length of time.

Yolles watched as Peter McDermott talked with the big Negro who sorted the garbage before incinerating it. McDermott had brought a sheet of the special Presidential Suite stationery and held it up for inspection. The Negro nodded and took the sheet, retaining it, but his expression was doubtful. He gestured to the dozens of overflowing bins crowded around them. There were also others, Yolles observed as they came in, lined up outside on hand trucks. He realized why, earlier on, McDermott had dismissed the possibility of locating a single piece of paper. Now, in response to a question, the Negro shook his head. McDermott returned to the two detectives.

"Most of this," he explained, "is yesterday's garbage, collected today. About a third of what came in had already been burned and whether what we want was in there or not, we've no means of knowing. As for the rest, Graham has to go through it, looking for things we salvage, like silverware and bottles. While he's doing that, he'll keep an eye open for a paper of the kind I've given him, but as you can see, it's a pretty formidable job. Before the garbage gets here, it's compressed and a lot of it is wet, which soaks everything else. I've asked Graham if he wants extra help, but he says there's even less chance if

339

someone else comes in who isn't used to working the way he does."

"Either way," the second detective said, "I wouldn't lay any bets."

Yolles conceded, "I suppose it's the best we can do. What arrangement did you make if your man finds anything?"

"He'll call upstairs right away. I'll leave instructions that I'm to be notified, whatever time it is. Then I'll call you."

Yolles nodded. As the three men left, Booker T. Graham had his hands in a mess of garbage on a large flat tray.

21

For Keycase Milne, frustration had piled upon frustration.

Since early evening he had maintained a watch upon the Presidential Suite. Near dinnertime—when he confidently expected the Duke and Duchess of Croydon to leave the hotel, as almost all visitors did—he had taken post on the ninth floor near the service stairs. From there he had a clear view of the entrance to the suite, with the advantage that he could avoid being observed himself by ducking quickly out of sight through the stairway door. He did this several times as elevators stopped and occupants of other rooms came and went, though on each occasion Keycase managed to catch a glimpse of them before his own departure. He also calculated, correctly, that at this time of day there would be little staff activity on the upper floors. In case of anything unforeseen, it was a simple matter to retreat to the eighth floor and, if necessary, his own room.

That part of his plan had worked. What had gone wrong was that through the entire evening the Duke and Duchess of Croydon had failed to leave their suite.

However, no room service dinner had been delivered, a fact which made Keycase linger hopefully.

Once, wondering if he had somehow missed the Croydons' departure, Keycase walked gingerly down the corridor and listened at the suite door. He could hear voices inside, including a woman's.

Later, his disappointment was increased by the arrival of visitors. They appeared to come in ones and twos and, after the first few, the doors to the Presidential Suite were left open. Soon after, room-service waiters appeared with trays of hors d'oeuvres, and a growing hum of conversation, mixed with the clink of ice and glasses, was audible in the corridor.

He was puzzled, later still, by the arrival of a broad-shouldered youngish man whom Keycase judged to be an official of the hotel. The hotelman's face was set grimly, as were those of two other men with him. Keycase paused long enough for a careful look at all three and, at first glance, guessed the second and third to be policemen. Subsequently he reassured himself that the thought was the product of his own too active imagination.

The three more recent arrivals left first, followed a half hour or so later by the remainder of the party. Despite the heavy traffic in the later stages of the evening, Keycase was certain he had been unobserved, except possibly as just another hotel guest.

With departure of the last visitor, silence was complete in the ninth floor corridor. It was now close to eleven P.M. and obvious that nothing more would happen tonight. Keycase decided to wait another ten minutes, then leave.

His mood of optimism earlier in the day had changed to depression.

He was uncertain whether he could risk remaining in the hotel another twenty-four hours. He had already considered the idea of entering the suite during the night or early tomorrow morning, then dismissed it. The hazard was too great. If someone awakened, no conceivable excuse could justify Keycase's presence in the Presidential Suite. He had also been aware since yesterday that he would have to consider the movements of the Croydons' secretary and the Duchess's maid. The maid, he learned, had a room elsewhere in the hotel and had not been in evidence tonight. But the secretary lived in the suite and was one more person who might be awakened by a night intrusion. Also, the dogs which Keycase had seen the Duchess exercising were likely to raise an alarm.

He was faced, then, with the alternative of waiting another day or abandoning the attempt to reach the Duchess's jewels.

Then, as he was on the point of leaving, the Duke and Duchess of Croydon emerged, preceded by the Bedlington terriers.

Swiftly, Keycase melted into the service stairway. His heart began to pulse faster. At last, when he had abandoned hope, the opportunity he coveted had come.

It was not an uncomplicated opportunity. Obviously the Duke and Duchess would not be away for long. And somewhere in the suite was the male secretary. Where? In a separate room with the door closed? In bed already? He looked a Milquetoast type who might retire early.

Whatever the risk of an encounter, it had to be taken. Keycase knew that if he failed to act now, his nerves would not survive another day of waiting.

He heard elevator doors open, then close. Cautiously, he returned to the corridor. It was silent and empty. Walking quietly, he approached the Presidential Suite.

His specially made key turned easily, as it had this afternoon. He opened one of the double doors slightly, then gently released the spring pressure and removed the key. The lock made no noise. Nor did the door as he opened it slowly.

A hallway was immediately ahead, beyond it a larger room. To the right and left were two more doors, both closed. Through the one on the right he could hear what sounded like a radio. There was no one in sight. The lights in the suite were turned on.

Keycase went in. He slipped on gloves, then closed and latched the outside door behind him.

He moved warily, yet wasting no time. Broadloom in the hallway and living room muffled his footsteps. He crossed the living room to a farther door which was ajar. As Keycase expected, it led to two spacious bedrooms, each with a bathroom, and a dressing room between. In the bedrooms, as elsewhere, lights were on. There was no mistaking which room was the Duchess's.

Its furnishings included a tallboy, two dressing tables and a walk-in closet. Keycase began, systematically, to search all four. A jewelbox, such as he sought, was in neither the tallboy nor the first dressing table. There were a number of items—gold evening purses, cigarette cases and expensive-looking compacts—which, with more time and in other circumstances, he would have garnered gladly. But now he was racing, seeking a major prize and discarding all else.

At the second dressing table he opened the first drawer. It contained nothing worth while. The second drawer yielded no better result. In the third, on top, was an array of negligees. Beneath them was a deep, oblong box of hand-tooled leather. It was locked.

Leaving the box in the drawer, Keycase worked with a knife and screwdriver to break the lock. The box was stoutly made and resisted opening. Several minutes passed. Conscious of fleeting time, he began to perspire.

At length the lock gave, the lid flew back. Beneath, in scintillating, breathtaking array were two tiers of jewels—rings, brooches, necklets, clips, tiaras; all of precious metal, and most were gem-encrusted. At the sight, Keycase drew in breath. So, after all, a portion of the Duchess's fabled collection had not been consigned to the hotel vault. Once more a hunch, an omen, had proved right. With both hands he reached out to seize the spoils. At the same instant a key turned in the lock of the outer door.

His reflex was instantaneous. Keycase slammed down the jewelbox lid and slid the drawer closed. On the way in, he had left the bedroom door slightly ajar; now he flew to it. Through an inch-wide gap he could see into the living room. A hotel maid was entering. She had towels on her arm and was headed for the Duchess's bedroom. The maid was elderly, and waddled. Her slowness offered a single slim chance.

Swinging around, Keycase lunged for a bedside lamp. He found its cord and yanked. The light went out. Now he needed something in his hand to indicate activity. Something! Anything!

Against the wall was a small attaché case. He seized it and stalked toward the door.

As Keycase flung the door wide, the maid recoiled. "Oh!" A hand went over her heart.

Keycase frowned. "Where have you been? You should have come here earlier."

The shock, followed by the accusation, made her flustered. He had intended that it should.

"I'm sorry, sir. I saw there were people in, and . . ."

He cut her short. "It doesn't matter now. Do what you have to, and there's a lamp needs fixing." He gestured into the bedroom. "The Duchess wants it working tonight." He kept his voice low, remembering the secretary.

"Oh, I'll see that it is, sir."

"Very well." Keycase nodded coolly, and went out.

In the corridor he tried not to think. He succeeded until he was in his own room, 830. Then, in bafflement and despair, he flung himself across the bed and buried his face in a pillow.

It was more than an hour before he bothered forcing the lock of the attaché case he had brought away.

Inside was pile upon pile of United States currency. All used bills, of small denominations.

With trembling hands he counted fifteen thousand dollars.

22

Peter McDermott accompanied the two detectives from the incinerator in the hotel basement to the St. Charles Street door.

"For the time being," Captain Yolles cautioned, "I'd like to keep what's happened tonight as quiet as possible. There'll be questions enough when we charge your man Ogilvie, whatever it's with. No sense in bringing the press around our necks until we have to."

Peter assured him, "If the hotel had any choice, we'd prefer no publicity at all."

Yolles grunted. "Don't count on it."

Peter returned to the main dining room to discover, not surprisingly, that Christine and Albert Wells had gone.

In the lobby he was intercepted by the night manager. "Mr. McDermott, here's a note Miss Francis left for you."

It was in a sealed envelope and read simply:

I've gone home. Come if you can.
                              —*Christine.*

He would go, he decided. He suspected that Christine was eager to talk over the events of the day, including this evening's astounding disclosure by Albert Wells.

Nothing else to do tonight at the hotel. Or was there? Abruptly, Peter remembered the promise he had made to Marsha Preyscott on leaving her at the cemetery so unceremoniously this afternoon. He had said he would telephone later, but he had forgotten until now. The crisis of the afternoon was only hours away. It seemed like days, and Marsha somehow remote. But he supposed he should call her, late as it was.

Once more he used the credit manager's office on the main floor and dialed the Preyscott number. Marsha answered on the first ring.

"Oh, Peter," she said, "I've been sitting by the telephone. I waited and waited, then called twice and left my name."

He remembered guiltily the pile of unacknowledged messages on his office desk.

"I'm genuinely sorry, and I can't explain, at least not yet. Except that all kinds of things have been happening."

"Tell me tomorrow."

"Marsha, I'm afraid tomorrow will be a very full day . . ."

"At breakfast," Marsha said. "If it's going to be that kind of day, you need a New Orleans breakfast. They're famous. Have you ever had one?"

"I don't usually eat breakfast."

"Tomorrow you will. And Anna's are special. A lot better, I'll bet, than at your old hotel."

It was impossible not to be charmed by Marsha's enthusiasms. And he had, after all, deserted her this afternoon.

"It will have to be early."

"As early as you like."

They agreed on 7:30 A.M.

A few minutes later he was in a taxi on his way to Christine's apartment in Gentilly.

He rang from downstairs. Christine was waiting with the apartment door open.

"Not a word," she said, "until after the second drink. I just can't take it all in."

"You'd better," he told her. "You haven't heard the half of it."

She had mixed daiquiris, which were chilling in the refrigerator. There was a heaped plate of chicken and ham sandwiches. The fragrance of freshly brewed coffee wafted through the apartment.

Peter remembered suddenly that despite his sojourn in the hotel kitchens, and the talk of breakfast tomorrow, he had eaten nothing since lunch.

"That's what I imagined," Christine said when he told her. "Fall to!"

Obeying, he watched as she moved efficiently around the tiny kitchen. He had a feeling, sitting here, of being at ease and shielded from whatever might be happening outside. He thought: Christine had cared about him enough to do what she had done. More important, there was an empathy between them in which even their silences, as now, seemed shared and understood.

He pushed away the daiquiri glass and reached for a coffee cup which Christine had filled. "All right," he said, "where do we start?"

They talked continuously for almost two hours, all the time their closeness growing. At the end, all they could decide on definitely was that tomorrow would be an interesting day.

"I won't sleep," Christine said. "I couldn't possibly. I know I won't."

"I couldn't either," Peter said. "But not for the reason you mean."

He had no doubts; only a conviction that he wanted this moment to go on and on. He took her in his arms and kissed her.

Later, it seemed the most natural thing in the world that they should make love.

FRIDAY

1

It was understandable, Peter McDermott thought, that the Duke and Duchess of Croydon should be rolling the chief house officer, Ogilvie—trussed securely into a ball—toward the edge of the St. Gregory roof while, far below, a sea of faces stared fixedly upward. But it was strange, and somehow shocking, that a few yards farther on, Curtis O'Keefe and Warren Trent were exchanging savage cuts with bloodstained dueling swords. Why, Peter wondered, had Captain Yolles, standing by a stairway door, failed to intervene? Then Peter realized that the policeman was watching a giant bird's nest in which a single egg was cracking open. A moment later, from the egg's interior, emerged an outsize sparrow with the cheery face of Albert Wells. But now Peter's attention was diverted to the roof-edge where a desperately struggling Christine had become entangled with Ogilvie, and Marsha Preyscott was helping the Croydons push the double burden nearer and nearer to the awful gulf below. The crowds continued to gape as Captain Yolles leaned against a doorpost, yawning.

If he hoped to save Christine, Peter realized, he must act himself. But when he attempted to move, his feet dragged heavily as if encased in glue, and while his body urged forward, his legs refused to follow. He tried to cry out, but his throat was blocked. His eyes met Christine's in dumb despair.

Suddenly, the Croydons, Marsha, O'Keefe, Warren Trent stopped and were listening. The sparrow that was

Albert Wells cocked an ear. Now Ogilvie, Yolles, and Christine were doing the same. Listening to what?

Then Peter heard: a cacophony as if all the telephones on earth were ringing together. The sound came closer, swelled, until it seemed that it would engulf them all. Peter put his hands over his ears. The dissonance grew. He closed his eyes, then opened them.

He was in his apartment. His bedside alarm showed 6:30 A.M.

He lay for a few minutes, shaking his head free from the wild, hodge-podge dream. Then he padded to the bath-room for a shower, steeling himself to remain under the spray with the cold tap "on" for a final minute. He emerged from the shower fully awake. Slipping on a towel robe, he started coffee brewing in the kitchenette, then went to the telephone and dialed the hotel number.

He was connected with the night manager who assured Peter that there had been no message during the night concerning anything found in the incinerator. No, the night manager said with a trace of tiredness, he had not checked personally. Yes, if Mr. McDermott wished, he would go down immediately and telephone the result, though Peter sensed a mild resentment at the unlikely errand so near the end of a long, tiring shift. The incinerator was some-where in the lower basement, wasn't it?

Peter was shaving when the return call came. The night manager reported that he had spoken with the incinerator employee, Graham, who was sorry, but the paper Mr. Mc-Dermott wanted had not turned up. Now, it didn't look as if it would. The manager added the information that Graham's night shift—as well as his own—was almost ended.

Later, Peter decided, he would pass the news, or rather the lack of it, to Captain Yolles. He remembered his opin-ion last night, which still held good, that the hotel had done all it could in the matter of public duty. Anything else must be the business of the police.

Between sips of coffee, and while dressing, Peter con-sidered the two subjects uppermost in his mind. One was Christine; the other, his own future, if any, at the St. Gregory Hotel.

After last night, he realized that whatever might be ahead, more than anything else he wished Christine to be a part of it. The conviction had been growing on him; now it was clear and definite. He supposed it might be said that he was in love, but he was guarded in attempting to define his deeper feelings, even to himself. Once before, what he had believed was love had turned to ashes. Perhaps it was better to begin with hope, and grope uncertainly toward an unknown end.

It might be unromantic, Peter reflected, to say that he was comfortable with Christine. But it was true and, in a sense, reassuring. He had a conviction that the bonds between them would grow stronger, not weaker, as time went by. He believed that Christine's feelings were similar to his own.

Instinct told him that what lay immediately ahead was to be savored, not devoured.

As to the hotel, it was hard to grasp, even now, that Albert Wells, whom they had assumed to be a pleasant, inconsequential little man, stood revealed as a financial mogul who had assumed control of the St. Gregory, or would today.

Superficially, it seemed possible that Peter's own position might be strengthened by the unexpected development. He had become friendly with the little man and had the impression that he himself was liked in return. But liking, and a business decision, were separate things. The nicest people could be hard-headed, and ruthless when they chose. Also, it was unlikely that Albert Wells would run the hotel personally, and whoever fronted for him might have definite views on the background records of personnel.

As he had before, Peter decided not to worry about events until they happened.

Across New Orleans, clocks were chiming seven-thirty as Peter McDermott arrived, by taxi, at the Preyscott mansion on Prytania Street.

Behind graceful soaring columns, the great white house stood nobly in early morning sunlight. The air around was fresh and cool, with traces still of a predawn mist. The

349

scent of magnolia hung fragrantly, and there was dew upon the grass.

The street and house were quiet, but from St. Charles Avenue and beyond could be heard distant sounds of the awakening city.

Peter crossed the lawn by the curving pathway of old red brick. He ascended the terrace steps and knocked at the double carved doorway.

Ben, the manservant who had functioned at dinner on Wednesday night, opened the door and greeted Peter cordially. "Good morning, sir. Please come in." Inside, he announced, "Miss Marsha asked me to show you to the gallery. She'll join you in a few minutes."

With Ben leading the way, they went up the broad curving staircase and along the wide corridor with frescoed walls where, on Wednesday night in semidarkness, Peter had accompanied Marsha. He asked himself: was it really so short a time ago?

In daylight the gallery appeared as well ordered and inviting as it had before. There were deep cushioned chairs, and planters bright with flowers. Near the front, looking down on the garden below, a table had been set for breakfast. There were two places.

Peter asked, "Is the house stirring early on my account?"

"No, sir," Ben assured him. "We're early people here. Mr. Preyscott, when he's home, doesn't like late starting. He always says there isn't enough of each day that you should waste the front end of it."

"You see! I told you my father was a lot like you."

At Marsha's voice, Peter turned. She had come in quietly behind them. He had an impression of dew and roses, and that she had risen freshly with the sun.

"Good morning!" Marsha smiled. "Ben, please give Mr. McDermott an absinthe Suissesse." She took Peter's arm.

"Pour lightly, Ben," Peter said. "I know absinthe Suissesse goes with a New Orleans breakfast, but I've a new boss. I'd like to meet him sober."

The manservant grinned. "Yessir!"

As they sat at the table, Marsha said, "Was that why you . . ."

"Why I disappeared like a conjurer's rabbit? No. That was something else."

Her eyes widened as he related as much as he could of the hit-and-run investigation without mentioning the Croydons' name. He declined to be drawn by Marsha's questioning, but told her, "Whatever happens, there will be some news today."

To himself, he reasoned: By now, Ogilvie was probably back in New Orleans and being interrogated. If retained in custody, he would have to be charged, with an appearance in court which would alert the press. Inevitably there would be a reference to the Jaguar which, in turn, would point a finger at the Croydons.

Peter sampled the fluffy absinthe Suissesse which had appeared before him. From his own bartending days he remembered the ingredients—herbsaint, white of an egg, cream, orgeat syrup, and a dash of anisette. He had seldom tasted them better mixed. Across the table Marsha was sipping orange juice.

Peter wondered: Could the Duke and Duchess of Croydon, in face of Ogilvie's accusation, continue to maintain their innocence? It was one more question which today might determine.

But certainly the Duchess's note—if it ever existed—was gone. There had been no further word from the hotel —at least, on that point—and Booker T. Graham would have long since gone off duty.

In front of both Peter and Marsha, Ben placed a Creole cream cheese Evangeline, garlanded with fruit.

Peter began to eat with enjoyment.

"Earlier on," Marsha said, "you started to say something. It was about the hotel."

"Oh, yes." Between mouthfuls of cheese and fruit, he explained about Albert Wells. "The new ownership is being announced today. I had a telephone call just as I was leaving to come here."

The call had been from Warren Trent. It informed Peter that Mr. Dempster of Montreal, financial representative of the St. Gregory's new owner, was en route to New Orleans. Mr. Dempster was already in New York where he would board an Eastern Airlines flight, arriving

351

at mid-morning. A suite was to be reserved, and a meeting between the old and new management groups was scheduled tentatively for eleven-thirty. Peter was instructed to remain available in case he was required.

Surprisingly, Warren Trent had sounded not in the least depressed and, in fact, brighter than in recent days. Was W.T. aware, Peter wondered, that the new owner of the St. Gregory was already in the hotel? Remembering that until an official changeover, his own loyalty lay with the old management, Peter related the conversation of last evening between himself, Christine, and Albert Wells. "Yes," Warren Trent had said, "I know. Emile Dumaire of Industrial Merchants Bank—he did the negotiating for Wells— phoned me late last night. It seems there was some secrecy. There isn't any more."

Peter also knew that Curtis O'Keefe, and his companion Miss Lash, were due to leave the St. Gregory later this morning. Apparently they were going separate ways since the hotel—which handled such matters for VIPs—had arranged a flight to Los Angeles for Miss Lash, while Curtis O'Keefe was headed for Naples, via New York and Rome.

"You're thinking about a lot of things," Marsha said. "I wish you'd tell me some. My father used to want to talk at breakfast, but my mother was never interested. I am."

Peter smiled. He told her the kind of day that he expected it to be.

As they talked, the remains of the cheeses Evangeline were removed, to be replaced by steaming, aromatic eggs Sardou. Twin poached eggs nestled on artichoke bottoms, appetizingly topped with creamed spinach and hollandaise sauce. A rosé wine appeared at Peter's place.

Marsha said, "I understand what you meant about today being very busy."

"And I understand what *you* meant by a traditional breakfast." Peter caught sight of the housekeeper, Anna, hovering in the background. He called out, "Magnificent!" and saw her smile.

Later, he gasped at the arrival of sirloin steaks with mushrooms, hot french bread and marmalade.

Peter said doubtfully, "I'm not sure . . ."

"There's *crêpes Suzette* to come," Marsha informed him, "and *café au lait*. When there were great plantations here, people used to scoff at the *petit dejeuner* of the continentals. They made breakfast an occasion."

"You've made it an occasion," Peter said. "This, and a good deal more. Meeting you; my history lessons; being with you here. I won't forget it—ever."

"You make it sound as if you're saying goodbye."

"I am, Marsha." He met her eyes steadily, then smiled. "Right after the *crêpes Suzette*."

There was a silence before she said, "I thought . . ."

He reached out across the table, his hand covering Marsha's. "Perhaps we were both daydreaming. I think we were. But it's quite the nicest daydream I ever had."

"Why does it have to be just that?"

He answered gently, "Some things you can't explain. No matter how much you like someone, there's a question of deciding what's best to do; of judgment . . ."

"And my judgment doesn't count?"

"Marsha, I have to trust mine. For both of us." But he wondered: Could it be trusted? His own instincts had proven less than reliable before. Perhaps, at this moment, he was making a mistake which years from now he would remember with regret. How to be sure of anything, when you often learned the truth too late?

He sensed that Marsha was close to tears.

"Excuse me," she said in a low voice. She stood up and walked swiftly from the gallery.

Sitting there, Peter wished he could have spoken less forthrightly, tempering his words with the gentleness that he felt for this lonely girl. He wondered if she would return. After a few minutes, when Marsha failed to, Anna appeared. "Looks like you'll be finishing breakfast alone, sir. I don't believe Miss Marsha'll be back."

He asked, "How is she?"

"She's cryin' in her room." Anna shrugged. "Isn't the first time. Don't suppose it'll be the last. It's a way she has when she doesn't get all she wants." She removed the steak plates. "Ben'll serve you the rest."

353

He shook his head. "No, thank you. I must go."

"Then I'll just bring coffee." In the background, Ben had busied himself, but it was Anna who took the *café au lait* and put it beside Peter.

"Don't go away worrying overmuch, sir. When she's past the most of it, I'll do the best I can. Miss Marsha has maybe too much time to think about herself. If her daddy was here more, maybe things'd be different. But he ain't. Not hardly at all."

"You're very understanding."

Peter remembered what Marsha had told him about Anna: how, as a young girl, Anna had been forced by her family to marry a man she scarcely knew; but the marriage had lasted happily for more than forty years until Anna's husband died a year ago.

Peter said, "I heard about your husband. He must have been a fine man."

"My husband!" The housekeeper cackled. "I ain't had no husband. Never been married in my whole life. I'm a maiden lady—more or less."

Marsha had said: *They lived with us here, Anna and her husband. He was the kindest, sweetest man I've ever known. If there was ever a perfect marriage, it belonged to them.* Marsha had used the portrayal to bolster her own argument when she asked Peter to marry her.

Anna was still chuckling. "My goodness! Miss Marsha's been taking you in with all her stories. She makes up a good many. A lot of the time she's play acting, which is why you don't need to worry none now."

"I see." Peter was not sure that he did, though he felt relieved.

Ben showed him out. It was after nine o'clock and the day was already becoming hot. Peter walked briskly toward St. Charles Avenue where he headed for the hotel. He hoped that the walk would overcome any somnolence he might feel from the trencherman's meal. He felt a genuine regret that he would not see Marsha again, and a sorrow concerning her for a reason he could not fully comprehend. He wondered if he would ever be wise about women. He rather doubted it.

2

Number four elevator was acting up again. Cy Lewin, its elderly daytime operator, was getting thoroughly sick of number four and its capriciousness, which had started a week or more ago and seemed to be getting worse.

Last Sunday the elevator had several times refused to respond to its controls, even though both cage and landing doors were fully closed. The relief man had told Cy that the same thing happened Monday night when Mr. McDermott, the assistant general manager, was in the car.

Then, on Wednesday, there had been trouble which put number four out of service for several hours. Malfunctioning of the clutch arrangement, Engineering said, whatever that meant; but the repair job had not prevented another hiatus the following day when on three separate occasions number four refused to start away from the fifteenth floor.

Now, today, number four was starting and stopping jerkily at every floor.

It was not Cy Lewin's business to know what was wrong. Nor did he especially care, even though he had heard the chief engineer, Doc Vickery, grumbling about "patching and patching" and complaining that he needed "a hundred thousand dollars to rip the elevators' guts out and begin again." Well, who wouldn't like that kind of money? Cy Lewin himself sure would, which was why every year he scraped together the price of a sweepstake ticket, though a fat lot of good it had ever done him.

But a St. Gregory veteran like himself was entitled to consideration, and tomorrow he would ask to be moved over to one of the other cars. Why not? He had worked twenty-seven years in the hotel and was running elevators before some of the young whippersnappers now around the place were born. After today, let someone else put up with number four and its contrariness.

It was a little before ten A.M., and the hotel was becoming busy. Cy Lewin took a load up from the lobby—mostly conventioneers with names on their lapels—stopping at intermediate floors until the fifteenth, which was the top of the hotel. Going down, the car was filled to capacity by the time he reached the ninth, and he highballed the rest of the way to the main lobby. On this latest trip he noticed that the jerkiness had stopped. Well, whatever *that* trouble was, he guessed it had fixed itself.

He could not have been more wrong.

High above Cy Lewin, perched like an eyrie on the hotel roof, was the elevator control room. There, in the mechanical heart of number four elevator, a small electrical relay had reached the limit of its useful life. The cause, unknown and unsuspected, was a tiny push rod the size of a household nail.

The push rod was screwed into a miniature piston head which, in turn, actuated a trio of switches. One switch applied and released the elevator brake, a second supplied power to an operating motor; the third controlled a generator circuit. With all three functioning, the elevator car moved smoothly up and down in response to its controls. But with only two switches working—and if the nonworking switch should be that which controlled the elevator motor—the car would be free to fall under its own weight. Only one thing could cause such a failure—the over-all lengthening of the push rod and piston.

For several weeks the push rod had been working loose. With movements so infinitesimal that a hundred might equal the thickness of a human hair, the piston head had turned, slowly but inexorably unscrewing itself from the push rod thread. The effect was twofold. The push rod and piston had increased their total length. And the motor switch was barely functioning.

Just as a final grain of sand will tip a scale, so, at this moment, the slightest further twisting of the piston would isolate the motor switch entirely.

The defect had been the cause of number four's erratic functioning which Cy Lewin and others had observed. A maintenance crew had tried to trace the trouble, but had not succeeded. They could hardly be blamed. There were more than sixty relays to a single elevator, and twenty elevators in the entire hotel.

Nor had anyone observed that two safety devices on the elevator car were partially defective.

At ten past ten on Friday morning, number four elevator was—in fact, and figuratively—hanging by a thread.

Mr. Dempster of Montreal checked in at half-past ten. Peter McDermott, notified of his arrival, went down to the lobby to extend official greetings. So far this morning, neither Warren Trent nor Albert Wells had appeared on the lower floors of the hotel, nor had the latter been heard from.

The financial representative of Albert Wells was a brisk, impressive person who looked like the seasoned manager of a large branch bank. He responded to a comment of Peter's about the speed of events being breathtaking with the remark, "Mr. Wells frequently has that effect." A bellboy escorted the newcomer to a suite on the eleventh floor.

Twenty minutes later Mr. Dempster reappeared in Peter's office.

He had visited Mr. Wells, he said, and spoken on the telephone with Mr. Trent. The meeting arranged tentatively for eleven-thirty was definitely to proceed. Meanwhile, there were a few people whom Mr. Dempster wished to confer with—the hotel's comptroller for one—and Mr. Trent had invited him to make use of the executive suite.

Mr. Dempster appeared to be a man accustomed to exercise authority.

Peter escorted him to Warren Trent's office and introduced Christine. For Peter and Christine it was their second meeting of the morning. On arrival at the hotel he had sought her out and, though the best they could do in the beleaguered surroundings of the executive suite was to touch hands briefly, in the stolen moment there was an excitement and an eager awareness of each other.

For the first time since his arrival, the man from Montreal smiled. "Oh yes, Miss Francis. Mr. Wells mentioned you. In fact, he spoke of you quite warmly."

"I think Mr. Wells is a wonderful man. I thought so before . . ." She stopped.

"Yes?"

"I'm a little embarrassed," Christine said, "about something which happened last night."

Mr. Dempster produced heavy-rimmed glasses which he polished and put on. "If you're referring to the incident of the restaurant bill, Miss Francis, it's unnecessary that you should be. Mr. Wells told me—and I quote his own words—that it was one of the sweetest, kindest things that was ever done for him. He knew what was happening, of course. There's very little he misses."

"Yes," Christine said, "I'm beginning to realize that."

There was a knock at the outer office door, which opened to reveal the credit manager, Sam Jakubiec. "Excuse me," he said when he saw the group inside, and turned to go. Peter called him back.

"I came to check a rumor," Jakubiec said. "It's going round the hotel like a prairie fire that the old gentleman, Mr. Wells . . ."

"It isn't rumor," Peter said. "It's fact." He introduced the credit man to Mr. Dempster.

Jakubiec clapped a hand to his head. "My God!—I checked his credit. I doubted his check. I even phoned Montreal!"

"I heard about your call." For the second time Mr. Dempster smiled. "At the bank they were vastly amused. But they've strict instructions that no information about Mr. Wells is ever to be given out. It's the way he likes things done."

Jakubiec gave what sounded like a moan.

"I think you'd have more to worry about," the man from Montreal assured him, "if you hadn't checked Mr. Wells' credit. He'd respect you for doing it. He does have a habit of writing checks on odd bits of paper, which people find disconcerting. The checks are all good, of course. You probably know by now that Mr. Wells is one of the richest men in North America."

A dazed Jakubiec could only shake his head.

"It might be simpler for you all," Mr. Dempster remarked, "if I explained a few things about my employer." He glanced at his watch. "Mr. Dumaire, the banker, and some lawyers will be here soon, but I believe we've time."

He was interrupted by the arrival of Royall Edwards. The comptroller was armed with papers and a bulging brief case. Once more the ritual of introductions was performed.

Shaking hands, Mr. Dempster informed the comptroller, "We'll have a brief talk in a moment, and I'd like you to

358

remain for our eleven-thirty meeting. By the way—you too, Miss Francis. Mr. Trent asked that you be there, and I know Mr. Wells will be delighted."

For the first time, Peter McDermott had a disconcerting sense of exclusion from the center of affairs.

"I was about to explain some matters concerning Mr. Wells." Mr. Dempster removed his glasses, breathed on the lenses and polished them once more.

"Despite Mr. Wells' considerable wealth, he has remained a man of very simple tastes. This is in no sense due to meanness. He is, in fact, extremely generous. It is simply that for himself he prefers modest things, even in such matters as clothing, travel, and accommodation."

"About accommodation," Peter said. "I was considering moving Mr. Wells to a suite. Mr. Curtis O'Keefe is vacating one of our better ones this afternoon."

"I suggest you don't. I happen to know that Mr. Wells likes the room he has, though not the one before it."

Mentally, Peter shuddered at the reference to the ha-ha room which Albert Wells had occupied before his transfer to 1410 on Monday night.

"He has no objection to others having a suite—me, for example," Mr. Dempster explained. "It is simply that he feels no need for such things himself. Am I boring you?"

His listeners, as one, protested that he was not.

Royall Edwards seemed amused. "It's like something from the Brothers Grimm!"

"Perhaps. But don't ever believe that Mr. Wells lives in a fairy tale world. He doesn't, any more than I do."

Peter McDermott thought: Whether the others realized it or not, there was a hint of steel beneath the urbane words.

Mr. Dempster continued, "I've known Mr. Wells a good many years. In that time I've come to respect his instincts both about business and people. He has a kind of native shrewdness that isn't taught at the Harvard School of Business."

Royall Edwards, who was a Harvard Business School graduate, flushed. Peter wondered if the riposte was accidental or if the representative of Albert Wells had done some swift investigating of the hotel's senior staff. It was entirely possible that he had, in which case Peter McDermott's record, including his Waldorf dismissal and subsequent black listing, would be known. Was this the reason, Peter wondered, behind his own apparent omission from the inner councils?

"I suppose," Royall Edwards said, "we can expect a good many changes around here."

"I'd consider it likely." Again Mr. Dempster polished his glasses; it seemed a compulsive habit. "The first change will be that I shall become president of the hotel company, an office I hold in most of Mr. Wells' corporations. He has never cared to assume titles himself."

Christine said, "So we'll be seeing a good deal of you."

"Actually very little, Miss Francis. I will be a figurehead, no more. The executive vice-president will have complete authority. That is Mr. Wells' policy, and also mine."

So after all, Peter thought, the situation had resolved itself as he expected. Albert Wells would not be closely involved with the hotel's management; therefore the fact of knowing him would carry no advantage. The little man was, in fact, twice removed from active management, and Peter's future would depend on the executive vice-president, whoever that might be. Peter wondered if it was anyone he knew. If so, it could make a great deal of difference.

Until this moment, Peter reasoned, he had told himself that he would accept events as they came, including—if necessary—his own departure. Now, he discovered, he wanted to remain at the St. Gregory very much indeed. Christine, of course, was one reason. Another was that the St. Gregory, with continued independence under new management, promised to be exciting.

"Mr. Dempster," Peter said, "if it isn't a great secret, who will the executive vice-president be?"

The man from Montreal appeared puzzled. He looked at Peter strangely, then his expression cleared. "Excuse me," he said, "I thought you knew. That's you."

4

Throughout last night, in the slow-paced hours when hotel guests were serenely sleeping, Booker T. Graham had labored alone in the incinerator's glare. That, in itself, was not unusual. Booker T. was a simple soul whose days and nights were like carbon copies of each other, and it never perturbed him that this should be so. His ambitions were simple too, being limited to food, shelter, and a measure of human dignity, though the last was instinctive and not a need he could have explained himself.

What had been unusual about the night was the slowness with which his work had gone. Usually, well before time to clock out and go home, Booker T. had disposed of the previous day's accumulated garbage, had sorted his retrievals, and left himself with half an hour when he would sit quietly, smoking a hand-rolled cigarette, until closing the incinerator down. But this morning, though his time on duty had been complete, the work was not. At the hour when he should have been leaving the hotel, a dozen or more tightly packed cans of garbage remained unsorted and undisposed.

The reason was Booker T.'s attempt to find the paper which Mr. McDermott wanted. He had been careful and thorough. He had taken his time. And so far he had failed.

Booker T. had reported the fact regretfully to the night manager who had come in, the latter looking unfamiliarly at the grim surroundings and wrinkling his nose at the all-pervading smell. The night manager had left as speedily as possible, but the fact that he had come and the message he had brought showed that—to Mr. McDermott—the missing paper was still important.

Regretful or not, it was time for Booker T. to quit and go home. The hotel objected to paying overtime. More to the point: Booker T. was hired to concern himself with garbage, not management problems, however remote.

He knew that during the day, if the remaining garbage was noticed, someone would be sent in to run the incinerator for an extra few hours and burn it off. Failing that, Booker T. himself would catch up with the residue when he returned to duty late tonight. The trouble was, with the first way, any hope of retrieving the paper would be gone forever, and with the second, even if found, it might be too late for whatever was required.

And yet, more than anything else, Booker T. wanted

361

to do this thing for Mr. McDermott. If he had been pressed, he could not have said why, since he was not an articulate man, either in thought or speech. But somehow, when the young assistant general manager was around, Booker T. felt more of a man—an individual—than at any other time.

He decided he would go on searching.

To avoid trouble, he left the incinerator and went to the time clock where he punched out. Then he returned. It was unlikely that he would be noticed. The incinerator was not a place which attracted visitors.

He worked for another three and a half hours. He worked slowly, painstakingly, with the knowledge that what he sought might not be in the garbage at all, or could have been burned before he was warned to look.

By mid-morning he was very tired and down to the last container but one.

He saw it almost at once when he emptied the bin—a ball of waxed paper which looked like sandwich wrappings. When he opened them, inside was a crumpled sheet of stationery, matching the sample Mr. McDermott had left. He compared the two under a light to be sure. There was no mistake.

The recovered paper was grease-stained and partially wet. In one place the writing on it had smeared. But only a little. The rest was clear.

Booker T. put on his grimed and greasy coat. Without waiting to dispose of the remaining garbage, he headed for the upper precincts of the hotel.

5

In Warren Trent's commodious office, Mr. Dempster had concluded his private talk with the comptroller. Spread around them were balance sheets and statements, which Royall Edwards was gathering up as others, arriving for the eleven-thirty meeting, came in to join them. The Pickwickian banker, Emile Dumaire, was first, a trifle flushed with self-importance. He was followed by a sallow, spindly lawyer who handled most of the St. Gregory's legal business, and a younger New Orleans lawyer, representing Albert Wells.

Peter McDermott came next, accompanying Warren Trent who had arrived from the fifteenth floor a moment earlier. Paradoxically, despite having lost his long struggle to maintain control of the hotel, the St. Gregory's proprietor appeared more amiable and relaxed than at any time in recent weeks. He wore a carnation in his buttonhole and greeted the visitors cordially, including Mr. Dempster whom Peter introduced.

For Peter, the proceedings had a chimeric quality. His actions were mechanical, his speech a conditioned reflex, like responding to a litany. It was as if a robot inside him had taken charge until such time as he could recover from the shock administered by the man from Montreal.

Executive vice-president. It was less the title which concerned him than its implications.

To run the St. Gregory with absolute control was like fulfillment of a vision. Peter knew, with passionate conviction, that the St. Gregory could become a fine hotel. It could be esteemed, efficient, profitable. Obviously, Curtis O'Keefe—whose opinion counted—thought so too.

There were means to achieve this end. They included an infusion of capital, reorganization with clearly defined areas of authority, and staff changes—retirements, promotions, and transplantings from outside.

When he had learned of the purchase of the hotel by Albert Wells, and its continued independence, Peter hoped that someone else would have the insight and impetus to make progressive changes. Now, he was to be given the opportunity himself. The prospect was exhilarating. And a little frightening.

There was a personal significance. The appointment, and what followed, would mean a restoration of Peter McDermott's status within the hotel industry. If he made a success of the St. Gregory, what had gone before would be forgotten, his account wiped clean. Hoteliers, as a group, were neither vicious nor shortsighted. In the end, achievement was what mattered most.

Peter's thoughts raced on. Still stunned, but beginning

to recover, he joined the others now taking their places at a long board table near the center of the room.

Albert Wells was last to arrive. He came in shyly, escorted by Christine. As he did, those already in the room rose to their feet.

Clearly embarrassed, the little man waved them down. "No, no! Please!"

Warren Trent stepped forward, smiling. "Mr. Wells, I welcome you to my house." They shook hands. "When it becomes your house, it will be my heartfelt wish that these old walls will bring to you as great a happiness and satisfaction as, at times, they have to me."

It was said with courtliness and grace. From anyone else, Peter McDermott thought, the words might have seemed hollow or exaggerated. Spoken by Warren Trent, they held a conviction which was strangely moving.

Albert Wells blinked. With the same courtesy, Warren Trent took his arm and personally performed the introductions.

Christine closed the outer door and joined the others at the table.

"I believe you know my assistant, Miss Francis; and Mr. McDermott."

Albert Wells gave his sly, birdlike smile. "We've had a bit to do with each other." He winked at Peter. "Will do some more, I reckon."

It was Emile Dumaire who "harrumphed" and opened the proceedings.

The terms of sale, the banker pointed out, had already been substantially agreed. The purpose of the meeting, over which both Mr. Trent and Mr. Dempster had asked him to preside, was to decide upon procedures, including a date for takeover. There appeared to be no difficulties. The mortgage on the hotel, due to be foreclosed today, had been assumed *pro tem* by the Industrial Merchants Bank, under guarantees by Mr. Dempster, acting on behalf of Mr. Wells.

Peter caught an ironic glance from Warren Trent who, for months, had tried unsuccessfully himself to obtain renewal of the mortgage.

The banker produced a proposed agenda which he distributed. There was a brief discussion of its contents, the lawyers and Mr. Dempster participating. They then moved on to deal with the agenda point by point. Through most of what followed, both Warren Trent and Albert Wells remained spectators only, the former meditative, the little man sunk into his chair as if wishing to meld into the background. At no point did Mr. Dempster refer to Albert Wells, or even glance his way. Obviously, the man from Montreal understood his employer's preference for avoiding attention and was used to making decisions on his own.

Peter McDermott and Royall Edwards answered questions, as they arose, affecting administration and finance. On two occasions Christine left the meeting and returned, bringing documents from the hotel files.

For all his pompousness, the banker ran a meeting well. Within less than half an hour, the principal business had been disposed of. The official transfer date was set for Tuesday. Other minor details were left for the lawyers to arrange between them.

Emile Dumaire glanced quickly around the table. "Unless there is anything else . . ."

"Perhaps one thing." Warren Trent sat forward, his movement commanding the attention of the others. "Between gentlemen, the signing of documents is merely a delayed formality confirming honorable commitments already entered into." He glanced at Albert Wells. "I assume that you agree."

Mr. Dempster said, "Certainly."

"Then please feel free to commence at once any actions you may contemplate within the hotel."

"Thank you." Mr. Dempster nodded appreciatively. "There are some matters we would like to set in motion. Immediately after completion on Tuesday, Mr. Wells wishes a directors' meeting to be held, at which the first business will be to propose your own election, Mr. Trent, as chairman of the board."

Warren Trent inclined his head graciously. "I shall be honored to accept. I will do my best to be suitably ornamental."

Mr. Dempster permitted himself the ghost of a smile.

"It is Mr. Wells' further wish that I should assume the presidency."

"A wish that I can understand."

"With Mr. Peter McDermott as executive vice-president."

A chorus of congratulations was directed at Peter from around the table. Christine was smiling. With the others, Warren Trent shook Peter's hand.

Mr. Dempster waited until the conversation died. "There remains one further point. This week I was in New York when the unfortunate publicity occurred concerning this hotel. I would like an assurance that we are not to have a repetition, at least before the change in management."

There was a sudden silence.

The older lawyer looked puzzled. In an audible whisper, the younger one explained, "It was because a colored man was turned away."

"Ah!" The older lawyer nodded understandingly.

"Let me make one thing clear." Mr. Dempster removed his glasses and began polishing them carefully. "I am not suggesting that there be any basic change in hotel policy. My opinion, as a businessman, is that local viewpoints and customs must be respected. What I am concerned with is that if such a situation arises, it should not produce a similar result."

Again there was a silence.

Abruptly, Peter McDermott was aware that the focus of attention had shifted to himself. He had a sudden, chilling instinct that here, without warning, a crisis had occurred—the first and perhaps the most significant of his new regime. How he handled it could affect the hotel's future and his own. He waited until he was absolutely sure of what he intended to say.

"What was said a moment ago"—Peter spoke quietly, nodding toward the younger lawyer—"is unfortunately true. A delegate to a convention in this hotel, with a confirmed reservation, was refused accommodation. He was a dentist—I understand, a distinguished one—and incidentally a Negro. I regret to say that I was the one who turned him away. I have since made a personal decision that the same thing will never happen again."

Emile Dumaire said, "As executive vice-president, I doubt if you'll be put in the position . . ."

"Or to permit a similar action by anyone else in a hotel where I am in charge."

The banker pursed his lips. "That's a mighty sweeping statement."

Warren Trent turned edgily to Peter. "We've been over all this."

"Gentlemen." Mr. Dempster replaced his glasses. "I made it clear, I thought, that I was not suggesting any fundamental change."

"But I am, Mr. Dempster." If there was to be a show-down, Peter thought, better to have it now, and done with. Either he would run the hotel or not. This seemed as good a time as any to find out.

The man from Montreal leaned forward. "Let me be sure I understand your position."

An inner cautioning voice warned Peter he was being reckless. He ignored it. "My position is quite simple. I would insist on complete desegregation of the hotel as a condition of my employment."

"Aren't you being somewhat hasty in dictating terms?"

Peter said quietly, "I assume your question to mean that you are aware of certain personal matters . . ."

Mr. Dempster nodded. "Yes, we are."

Christine, Peter observed, had her eyes intently on his face. He wondered what she was thinking.

"Hasty or not," he said, "I think it's fair to let you know where I stand."

Mr. Dempster was once more polishing his glasses. He addressed the room at large. "I imagine we all respect a firmly held conviction. Even so, it seems to me that this is the kind of issue where we might temporize. If Mr. McDermott will agree, we can postpone a firm decision now. Then, in a month or two, the subject can be reconsidered."

If Mr. McDermott will agree. Peter thought: With diplomatic skill, the man from Montreal had offered him a way out.

It followed an established pattern. Insistence first, conscience appeased, a belief declared. Then mild concession. A reasonable compromise reached by reasonable men. *The*

367

subject can be reconsidered. What could be more civilized, more eminently sane? Wasn't it the moderate, nonviolent kind of attitude which most people favored? The dentists, for example. Their official letter, with the resolution deploring the hotel's action in the case of Dr. Nicholas, had arrived today.

It was also true: there *were* difficulties facing the hotel. It was an unpropitious time. A change of management would produce a crop of problems, never mind inventing new ones. To wait, perhaps, would be the wisest choice.

But then, the time for drastic change was never right. There were always reasons for not doing things. Someone, Peter remembered, had said that recently. Who?

Dr. Ingram. The fiery dentists' president who resigned because he believed that principle was more important than expediency, who had quit the St. Gregory Hotel last night in righteous anger.

Once in a while, Dr. Ingram had said, *you have to weigh what you want against what you believe in . . . You didn't do it, McDermott, when you had the chance. You were too worried about this hotel, your job . . . Sometimes, though, you get a second chance. If it happens to you—take it.*

"Mr. Dempster," Peter said, "the law on civil rights is perfectly clear. Whether we delay or circumvent it for a while, in the end the result will be the same."

"The way I hear it," the man from Montreal remarked, "there's a good deal of argument about States' rights."

Peter shook his head impatiently. His gaze swung round the table. "I believe that a good hotel must adapt itself to changing times. There are matters of human rights that our times have awakened to. Far better that we should be ahead in realizing and accepting these things than that they be forced upon us, as will happen if we fail to act ourselves. A moment ago I made the statement that I will never be a party again to turning away a Dr. Nicholas. I am not prepared to change my mind."

Warren Trent snorted. "They won't all be Dr. Nicholas."

"We preserve certain standards now, Mr. Trent. We shall continue to preserve them, except that they will be more embracive."

I warn you! You will run this hotel into the ground."
'There seem to be more ways than one of doing that."

At the rejoinder, Warren Trent flushed.

Mr. Dempster was regarding his hands. "Regrettably, we seem to have reached an impasse. Mr. McDermott, in view of your attitude, we may have to reconsider . . ." For the first time, the man from Montreal betrayed uncertainty. He glanced at Albert Wells.

The little man was hunched down in his chair. He seemed to shrink as attention turned toward him. But his eyes met Mr. Dempster's.

"Charlie," Albert Wells said, "I reckon we should let the young fellow do it his way." He nodded toward Peter.

Without the slightest change of expression, Mr. Dempster announced, "Mr. McDermott, your conditions are met."

The meeting was breaking up. In contrast to the earlier accord, there was a sense of constraint and awkwardness. Warren Trent ignored Peter, his expression sour. The older lawyer looked disapproving, the younger noncommittal. Emile Dumaire was talking earnestly with Mr. Dempster. Only Albert Wells seemed slightly amused at what had taken place.

Christine went to the door first. A moment later she returned, beckoning Peter. Through the doorway he saw that his secretary was waiting in the outer office. Knowing Flora, it would be something out of the ordinary that had brought her here. He excused himself and went outside.

At the doorway, Christine slipped a folded piece of paper into Peter's hand. She whispered, "Read it later." He nodded and thrust the paper into a pocket.

"Mr. McDermott," Flora said, "I wouldn't have disturbed you . . ."

"I know. What's happened?"

"There's a man in your office. He says he works in the incinerator and has something important that you want. He won't give it to me or go away."

Peter looked startled. "I'll come as quickly as I can."

"Please hurry!" Flora seemed embarrassed. "I hate to say this, Mr. McDermott, but the fact is . . . well, he *smells*."

6

A few minutes before midday, a lanky, slow-moving maintenance worker named Billyboi Noble lowered himself into a shallow pit beneath the shaft of number four elevator. His business there was routine cleaning and inspection, which he had already performed this morning on elevators numbers one, two, and three. It was a procedure for which it was not considered necessary to stop the elevators and, as Billyboi worked, he could see the car of number four—alternately climbing and descending—high above.

7

Momentous issues, Peter McDermott reflected, could hinge upon the smallest quirk of fate.

He was alone in his office. Booker T. Graham, suitably thanked and glowing from his small success, had left a few minutes earlier.

The smallest quirk of fate. ·

If Booker T. had been a different kind of man, if he had gone home—as others would have done—at the appointed time, if he had been less diligent in searching, then the single sheet of paper, now staring up at Peter from his desk blotter, would have been destroyed.

The "ifs" were endless. Peter himself had been involved.

His visits to the incinerator, he gathered from their conversation, had had the effect of inspiring Booker T. Early this morning, it appeared, the man had even clocked out and continued to work without any expectation of overtime. When Peter summoned Flora and issued instructions that the overtime be paid, the look of devotion on Booker T.'s face had been embarrassing.

Whatever the cause, the result was here.

The note, face upward on the blotter, was dated two days earlier. Written by the Duchess of Croydon on Presidential Suite stationery, it authorized the hotel garage to release the Croydons' car to Ogilvie *"at any time he may think suitable."*

370

Peter had already checked the handwriting.

He had asked Flora for the Croydons' file. It was open on his desk. There was correspondence about reservations, with several notes in the Duchess's own hand. A handwriting expert would no doubt be precise. But even without such knowledge, the similarity was unmistakable.

The Duchess had sworn to police detectives that Ogilvie removed the car without authority. She denied Ogilvie's accusation that the Croydons paid him to drive the Jaguar away from New Orleans. She had suggested that Ogilvie, not the Croydons, had been driving last Monday night at the time of the hit-and-run. Questioned about the note, she challenged, "Show it to me!"

It could now be shown.

Peter McDermott's specific knowledge of the law was confined to matters affecting a hotel. Even so, it was obvious that the Duchess's note was incriminating in the extreme. Equally obvious was Peter's own duty—to inform Captain Yolles at once that the missing piece of evidence had been recovered.

With his hand on the telephone, Peter hesitated.

He felt no sympathy for the Croydons. From the accumulated evidence, it seemed clear that they had committed a dastardly crime, and afterward compounded it with cowardice and lies. In his mind, Peter could see the old St. Louis cemetery, the procession of mourners, the larger coffin, the tiny white one behind . . .

The Croydons had even cheated their accomplice, Ogilvie. Despicable as the fat house detective was, his crime was less than theirs. Yet the Duke and Duchess were prepared to inflict on Ogilvie the larger blame and punishment.

None of this made Peter hesitate. The reason was simply a tradition—centuries old, the credo of an innkeeper—of politeness to a guest.

Whatever else the Duke and Duchess of Croydon might be, they were guests of the hotel.

He would call the police. But he would call the Croydons first.

Lifting the telephone, Peter asked for the Presidential Suite.

371

8

Curtis O'Keefe had personally ordered a late room service breakfast for himself and Dodo, and it had been delivered to his suite an hour ago. Most of the meal, however, still remained untouched. Both he and Dodo had made a perfunctory attempt to sit down together to eat, but neither, it seemed, could muster an appetite. After a while, Dodo asked to be excused, and returned to the adjoining suite to complete her packing. She was due to leave for the airport in twenty minutes, Curtis O'Keefe, an hour later.

The strain between them had persisted since yesterday afternoon.

After his angry outburst then, O'Keefe had been immediately and genuinely sorry. He continued to resent bitterly what he considered to be the perfidy of Warren Trent. But his tirade against Dodo had been inexcusable, and he knew it.

Worse, it was impossible to repair. Despite his apologies, the truth remained. He *was* getting rid of Dodo, and her Delta Air Lines flight to Los Angeles was due to leave this afternoon. He *was* replacing her with someone else—Jenny LaMarsh who, at this moment, was waiting for him in New York.

Last night, contritely, he had laid on an elaborate evening for Dodo, taking her first to dine superbly at the Commander's Palace, and afterward to dance and be entertained at the Blue Room of the Roosevelt Hotel. But the evening had not gone well, not through any fault of Dodo's, but, perversely, through his own low spirits.

She had done her best to be gay good company.

After her obvious unhappiness of the afternoon, she had, it seemed, resolved to put hurt feelings behind her and be engaging, as she always was. "Gee, Curtie," Dodo exclaimed at dinner, "a lotta girls would give their Playtex girdles to have a movie part like I got." And later, placing her hand over his, "You're still the sweetest, Curtie. You always will be."

The effect had been to deepen his own depression which, in the end, proved contagious to them both.

Curtis O'Keefe attributed his feelings to the loss of the hotel, though usually he was more resilient about such matters. In his long career he had experienced his share of business disappointments and had schooled himself to bounce back, getting on with the next thing, rather than waste time in lamenting failures.

But on this occasion, even after a night's sleep, the mood persisted.

It made him irritable with God. There was a distinct sharpness, plus an undertone of criticism, in his morning prayers. . . . *Thou hast seen fit to place thy St. Gregory Hotel in alien hands . . . No doubt thou hast thine own inscrutable purpose, even if experienced mortals like thy servant can perceive no reason . . .*

He prayed alone, taking less time than usual, and afterward found Dodo packing his bags as well as her own. When he protested, she assured him, "Curtie, I like doing it. And if I didn't this time, who would?"

He felt disinclined to explain that none of Dodo's predecessors had ever packed or unpacked for him, or that he usually summoned someone from a hotel housekeeping department to do the job, as from now on, he supposed, he would have to do once more.

It was at that point he telephoned room service to order breakfast, but the idea hadn't worked despite the fact that when they sat down, Dodo tried again. "Gee, Curtie, we don't have to be miserable. It isn't like we'll never see each other. We can meet in L.A. lots of times."

But O'Keefe, who had traveled this road before, knew that they would not. Besides, he reminded himself, it was not parting with Dodo, but the loss of the hotel which really concerned him.

The moments slipped by. It was time for Dodo to leave. The bulk of her luggage, collected by two bellboys, had gone down to the lobby several minutes earlier. Now, the bell captain arrived for the remaining hand baggage, and to escort Dodo to her specially chartered airport limousine.

Herbie Chandler, aware of Curtis O'Keefe's importance, and sensitive as always to potential tips, had supervised this call himself. He stood waiting at the corridor entrance to the suite.

373

O'Keefe checked his watch and walked to the connecting doorway. "You've very little time, my dear."

Dodo's voice floated out. "I have to finish my nails, Curtie."

Wondering why all women left attending to their finger nails until the very last minute, Curtis O'Keefe handed Herbie Chandler a five-dollar bill. "Share this with the other two."

Chandler's weasel face brightened. "Thank you very much, sir." He would share it all right, he reflected, except that the other bellboys would get fifty cents each, with Herbie retaining the four dollars.

Dodo walked out from the adjoining room.

There should be music, Curtis O'Keefe thought. A blazoning of trumpets and the stirring sweep of strings.

She had on a simple yellow dress and the big floppy picture hat she had worn when they arrived on Tuesday. The ash-blond hair was loose about her shoulders. Her wide blue eyes regarded him.

"Goodbye, dearest Curtie." She put her arms around his neck and kissed him. Without intending to, he held her tightly.

He had an absurd impulse to instruct the bell captain to bring back Dodo's bags from downstairs, to tell her to stay and never to leave. He dismissed it as sentimental foolishness. In any case, there was Jenny LaMarsh. By this time tomorrow . . .

"Goodbye, my dear. I shall think of you often, and I shall follow your career closely."

At the doorway she turned and waved back. He could not be sure, but he had an impression she was crying. Herbie Chandler closed the door from outside.

On the twelfth-floor landing, the bell captain rang for an elevator. While they waited, Dodo repaired her make-up with a handkerchief.

The elevators seemed slow this morning, Herbie Chandler thought. Impatiently he depressed the call button a second time, holding it down for several seconds. He was still tense, he realized. He had been on tenterhooks ever since the session yesterday with McDermott, wondering just how and when the call would come—a direct summons from Warren Trent perhaps?—which would mark the end of Herbie's career at the St. Gregory Hotel. So far there had been no call and now, this morning, the rumor was around that the hotel had been sold to some old guy whom Herbie had never heard of.

How would that kind of change affect him personally? Regretfully, Herbie decided there would be no advantage for himself—at least, if McDermott stayed on, which seemed probable. The bell captain's dismissal might be delayed a few days, but that was all. McDermott! The hated name was like a sting inside him. If I had guts enough, Herbie thought, I'd put a knife between the bastard's shoulder blades.

An idea struck him. There were other ways, less drastic but still unpleasant, in which someone like McDermott could be given a rough time. Especially in New Orleans. Of course, that kind of thing cost money, but there was the five hundred dollars which McDermott had turned down so smugly yesterday. He might be sorry that he had. The money would be worth spending, Herbie reflected, just for the pleasure of knowing that McDermott would writhe in some gutter, a mess of blood and bruises. Herbie had once seen someone after they received that kind of beating. The sight was not pretty. The bell captain licked his lips. The more he thought about it, the more the idea excited him. As soon as he was back on the main floor, he decided, he would make a telephone call. It could be arranged quickly. Perhaps tonight.

An elevator had arrived at last. Its doors opened.

There were several people already inside who eased politely to the rear as Dodo entered. Herbie Chandler followed. The doors closed.

It was number four elevator. The time was eleven minutes past noon.

9

It seemed to the Duchess of Croydon as if she was waiting for a slow-burning fuse to reach an unseen bomb. Whether the bomb would explode, and where, would only

375

be known when the burning reached it. Nor was it certain
how long, in time, the fuse would take.

Already it had been fourteen hours.

Since last night, when the police detectives left, there
had been no further word. Troublesome questions remained
unanswered. What were the police doing? Where was Ogilvie? The Jaguar? Was there some scrap of evidence which,
for all her ingenuity, the Duchess had overlooked? Even
now, she did not believe there was.

One thing seemed important. Whatever their inner tensions, outwardly the Croydons should maintain an appearance of normalcy. For this reason, they had breakfasted
at their usual time. Urged on by the Duchess, the Duke
of Croydon exchanged telephone calls with London and
Washington. Plans were begun for their departure tomorrow from New Orleans.

At mid-morning, as she had most other days, the Duchess left the hotel to exercise the Bedlington terriers. She
had returned to the Presidential Suite half an hour ago.

It was almost noon. There was still no news concerning
the single thing that mattered most.

Last night, considered logically, the Croydons' position
seemed unassailable. And yet, today, logic seemed more
tenuous, less secure.

"You'd almost think," the Duke of Croydon ventured,
"that they're trying to wear us down by silence." He was
standing, looking from the window of the suite living room,
as he had so many times in recent days. In contrast to
other occasions, today his voice was clear. Since yesterday, though liquor remained available in the suite, he had
not wavered in his abstinence.

"If that's the case," the Duchess responded, "we'll see
to it that . . ."

She was interrupted by the jangling of the telephone.
It honed their nervousness to an edge, as had every other
call this morning.

The Duchess was nearest to the phone. She reached out
her hand, then abruptly stopped. She had a sudden premo-
nition that this call would be different from the rest.

The Duke asked sympathetically, "Would you rather
me do it?"

She shook her head, dismissing the momentary weakness. Lifting the telephone, she answered, "Yes?"

A pause. The Duchess acknowledged, "This is she." Covering the mouthpiece, she informed her husband, "The man from the hotel—McDermott—who was here last night."

She said into the telephone, "Yes, I remember. You were present when those ridiculous charges . . ."

The Duchess stopped. As she listened, her face paled. She closed her eyes, then opened them.

"Yes," she said slowly. "Yes, I understand."

She replaced the receiver. Her hands were trembling.

The Duke of Croydon said, "Something has gone wrong." It was a statement, not a question.

The Duchess nodded slowly. "The note." Her voice was scarcely audible. "The note I wrote has been found. The hotel manager has it."

Her husband had moved from the window to the center of the room. He stood, immobile, his hands loosely by his sides, taking time to let the information sink in. At length he asked, "And now?"

"He's calling the police. He said he decided to notify us first." She put a hand to her forehead in a gesture of despair. "The note was the worst mistake. If I hadn't written it . . ."

"No," the Duke said. "If it wasn't that, it would have been something else. None of the mistakes were yours. The one that mattered—to begin with—was mine."

He crossed to the sideboard which served as a bar, and poured a stiff Scotch and soda. "I'll just have this, no more. Be a while before the next, I imagine."

"What are you going to do?"

He tossed the drink down. "It's a little late to talk of decency. But if any shreds are left, I'll try to salvage them." He went into the adjoining bedroom, returning almost at once with a light raincoat and a Homburg hat.

"If I can," the Duke of Croydon said, "I intend to get to the police before they come to me. It's what's known, I believe, as giving yourself up. I imagine there isn't much time, so I'll say what I have to say quickly."

The Duchess's eyes were on him. At this moment, to speak required more effort than she could make.

In a controlled, quiet voice the Duke affirmed, "I want you to know that I'm grateful for all you did. It was a mistake both of us made, but I'm still grateful. I'll do all I can to see that you're not involved. If, in spite of that, you are, then I'll say that the whole idea—after the accident—was mine and that I persuaded you."

The Duchess nodded dully.

"There's just one other thing. I suppose I shall need some kind of lawyer chap. I'd like you to arrange that, if you will."

The Duke put on the hat and with a finger tapped it into place. For one whose entire life and future had collapsed around him a few moments earlier, his composure seemed remarkable.

"You'll need money for the lawyer," he reminded her. "Quite a lot, I imagine. You could start him off with some of that fifteen thousand dollars you were taking to Chicago. The rest should go back into the bank. Drawing attention to it doesn't matter now."

The Duchess gave no indication of having heard.

A look of pity crossed her husband's face. He said uncertainly, "It may be a long time . . ." His arms went out toward her.

Coldly, deliberately, she averted her head.

The Duke seemed about to speak again, then changed his mind. With a slight shrug he turned, then went out quietly, closing the outer door behind him.

For a moment or two the Duchess sat passively, considering the future and weighing the exposure and disgrace immediately ahead. Then, habit reasserting itself, she rose. She would arrange for the lawyer, which seemed necessary at once. Later, she decided calmly, she would examine the means of suicide.

Meanwhile, the money which had been mentioned should be put in a safer place. She went into her bedroom.

It took only a few minutes, first of unbelief, then of frantic searching to discover that the attaché case was gone. The cause could only be theft. When she considered the possibility of informing the police, the Duchess of Croydon convulsed in demented, hysterical laughter.

If you wanted an elevator in a hurry, the Duke of Croydon reflected, you could count on it being slow in coming.

He seemed to have been waiting on the ninth floor landing for several minutes. Now, at last, he could hear a car approaching from above. A moment later its doors opened at the ninth.

For an instant the Duke hesitated. A second earlier he thought he had heard his wife cry out. He was tempted to go back, then decided not.

He stepped into number four elevator.

There were several people already inside, including an attractive blond girl and the hotel bell captain who recognized the Duke.

"Good day, your Grace."

The Duke of Croydon nodded absently as the doors slid closed.

10

It had taken Keycase Milne most of last night and this morning to decide that what had occurred was reality and not an hallucination. At first, on discovering the money he had carried away so innocently from the Presidential Suite, he assumed himself to be asleep and dreaming. He had walked around his room attempting to awaken. It made no difference. In his apparent dream, it seemed, he was awake already. The confusion kept Keycase genuinely awake until just before dawn. Then he dropped into a deep, untroubled sleep from which he did not stir until mid-morning.

It was typical of Keycase, however, that the night had not been wasted.

Even while doubting that his incredible stroke of fortune was true, he shaped plans and precautions in case it was.

Fifteen thousand dollars in negotiable cash had never before come Keycase's way during all his years as a professional thief. Even more remarkable, there appeared only two problems in making a clean departure with the money intact. One was when and how to leave the St. Gregory Hotel. The other was transportation of the cash.

Last night he reached decisions affecting both.

In quitting the hotel, he must attract a minimum of attention. That meant checking out normally and paying his bill. To do otherwise would be sheerest folly, proclaiming dishonesty and inviting pursuit.

It was a temptation to check out at once. Keycase resisted it. A late night checkout, perhaps involving discussion as to whether or not an extra room day should be charged, would be like lighting a beacon. The night cashier would remember and could describe him. So might others if the hotel was quiet, as most likely it would be.

No!—the best time to check out was mid-morning or later, when plenty of other people would be leaving too. That way, he could be virtually unnoticed.

Of course, there was danger in delay. Loss of the cash might be discovered by the Duke and Duchess of Croydon, and the police alerted. That would mean a police stake-out in the lobby and scrutiny of each departing guest. But, on the credit side, there was nothing to connect Keycase with the robbery, or even involve him as a suspect. Furthermore, it seemed unlikely that the baggage of every guest would be opened and searched.

Also, there was an intangible. Instinct told Keycase that the presence of so large a sum in cash—precisely where and how he had found it—was peculiar, even suspicious. *Would* an alarm be raised? There was at least a possibility that it might not.

On reflection, to wait seemed the lesser risk.

The second problem was removal of the money from the hotel.

Keycase considered mailing it, using the hotel mail chute and addressing it to himself at a hotel in some other city where he would appear in a day or two. It was a method he had used successfully before. Then, ruefully, he decided the sum was too large. It would require too many separate packages which, in themselves, might create attention.

The money would have to be carried from the hotel. How?

Obviously, not in the attaché case which he had brought here from the Duke and Duchess of Croydon's suite. Before anything else was done, that must be destroyed. Keycase set out carefully to do so.

The case was of expensive leather and well constructed. Painstakingly, he took it apart, then, with razor blades, cut it into tiny portions. The work was slow and tedious. Periodically, he stopped to flush portions down the toilet, spacing out his use of the toilet, so as not to attract attention from adjoining rooms.

It took more than two hours. At the end, all that remained of the attaché case were its metal locks and hinges. Keycase put them in his pocket. Leaving his room, he took a walk along the eighth-floor corridor.

Near the elevators were several sand urns. Burrowing into one with his fingers, he pushed the locks and hinges well down. They might be discovered eventually, but not for some time.

By then, it was an hour or two before dawn, the hotel silent. Keycase returned to his room where he packed his belongings, except for the few things he would need immediately before departure. He used the two suitcases he had brought with him on Tuesday morning. Into the larger, he stuffed the fifteen thousand dollars, rolled in several soiled shirts.

Then, still dazed and unbelieving, Keycase slept.

He had set his alarm clock for ten A.M., but either he slept through its warning or it failed to go off. When he awoke, it was almost 11:30, with the sun streaming brightly into the room.

The sleep accomplished one thing. Keycase was convinced at last that the happenings of last night were real, not illusory. A moment of abject defeat had, with Cinderella magic, turned into shining triumph. The thought sent his spirits soaring.

He shaved and dressed quickly, then completed his packing and locked both suitcases.

He would leave the suitcases in his room, he decided,

while he went down to pay his bill and reconnoiter the lobby.

Before doing so, he disposed of his surplus keys—for rooms 449, 641, 803, 1062, and the Presidential Suite. While shaving, he had observed a plumber's inspection plate low on the bathroom wall. Unscrewing the cover, he dropped the keys in. One by one he heard them strike bottom far below.

He retained his own key, 830, for handing in when he left his room for the last time. The departure of "Byron Meader" from the St. Gregory Hotel must be normal in every way.

The lobby was averagely busy, with no sign of unusual activity. Keycase paid his bill and received a friendly smile from the girl cashier. "Is the room vacant now, sir?"

He returned the smile. "It will be in a few minutes. I have to collect my bags, that's all."

Satisfied, he went back upstairs.

In 830 he took a last careful look around the room. He had left nothing; no scrap of paper, no unconsidered trifle such as a match cover, no clue whatever to his true identity. With a damp towel, Keycase wiped the obvious surfaces which might have retained fingerprints. Then, picking up both suitcases, he left.

His watch showed ten past twelve.

He held the larger suitcase tightly. At the prospect of walking through the lobby and out of the hotel, Keycase's pulse quickened, his hands grew clammy.

On the eighth-floor landing he rang for an elevator. Waiting, he heard one coming down. It stopped at the floor above, started downward once more, then stopped again. In front of Keycase, the door of number four elevator slid open.

At the front of the car was the Duke of Croydon.

For a horror-filled instant, Keycase had an impulse to turn and run. He mastered it. In the same split second, sanity told him that the encounter was accidental. Swift glances confirmed it. The Duke was alone. He had not even noticed Keycase. From the Duke's expression, his thoughts were far away.

The elevator operator, an elderly man, said, "Going down!"

Alongside the operator was the hotel bell captain, whom Keycase recognized from having seen him in the lobby. Nodding to the two bags, the bell captain inquired, "Shall I take those, sir?" Keycase shook his head.

As he stepped into the elevator, the Duke of Croydon and a beautiful blond girl eased nearer the rear to make room.

The gates closed. The operator, Cy Lewin, pushed the selector handle to "descend." As he did, with a scream of tortured metal, the elevator car plunged downward, out of control.

11

He owed it to Warren Trent, Peter McDermott decided, to explain personally what had occurred concerning the Duke and Duchess of Croydon.

Peter found the hotel proprietor in his main mezzanine office. The others who had been at the meeting had left. Aloysius Royce was with his employer, helping assemble personal possessions, which he was packing into cardboard containers.

"I thought I might as well get on with this," Warren Trent told Peter. "I won't need this office any more. I suppose it will be yours." There was no rancor in the older man's voice, despite their altercation less than half an hour ago.

Aloysius Royce continued to work quietly as the other two talked.

Warren Trent listened attentively to the description of events since Peter's hasty departure from St. Louis cemetery yesterday afternoon, concluding with the telephone calls, a few minutes ago, to the Duchess of Croydon and the New Orleans police.

"If the Croydons did what you say," Warren Trent pronounced, "I've no sympathy for them. You've handled it well." He growled an afterthought. "At least we'll be rid of those damn dogs."

"I'm afraid Ogilvie is involved pretty deeply."

383

The older man nodded. "This time he's gone too far. He'll take the consequences, whatever they are, and he's finished here." Warren Trent paused. He seemed to be weighing something in his mind. At length he said, "I suppose you wonder why I've always been lenient with Ogilvie."

"Yes," Peter said, "I have."

"He was my wife's nephew. I'm not proud of the fact, and I assure you that my wife and Ogilvie had nothing in common. But many years ago she asked me to give him a job here, and I did. Afterward, when she was worried about him once, I promised to keep him employed. I've never, really, wanted to undo that."

How did you explain, Warren Trent wondered, that while the link with Hester had been defective and tenuous, it was the only one he had.

"I'm sorry," Peter said. "I didn't know . . ."

"That I was ever married?" The older man smiled. "Not many do. My wife came with me to this hotel. We were both young. She died soon after. It all seems a long time ago."

It was a reminder, Warren Trent thought, of the loneliness he had endured across the years, and of the greater loneliness soon to come.

Peter said, "Is there anything I can . . ."

Without warning, the door from the outer office flew open. Christine stumbled in. She had been running, and had lost a shoe. She was breathless, her hair awry. She barely got the words out.

"There's been . . . terrible accident! One of the elevators. I was in the lobby . . . It's horrible! People are trapped . . . They're screaming."

At the doorway, already on the run, Peter McDermott brushed her aside. Aloysius Royce was close behind.

12

Three things should have saved number four elevator from disaster.

One was an overspeed governor on the elevator car. It

was set to trip when the car's speed exceeded a prescribed safety limit. On number four—though the defect had not been noticed—the governor was operating late.

A second device comprised four safety clamps. Immediately the governor tripped, these should have seized the elevator guide rails, halting the car. In fact, on one side of the car two clamps held. But on the other side—due to delayed response of the governor, and because the machinery was old and weakened—the clamps failed.

Even then, prompt operation of an emergency control inside the elevator car might have averted tragedy. This was a single red button. Its purpose, when depressed, was to cut off all electric power, freezing the car. In modern elevators the emergency button was located high, and plainly in view. In the St. Gregory's cars, and many others, it was positioned low. Cy Lewin reached down, fumbling awkwardly to reach it. He was a second too late.

As one set of clamps held and the other failed, the car twisted and buckled. With a thunder of wrenching, tearing metal, impelled by its own weight and speed, plus the heavy load inside, the car split open. Rivets sheared, paneling splintered, metal sheeting separated. On one side—lower than the other because the floor was now tilted at a steep angle—a gap several feet high appeared between floor and wall. Screaming, clutching wildly at each other, the passengers slid toward it.

Cy Lewin, the elderly operator, who was nearest, was first to fall through. His single scream as he fell nine floors was cut off when his body hit the sub-basement concrete. An elderly couple from Salt Lake City fell next, clasping each other. Like Cy Lewin, they died as their bodies smashed against the ground. The Duke of Croydon fell awkwardly, striking an iron bar on the side of the shaft, which impaled him. The bar broke off, and he continued to fall. He was dead before his body reached the ground.

Somehow, others held on. While they did, the remaining two safety clamps gave way, sending the wrecked car plummeting the remaining distance down the shaft. Part way, a youngish conventioneer dentist slipped through the gap, his arms flailing. He was to survive the accident, but die three days later of internal injuries.

Herbie Chandler was more fortunate. He fell when the car was near the end of its descent. Tumbling into the adjoining shaft, he sustained head injuries from which he would recover, and sheared and fractured vertebrae which would make him a paraplegic, never walking again for the remainder of his life.

A middle-aged New Orleans woman lay, with a fractured tibia and a shattered jaw, on the elevator floor.

As the car hit bottom, Dodo was last to fall. An arm was broken and her skull cracked hard against a guide rail. She lay unconscious, close to death, as blood gushed from a massive head wound.

Three others—a Gold Crown Cola conventioneer, his wife, and Keycase Milne—were miraculously unhurt.

Beneath the wrecked elevator car, Billyboi Noble, the maintenance worker who, some ten minutes earlier, had lowered himself into the elevator pit, lay with legs and pelvis crushed, conscious, bleeding, and screaming.

13

Running with a speed he had never used in the hotel before, Peter McDermott raced down the mezzanine stairs.

The lobby, when he reached it, was a scene of pandemonium. Screams resounded through the elevator doors and from several women nearby. There was confused shouting. In front of a milling crowd, a white-faced assistant manager and a bellboy were attempting to pry open the metal doors to number four elevator shaft. Cashiers, room clerks, and office workers were pouring out from behind counters and desks. Restaurants and bars were emptying into the lobby, waiters and bartenders following their customers. In the main dining room, lunchtime music had stopped, the musicians joining the exodus. A line of kitchen workers was streaming out through a service doorway. An excited babel of questions greeted Peter.

As loudly as he could, he shouted above the uproar, "Quiet!"

There was a momentary silence in which he called out again, "Please stand back and we will do everything we can." He caught a room clerk's eye. "Has someone called the Fire Department?"

"I'm not sure, sir. I thought . . ."

Peter snapped, "Do it now!" He instructed another, "Get onto the police. Tell them we need ambulances, doctors, someone to control the crowd."

Both men disappeared, running.

A tall, lean man in a tweed jacket and drill trousers stepped forward. "I'm a Marine officer. Tell me what you want."

Peter said gratefully, "The center of the lobby must be kept clear. Use hotel staff to form a cordon. Keep a passageway open to the main entrance. Fold back the revolving doors."

"Right!"

The tall man turned away and began cracking commands. As if appreciative of leadership, others obeyed. Soon, a line of waiters, cooks, clerks, bellboys, musicians, some conscripted guests, extended across the lobby and to the St. Charles Avenue door.

Aloysius Royce had joined the assistant manager and bellboy attempting to force the elevator doors. He turned, calling to Peter. "We'll never do this without tools. We have to break in somewhere else."

A coveralled maintenance worker ran into the lobby. He appealed to Peter. "We need help at the bottom of the shaft. There's a guy trapped under the car. We can't get him out or get at the others."

Peter snapped, "Let's get down there!" He sprinted for the lower service stairs, Aloysius Royce a pace behind.

A gray brick tunnel, dimly lighted, led to the elevator shaft. Here, the cries they had heard above were audible again, but now with greater closeness and more eerily. The shattered elevator car was directly in front, but the way to it barred by twisted, distorted metal from the car itself and installations it had hit on impact. Near the front, maintenance workers were struggling with pry bars. Others stood helplessly behind. Screams, confused shouts, the rumble of nearby machinery, combined with a steady moaning from the car's interior.

Peter shouted to the men not occupied, "Get more lights in here!" Several hurried away down the tunnel.

He instructed the man in coveralls who had come to the lobby, "Get back upstairs. Guide the firemen down."

Aloysius Royce, on his knees beside the debris, shouted, "And send a doctor—now!"

"Yes," Peter said, "take someone to show him the way. Have an announcement made. There are several doctors staying in the hotel."

The man nodded and ran back the way they had come.

More people were arriving in the corridor, beginning to block it. The chief engineer, Doc Vickery, shouldered his way through.

"My God!" The chief stood staring at the scene before him. "My God!—I told them. I warned if we didn't spend money, something like this . . ." He seized Peter's arm. "You heard me, laddie. You've heard me enough times . . ."

"Later, chief." Peter released his arm. "What can you do to get those people out?"

The chief shook his head helplessly. "We'd need heavy equipment—jacks, cutting tools . . ."

It was evident that the chief was in no condition to take charge. Peter instructed him, "Check on the other elevators. Stop all service if you have to. Don't take chances of a repetition." The older man nodded dumbly. Bowed and broken, he moved away.

Peter grasped the shoulder of a gray-haired stationery engineer whom he recognized. "Your job is to keep this area clear. Everyone is to move out of here who is not directly concerned."

The engineer nodded. As he began to order others back, the tunnel cleared.

Peter returned to the elevator shaft. Aloysius Royce, by kneeling and crawling, had eased himself under part of the debris and was holding the shoulders of the injured, screaming maintenance man. In the dim light it was clear that a mass of wreckage rested on his legs and lower abdomen.

"Billyboi," Royce was urging, "you'll be all right. I promise you. We'll get you out."

The answer was another tortured scream.

Peter took one of the injured man's hands. "He's right. We're here now. Help is coming."

Distantly, high above, he could hear a growing wail of sirens.

14

The room clerk's telephone summons reached the Fire Alarm Office in City Hall. His message had not concluded when two high-pitched beeps—a major alarm alert—sounded in every city fire hall. On radio, a dispatcher's calm voice followed.

"Striking box zero zero zero eight for alarm at St. Gregory Hotel, Carondelet and Common."

Automatically, four fire halls responded—Central on Decatur, Tulane, South Rampart, and Dumaine. In three of the four, non-duty-watchmen were at lunch. At Central, lunch was almost ready. The fare was meatballs and spaghetti. A fireman, taking his turn as cook, sighed as he turned off the gas and ran with the rest. Of all the godforsaken times for a midtown, high property alarm!

Clothing and longboots were on the trucks. Men kicked off shoes, climbing aboard while rigs were rolling. Within less than a minute of the double beeps, five engine companies, two hook and ladders, a host tender, emergency, rescue and salvage units, a deputy chief and two district chiefs were on the way to the St. Gregory, their drivers fighting busy midday traffic.

A hotel alert rated everything in the book.

At other fire halls, sixteen more engine companies and two hook and ladders stood by for a second alarm.

The Police Complaint Department in the Criminal Justice Courts received its warning two ways—from the Fire Alarm Office and directly from the hotel.

Under a notice, *"Be Patient With Your Caller,"* two women communications clerks wrote the information on message blanks, a moment later handed them to a radio dispatcher. The message went out: All ambulances—Police and Charity Hospital—to the St. Gregory Hotel.

389

Three floors below the St. Gregory lobby, in the tunnel to the elevator shaft, the noise, hasty commands, moans and cries continued. Now, penetrating them, were crisp, swift footsteps. A man in a seersucker suit hurried in. A young man. With a medical bag.

"Doctor!" Peter called urgently. "Over here!"

Crouching, crawling, the newcomer joined Peter and Aloysius Royce. Behind them, extra lights, hastily strung, were coming on. Billyboi Noble screamed again. His face turned to the doctor, eyes pleading, features agony-contorted. "Oh, God! Oh, God! Please give me something . . ."

The doctor nodded, scrabbling in his bag. He produced a syrette. Peter pushed back Billyboi's coverall sleeve, holding an arm exposed. The doctor swabbed hastily, jabbed the needle home. Within seconds the morphine had taken hold. Billyboi's head fell back. His eyes closed.

The doctor had a stethoscope to Billyboi's chest. "I haven't much with me. I came off the street. How quickly can you get him out?"

"As soon as we've help. It's coming."

More running footsteps. This time, a heavy pounding of many feet. Helmeted firemen streaming in. With them, bright lanterns, heavy equipment—axes, power jacks, cutting tools, lever bars. Little talk. Short, staccato words. Grunts, sharp orders. "Over here! A jack under there. Get this heavy stuff moving!"

From above, a tattoo of ax blows crashing home. The sound of yielding metal. A stream of light as shaft doors opened at the lobby level. A cry, "Ladders! We need ladders here!" Long ladders coming down.

The young doctor's command: "I *must* have this man out!"

Two firemen struggling to position a jack. Extended, it would take the weight from Billyboi. The firemen groping, swearing, maneuvering to find clearance. The jack too large by several inches. "We need a smaller jack! Get a smaller jack to start, to get the big one placed." The demand repeated on a walkie-talkie. "Bring the small jack from the rescue truck!"

The doctor's voice again, insistently. *"I must have this man out!"*

Peter's voice. "That bar there! The one higher. If we move it, it will lift the lower, leave clearance for the jack."

A fireman cautioning. "Twenty tons up there. Shift something, it can all come down. When we start, we'll take it slow."

"Let's try!" Aloysius Royce.

Royce and Peter, shoulders together, backs under the higher bar, arms interlocked. Strain upward! Nothing. Strain harder again! Still harder! Lungs bursting, blood surging, senses swimming. The bar moving, but barely. Even harder! Do the impossible! Consciousness slipping. Sight diminishing. A red mist only. Straining. Moving. A shout, "The jack is in!" The straining ended. Down. Pulled free. The jack turning, lifting. Debris rising. "We can get him out!"

The doctor's voice, quietly. "Take your time. He just died."

The dead and injured were brought upward by the ladder one by one. The lobby became a clearing station, with hasty aid for those still living, a place of pronouncement for the dead. Furniture was pushed clear. Stretchers filled the central area. Behind the cordon, the crowd—silent now —pressed tightly. Women were crying. Some men had turned away.

Outside, a line of ambulances waited. St. Charles Avenue and Carondelet, between Canal and Gravier Streets, were closed to traffic. Crowds were gathering behind police blockades at both ends. Singly, the ambulances raced away. First, with Herbie Chandler; next, the injured dentist who would die; a moment later, the New Orleans woman with injuries to leg and jaw. Other ambulances drove more slowly to the city morgue. Inside the hotel, a police captain questioned witnesses, seeking names of victims.

Of the injured, Dodo was brought up last. A doctor, climbing down, had applied a compression dressing to the gaping head wound. Her arm was in a plastic splint. Key-case Milne, ignoring offers of help himself, had stayed with Dodo, holding her, guiding rescuers to where she lay. Key-

391

case was last out. The Gold Crown Cola conventioneer and his wife preceded him. A fireman passed up the bags —Dodo's and Keycase's—from the elevator's wreckage to the lobby. A uniformed city policeman received and guarded them.

Peter McDermott had returned to the lobby when Dodo was brought out. She was white and still, her body blood-soaked, the compression dressing already red. As she was laid on a stretcher, two doctors worked over her briefly. One was a young intern, the other an older man. The younger doctor shook his head.

Behind the cordon, a commotion. A man in shirtsleeves, agitated, shouting. "Let me pass!"

Peter turned his head, then motioned to the Marine officer. The cordon parted. Curtis O'Keefe came rushing through.

His face distraught, he walked beside the stretcher. When Peter last saw him, he was on the street outside, pleading to be allowed in the ambulance. The intern nodded. Doors slammed. Its siren screaming, the ambulance raced away.

16

With shock, barely believing his own deliverance, Keycase climbed the ladder in the elevator shaft. A fireman was behind. Hands reached down to help him. Arms gave support as he stepped into the lobby.

Keycase found that he could stand and move unaided. His senses were returning. Once more, his brain was alert. Uniforms were all around. They frightened him.

His two suitcases! If the larger one had burst open! . . . But no. They were with several others nearby. He moved toward them.

A voice behind said, "Sir, there's an ambulance waiting." Keycase turned, to see a young policeman.

"I don't need . . ."

"Everyone must go, sir. It's for a check. For your own protection."

Keycase protested, "I must have my bags."

392

"You can collect them later, sir. They'll be looked after."

"No, now."

Another voice cut in. "Christ! If he wants his bags, let him take them. Anyone who's been through that's entitled . . ."

The young policeman carried the bags and escorted Keycase to the St. Charles Avenue door. "If you'll wait here, sir, I'll see which ambulance." He set the bags down.

While the policeman was gone, Keycase picked them up and melted into the crowd. No one observed him as he walked away.

He continued to walk, without haste, to the outdoor parking lot where he had left his car yesterday after his successful pillaging of the house in Lakeview. He had a sense of peace and confidence. Nothing could possibly happen to him now.

The parking lot was crowded, but Keycase spotted his Ford sedan by its distinctive green-on-white Michigan plates. He was reminded that on Monday he had been concerned that the license plates might attract attention. Obviously, he had worried needlessly.

The car was as he had left it. As usual, the motor started at a touch.

From downtown, Keycase drove carefully to the motel on Chef Menteur Highway where he had cached his earlier loot. Its value was small, compared with the glorious fifteen thousand dollars cash, but still worth while.

At the motel, Keycase backed the Ford close to his rented room and carried in the two suitcases he had brought from the St. Gregory. He drew the motel room drapes before opening the larger case to assure himself that the money was still there. It was.

He had stored a good many of his personal effects at the motel, and now he repacked his several suitcases to get these in. At the end, he found that he was left with the two fur coats and the silver bowl and salver he had stolen from the house in Lakeview. There was no room to include them, except by repacking once more.

Keycase knew that he should. But in the past few minutes, he had become aware of an overwhelming fatigue—

393

a reaction, he supposed, from the events and tensions of today. Also, time had run on, and it was important that he get clear of New Orleans as quickly as possible. The coats and silver, he decided, would be perfectly safe, unpacked, in the trunk of the Ford.

Making sure he was unobserved, he loaded the suitcases into the car, placing the coats and silver beside them.

He checked out of the motel and paid a balance owing on his bill. Some of his tiredness seemed to lift as he drove away.

His destination was Detroit. He planned to make the drive in easy stages, stopping when he felt like it. On the way he would do some serious thinking about the future. For a number of years Keycase had promised himself that if ever he acquired a reasonably substantial sum of money, he would use it to buy a small garage. There, abandoning his itinerant life of crime, he would settle down to work honestly through the sunset of his days. He possessed the ability. The Ford beneath his hands was proof. And fifteen thousand dollars was ample for a start. The question was: Was this the time?

Keycase was already debating the proposition as he drove across north New Orleans, heading for the Pontchartrain Expressway and the road to freedom.

There were logical arguments in favor of settling down. He was no longer young. Risks and tension tired him. He had been touched, this time in New Orleans, by the disabling hand of fear.

And yet . . . events of the past thirty-six hours had given him fresh confidence, a new *élan*. The successful house robbery, the Aladdin's haul of cash, his survival of the elevator disaster barely an hour ago—all these seemed symptoms of invincibility. Surely, combined, they were an omen telling him the way to go?

Perhaps after all, Keycase reflected, he should continue the old ways for a while. The garage could come later. There was really plenty of time.

He had driven from Chef Menteur Highway onto Gentilly Boulevard, around City Park, past lagoons and ancient, spreading oaks. Now, on City Park Avenue, he was approaching Metarie Road. It was here that the newer cemeteries of New Orleans—Greenwood, Metarie, St. Patrick, Fireman's, Charity Hospital, Cypress Grove—spread a sea of tombstones as far as vision went. High above them all was the elevated Pontchartrain Expressway. Keycase could see the Expressway now, a citadel in the sky, a haven beckoning. In minutes he would be on it.

Approaching the junction of Canal Street and City Park Avenue, last staging point before the Expressway ramp, Keycase observed that the intersection's traffic lights had failed. A policeman was directing traffic from the center of the road on the Canal Street side.

A few yards from the intersection, Keycase felt a tire go flat.

Motor Patrolman Nicholas Clancy, of the New Orleans Police, had once been accused by his embittered sergeant of being "the dumbest cop on the force, bar none."

The charge held truth. Despite long service which had made him a veteran, Clancy had never once advanced in rank or even been considered for promotion. His record was inglorious. He had made almost no arrests, and none that was major. If Clancy chased a fleeing car, its driver was sure to get away. Once, in a melee, Clancy had been told to handcuff a suspect whom another officer had captured. Clancy was still struggling to free his handcuffs from his belt when the suspect was blocks away. On another occasion, a much-sought bank bandit who had got religion, surrendered to Clancy on a city street. The bandit handed over his gun which Clancy dropped. The gun went off, startling the bandit into changing his mind and fleeing. It was another year and six more holdups before he was recaptured.

Only one thing, over the years, saved Clancy from dismissal—an extreme good nature which no one could resist, plus a sad clown's humble awareness of his own shortcomings.

Sometimes, in his private moments, Clancy wished that he could achieve one thing, attain some single worthwhile moment, if not to balance the record, at least to make it less one-sided. So far he had signally failed.

One solitary thing in line of duty gave Clancy not the

slightest trouble—directing traffic. He enjoyed it. If, somehow, Clancy could have reached back into history to prevent the invention of the automatic traffic light, he would have done so gladly.

Ten minutes ago, when he realized that the lights at Canal and City Park Avenue had failed, he radioed the information in, parked his motorcycle, and took over the intersection. He hoped that the street lighting repair crew would take its time in coming.

From the opposite side of the avenue, Clancy saw the gray Ford sedan slow and stop. Taking his time, he strolled across. Keycase was seated, motionless, as when the car stopped.

Clancy surveyed the offside rear wheel which was resting on its rim.

"Flat tire?"

Keycase nodded. If Clancy had been more observant, he would have noticed that the knuckle joints of the hands on the steering wheel were white. Keycase, through a veil of bitter self-recrimination, was remembering the single, simple factor his painstaking plans had overlooked. The spare tire and jack were in the trunk. To reach them, he must open the trunk, revealing the fur coats, the silver bowl, the salver and the suitcases.

He waited, sweating. The policeman showed no sign of moving.

"Guess you'll have to change the wheel, eh?"

Again Keycase nodded. He calculated. He could do it fast. Three minutes at the most. Jack! Wheel wrench! Spin the nuts! Wheel off! The spare on! Fasten! Throw wheel, jack and wrench on the back seat! Slam the trunk closed! He could be away. On the Expressway. *If only the cop would go.*

Behind the Ford, other cars were slowing, some having to stop before easing into the center lane. One pulled out too soon. Behind him, rubber squealed. A horn blasted in protest. The cop leaned forward, resting his arms on the door beside Keycase.

"Gets busy around here."

Keycase swallowed. "Yes."

The cop straightened up, opening the door. "Ought to start things moving."

Keycase drew the keys from the ignition. Slowly, he stepped down to the road. He forced a smile. "It's all right, officer. I can handle it."

Keycase waited, holding his breath as the cop surveyed the intersection.

Clancy said good naturedly, "I'll give you a hand."

An impulse seized Keycase to abandon the car and run. He dismissed it as hopeless. With resignation, he inserted the key and opened the trunk.

Scarcely a minute later, he had the jack in place, wheel nuts were loosened, and he was raising the rear bumper. The suitcases, fur coats and silver were heaped to one side in the trunk. As he worked, Keycase could see the cop contemplating the collection. Incredibly, so far, he had said nothing.

What Keycase could not know was that Clancy's reasoning process took time to function.

Clancy leaned down and fingered one of the coats.

"Bit hot for these." The city's shade temperature for the past ten days had hovered around ninety-five.

"My wife . . . sometimes feels the cold."

Wheel nuts were off, the old wheel free. With a single movement, Keycase opened the rear car door and flung the wheel inside.

The cop craned around the trunk lid, inspecting the car's interior.

"Little lady not with you, eh?"

"I . . . I'm picking her up."

Keycase's hands strove frantically to release the spare wheel. The locknut was stiff. He broke a finger nail and skinned his fingers freeing it. Ignoring the hurt, he hefted the wheel from the trunk.

"Looks kind of funny, all this stuff."

Keycase froze. He dare not move. He had come to Golgotha. Intuition told him why.

Fate had presented him a chance, and he had thrown it away. It mattered not that the decision had been solely in his mind. Fate had been kind, but Keycase had spurned the kindness. Now, in anger, fate had turned its back.

397

Terror struck as he remembered what, a few minutes earlier, he had so readily forgotten—the awful price of one more conviction; the long imprisonment lasting, perhaps, for the remainder of his life. Freedom had never seemed more precious. The Expressway, so close, seemed half a world away.

At last Keycase knew what the omens of the past day and a half had really meant. They had offered him release, a chance for a new and decent life, an escape to tomorrow. If he had only known.

Instead, he had misread the portents. With arrogance and vanity, he had interpreted fate's kindness as his own invincibility. He had made his decision. This was the result. Now it was too late.

Was it? Was it ever too late—at least for hope? Keycase closed his eyes.

He vowed—with a deep resolve which, given the opportunity, he knew he would keep—that if, through merest chance, he should escape this moment, he would never again, in all his life, do one more dishonest thing.

Keycase opened his eyes. The cop was walking to another car whose driver had stopped to ask directions.

With movements swifter than he believed possible, Keycase thrust the wheel on, replaced the nuts and released the jack which he threw into the trunk. Even now, instinctively as a good mechanic should, Keycase gave the wheel nuts an extra tightening when the wheel was on the ground. He had the trunk repacked when the cop returned.

Clancy nodded approvingly, his earlier thought forgotten. "All finished, eh?"

Keycase slammed the trunk lid down. For the first time, Motor Patrolman Clancy saw the Michigan license plate.

Michigan. Green on white. In the depths of Clancy's brain, memory stirred.

Had it been today, yesterday, the day before? . . . His platoon commander, on parade, reading the latest bulletins aloud . . . Something about green and white . . .

Clancy wished he could remember. There were so many bulletins—wanted men, missing persons, cars, robberies. Every day the bright, eager youngsters on the force scribbled swiftly in their notebooks, memorizing, getting the information down. Clancy tried. He always had. But inevitably, the lieutenant's brisk voice, the slowness of his own handwriting, left him far behind. *Green and white.* He wished he could remember.

Clancy pointed to the plate. "Michigan, eh?"

Keycase nodded. He waited numbly. There was just so much that the human spirit could absorb.

"Water Wonderland." Clancy read aloud the legend on the plate. "I hear you got some swell fishing."

"Yes . . . there is."

"Like to get there one day. Fisherman myself."

From behind, an impatient horn. Clancy held the car door open. He seemed to remember he was a policeman. "Let's get this lane clear." *Green and white.* The errant thought still bothered him.

The motor started. Keycase drove forward. Clancy watched him go. With precision, neither too fast nor too slow, his resolve steadfast, Keycase nosed the car on the Expressway ramp.

Green and white. Clancy shook his head and returned to directing traffic. Not for nothing had he been called the dumbest cop on the force, bar none.

17

From Tulane Avenue, the sky-blue and white police ambulance, its distinctive blue light flashing, swung into the emergency entrance driveway of Charity Hospital. The ambulance stopped. Swiftly its doors were opened. The stretcher bearing Dodo was lifted out, then, with practiced speed, wheeled by attendants through a doorway marked ADMISSION OUTPATIENTS WHITE.

Curtis O'Keefe followed close behind, almost running to keep up.

An attendant in the lead called, "Emergency! Make way!" A busy press of people in the admitting and discharge lobby fell back to let the small procession pass. Curious eyes followed its progress. Most were on the white, waxen mask of Dodo's face.

Swinging doors marked ACCIDENT ROOM opened to admit the stretcher. Inside were nurses, doctors, activity, other stretchers. A male attendant barred Curtis O'Keefe's way. "Wait here, please."

O'Keefe protested, "I want to know . . ."

A nurse, going in, stopped briefly. "Everything possible will be done. A doctor will talk to you as soon as he can." She continued inside. The swinging doors closed.

Curtis O'Keefe remained facing the doors. His eyes were misted, his heart despairing.

Less than half an hour ago, after Dodo's leavetaking, he had paced the suite living room, his thoughts confused and troubled. Instinct told him that something had gone from his life that he might never find again. Logic mocked him. Others before Dodo had come and gone. He had survived their departure. The notion that this time might be different was absurd.

Even so, he had been tempted to follow Dodo, perhaps to delay their separation for a few hours, and in that time to weigh his feelings once again. Rationality won out. He remained where he was.

A few minutes later he had heard the sirens. At first he had been unconcerned. Then, conscious of their growing number and apparent convergence on the hotel, he had gone to the window of his suite. The activity below made him decide to go down. He went as he was—in shirtsleeves, without putting on a coat.

On the twelfth-floor landing, as he waited for an elevator, disquieting sounds had drifted up. After almost five minutes, when an elevator failed to come and other guests were milling on the landing, O'Keefe decided to use the emergency stairs. As he went down, he discovered others had had the same idea. Near the lower floors, the sounds becoming clearer, he employed his athlete's training to increase his speed.

In the lobby he learned from excited spectators the essential facts of what had occurred. It was then he prayed with intensity that Dodo had left the hotel before the accident. A moment later he saw her carried, unconscious, from the elevator shaft.

The yellow dress he had admired, her hair, her limbs, were a mess of blood. The look of death was on her face.

400

In that instant, with searing, blinding insight, Curtis O'Keefe discovered the truth he had shielded from himself so long. He loved her. Dearly, ardently, with a devotion beyond human reckoning. Too late, he knew that in letting Dodo go, he had made the greatest single error of his life.

He reflected on it now, bitterly, surveying the accident-room doors. They opened briefly as a nurse came out. When he approached her, she shook her head and hurried on.

He had a sense of helplessness. There was so little he could do. But what he could, he would.

Turning away, he strode through the hospital. In busy lobbies and corridors, he breasted crowds, followed sign-boards and arrows to his objective. He opened doors marked PRIVATE, ignored protesting secretaries. He stopped before the Director's desk.

The Director rose angrily from his chair. When Curtis O'Keefe identified himself, the anger lessened.

Fifteen minutes later the Director emerged from the accident room accompanied by a slight, quietly spoken man whom he introduced as Dr. Beauclaire. The doctor and O'Keefe shook hands.

"I understand that you are a friend of the young lady —I believe, Miss Lash."

"How is she, Doctor?"

"Her condition is critical. We are doing everything we can. But I must tell you there is a strong possibility she may not live."

O'Keefe stood silent, grieving.

The doctor continued, "She has a serious head wound which appears superficially to be a depressed skull fracture. There is a likelihood that fragments of bone may have entered the brain. We shall know better after X rays."

The Director explained, "The patient is being resuscitated first."

The doctor nodded. "We have transfusions going. She lost a good deal of blood. And treatment has begun for shock."

"How long . . ."

"Resuscitation will be at least another hour. Then, if

401

X rays confirm the diagnosis, it will be necessary to operate immediately. Is the next-of-kin in New Orleans?"

O'Keefe shook his head.

"It makes no difference, really. In this kind of emergency, the law permits us to proceed without permission."

"May I see her?"

"Later, perhaps. Not yet."

"Doctor, if there's anything you need—a question of money, professional help . . ."

The Director interrupted quietly. "This is a free hospital, Mr. O'Keefe. It's for indigents and emergencies. All the same, there are services here that money couldn't buy. Two university medical schools are next door. Their staffs are on call. I should tell you that Dr. Beauclaire is one of the leading neurosurgeons in the country."

O'Keefe said humbly, "I'm sorry."

"Perhaps there is one thing," the doctor said.

O'Keefe's head came up.

"The patient is unconscious now, and under sedation. Earlier, there were some moments of lucidity. In one of them she asked for her mother. If it's possible to get her mother here . . ."

"It's possible." It was a relief that at least there was something he could do.

From a corridor pay phone, Curtis O'Keefe placed a collect call to Akron, Ohio. It was to the O'Keefe-Cuyahoga Hotel. The manager, Harrison, was in his office.

O'Keefe instructed, "Whatever you are doing, leave it. Do nothing else until you have completed, with the utmost speed, what I am about to tell you."

"Yes, sir." Harrison's alert voice came down the line.

"You are to contact a Mrs. Irene Lash of Exchange Street, Akron. I do not have the number of a house." O'Keefe remembered the street from the day that he and Dodo had telegraphed the basket of fruit. Was it only last Tuesday?

He heard Harrison call to someone in his office, "A city directory—fast!"

O'Keefe continued, "See Mrs. Lash yourself. Break the news to her that her daughter, Dorothy, has been injured in an accident and may die. I want Mrs. Lash flown to

New Orleans by the fastest possible means. Charter if necessary. Disregard expense."

"Hold it, Mr. O'Keefe." He could hear Harrison's crisp commands. "Get Eastern Airlines—the sales department in Cleveland—on another line. After that, I want a limousine with a fast driver at the Market Street door." The voice returned, more strongly. "Go ahead, Mr. O'Keefe."

As soon as the arrangements were known, O'Keefe directed, he was to be contacted at Charity Hospital.

He hung up, confident that the instructions would be carried through. A good man, Harrison. Perhaps worthy of a more important hotel.

Ninety minutes later, X rays confirmed Dr. Beauclaire's diagnosis. A twelfth-floor operating room was being readied. The neurosurgery, if continued to a conclusion, would take several hours.

Before Dodo was wheeled into the operating room, Curtis O'Keefe was permitted to see her briefly. She was pale and unconscious. It seemed to his imagination as if all her sweetness and vitality had flown.

Now the O.R. doors were closed.

Dodo's mother was on her way. Harrison had notified him. McDermott of the St. Gregory, whom O'Keefe had telephoned a few minutes ago, was arranging for Mrs. Lash to be met and driven directly to the hospital.

For the moment there was nothing to do but wait.

Earlier, O'Keefe had declined an invitation to rest in the Director's office. He would wait on the twelfth floor, he decided, no matter for how long.

Suddenly, he had a desire to pray.

A door close by was labeled LADIES COLORED. Next to it was another marked RECOVERY ROOM STORAGE. A glass panel showed that it was dark inside.

He opened the door and went in, groping his way past an oxygen tent and an iron lung. In the semidarkness he found a clear space where he knelt. The floor was a good deal harder on his knees than the broadloom he was used to. It seemed not to matter. He clasped his hands in supplication and lowered his head.

Strangely, for the first time in many years, he could find no words for what was in his heart.

Dusk, like an anodyne to the departing day, was settling over the city. Soon, Peter McDermott thought, the night would come, with sleep and, for a while, forgetfulness. Tomorrow, the immediacy of today's events would begin receding. Already, the dusk marked a beginning to the process of time which, in the end, healed all things.

But it would be many dusks and nights and days before those who were closest to today's events would be free from a sense of tragedy and terror. The waters of Lethe were still far distant.

Activity—while not a release—helped the mind a little. Since early this afternoon, a good deal had occurred.

Alone, in his office on the main mezzanine, Peter took stock of what had been done and what remained.

The grim, sad process of identifying the dead and notifying families had been completed. Where the hotel was to aid with funerals, arrangements had begun.

The little that could be done for the injured, beyond hospital care, had been put in hand.

Emergency crews—fire, police—had long since left. In their place were elevator inspectors, examining every piece of elevator equipment the hotel possessed. They would work into tonight and through tomorrow. Meanwhile, elevator service had been partially restored.

Insurance investigators—gloomy men, already foreseeing massive claims—were intensively questioning, taking statements.

On Monday, a team of consultants would fly from New York to begin planning for replacement of all passenger elevator machinery with new. It would be the first major expenditure of the Albert Wells-Dempster-McDermott regime.

The resignation of the chief engineer was on Peter's desk. He intended to accept it.

The chief, Doc Vickery, must be honorably retired, with the pension befitting his long years of service to the hotel. Peter would see to it that he was treated well.

M. Hèbrand, the chef de cuisine, would receive the

same consideration. But the old chef's retirement must be accomplished quickly, with André Lemieux promoted to his place.

On young André Lemieux—with his ideas for creation of specialty restaurants, intimate bars, an overhaul of the hotel's entire catering system—much of the St. Gregory's future would depend. A hotel did not live by renting rooms alone. It could fill its rooms each day, yet still go bankrupt. Special services—conventions, restaurants, bars—were where the mother lode of profit lay.

There must be other appointments, a reorganization of departments, a fresh defining of responsibilities. As executive vice-president, Peter would be involved much of the time with policy. He would need an assistant general manager to supervise the day-to-day running of the hotel. Whoever was appointed must be young, efficient, a disciplinarian when necessary, but able to get along with others older than himself. A graduate of the School of Hotel Administration might do well. On Monday, Peter decided, he would telephone Dean Robert Beck at Cornell. The dean kept in touch with many of his bright ex-students. He might know such a man, who was available now.

Despite today's tragedy, it was necessary to think ahead.

There was his own future with Christine. The thought of it was inspiring and exciting. Nothing between them had been settled yet. But he knew it would be. Earlier, Christine had left for her Gentilly apartment. He would go to her soon.

Other—less palatable—unfinished business still remained. An hour ago, Captain Yolles of the New Orleans Police had dropped into Peter's office. He had come from an interview with the Duchess of Croydon.

"When you're with her," Yolles said, "you sit there wondering what's under all that solid ice. Is it a woman? Does she *feel* about the way her husband died? I saw his body. My God!—no one deserved that. For that matter, she saw him too. Not many women could have faced it. Yet, in her, there isn't a crack. No warmth, no tears. Just her head tilted up, that way she has, and the haughty look she gives you. If I tell you the truth—as a man—I'm attracted to her. You get to feeling you'd like to know

405

what she's really like." The detective stopped, considering.

Later, answering Peter's question, Yolles said, "Yes, we'll charge her as an accessory, and she'll be arrested after the funeral. What happens beyond that—whether a jury will convict if the defense claims that her husband did the conniving, and he's dead . . . Well, we'll see."

Ogilvie had already been charged, the policeman revealed. "He's booked as an accessory. We may throw more at him later. The D.A. will decide. Either way, if you're keeping his job open, don't count on seeing him back in less than five years."

"We're not." Reorganization of the hotel's detective force was high on Peter's list of things to do.

When Captain Yolles had gone, the office was quiet. By now, it was early evening. After a while, Peter heard the outer door open and close. A light tap sounded on his own. He called, "Come in!"

It was Aloysius Royce. The young Negro carried a tray with a martini pitcher and a single glass. He set the tray down.

"I thought maybe you could do with this."

"Thanks," Peter said. "But I never drink alone."

"Had an idea you'd say that." From his pocket, Royce produced a second glass.

They drank in silence. What they had lived through today was still too close for levity or toasts.

Peter asked, "Did you deliver Mrs. Lash?"

Royce nodded. "Drove her right to the hospital. We had to go in through separate doorways, but we met inside and I took her to Mr. O'Keefe."

"Thank you." After Curtis O'Keefe's call, Peter had wanted someone at the airport on whom he could rely. It was the reason he had asked Royce to go.

"They'd finished operating when we got to the hospital. Barring complications, the young lady—Miss Lash—will be all right."

"I'm glad."

"Mr. O'Keefe told me they're going to be married. As soon as she's well enough. Her mother seemed to like the idea."

Peter smiled fleetingly. "I suppose most mothers would."

There was a silence, then Royce said, "I heard about the meeting this morning. The stand you took. The way things turned out."

Peter nodded. "The hotel is desegregated. Entirely. As of now."

"I suppose you expect me to thank you. For giving us what's ours by right."

"No," Peter said. "And you're being prickly again. I wonder, though, if you might decide now to stay with W.T. I know he'd like it, and you'd be entirely free. There's legal work for the hotel. I could see that some of it came your way."

"I'll thank you for that," Royce said. "But the answer's no. I told Mr. Trent this afternoon—I'm leaving, right after graduation." He refilled the martini glasses and contemplated his own. "We're in a war, you and me—on opposite sides. It won't be finished in our time, either. What I can do, with what I've learned about the law, I intend to do for my people. There's a lot of in-fighting ahead—legal, some of the other kind too. It won't always be fair, on our side as well as yours. But when we're unjust, intolerant, unreasonable, remember—we learned it from you. There'll be trouble for all of us. You'll have your share here. You've desegregated, but that isn't the end. There'll be problems—with our people who won't like what you've done, with Negroes who won't behave nicely, who'll embarrass you because some are the way they are. What'll you do with the Negro loudmouth, the Negro smart-aleck, the Negro half-drunk Romeo? We've got 'em, too. When it's white people who behave like that, you swallow hard, you try to smile, and most times you excuse it. When they're Negroes—what'll you do then?"

"It may not be easy," Peter said. "I'll try to be objective."

"You will. Others won't. All the same, it's the way the war will go. There's just one good thing."

"Yes?"

"Once in a while there'll be truces." Royce picked up the tray with the pitcher and the empty glasses. "I guess this was one."

407

Now it was night.

Within the hotel, the cycle of another innkeeping day had run its course. This had differed from most, but beneath unprecedented events, routines had continued. Reservations, reception, administration, housekeeping, engineering, garage, treasury, kitchens . . . all had combined in a single, simple function. To welcome the traveler, sustain him, provide him with rest, and speed him on.

Soon, the cycle would begin again.

Wearily, Peter McDermott prepared to leave. He switched off the office lights and, from the executive suite, walked the length of the main mezzanine. Near the stairway to the lobby he saw himself in a mirror. For the first time, he realized that the suit he was wearing was rumpled and soiled. It became that way, he reflected, under the elevator debris where Billyboi died.

As best he could, he smoothed the jacket with his hand. A slight rustling made him reach into a pocket where his fingers encountered a folded paper. Taking it out, he remembered. It was the note which Christine had given him as he left the meeting this morning—the meeting where he had staked his career on a principle, and won.

He had forgotten the note until now. He opened it curiously. It read: *It will be a fine hotel because it will be like the man who is to run it.*

At the bottom, in smaller lettering, Christine had written: *P.S. I love you.*

Smiling, the length of his stride increasing, he went downstairs to the lobby of his hotel.

ABOUT THE AUTHOR

Born in Luton, England, in 1920, ARTHUR HAILEY was educated in English schools until age fourteen. After a brief career as an office boy, he joined the British Royal Air Force in 1939 and served through World War II, rising through the ranks to become a pilot and flight lieutenant. In 1947 Mr. Hailey emigrated to Canada, where he was successively a real estate salesman, business paper editor and a sales and advertising executive. He became, and still is, a Canadian citizen. In 1956 Arthur Hailey scored his first writing success with a TV drama, "Flight into Danger," which later became a motion picture and a novel, *Runway Zero-Eight.* Since then, as a novelist and one of the great storytellers of our time, he has acquired a worldwide following of devoted readers and his books are published in twenty-seven languages. The sensational Hailey bestsellers include: *Hotel, Airport, Wheels, The Final Diagnosis, In High Places* and—his latest—*The Moneychangers.* Arthur Hailey and his wife, Sheila, make their home at Lyford Cay in the Bahamas, where their children, Jane, Steven and Diane, join them during college vacations.

ARTHUR HAILEY

Year after year Arthur Hailey has given his readers meticulously-researched, brilliant novels making his name synonymous with sheer entertainment and edge-of-the-chair suspense. AIRPORT. HOTEL. WHEELS. THE MONEYCHANGERS. Timely, memorable stories about people today and the worlds they work in. Stories that appeal to everyone. That's the way the big bestsellers keep coming from Arthur Hailey.

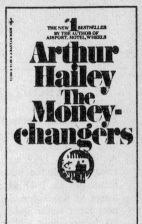

THE #1 BESTSELLER
BY THE AUTHOR OF
AIRPORT, HOTEL, WHEELS

Arthur Hailey The Moneychangers